THE BROTHER'S CURSE

BY CHRISTINE M. GERMAIN

This is a work of fiction. Names, characters, places, and incidents either are the product of the author's imagination or are used fictitiously. Any resemblance to actual persons, living or dead, events, or locales is entirely coincidental.

Copyright © 2020 by Christine M. Germain

All rights reserved. No part of this book may be reproduced or used in any manner without written permission of the copyright owner except for the use of quotations in a book review. For more information, email address: christinegermain58@gmail.com

Twitter: Christine M. Germain @CJReau

ISBN 978-1-7354-7890-6 (paperback)
ISBN 978-1-7354-7891-3 (Hardback)

DEDICATED

To My Loving Mother Margareth & Busta Brown

TABLE OF CONTENT

SHAPESHIFTER DEMONS 8
PROLOGUE TALE OF THE BROTHERS 9
- **CHAPTER 1:** DEAD BODIES 11
- **CHAPTER 2:** HOME SWEET HELL 21
- **CHAPTER 3:** IT'S COMING FOR YOU 35
- **CHAPTER 4:** TERROR AWAITS 47
- **CHAPTER 5:** THE FINAL GOODBYE 57
- **CHAPTER 6:** JASON 69
- **CHAPTER 7:** CHOOSE WISELY 77
- **CHAPTER 8:** WARNING SIGNS 85
- **CHAPTER 9:** DOOMSDAY 97
- **CHAPTER 10:** THE STONE 109
- **CHAPTER 11:** WHO'S NEXT 121
- **CHAPTER 12:** HE DEVOURS YOU 133
- **CHAPTER 13:** THE BROTHERS TALE 141
- **CHAPTER 14:** KILLER CREEK LANE 155
- **CHAPTER 15:** BOOGEYMAN 165
- **CHAPTER 16:** EVIL LURKED WITHIN 175

CHAPTER 17:	GONE	187
CHAPTER 18:	SKIN DEEP	189
CHAPTER 19:	TOUCH OF THE BEAST	197
CHAPTER 20:	DEADLY PILEUP	205
CHAPTER 21:	LAZURKISMURMA	215
CHAPTER 22:	THE BOOK	223
CHAPTER 23:	BODY COUNT	233
CHAPTER 24:	DARKNESS	241
CHAPTER 25:	THE BROTHER'S CURSE	253
CHAPTER 26:	THE END IS NEAR	265
CHAPTER 27:	HER LAST WISH	279
CHAPTER 28:	FRIGHT NIGHT	291
CHAPTER 29:	BLOODY BIRTHDAY	299
CHAPTER 30:	THE SHERIFF	307
CHAPTER 31:	TILLY	315
CHAPTER 32:	THE CHOSEN	323
CHAPTER 33:	SHE WHO HOLDS THE STONE	333

EPILOGUE 341
ABOUT AUTHOR 343

THE BROTHER'S CURSE

SHAPESHIFTER DEMONS

Armed with the ability to change shape, shapeshifter demons use the power of human flesh shifting to achieve their goals by transforming and masking their identity to take on the form of one close to them to manipulate and kill by flaying the person alive. Often being high-ranking in the hierarchy of evil, shapeshifter demons possess maximal other powers and can only be defeated with the blood of the girl that owns the purple amethyst stone necklace.

PROLOGUE
TALE OF THE BROTHERS

THE YEAR "1825"

Before being abandoned in a burning church, two twin baby boys were cursed with the spell of demonic immortality by their wicked and mighty father named Mastema. Mastema is a 17th-century flesh-eating, human shape-shifter known to manipulate and cause great pain to anyone who comes across him. A diabolical demon to humanity, Mastema hunted and searched for sorceress energy, ultimately slaughtering almost all Wiccan women in the peaceful village of Wickerlake Cove.

Foreseeing his demise after killing almost all of Colette Francis Courier's powerful

French coven, Mastema implements a specific duty for his sons before he is forever cast away into the purple crystal amethyst stone.

By placing the immortal curse on his sons, they will continue in the hunt for the girl of the last Wiccan generation that destroyed and locked Mastema up along with the evil entities that were part of his army called "The first coming flesh-eating human Shape-shifters."

To be successful with their duties, the brothers must retrieve the purple crystal amethyst chariot stone and the chosen girl's blood on her 25th birthday. The brothers must summon their father two hundred years from now by resurrecting the shifters locked away in the chariot stone.

It is up to Mastema's sons to find the stone and bring it to the church with the girl, and if for any reason, one of the brothers falls in love with her, there will be severe and deadly consequences.

May the Best Brother Win

CHAPTER ONE

DEAD BODIES

LAKEVIEW FALLS, MICHIGAN
OCTOBER 9TH, 2025

Various news networks play on three flatscreen television sets mounted on the beige walls in the Lakeview Falls County Sheriff's main lobby. A loud commotion echo throughout the station as the rookie deputies' eyes fixate on the live nationwide news coverage reporting on horrific and brutal murders unfolding all over the state of Michigan.

Nervously exiting his office is Sheriff Thomas Mills, a husky middle-aged divorcee with two sons. The six-foot-two head chief has been Lakeview Falls' enforcer for over ten years and has been under harsh scrutiny for his inability to solve recent mysterious deaths surfacing around town.

Sheriff Mills scowls as he storms past the empty cubicles, heading towards the main lobby to see all of his deputies missing from their working stations. "Where the hell are these idiots?" he utters under his breath.

When he reaches the main lobby, Sheriff Mills places both hands on each side of his hips, taps his foot against the hard marble floor, and glares at his entire squad who are engaged in deep conversation. Advancing towards them, he sees five officers staring out the window, where one female reporter stood in front of the sheriff's station, setting up her equipment with her cameraman.

"What in God's name is that woman doing? Jesus Christ! Those 666 news reporters need to get off my ass!" Sheriff Mills hollers as he extends his hands, pushing the front door open.

As he exits the station, the crisp autumn air entwines its soft fingers through his clothes and hair as he walks towards the reporter. Her long wavy auburn hair blows as she grasps her microphone tightly in her hands, staring into the camera.

"Good afternoon, this is Susan Kerbs with 666KR News, and we are here live in Lakeview Falls where horrific mass murders continue to plague this eerie small suburban town. One by one, middle-class families, slaughtered in their homes, and from each family, a son missing or flayed. None of this makes any sense Sheriff Mills; are there any answers to why the abductor is taking only young males, all in their late teens and early twenties, and wiping out the rest of the families?"

Extending the microphone up to the Sheriff's mouth, the reporter impatiently waits for a response.

He brushes his hand over his salt-and-pepper beard, while staring into the camera. "At this time, we have in counting about twenty young males missing in the past 48 hours. We are working hard to hunt down the abductor that is still on the loose; I promise you so help me God, we will find this son of a bitch!" he says while his eyes fixate on the camera lens.

Suddenly, a loud static noise coming from the sheriff's hands-free walkie-talkie startles him. On the other end of the line, a deputy frantically shouts in a high pitch, tone.

"Sheriff Mills, you have to come down here! We've got hanging bodies all over the place! Lots of them!" the deputy says, disappearing from the other line.

Speechless, Sheriff Mills' eyes search for any officers outside of the department. He then notices Deputy Matthew Scott, patrolling at the corner of Fearman Lane. The twenty-six-year-old Mexican American joined the Sheriff's department eight months ago as a rookie assistant working alongside Sheriff Mills. Matthew, who is usually called Matty or Matt by his friends, is five foot eleven with dark brown eyes and a muscular toned body that compliments his height.

Wearing his jet black hair in a wavy crop fade, Deputy Scott always keeps a sharp well-groomed appearance. Dressed in a two-tone colored uniform that consists of a light khaki button-down short sleeve shirt and dark brown pleated pants, matching with his polished brown men shoes, Matt looks professional at all times. Fixing his seven-point-metal badge with a gold nameplate that read, "Scott," Deputy Matthew Scott stood patrolling the area when he suddenly sees a frantic officer scurrying over to Sheriff Mills.

"Sheriff Mills!" One male deputy exclaims as sweat drips down his forehead, "we just received an emergency call about those missing boys," with a frightened expression, the officer's breathing becomes more rapid.

"We have to go now, Sheriff!" he demands as he heads back to his patrol car.

Clicking on his walkie talkie, Sheriff Mills contacts an officer at the crime scene. "This is Sheriff Thomas Mills. What's your twenty? Copy that."

"Sheriff Mills, location intersection 402 Deerfield; Roger that," a female officer responds on the other end.

"Ten-four, on my way," Sheriff Mills responds, ending the conversation.

"I'm sorry, but I can't answer any more of your questions at this time," Sheriff Mills says to the reporter while putting on his tinted sunglasses, walking away from her.

"Sheriff Mills, is it a lead on the missing boys?" the female reporter asks, holding onto her microphone while chasing Sheriff Mills to his patrol car with her cameraman following behind.

"I can't comment on that, excuse me," he replies, slightly snubbing the camera guy out of his way.

Forming an A shape with his index and middle finger, Sheriff Mills places them in his mouth, releasing an ear-piercing whistle, getting his rookie assistant's attention.

THE BROTHER'S CURSE

"Deputy Scott! Get in the car right now!" Sheriff Mills hollers while sprinting towards his patrol car.

"But sir, I'm still patrolling."

"Get in the damn car Scott!"

"Yes, Sheriff!"

Checking his rearview mirror, Sheriff Mills turns his siren on and drives off, heading to the rural Holloway interstate in a small town called Deerfield.

❄ ❄ ❄

DEERFIELD MICHIGAN

Arriving at the crime scene, both Sheriff Mills and Deputy Scott's jaws drop in horror as they see ten dead bodies of young men hanging from each light pole, naked with their skin stripped off. The deputies can tell the bodies were rotting for a few days due to a yellow-green slime trickling down the masses from the horrendous smell that fermented the entire interstate, making it unbearable to breathe.

"What in the hell," Sheriff Mills mutters in disgust, noticing some officers regurgitating on the side of the road.

The sight, so revolting, makes Deerfield's local lieutenant, Mitch Macmore cover his mouth as he approaches Sheriff Mills' patrol car, handing him a face mask.

"Good Afternoon, Sheriff, you might want to put these on; this isn't a pretty scene," he says to him, looking over at the passenger side.

The lieutenant notices Deputy Scott's fingers trembling rapidly. "Son, are you sure you're up for big boy work? This scene isn't for the faint of heart."

"I'll be fine lieutenant, I can handle anything," Deputy Scott replies with a side-eye.

"Sure thing tough guy, suit yourself; don't say I didn't warn you," Lieutenant Macmore says to Deputy Scott as he walks away from the patrol car.

"Are you ready to go, Deputy?" Sheriff Mills asks as he opens his car door.

"Yes, Sheriff Mills," Deputy Scott responds swiftly, putting his mask on.

"Here," Sheriff Mills says, handing him an extra face mask.

Both men exit the patrol car. The smell instantly hits their nostrils like a thick cloud of smoke, "Jesus Christ! That smells awful!" Sheriff Mills says, making gagging sounds as he walks towards the crime scene.

Walking under the yellow "Do not cross" sign with Deputy Scott, they advance towards the first hanging body.

"Christ!" Sheriff Mills exclaims, staring at the mutilated corpse, "what kind of monster would do such a thing?"

"Sheriff Mills!" a male police officer calls out, rushing over to him. "Thank you for getting here; this is the first break we've had in a few weeks."

Slowly walking pass each hanging body, Sheriff Mills' stomach churns, he looks downwards, avoiding eye contact with the dead. "So are we assuming that these are the young men that have been reported missing?" Sheriff Mills asks the officer.

"Yes, Sheriff, we are one hundred percent sure that these are the same young boys."

"Who found them?" Sheriff Mills asks, releasing a slight cough.

"We received an anonymous call from someone in the area complaining about the smell," the police officer says, flipping through his white notepad.

Suddenly, from across the road, an old raggedy woman lurking around the bushes walks towards the officers in a cloaked dingy white gown screaming,

"The Shifters have woken!"

Sheriff Mills stares at the deranged woman with a disturbed expression painted all over his face, as she walks towards deputy Scott with a possessed look on her face.

"They are coming for her, and they won't stop till they find it!" the older woman says, sneering at the young deputy.

"Get her out of here!" Sheriff Mills angrily hollers, waving to other officers around.

Deputy Scott stood frozen with his eyes wide open as the woman inches closer, whispering in his ears with a wicked smirk, exposing her stained rotted teeth with two missing on the bottom.

"She who holds the stone will put everyone's lives in terrible danger! You're going to die a very, very terrible death, I can see it."

Two officers immediately run towards the old woman and quickly pulls her away from Deputy Scott. "Excuse me, ma'am, this is an official crime scene you have to leave right now!"

"They will find her, and you will all be dead!" the old woman says and gives off an unearthly yell, scurrying into the bushes.

"What the hell was that about?" Sheriff Mills asks, walking towards Deputy Scott. "Are you okay, Deputy Scott?"

"Yes, Sheriff," trying to act brave, Deputy Scott sounded like he is on the verge of tears. "That lady was super creepy."

"Tell me about it. It was like watching an episode of the walking dead," Sheriff Mills says to him with a haunted expression.

Sensing a sudden vibration, Deputy Scott feels his cell phone go off in his pants pocket. Pulling it out, he sees the call is from his girlfriend of eight years, Gabriela Santos.

"I'm sorry, Sheriff, I have to take this call," he says, quickly excusing himself.

"Sure, but make it fast we have a lot of work ahead of us," Sheriff Mills says as he walks over to speak to another officer.

"Hey, babe! I'm sorry I didn't get to call you, it's been a little hectic at work. There is some crazy shit happening on the other side of town." Matt says walking away from the scene.

"That's okay, Matty," Gabby replies on the other end of the line, watching Trey struggle to hang a welcome home banner on the wall at her family-owned restaurant at Lakeside diner.

"Trey, you have it slanted," she scowls.

"Gabby, this is a bad idea," Trey clicks his teeth, rearranging the banner, "you know Crystal is going to hate all of this," Trey says, taking a step down from the booth.

Trey Delgado is one of Crystal's childhood friends. A gay rights activist at Lakeview Falls University. Trey is a mixture of Jewish and African American. Five-foot-seven, with light brown eyes, full lips, and dark brown short curly hair, Trey portrays both the masculine and feminine side. Revealing that he was a proud gay man a few years ago, Trey embraces his sexuality through his blunt sassiness.

Placing paper plates one by one on each table, Trey releases a sigh. "Gabby, do you think that Crystal is up for a party after what happened last year to her parents?"

"Trey, why are you so paranoid? Crystal deserves to have a night to unwind with friends who care about her."

"Gabriella, I don't think a party is the smartest idea, plus, you know Crystal loathes surprises."

Overhearing Trey on the other line, Matt tries to talk Gabriela out of hosting the party.

"Seriously, Gabby? Trey is right; I don't know if throwing a party for her is the right thing at this moment. I'm pretty sure she's not thrilled to come back to this shit hole of a town."

"It hasn't been easy for her Matt, Crystal has been through a lot since her parents died," Gabriela says to him while fixing mini red velvet cupcakes with vanilla frosting on a silver tray.

"Exactly my point, that's why I don't think it's a good idea Gabby, maybe Crystal needs some time to adjust being back home."

"Matty, a small party with close friends isn't going to ruin Crystal's night. If anything, maybe it will make her feel better."

Meanwhile, at the crime scene staring at Matt with his hands on his hips, Sheriff Mills clicks his teeth in annoyance. **"Get off your goddamn phone, Scott! Or I'll have your ass patrolling parking meters!"**

Startled, Matt removes the receiver part of his cell phone away from his ears. "Yes, Sheriff!" he responds to Sheriff Mills.

"Ok, babe," holding the phone to his ears again, "I gotta go. Sheriff Mills is losing his shit. I hope Crystal doesn't get pissed about this party. Oh, and before I forget, I'm going be a little late coming to the diner, there are a few things I have to do with the

Sheriff before I leave. There is some crazy shit going down in Deerfield; we have some psychopath on the loose, slaughtering young guys all over town. Crystal couldn't have picked a better time to come back home."

"That's awful, please be careful Matty," Gabriela says with a sense of uneasiness.

"Gabby, baby I'm going to be fine. You worry too much. I will call you as soon as I'm on my way to the restaurant. I'll see you later; I love you."

"I love you too, Matty, and don't forget to pick up Crystal's cake at Delia's bakery before you come to the party."

"Yes, of course, babe, I won't forget."

Ending his call with Gabby, Matt looks intensely at the carnage hanging off the poles while deputies line up number cards in front of each deceased body.

"Sheriff Mills! How are we going to get these bodies down?" a female deputy asks, holding her hands up to her face.

"Dammit! Call the fire department and the coroners!" he orders.

"Hey! Listen up, everyone!" Sheriff Mills shouts, striking his hands together, alerting the deputies at the scene.

"We've got a long day ahead of us. I will be issuing a curfew for the entire county, including Lakeview Falls. We will have to close down a few roads like Fall Park Lane. I think you all should take a safer shortcut to get home," Sheriff Mills announces.

Listening to Sheriff Mills' announcement, Matt could not help but feel worried his once wholesome town had falling prey to a serial killer or supernatural being. Not only would these tragic events scare the entire village, but they will also affect the people in his life, including his girlfriend Gabriela and his closest friends. He can only hope that whatever is out there doing these horrendous murders will be stopped before it gets worse.

"Sheriff," Deputy Scott says, approaching him, " I know this might not be the best time to ask you this, but—May I leave, sir? I have a surprise party to go to."

"Surprise Party!" Sheriff Mills scowls, "Are you shitting me, Deputy?"

"I'm sorry, Sheriff, is just that Crystal's coming back home tonight and..."

"Francois?" Sheriff Mills asks with a puzzled expression.

"Yes, Sheriff," Deputy Scott replies.

Surprised by the sudden news, Sheriff Mills remembers the fatal event that occurred a year prior. Determined to solve the Francois case, Sheriff Mills promised Crystal and her younger sister that he would catch the person who murdered her beloved parents.

The gleaming sun hits Sheriff Mills' eyes, forcing him to turn the opposite direction, "I didn't think Crystal would be back so soon after— you know?"

"I didn't expect it either Sheriff. I'm not sure how she will handle everything that's happening right now. This town is always full of surprises and not the good ones," Deputy Scott says as he walks towards his car.

"Hey! If you see my sons, tell them curfew is in effect and get their asses home by 8 pm," Sheriff Mills says, watching Deputy Scott enter his vehicle.

"You got it, Sheriff," Deputy Scott responds before driving off.

Drenched in sweat, a rookie deputy advances towards Sheriff Mills by the side of the road. "Sir, the fire department is here now," the deputy informs him.

"Great, let's get these bodies down, boys!"

CHAPTER TWO

HOME SWEET HELL

EARLY EVENING

Arriving at Plainfield International airport in Lakeview Falls is twenty-four-year-old Crystal Jade Francois, an attractive Haitian American woman, and native of the small town. Boarding off the airplane carrying her handbag, Crystal advances down the brightly lit jetway making her way through the large crowd, dressed in dark blue faded jeans, a white cashmere sweater, and a pair of black ankle boots. Her jet black curly hair worn in a ponytail updo complements her dark brown doe eyes and heart-shaped lips.

Entering the baggage claim area, Crystal feels a sudden rush of anxiety coursing through her veins. A swarm of negativity envelopes her inner thoughts as she immediately regrets returning to a place she so desperately wanted to flee. She couldn't help but feel more depressed than excited to be back home in Lakeview Falls.

Crystal's dreams of leaving the small town had finally come true six years ago when she received a full scholarship to Thornwell College in Hudson Valley, New York, where she studies advanced criminology. Academically excelling in her course, the young grad student-focused intensely on her last year of school, hoping to make her parents proud.

Upon finishing her junior year at the University one year ago, Crystal receives a call from her aunt with the terrible news that her parents were mutilated and left in the trunk of their car on the side of the rural road. The story of her parent's murder not only devastated her, but it also changed the course of her life.

Searching for answers to who may have murdered them on that fateful night, the local Sheriff's department came up empty with no leads. The murder of Crystal's parents is a cold case, deeming it as a mystery killing that cannot be solved.

Since their passing, Crystal's younger sister Alexandria decided to move out of her dorm room she shared with her boyfriend at Lakeview Falls University to live at home. Having written out a will before their deaths, Robert and Desiree Francois stated that the family home and trust funds are for both daughters.

Assisting with the Francois residents' household finances is their godmother Jacqueline Porter. She is the younger sister of their mother, Desiree. Aunty J visited the house from time to time to check up on Alexandria while Crystal was away at college.

❈ ❈ ❈

Exiting the airport with her two suitcases, Crystal waits impatiently near the pickup terminal. She is deafened by the loud echoing sounds of a car horn. Her head shifts to see her sister, Alexandria, flashing her a grin from a distance, waving outside her car window. Born one year apart, Alexandria shares the same beauty as her older sister. She has vibrant dark skin like chocolate, full red painted lips, hazel brown eyes, and a natural curly afro with light brown highlights that shines so brightly when the sun sets on her.

Pulling her car up on the ramp, Alex hollers at her sister, "Get in the car, big head. I'm starving!" she giggles.

Placing her suitcases in the back seat of the car, Crystal hops in the passenger side, making a goofy face. "Gosh, it's so great to see you too, Alex," Crystal replies sarcastically.

Leaving the airport, Alexandria takes the Satansway interstate. Noticing a sudden silence from her sister who stared quietly out the window, Alex quickly gets her attention. "So, how was your flight?" she asks.

"It was long and exhausting. Ever since I got off that plane, all I've wanted to do is go home put on some Netflix, order take out, and relax solo."

"Netflix all by yourself? That sounds pretty damn boring, Crystal, especially your first day back home. You need to stop acting like some weird introvert."

"Whatever, Alex, I'm not in the mood to hang out with anyone. Can you please let me be boring alone and stop judging me?"

"Jesus, why are you acting like a crabby bitch?" Alex asks her when suddenly she receives a text message on her cell phone.

Taking her eyes off the road, she quickly clicks on the message from her sister's best friend Gabriela that read in bold letters, **"Hey Alex, Trey and I are done setting everything up. Matt is picking up the cake also. Please, Alex, whatever you do, don't take Crystal home first; she will never come back out. See you soon."**

Responding to the text message, Alex misses a red light. Hearing the roaring sounds of a commercial truck, she quickly looks up panic-stricken. Grasping hold of the steering wheel, Alexandria shrieks as she nearly collides with a large delivery truck. Slamming the car breaks as quickly as possible, Alex watches the truck driver swerve to the opposite side, honking his horn and flipping her the bird at the same time.

"What the hell is the matter with you, Alex?" she screams angrily at her sister.

Crystal's heart pounds in her ears, blocking out all other sounds as she glares intensely at Alexandria. "Are you crazy? Texting and driving? How stupid can you be? I don't know about you, but I'm not trying to die my first day back home!"

"Oh my God, Crystal, I'm sorry, I didn't realize I ran a red light, " Alex said, apologizing profusely to Crystal with a frown expression.

"You didn't realize it because you were too busy on your damn phone Alex! Can you put it down and try to get us home in one piece, please?" Crystal replies. Releasing a sigh of annoyance, Crystal shifts her gaze towards the side window.

THE BROTHER'S CURSE

"I will get us home safe right after I pick up the food I ordered for us at the Lakeside Diner. I remember how much you love those double bacon cheeseburgers."

"Alex, you know I stopped eating red meat a year ago, right? So what's the deal?" Crystal suspiciously asks her sister, squinting one eye. "You never offer to buy me food. What are you up to?"

"I'm not up to anything big head, why are you so suspicious? Can't a girl just be hungry? I figured since I'm already driving, I can pick something up for us on our way back home."

"Fine, I won't argue. Since you are paying for this wonderful meal, I will keep my mouth shut," Crystal replies, putting her finger over her mouth.

"Good, you talk too much," Alexandria smirks.

Suddenly feeling her cell phone vibrate in her purse, Crystal reaches into her handbag and pulls out her glitter designed smartphone. Ecstatic to see it's a call from her Aunty J, Crystal quickly answers the phone, putting her on speakerphone.

"Hi, Aunty J," she exclaims with excitement.

"Hello, my darling, you have no idea how happy I am to hear your sweet voice. I've missed you so much. How was your flight?"

"It was a good Aunty J; I am glad to be back home. I've missed you, and of course, my annoying little sister," Crystal says, grinning while Alexandria sticks her tongue out at her.

"I can't wait to see you, my dear," her aunt says with a soft-spoken tone, "by the way, are you girls heading to the house now?" she asks.

"No, Aunty J, I'm taking Crystal to her surprise party!" Alexandria says quickly, realizing she blew her cover, slamming her hands over the steering wheel, she squeals.

"Oh shit! I wasn't supposed to say that," gritting her teeth. Alex shakes her head from side to side, disappointed with herself.

"Aha!" Crystal points her index finger at her sister, "I knew you were hiding something, double bacon cheeseburger, my ass."

"A party? Well, that sounds like fun. I'm sure your friends will be excited to see you, Crystal," her aunt says to her.

"I know, I just wasn't ready to see anyone my first day back," Crystal mutters under her breath.

"I don't want to take up your time since you are on the road girls, I have a date in an hour, and I'm getting myself ready as we speak."

"A date, huh?" Crystal wittingly replies, winking her eye at Alexandria. "Who's the mystery guy?"

"He's just someone I've been seeing for a few months."

"Ooo, Aunty J is getting her groove back, is he nice?" Alex asks her.

"Yes, he's a nice guy Alexandria."

"Is he big?" Alexandria asks as a burst of laughter escapes her lips.

"Damn Alex," Crystal clicks her teeth with a side-eye, "why would you ask her that? You are so nasty."

"Alexandria, I'm going to pretend I didn't hear that," Aunty J says awkwardly clearing her throat. "Enough about my love life. I called because your neighbor Joe McGregor stopped by the house a few minutes ago. He informed me that he is taking an emergency trip and will be out of town for a while. He asked me if it was okay to drop off his house keys with us. He also said he's sending someone by the house to pick them up. I tried to ask Mr. McGregor, who was coming to pick up the keys, but he seemed to be in a hurry. That man was acting a bit strange."

"Mr. McGregor is strange," Alexandria responds to her aunt.

"I wonder why he would drop his keys off at our house? He hates us," Crystal says, confused by her neighbor's behavior.

"No, Mr. McGregor doesn't hate us. He hates me!" Alex interrupts her sister.

"Why on earth would that old man hate you, Alex?" Aunty J asks her with a slight giggle.

"Because one night Alex got drunk and took a shit in his flower garden," Crystal responds to her aunt, unable to control her laughter.

"That's not funny Crystal. I had to go," Alexandria says in a whining voice.

"You're disgusting, Alex; what did you use for toilet paper?" Crystal asks her sister, twitching her nose in disgust.

Extending her arms, Alexandria reaches over and pinches Crystal on her left arm. "You are such a jerk," Alexandria snickers.

"Ouch! That hurts," Crystal groans in pain while brushing her hand over her arms.

"Girls, I would love to stay on the phone and chit chat, but I have to go, I left Mr. McGregor's house keys on the kitchen counter. I will stop by the house in a few days; I love you both. Please be careful on the road," Aunty J says to them.

"We Love you too, Aunty J," Crystal responds, ending the phone call.

"That is so weird," Crystal mutters with an odd expression on her face.

"What's weird, Crystal?" Alexandria questions her sister squinting her eyes.

"Remember when Mom and Dad used to talk about how Mr. McGregor is a paranoid hermit crab that has never left his house or Lakeview Falls in years?"

"Yes, and what's your point, Crystal?" Alexandria replies, shrugging her shoulders.

"Don't you think it's weird that all of sudden he's taking a trip away from Lakeview Falls?"

"Crystal, you need to relax that criminology brain of yours and stop trying to play inspector gadget. Maybe Mr. McGregor had something important to do. It's not that serious; he's an old man who probably needed a vacation."

"I guess you're right Alex; I wonder who's going to watch over his house while he's gone."

"Who cares, Crystal! I'm surprised Mr. McGregor even has any friends. Whoever it is, will probably lock their ass up in that house just like he did."

"So, there's a party for me, huh? Whoever told you should have known that you're terrible at keeping secrets, Alex."

With a pouty lip, Alexandria feels a sense of guilt for ruining the surprise. "You're right, I screwed up. I got excited. I know deep down inside you're not happy you left New York to move back to Lakeview Falls. It's written all over your face Crystal, but I'm happy you did because I've missed you so much."

Giving her sister a warm-hearted smile, Crystal reaches over and brushes her hands against her lap. "I missed you too, Alex."

"I know things haven't been easy since Mom and Dad died; it's been pretty lonely at the house without you, Crystal."

A saddened expression surfaces on Crystal's face, she had no idea that being away from home would have affected her sister in that way.

"Alex, the day of Mom and Dad's funeral was an adamant time for us. My focus should have been more on our family: on us. I should have stayed here."

"Crystal, you worked so hard to get into that school in New York. It would have been selfish on my part if I asked you to stay."

Patting Alexandria's lap, Crystal's eyes gleam with admiration towards her sister. After the pain they have gone through with losing their parents, Crystal appreciated how understanding her sister is towards her career and dreams of success.

Emotions begin to stir within Crystal, prompting her to change the subject quickly. "Are you going to tell me who planned this party?" Crystal asks suspiciously, gawking at her sister.

"Crystal," Alex whines, "I already ruin the surprise, now you want me to be a snitch?"

"Who planned it, Alex?"

"Gabby!" she confesses, shaking her head with disappointment, "Gabby set it all up, shoot, she's going to kill me; I can already see it."

"Relax, Alex, I won't say anything. I will play along. Gabby is something else; out of everyone besides Trey, she should know that I hate surprises," Crystal says, feeling annoyed.

"Well, now that the cat is out of the bag, have you heard from John yet?" Alex asks, winking her right eye.

Unable to respond, Crystal remains silent as she looks out the window, thinking about a blooming friendship with John that slowly turned into a full-fledge long-distance romantic relationship just two years ago.

John Pheiffer, also known as JP, is a handsome twenty-four-year-old college graduate. Born half Italian and half Mexican, John has a muscular built from playing sports in his high school years. John, who is six-foot-tall with amber, green eyes, possesses an alluring visage. His short golden brown wavy hair, sharp facial features, and full lips stand out, especially the small dimple he has on his right cheek.

Moving to Lakeview Falls seven years ago, John met Crystal at Lakeview Falls high school at the beginning of their senior year. They quickly became close friends—keeping their friendship strictly platonic while Crystal was dating Terrance Johnson at the time. Crystal and John built trust and mutual respect for one another.

Soon after they graduated high school, Crystal called it quits with Terrance and left Lakeview Falls. Their post-breakup gave John the courage to show how he felt about Crystal. Making her his number one priority, John stayed in touch with Crystal while away at College. During seasonal breaks from grad school, John traveled on the weekends to visit Crystal, which brought them closer and soon turned into a loving romantic relationship between the two.

Reminiscing in her head about their summer together three months ago, Crystal felt uncertain of where her and John's relationship was going. Taking a deep breath, she expresses her concerns to Alexandria.

"I don't know what's going on with John, I have been trying to call him since I got off the plane and he hasn't called me back. It doesn't make any sense why he's acting this way."

"I'm sure he has a good reason for why you haven't heard from him. Aren't you guys officially dating now?"

"Yes, that's why I don't understand his behavior. Between you and me, this summer, John told me that he's in love with me; I told him the same."

"In love? Wow, that is a big step, Crystal. Those three words alone are powerful. Did you sleep with him?"

Unable to respond, Crystal looks away, gritting her teeth.

"You did sleep with him," Alexandria gasps as her eyes widen in shock, "my sister is finally out of the virgin loop. Is it big?"

Giving her sister the side-eye in disgust, she replies, "First of all, that's none of your business, second, what's with the perverted question Alex? It's so inappropriate."

Shrugging her shoulders, Alexandria flashes Crystal a sly smirk. "No, it's not."

"Yes, it is, Alex. You can't just blatantly ask a female how big their boyfriend's dick size is."

"But you're not just anyone; you're my sister. Aren't we supposed to share this information?"

Crystal shakes her head, disapproving. "Well, since you put it that way, I guess it's okay to ask you about Derrick's dick size, huh?"

"Now slow down," Alexandria says, raising her hand, quickly cutting her off, "we are talking about you right now, not me."

"Ha! That's what I thought."

"I can't believe you are finally a woman," Alexandria continues teasing her sister while entering Lakeside Diners parking lot.

"Shut up, Alex, you're so dramatic."

"I am dramatic, but that doesn't change the fact that I've seen a penis before you, and you're older than me."

"By one year..." Crystal corrects her.

"I still had sex before you, Crystal."

Crystal slowly gives her sister a round of applause. "Congratulations, Alex, that still doesn't help the fact that I slept with my boyfriend, and now he's ignoring me."

"John never seemed like the type of guy to act like an asshole; I can't believe he is ghosting you," Alexandria says, frowning at Crystal.

"Me neither, this town isn't big enough to ghost anyone," Crystal says to her sister, glancing out the window, staring at the neon red lights that shine outside the restaurant.

❈ ❈ ❈

Meanwhile, as Crystal's close friends from high school mingle amongst each other, conversing while enjoying great music, assorted platters of fusion food and drinks. Gabriela admires her and Trey's hard work putting the party together. The decorated diner has an amber glow; pink and white ribbons are hung across the off white walls, symbolizing strength and love, which are two admirable traits that Crystal possesses.

Among her friends, awaiting Crystal's arrival are Terrance, Victoria, Phillip, and Justin Mills, both sons of Sheriff Mills. Echoes of excitement and laughter fill the air while Trey worriedly walks away from the group, checking the time on his smartwatch.

Noticing that Matt is running late, Trey scurries over to Gabriela with concern. Waving his hands repeatedly at her, Trey stares awkwardly at Gabby while she stood in a daze, gazing at the hors d' oeuvres on a silver platter.

"Earth to Gabriela!" Trey hollers, finally getting her attention. "How long is it going to take Matt to get here with the cake?" Trey asks, giving a much-needed attitude.

"Trey, calm down, Matt said as soon as he picks it up, he is coming straight here. If it makes you happy, I will try and call him again," Gabriela says to him, taking her phone out of her jeans pocket.

Making a call to her boyfriend, Gabriela and Trey are interrupted by Victoria, who approaches them flashing a plastic smile. Victoria is Lakeview Falls' biggest snobs, her only high quality is absolutely nothing. Victoria only has her beauty that covers up the narcissistic attitude she displays when she doesn't get her way.

Half Vietnamese and half black, Victoria Lawson always dresses the part of an uptight fashionista, her straight black elbow-length hair, slanted light brown eyes, and small perky lips adds an exotic touch to her mixed-race looks. Dating Phillip Mills for over three years, Victoria maintains a cordial friendship with his friends, especially Crystal.

Pointing towards the front window of the diner, Victoria blurts out, "Hey, guys, I just saw Alexandria pull into the parking lot."

Racing over to the multicolored touch screen jukebox, Trey quickly uses the voice command music system to turn it off while Gabriela alerts everyone on Crystal's arrival.

"Okay, everyone, Crystal and Alex just parked up! Get ready," Gabriela shouts as she keeps herself hidden behind the bar counter.

As everyone takes a hiding spot behind the booths, they hear Crystal and her sister Alexandria enter the diner. Suddenly shining a bright light on Crystal, her friends jump out of their hiding spots, screaming.

"SURPRISE!" they shout, throwing colorful confetti at her.

Placing her hands over her chest, Crystal gasps, giving them a goofy smile. "Oh my God, you guys shouldn't have!" she exclaims, trying her hardest to pretend she has no idea about the party.

Strutting over to Alexandria, Trey snatches her arm, pulling her away from Crystal. "You told her, didn't you, Alex?"

"I am so sorry, Trey," she apologizes.

"Alexandria I swear you have a big ass mouth," Trey curses under his breath

"I slipped up Trey. I didn't do it on purpose," Alex replies with her head hung low.

On the other side of the diner, the rest of the gang surrounds Crystal, welcoming her with heartfelt embraces. Overwhelmed by the love of her friends, Crystal takes a moment of silence to absorb it all.

Gabriela's eyes well up as she makes her way through the crowd. Her arms widen as she welcomes Crystal in a sweet embrace. "Welcome home, Crystal; you have no idea how much I've missed you."

Wrapping her arms around her best friend, Crystal becomes emotional. "Gabby, I can't believe you did all of this for me. Thank you," Crystal says, unable to hold back her tears.

"After everything you have been through Crystal, I wanted you to have the best welcome home party. I've been looking forward to this day, and I'm so happy that your home. I've missed you so much, I mean—" Gabby turns, observing everyone's eyes locked on them, smiling, "we've all missed you, Crystal."

Disconnecting from their embrace, Crystal directs her gaze to the rest of her friends as she walks to the center of the room. "Can I please have everyone's attention."

As everyone circles Crystal, Trey passes around glasses of sparkling champagne. Holding their drinks, they continue to listen to her speech.

"I want to thank you all for coming. It's been a while since I've seen all of you. I'm so happy to be back home." Feeling a bit overwhelmed by all the attention, Crystal still keeps a smile on her face.

Raising her glass of champagne, Gabby makes a toast. "To Crystal! Welcome back home."

"To Crystal," everyone responds, raising their glass to her.

Taking a sip of her champagne, Crystal is taken by surprise by a sudden tap on the shoulder. Swiftly turning around, she is shocked to see that it is her ex-boyfriend Terrance Johnson. The twenty-six-year-old post-grad and also martial arts instructor is Lakeview Falls' prominent athlete and motivator for the residents. Since tragedy saturated the town for many years, Terrance reached out to the youths, teaching them self defense mechanisms that could help keep them safe.

Terrance Johnson moved to Lakeview Falls in his sophomore year of high school, winning Crystal's heart. The two dated for two and a half years until Crystal broke it off right after their senior graduation to pursue her dreams at Law school in New York.

Still maintaining the same good looks he had as a teenager, Terrance captured everyone with his charismatic and witty personality. His tall, chiseled, muscular build brings out his smooth brown skin tone.

His hazel brown eyes look at her curiously, his lips turn into a grin. "Hey CJ," he says, calling her by the nickname he gave her when they dated.

Caught off guard, Crystal swiftly swallows the remainder of the champagne that lingered in her mouth. "Terrance," she hiccups.

"Damn," he says, letting out a chuckle, "that must be some good champagne there," he says pointing his finger directly at her glass.

"Excuse me," she says, gently patting her chest. "What a surprise, how are you?" she asks awkwardly, smiling at him.

"I'm great, now that you are here," he says flirtatiously.

Despite their breakup, Terrance wanted to make amends with Crystal. Reaching out with his arms extended, Terrance welcomes Crystal with a warm-hearted, friendly embrace and a soft kiss on her left cheek.

Disconnecting herself from his tight hold, Crystal smiles. "It's nice to see you again Terrance. It has been a long time."

"Yes, it has been a long time. Maybe we can get together sometime?" Terrance asks her, hoping she accepts his invitation.

Waiting for her response, Terrance notices Crystal's eyes shifting towards Gabriela, who worriedly paces back and forth by the Jukebox.

"Crystal, did you hear what I said?" Terrance asks, trying to get her attention.

"I'm sorry Terrance, can we continue this conversation another time?" Crystal says, excusing herself to check on Gabriela.

Approaching her best friend, Crystal sees Gabby's hands trembling while typing a message on her cell phone. "Gabby, what's wrong?"

Looking up at Crystal, Gabby feels a sense of anxiety as she impatiently waits for a text reply. "I've been trying to reach Matt, and he isn't answering my calls. He was supposed to be here an hour ago."

"Maybe he is stuck in traffic Gabby," Crystal says, placing her hands on her back.

"I don't know what it is, Crystal; I have this weird feeling in the pit of my stomach. Something doesn't feel right about this. It's not like him not to contact me," Gabby says with a saddened expression.

"Don't worry, Gabby; I'm sure Matt is fine."

Gabriela wanted to believe that Crystal was right, but her gut feeling was telling her something different. Glaring at her phone, she mutters to herself.

"If Matt is fine, then where the hell is he?"

CHAPTER THREE

IT'S COMING FOR YOU

FALL PARK LANE

A musk scent fills the cold night air as headlights from a car creeps through the fog. After leaving Delia's bakery to pick up the custom made cake that Gabriela ordered for Crystal's welcome back party, Matt decides to take a quicker route to Lakeside diner. Driving down the narrow rural trail on Fall Park Lane, Matt fails to remember the lane is off-limits due to a horrible incident of multiple mutilated bodies discovered a few weeks prior.

He drives at a speed of 90 mph, ignoring the Sheriff's department warning about speeding after-hours down rural roads. The law in Michigan forbids deputies to go above 50 mph. Matt knew he was breaking the rules. He was Instructed by his chief to conduct himself as a man of the law when he is in uniform.

Making a sharp right turn down the eerie dark, forest pathway, Matt is blindsided by a foggy mist. Straining his eyes as if he is peering at a pond of gray murk, the young deputy continues to drive down the trail. Feeling an instant vibration from his cell phone that is lodged in his pants pocket, Matt pulls it out and sees he has eight missed calls and text messages from Gabriela.

Releasing a sigh, Matt places the cell phone on the passenger seat while driving with one hand on the steering wheel. Directing his gaze back on the wooded trail, Matt is startled by a shadowy human figure standing in a frozen stance in the middle of the road.

"Holy Shit!" Matt shouts as he presses his foot quickly on the brakes.

Swirling his car from left to right, he is unable to control his vehicle. His eyes widen in fear while his mouth opens in a silent scream as the patrol car slams directly into the figure with an earth-shattering **"BOOM!"**

In an instant, Matt's body lunges forward, hitting his chest against the steering wheel with a thud. The person is thrown violently across the road. Their body lays flat on the concrete ground while Matt slumps backward in his seat, panic-stricken.

Wiping the excessive sweat that drips down his forehead, a wheezing sound escapes his lips as fear begins to settle in. Grabbing his cell phone, Matt tries to call Sheriff Mills but realizes he has no reception.

Leaning over for his walkie-talkie, Matt detaches the portable handset and presses down on the side button, alerting an emergency dispatcher. He breathes heavily, listening to his heartbeat race rapidly by the minute. The adrenaline rush from the accident sends tremors up and down his spine. Visibly shaken and terrified, Matt impatiently waits for a response. Suddenly, he hears a dispatcher on the other line.

"This is Lisa Harrow, dispatcher number 501826. What is your emergency?"

"I need help!" he yells loudly into the walkie talkie. "This is Deputy Matthew Scott from Lakeview Falls Sheriff's department. There's been an accident; I hit someone! I am on Fall Park Lane; I repeat Fall Park Lane! I need you to contact my head chief Sheriff Thomas Mills and send an ambulance, please! Copy!"

"We will send someone to you as soon as possible Deputy Scott. Stay where you are!" the female dispatcher replies on the other end of the line.

"Okay, thank you, and please hurry!" Ending the call, Matt lowers his head, dropping the walkie talkie on the passenger seat.

Matt lifts his head and froze, staring at the middle of the road. Every muscle in his body goes numb as he stares at the person he hit, standing a few feet away from his patrol car, grimacing at him.

The man's mangled body stands in a crooked slant. He rocks back and forth, gawking at the young deputy. With both of his arms severed, blood slowly oozes down his forehead, dripping onto the cold granite concrete ground.

On the verge of tears, Matt stares intensely at the man standing in an awkward position. Even though his fears are rooted deep within him, his sense of bravery made him want to make sure the man he hit is okay. Muttering a Santa Maria prayer to himself, Matt cautiously exits his patrol car.

As Matt takes a few steps away from his vehicle, his feet slowly graze on the wet ground, gradually inhaling the crisp air into his mouth. Feeling knots in the pit of his stomach, he notices the figure eyeing him in a cold and malice glare.

"Sir!" Matt shouts inching closer towards the man, "Are you okay?" he asks nervously, keeping his hand beside his gun belt. "I called for help; an ambulance will be here soon to take you to the hospital."

Shivering from the brisk breeze, Matt shudders. A surge of intuition courses through his veins, waiting for the man to respond. The eerie silence is interrupted by the man's gaping mouth, releasing a low base growl, breathing in and out.

From a short distance, Matt is paralyzed in sheer horror, gazing at the giant skinless demon. It's pale, slimy disfigured face looks at Matt up and down with its fiery red eyes. The monster listens to the pulsating sounds of Matt's heartbeat with its bat wing-shaped ears. It snarls while two distinctive grey horns protrude from the top of its skull.

"What the fuck!" Matt exclaims as he backs away immediately, drawing his gun at the demon. "Stay back! I swear to God I will shoot you!" he says, clenching his pistol tightly in his hand, pointing it at the creature.

THE BROTHER'S CURSE

Frightened, Matt can feel his bowels loosen as he freely urinates through his pants, engulfed in fear as the demon sprints towards him at full speed, grappling him by the back of his neck. No time to react, Matt is held in a firm grip, staring dead into the creature's bloodshot eyes.

"Please don't kill me, please, please don't!" Matt whimpers softly, pleading to the demon to spare his life.

Complete hopelessness converts into tears that rain down Matt's face at lightning speed. The offensive decaying smell released from the demon's skinless body forces him to regurgitate in his mouth, swallowing his vomit.

As the demon's face gradually splits open from its temple down to its jawbone, the creature exposes one hundred sharp razor blade teeth. Releasing a bone-chilling scream, Matt slowly closes his eyes as the demon latches its jaws into his face, ripping his skin clean off.

Gnawing the remaining ligaments of Matt's face, the demon extends its long grey tongue, licking fresh blood from its chin. Unleashing a euphoric sexual moan enticed by the taste of male flesh in its mouth, the grotesque creature rips Matt apart, limb by limb scattering him all over the wet rural road.

❋ ❋ ❋

MEANWHILE AT FEARMAN STREET

The street lights enshroud with an eerie, mystical glow while the air is thick with smog. Across the street at the Town Hall Circle, one lamppost flickers like a candle threatening to extinguish itself at any moment. Entering Lakeside Diner's spacious parking lot, Sheriff Mills pulls into his private parking spot reserved only.

Leaning towards his car's back seat, Sheriff Mills stretches his arms out to grab a small-flowered printed gift box with a pink bow tie neatly wrapped around it. Shifting his hip to the right, reaching for the gift, Sheriff Mills is startled by the sound of a **toot** that exits from his rear end.

Instantly smelling the pungent odor that spreads vigorously inside the vehicle, Sheriff Mills' hands flutter from side to side as his face scrunches up in disgust, "HooWee!" he exclaims in a high pitch tone. "I shouldn't have eaten those two-day-old burritos," he mutters to himself, quickly exiting the patrol car.

Tucking the gift box under his arm, Sheriff Mills proceeds towards the diner, whistling a western tune. Fiddling his car keys between his fingers, Sheriff Mills walks up the concrete steps to the main entrance, where he hears echoes of laughter coming from the opposite side of the door. Grabbing the polished brass handle, Sheriff Mills enters the restaurant and sees everyone dancing to an upbeat tune on the jukebox.

Noticing Sheriff Mills from a distance, his older son, twenty-seven-year-old Justin Ryan Mills, quickly approaches him. A spitting image of his father, Justin's clear, youthful skin is the kind you see in magazines with airbrushed models. Known for being the family's backbone, Justin has an optimistic and mature demeanor that sets him apart from the dysfunctional family turmoil he has to deal with behind closed doors.

Recently graduating from the police academy, Justin decides to follow in his father's footsteps in the law force, becoming a newly appointed deputy. As a rookie officer, Justin knew one thing in life: to be a protector to his family and to his town that has suffered devastation.

 Justin's deep blue sparkling eyes search his father's confusingly as a tiny scar stretches above his left eyebrow. "Dad, what are you doing here? I thought you were working late?"

"I thought so too, but plans changed, I had to let everyone go home early after we took all those damn bodies down from the lamppost," Sheriff Mills responds, removing his olive green four dent style uniform hat, stroking his thick head of hair slicking it back.

"Jesus, Dad, can you lower your voice?" Justin quietly says to his father, checking to see if anyone heard him.

"Well, you asked me a question, moron," he groans inwardly at his son.

Running his fingers through his short wavy dirty blonde hair, a sigh of annoyance escapes Justin's lips. "Dad, why are you here?"

Sheriff Mills smile widens, crinkling slightly at the corners. "I'm here because I heard you all were throwing Crystal a welcome home party, and I thought it would be nice to drop by and say hello."

"Dad, it's a small get together just for close friends, that means no parents allowed."

"I'm her godfather for Christ sakes; her parents were dear friends of mine, God rest their souls. You know you have some nerve questioning me. Let's not forget who is in charge in this family; now, can you please get the hell out of my way so I can give her this nice gift I brought," Sheriff Mills says, slowly pushing his son aside.

"Dad, maybe you should give that to Crystal some other time."

"What the hell is your problem, Justin? You're all fidgety and acting like a nervous wreck."

"Look, Phillip is here, and I don't want you guys to fight in public."

"Fight?" he bursts into laughter, "It's not my fault your brother still has a stick up his ass because his mom left us many moons ago. He needs to get over it and stop acting like a child."

"Phillip has been struggling a lot since that happened, and even though he puts on a clown act as if nothing phases him, I know he isn't happy."

"Save me the dramatics son; I don't care if Phillip's mad that I showed up. It's bad enough that the two of you are grown men still living under my roof. If he doesn't like to mingle with his pops, then let him act like a little ass hat. He has his hands full these days with little Miss Saigon over there," the Sheriff finishes, directing his eyes to Victoria. Sheriff Mills clicks his teeth, watching her wave at him from across the room.

"Come on, Dad," Justin exclaims, lifting his shoulders and shrugging, "Victoria is not that bad."

"Not that bad? Have you seen what she does to our bathroom sink in the mornings? Jesus Christ, the last thing I need is for that girl to officially become a Mills, then my life will surely be in the goddamn pits."

"She might not be the cleanest person when it comes to tidying up Dad, but she cooks for us."

"I'm tired of eating Vietnamese curry chicken every day; I'm more of a roast beef and cabbage kind of guy. At this point, I don't mind cooking for myself. Speaking of, when exactly do you plan on moving out of my house?"

Giving his father a sly smirk, Justin pats him on the back aggressively. "Enjoy the party, Dad."

"Thank you, son, I knew that would shut you up," nodding his head slightly, Sheriff Mills snickers, flick finger slapping his son against his forehead, walking away.

Advancing towards Crystal, Sheriff Mills grips the gift box tightly in his hands, taking a deep breath. Wiping the excessive sweat from his forehead, he comes up from behind, tapping her on the shoulders, clearing his throat.

A delighted smile stretches across Crystal's face. "Uncle Thomas!" she ecstatically says, spreading her arms wide, welcoming him in.

Gently embracing his goddaughter, Sheriff Mills couldn't help but think back to how devastated he was when he discovered Robert and Desiree's murder. The friendship he had built with Crystal's parents stems from the late 1970s when he first met her father, Robert Francois, at Lakeview Falls University.

Becoming close friends quickly, Thomas and Robert formed a bond of brotherhood for many years. Both married with children, Robert formally asked Thomas to be the godfather of his two daughters. Accepting, Thomas Mills promised his best friend that he would protect and look after Crystal and Alexandria no matter what.

Enraptured by her presence, Sheriff Mills takes a step back to take a long look at his goddaughter. "Crystal, my dear; it is great to see you."

"It's great to see you too, Uncle Thomas," she giggles, " I didn't think I would see you so soon."

"Matthew told me you were moving back, and of course, as your godfather, I have to make sure that you are okay. If there is anything you need, Crystal, do not hesitate to contact me."

"Thank you, Uncle Thomas, I appreciate it," with a soft smile, Crystal gently places her hands on Sheriff Mills' arms when Gabby suddenly interrupts them.

"Sheriff Mills, have you heard from Matt? I've been trying to get in contact with him, but he hasn't returned my phone calls."

"I saw him an hour ago; I thought he would have been here already since he was rushing to leave work."

Checking his voice command wristwatch, Sheriff Mills feels a vibration from his portable walkie-talkie that goes off, alarming the crowd. A loud static sound echoes, causing everyone to stop dancing.

"Sheriff Mills! I am Dispatcher Carol Tugney at Michigan's emergency department; I have just received an alert that there has been an accident at Fall Park Lane Forest, an off-duty male officer called in asking for immediate help. His Deputy number is LVF4608942, I REPEAT! His number is LVF4608942."

The sudden shock of hearing the dispatcher call out the numbers instantly made Gabriela' pulse beat in her ears, blocking out all other sounds around her. "Oh my God!" she gasps, "that's Matty's number!" she squeals frantically.

Fear becomes tangible as everyone inside the diner tries to remain calm. Immediately heading over to the jukebox, Trey bends over and reaches behind the music system, forcefully pulling the plug out from the outlet. A feeling of dread engulfs Sheriff Mills when he hears the name Fall Park Lane; Just hours before, he had warned his entire unit to stay away from that trail for safety reasons. Steadying his breath, Sheriff Mills calmly responds to the dispatcher.

"Copy that, I'm on my way," Sheriff Mills says worriedly, placing his walkie talkie back on his belt, his head shakes from side to side. "I told that kid to stay off that road; what the hell was he doing driving over there?" he whispers to himself.

Tears well up in Gabriela's light brown eyes while shifting her gaze to Sheriff Mills. "Did something happen to Matt?"

"Gabriela, I don't know; if I hear anything, I will give you a call. For now, I think you should go home," Sheriff Mills replies, advancing towards the center of the diner.

"Excuse me, everyone!" he whistles loudly, getting everyone's attention. "I'm sorry to be the bearer of bad news, but I am officially declaring a town curfew, starting now! I would suggest that you all go home where it's safer."

Baffled, Justin walks up to his father with an intense glare. "Dad, what the hell is going on?"

"Listen to me." Inching closer to his son's ears; Sheriff Mills whispers, "I think Matt is in trouble, and I can't have everyone in a panic state. Two days ago, I found three male bodies in Fall Park forests, which means that whoever is killing these men is still on the loose. Please step up and make sure your friends, including Crystal, go straight home. You hear me?"

"Dad, let me come with you," Justin pleads with a stern expression following him to the front entrance. "It's not safe to go there by yourself, Dad."

"Son, I've been doing this job for over twenty-five years; I will be fine. Stop talking and go home! Now!" Sheriff Mills yells, pushing the exit door open.

Shoving Justin out of her way, Gabriela chases after Sheriff Mills. The crisp breeze sends her long silky black locks fluttering back. Desperately pushing negative thoughts out of her mind, Gabriela advances towards the patrol car, grabbing hold of Sheriff Mills' arms, searching his face for a hidden sign.

"I'm not going home, not until I find out my boyfriend is okay," she cries out.

"Gabriela, let go of me, please! That's unless you want to sit in my station for being aggressive with a Sheriff."

"I'm sorry, Sheriff Mills."

Unleashing her grip from Sheriff Mills, Gabby notices everyone rushing out of the diner, including Justin, who advances in their direction. Unlocking his car door, Sheriff Mills enters his vehicle, slamming the door shut. Turning on the ignition, he quickly pulls out of the parking lot and drives off Fearman Street.

"Sheriff Mills! Come Back!" Gabriela hollers, watching the patrol car speed down the Town Hall Circle.

"Gabby! Go home! I will catch up with my dad!" Justin says, pulling out the keys to his dark blue jeep.

"Don't tell me what to do, Justin! I'm going to find Matt."

"Gabby, come with me and let Sheriff Mills handle it," Crystal says, proceeding down the concrete stairs.

"Can everyone shut up! Matt could be hurt!"

"You don't know that Gabriela," Trey responds, wrapping his arms around her, "I'm sure Matt is fine. Maybe his car broke down or something."

"You guys heard what my dad said, go home! If anything comes up, I will let you know!"

"Justin! Where the hell are you going?" Phillip asks, rushing towards the mustang, holding Victoria's hand.

"Dad set a curfew; I suggest you and Victoria drive back to the house. Something's up with Matt, it doesn't sound good."

"Screw what Dad said!" Phillip responds, raising his voice at his brother. "Since when do you take orders from him? Matt is our friend. We have every right to know what's going on!"

"If Dad says you shouldn't go, that means you shouldn't go. Why are you so damn stubborn, Phillip?"

Shaking his head with disapproval, Phillip brushes his hand over his short dark brown locks letting out a grunt. "Gabby! Trey! You guys can take a ride in my car!" Phillip shouts, stomping pass his brother.

Grappling his brother's wrist, Justin pulls him away from Victoria. "You can't be serious, Phillip! We all can't go there; this isn't a joke. What if there is something there that we are not supposed to see? Huh?"

Like a raging bull, Gabriela storms towards Justin. "If you don't get out of Phillip's way, I will chop your Pelotas off!" she threatens, giving Justin a long, long sinister glare.

"Instead of everyone bickering, why can't we just leave already? All we are doing is wasting time in this parking lot," Terrance says, inching towards his red mustang.

Agreeing with Terrance, the group decides to follow Justin to Fall park Lane. As everyone enters their vehicles, Crystal enters the passenger side of her sister's mini coop, shutting the door. Releasing a long sigh, Alexandria starts her vehicle and follows behind Phillip's car.

An uneasy feeling stirs in the pit of Crystal's stomach as her face displays a wave of gloom. "You see Alex, this is why I hate surprises," she says, frowning inwardly at her sister.

CHAPTER FOUR

TERROR AWAITS

FALL PARK FORESTS

Lightning strikes with a golden gleam, releasing a loud crack of thunder from the distant sky. A frigid breeze creates a dreadful, evil, and haunting aura surrounding the abandoned rural forest pathway. Whizzing through a red light at the intersection of South Skinner and Grimm Field, Sheriff Mills cautiously makes a narrow turn into Fall Park Lane.

Peering through the dark maze with sweat running in his eyes, Sheriff Mills is confused by the dangerous unknowns that lie at the end of the trail. The wooded forest is cloaked in darkness as trees stood still like statues in a museum while shrill cries of cicadas echo on autumn leaves barely hanging from its branches.

Pulling over, Sheriff Mills steps out of his patrol car. Trudging down the forest path's soft, damp moss, a pungent metallic smell ferment in the air, hitting his nostrils instantly. Shielding his face with his forearm, Sheriff Mills sees an ongoing trail of fresh blood on the granite ground.

A tremor takes over his body while continuing down the pathway. Reaching the trail's center, he sees Deputy Scott's patrol car's bright headlights abandoned by a hollow tree. Noticing the driver's side door wide open, Sheriff Mills takes slow steps closer towards the vehicle.

Immediately drawing his semi-automatic pistol, Sheriff Mills uses his left hand to hold up his small silver flashlight. Fear rises from behind the Sheriff's eyes as he aims his gun towards the front of the car. In sheer horror, he shrieks at the sight of Deputy Scott's mutilated corpse scattered across the ground while two opossums stood beside his head, nibbling on an ear.

Sheriff Mills couldn't scream; he could only open his mouth to find that even words have deserted him. The nightmare standing in front of him is more than unbearable; it's horrific. Every minute feels as though he is out of touch with reality; no matter how hard he wants to believe it is not Matthew, he knows it is.

Shooing the revolting mammal away from the torn limbs, Sheriff Mills is disturbed by an overpowering zzzz of bloodthirsty mosquitoes that start coming at a high number, hovering over Deputy Scott's corpse. The gruesome sight of swarming fresh larva emerging from the upper torso part of the young deputy's body, causes Sheriff Mills to look away, regurgitating thick yellow bile onto his brown leather boots.

Forcing himself to take deep breaths, Sheriff Mills feels water creep out of his eyes. Suddenly, there is an aura of grey around him. It is a fog that will not rise nor fade.

"Goddammit," he mumbles as more tears trickle down his cheeks.

Taking hold of his walkie-talkie, Sheriff Mills makes the call he dreads as a chief of police. Pressing down on his alert button, he contacts Michigan's emergency line.

"Michigan's Emergency Patrol hotline, this is Dispatcher Cassidy Tooter, state number 69960. What is your emergency?"

Sheriff Mills' heart frantically beats; he opens his mouth, trying to concentrate on what he is going to say. There are no words to describe how heartbroken he is at losing such a fine young man like Matthew. The pain of another life taken in a matter of hours will send everyone on edge, including his son, Justin and rookie deputies who just started the job.

TERROR AWAITS

Sniffling, Sheriff Mills wipes his hand across his nose. He releases a sorrowful sigh. "This is Sheriff Thomas Mills from Lakeview Falls local department, I'm reporting the murder of one of my men, Deputy Matthew Scott. I found his body dismembered at the Fall park Lane Forest pathway; I need assistance with removing the deceased as soon as possible."

"Sheriff, can you describe the condition of the body before we send the coroners?"

"WHAT!" he shouts, appalled by the dispatcher's question, "are you on drugs? Did you not hear me say dismembered body? Get me some goddamn help!"

Swiftly ending the conversation, the distraught Sheriff angrily smashes the walkie-talkie repeatedly against the cold granite ground. A roar of rage escapes his lips while kneeling on one leg to inspect for any evidence of who or what might have killed Deputy Scott.

Sheriff Mills' eyes then fixates on the small red and black skull tattoo with the wording above that says: **"LVF Deputy 4 Life,"** displaying on Matthew's dismembered arm.

Grief sweeps through the Sheriff's system as he slowly buries his face in his hands. In that moment, he reflects on the day Matthew graduated from the police academy, becoming the newest Deputy of Lakeview Falls.

❈ ❈ ❈

EIGHT MONTHS AGO

Surrounded by friends and family inside Lakeside Diner, Matthew Antonio Scott ecstatically cuts the first slice of his vanilla and strawberry frosted sponge cake. The three-tier pastry was custom made with Matthew's decorative caricature wearing his uniform, giving a thumbs up.

Standing beside him with an adoring expression, Gabriela Santos admired how driven her boyfriend was at becoming a man of the law. Caressing his back, Gabriela began to sing **"For He's a**

Jolly- Good Fellow," which prompts everyone else to follow her lead. Matt's infectious smile widens while gazing at his fellow officers who also came to congratulate him on his big day.

His parents Mateo and Martina Scott were ecstatic when their only son became the first Mexican American officer to achieve his goals. Joining the sheriff's department, Matthew had finally accomplished his dream at the age of twenty-five.

Raising his glass of champagne for a toast, Matt quickly glances over at his best friend Derrick, who lifts his left arm to salute him with a sly smirk. Nodding to Derrick with a wink of an eye, Matt proceeds with his heartfelt speech.

"Can I have everyone's attention, please," Matt asks in a soft-spoken tone, tapping the glass with a dessert fork. "I want to thank you all for coming and sharing this exciting new chapter of my life. When I first joined the police academy, I knew it was going to be a challenge, but with the support from my wonderful parents and friends, including my best friend, Derrick who busted my balls to join him in the force, I don't think I could have gone through with this."

Shifting his gaze to Gabriela, Matt had a sharp dimpled face that seemed to devour her heart. The love he had for Gabby was pure and raw. Placing his hands gently on the sides of her face, he stroke his fingers through her silky long black locks.

"I want to thank you, Gabriela, for being an amazing woman. From the moment I met you, I knew that you were my one and only. There was no doubt that I wanted to spend my life with you. I promise that I will do everything I can to make our forever come true."

Biting her lower lip, Gabriela couldn't fight the warm tears that began trickling down her rosy cheeks. Everyone stood in awe, listening to Matt profess his undying love for Gabby. A sobbing whimper suddenly escapes Martina Scott's lips as she pulls out a handkerchief to dry her eyes.

"Gabby," Matt says, taking hold of her hand.

"I want to thank you for being my better half and for always standing by my side throughout this ordeal. Te quiero muchísimo Gabriela," he expresses, kissing her gently on the lips.

"Hey, what about all of us?" Sheriff Mills hollers jokingly, giving Matt a goofy smile, "What are we? Chop liver?" he asks, letting out a short random laugh.

A delighted expression spreads across Matt's face, smiling at his fellow officers. "How can I forget about you guys? You're my family through thick and thin, and I hope to make you all proud, including you, Sheriff Mills. I wish us all many years of kicking ass at this department," he says and raises his glass to his squad and Sheriff Mills with a warm-hearted smile.

❅ ❅ ❅

BACK AT THE SCENE

Sheriff Mills' eyes snap open, realizing that Matt was never coming back. The young deputy's memories will forever live on in his heart, and everyone else he touched with his loving and self-compassion. Worried about the reaction Matt's death will have on everyone, Sheriff Mills prepares himself for what's to come.

A murder like Matthew's will hit everyone in the worst way. The media outlets and state government would come down hard on the Sheriff's department, blaming them for not protecting their own. Sheriff Mills knew he would face backlash for not working hard enough in finding who or what had been killing innocent men all over town.

Removing his uniform hat, Sheriff Mills runs his fingers through his hair, huffing under his breath with aggravation. Rising from the ground, he hears the loud screeching of the tires heading in his direction. In a panic, Sheriff Mills' head swivels around, drawing his gun immediately.

Staring at the bright headlights, he recognizes the license plate belonging to his son Justin. In annoyance, Sheriff Mills grunts with a heavy sigh while staring at his son and two other cars behind his, parking up by the side of the forest road.

Clutching his pistol against his chest, he watches both Justin and Phillip exit their vehicles. Cold air biting into his lungs, Sheriff Mills runs at high speed in their direction, quickly blocking his sons from advancing further towards the area where Matt's mutilated remains are.

Cautiously putting his pistol back in his gun belt holster, Sheriff Mills extends his arms, placing his rough hands against their chest as a warning to stop.

"What in the hell are you two idiots doing here?" he asks his son with an unpleasant expression.

"Dad, I know what you said but—- but," Justin stutters trying to explain himself.

Irritated, Sheriff Mills feels his temperature rise quickly; his head spins, threatening to explode. "But nothing Justin! I told you and the rest of your Scooby gang to go straight home!"

"Why do you always have to yell at us like we're little kids?" Phillip shouts, raising his arms in the air.

"Because you don't Listen! You don't fucking Listen!" he yells. In vexation, Sheriff Mills forcefully thrust his sons.

Stumbling backward, both brothers see the intensity in their father's eyes. Justin and Phillip knew at that moment that the anger bottled up in their farther was not because they disobeyed his orders; it is because something terrible was lying at the end of the trail that he didn't want them to see.

"Dad, we had to come; we are all worried about Matt, plus, Gabby threatened to cut my balls off if we didn't bring her here. I believe her. I tend to steer clear from Latin women when they're angry," Justin says, scrunching his face.

"Look at me, Justin!" he says with a scowl, "does my face look like I give a shit about anything you are saying? You both need to get in your car and leave right this instant! If you let Gabriela get out of that car, she's going to regret it because in a few minutes, the coroners will be here with a body bag."

"A body bag? Dad, what happened to Matt, where is he?" Phillip questions his father, trying to push him out of his way.

"Phillip! I'm not going to repeat myself, get in your damn car and leave! Take Gabriela home. Now!"

"No, Dad, I'm not going anywhere!" Phillip raises his voice in anger as he stares directly into his father's light brown eyes.

"You better lower your voice when you speak to me, boy! I am still your father."

"What are you hiding, Dad?" Justin asks suspiciously, "I can see Matt's car by that tree. What happened to him?"

"Screw you, Dad! I want to see what's at the end of that trail!" Shoving his father to the side, Phillip scurried towards Matt's vehicle.

Shifting his gaze away from Justin, Sheriff Mills tries to stop Phillip when Justin grabs hold of his arm. "Dad just let him go!"

"Phillip, if you go any further, you are going to regret it! I promise you!" Sheriff Mills yells aggressively.

Edging a cautious inch closer to the patrol car, Phillip stretches out his neck and is taken back by the horrendous odor. A sickening aura of death circles him, he tries not to breathe, but he knows it is impossible.

Taking a single step, Phillip squeals, "Oh, Shit!" and he covers his mouth, horrified by the gruesome scene.

Meanwhile, seated in Phillip's car's back seat, Gabby glances out the front window and sees Phillip frantically running back to his father, who stood arguing with Justin. Observing the traumatized expression on Phillip's face worried her. If Phillip looks frightened, then she knows something terrible has happened to her beloved boyfriend.

A sudden quiver creeps through Gabby's body as she wraps her arms around her stomach, feeling faint. Slowly dragging in air, she eases it out, reaching for the car door handle when she is stopped abruptly by Trey, who tightly clasps her hand.

"Gabby, what are you doing?" Trey asked hesitantly.

THE BROTHER'S CURSE

Flinching her hand back In frustration, Gabby gives Trey a good stare. "What does it look like, Trey? I'm going to see what's going on; I need to know where Matt is."

"Gabriela, I don't think that's a good idea. Maybe we should let Sheriff Mills handle this."

"Trey, let go of my arm!" Gabriela hollers, removing Trey's hands off her.

Gripping the handle, Gabby immediately exits Phillip's vehicle, slamming the door behind her. Stomping her way towards Sheriff Mills, her face is flushed with anger, "Sheriff Mills! Where's Matt?"

Extending his hand out, Sheriff Mills shields her from getting through. "Whoa! Gabriela, you can't go any further. Please turn around and get back in the car. That's an order!"

"Something happened to Matt, right? Right?" she shouts with a high pitch tone. "Answer Me!"

"Gabby, my dad is right," Phillip says, intervening, "I will take you home, okay."

"NO! Now get the hell out of my way, Phillip!"

"I can't do that, Gabby!"

Striking her foot against his shin with a powerful force, Phillip feels an intense pain as Gabriela pushes him away. Fighting the throbbing ache in his knee, Phillip hurls himself towards Gabriela, grappling her forearm.

"Gabby, please stop! Don't go near there!" Phillip pleads with her.

Spinning her around, Gabriela slaps her right palm across Phillip's face. Her eyes widen in anger; she runs further away towards the trail, but Phillip follows, tripping and stumbling over his own two feet. Tears run down her cheeks in blankets as she begins to scream out.

"Matt! Matt! Where are you?"

"Gabriela! Stop this instant! I'm warning you!" Sheriff Mills hollers, taking out his gun and shooting one round in the air.

Grabbing the gun from his father, Justin shouts, "Dad, what the hell are you doing?"

Reaching the end of the trail, Gabriela's memories of her and Matt flood her mind like waves of destruction, breaking her hope and joy. The frantic beat of her heart is like a train on a rickety track.

Gabriela's ragged breath moves in and out of her mouth, gasping in intervals as she approaches Matt's patrol car. Terror-stricken, Gabriela's jaw drops at the sight of her boyfriend's mutilated corpse, lying beside the Vanilla frosted cake with a raspberry colored wording that reads, **"Welcome Home, Crystal."** Letting out a blood-curdling scream, Gabriela falls to her knees.

CHAPTER FIVE

THE FINAL GOODBYE

LAKEVIEW FALLS CEMETERY
FIVE DAYS LATER

CRYSTAL NARRATES

The smell of wet roses sweeps into my nose; the sky is dark grey, and dreary as the rain falls rapidly to the turf-grass lawn. Grief hangs in the air like a thick wool blanket covering us as we grieve our beloved friend's passing. All around are tear-stained faces sobbing as I glance at Matt's family, who look so hurt and heartbroken. His death leaves a massive hole in all of our hearts that might not ever be repairable. Matt was one of the most caring and selfless people I have ever met in my life, and for that, I will always cherish the moments we had in this lifetime.

As I stood in silence, holding Gabriela's hands, I thought to myself how much I'm not too fond of funerals and losing loved ones. I couldn't help but feel as though this entire situation was all my fault. Maybe, if I didn't come back home, Gabby wouldn't have decided to throw that party; and Matthew would still be here; he would be alive.

THE BROTHER'S CURSE

Everything seems foggy and eerie as I look around at all of the tombstones surrounding us. All I could remember at that moment was when I stood here one year ago, saying my final goodbye to my mother and father. As Trey and I remain silent at the memorial service, we hear Gabby's heartbreaking onslaught of sobs. I wish I could make her feel better and take away her pain, be the best friend that tells her everything will be okay, but I can't; all I could do is comfort her in her grieving state.

When you lose someone you love with all of your heart, no one can tell you it will get better, only time can do that. Whoever or whatever killed Matt is still out there. I can't help but ask myself if it's the same monster that killed my parents also. Trying to hold me together even though I am full of despair, I continue questioning; what purpose do I have when it comes to living in this dreadful town?

The moment I stepped foot in Lakeview Falls again, I knew I didn't belong here anymore. Events occurring are almost like a domino effect because I decided to be closer to the people I love. The gut feeling I have in the pit of my stomach tells me that something wanted me back here; I have no idea what it is. **I fear that this is far from over.**

❆ ❆ ❆

Flocks of crows croak like the roaring of some terrible beast casting a relentless misery on all who trespass in their territory. The wind blows bitterly across the black silk sheet-like covering placed over Matt's casket, while Father Joel Harbor delivers a heartfelt eulogy.

"Matthew Antonio Scott was a fine young man, taken away from us too soon. He was a son, a partner, and a friend to all who knew him. His love and passion and, most importantly, his dedication and selfless acts protecting this town, and our residents. May he always be remembered. Let us all bow our heads in a moment of silence."

While everyone remains still, soundless with heaviness in their hearts, Trey's eyes fixate on the casket before he lowers his head, muttering, "I knew Matt shouldn't have bought that cake."

Standing beside Trey, Victoria clicks her teeth in disgust, "Jesus Christ Trey, nobody gives a shit about the cake."

"Dude!" We're at a funeral!" Phillip snarls, squinting his right eye that was slightly bruised by Gabriela's slap.

"Yes, Phillip, we are at a funeral, a funeral that did not have to happen if Matt didn't drive down the wrong road. This shit would have never happened if your father was more clear about the closed-off roadways!" Trey shouts in rage.

"You better calm down and keep your mouth shut, Trey," Phillip scowls, pointing his finger in his face.

Taking a step towards Phillip, Trey rolls up his suit jacket sleeve, clenching his fist. "Make me, Phillip, come on!" he says.

"Hey, what is wrong with you two?" Crystal mutters, grabbing hold of Trey's hand, "Seriously, this is not the right time for an argument. You need to show some respect for Matt and his family."

A sigh escapes Trey's lips. "You're right Crystal, I'm sorry; it's hard to process everything that is happening."

"I know Trey, but we all have to be strong for Gabby right now, this is not easy for her either."

Crystal's eyes begin to well up while caressing Trey's back; she can feel the anger raging within her best friend. Trey is never one to become irate or come out of character, but at this moment, it all seems as though everyone's emotions were at its all-time high. For Gabby, Matt's death is like being trapped in another world where she cannot breathe or escape.

While Trey takes a few moments to calm himself, Phillip and Victoria excuse themselves from the funeral while the priest finishes the eulogy. Avoiding another altercation, they quickly give their condolences to Matt's parents then proceed out of the cemetery.

As Gabriela watches Matthew's coffin lowered into the cold, hard earth, her eyes swell with saturated grief. Nothing else matters to her, now that he isn't here anymore. Her body stood stiff like the porcelain statues displayed throughout the cemetery. Lowering her head, she whimpers, "I can't believe my Matty is gone."

THE BROTHER'S CURSE

"I can't believe it either, Gabby; I'm so sorry. Matt was a one of a kind guy, and he loved you more than anything in this world, you know that, right?"

"I shouldn't have made him go, Crystal; he told me not to have that party for you, and I didn't listen. He wanted you to settle down first when you got home before being bombarded with surprise parties. I'm so stupid."

"Gabby, this isn't your fault," Crystal softly says, gently placing her hand on her shoulder. "You couldn't have known what was going to happen to him; please don't blame yourself."

Suddenly, Gabriela's almond-shaped eyes gleam with darkness as she swiftly turns to face Crystal. "You're right, Crystal, I shouldn't blame myself. I should blame you!" she says, brushing Crystal's hands off her shoulders.

Flabbergasted, Crystal did not know how to react; she pauses, staring long and hard at Gabriela when Trey abruptly interrupts. "Gabby, how can you say that? Crystal had nothing to do with Matt's death; I know you're upset right now, but you need to calm down."

"Shut up, Trey!" Gabriela angrily yells out, backing away from the two of them.

"You know what Crystal? If you didn't decide to come back home, none of this would have happened."

A solemn tear falls down Crystal's cheek; her body looks calm compared to how tangled her mind is, hearing her best friend lash out at her in such a harsh matter. Crystal folds her arms and purses her lips, infuriated by Gabriela's attitude towards her.

"Gabby, how can you say this to me? After everything I've been through, do you think that my presence is what caused Matt's death? My parents died! I had no choice but to come back home. If you were a real friend like you claim to be, you would not be this nasty to me."

"I have every right to feel the way I feel, Crystal!"

"The way you are reacting is uncalled for Gabby; not for nothing, you're the one who decided to throw that party for me. I didn't ask for any of this. You know that I'm not fond of surprises, Gabriela, and you still went along with it. Maybe you need to re-evaluate your attitude before you say something else you might regret."

Furrowing her eyebrows, Gabriela rolls her eyes. "I need space away from you Crystal, I can't continue this conversation. I'm too upset, and it's hard to think straight."

"That's fine with me, Gabby; you should go and let off your steam somewhere else."

Making no reply, Gabriela ignores Crystal and kindly asks Trey to take her to her family's restaurant. Tightly wrapping her black scarf around her neck, Gabby walks along the cobblestone trail along with everyone else who said their final farewell, exiting the cemetery.

Watching Gabriela heading towards his vehicle, Trey's eyes shift to Crystal, who is visibly distraught. "Crystal, are you okay?"

"Yes, I will be fine, Trey," Crystal sniffles, trying to hold back her sobs.

"Gabby didn't mean what she said Crystal, she's distraught, and I think she needs some time to cool off. I'm sure once she realizes how much she upset you, she will apologize," he says, shuffling his hand in his coat pocket.

"Yeah, I guess so," Crystal mutters softly as her eyes slowly disconnect from Trey.

"Are you going to be okay by yourself, Crystal?"

"I'll be fine, Trey," she sighs.

"I can take her home Trey," John says, approaching Crystal from behind.

Surprised, Crystal turns around and gazes into his amber-green eyes; time stood still like never before. Her heartbeat is rapid, while her hands begin to tremble. She gives Trey a nod. "It's alright, Trey; I need to speak to John. Take care of Gabby."

"I will call you later," he says, kissing her on her forehead.

Leaving Crystal alone with John, Trey makes his way to his vehicle. Silence prevails as the two stood staring at each other. John's hand moves across his neck as he clears his throat, feeling a sense of awkwardness.

John lets out a shaky breath. "It's terrible what happened to Matt; I still can't believe he's gone."

"I can't believe it either John; he didn't deserve this."

"Gabby must be a mess."

"Of course she is John," Crystal exclaims with a wrathful tone in her voice, "she just lost her boyfriend. I'm sure if it were you that lost someone you loved, you would be the same way too or maybe not, since you don't know how a relationship works anyway."

"What?" he mutters in confusion, his eyes searching hers. He inches closer. "Crystal, what do you mean by that?"

"You know damn well what I mean, John, do not pretend that you had no idea I was coming back home! I've been trying to reach you since I got off that plane. It's been a whole week, and you haven't had the decency to return any of my phone calls!"

"Manten tu Voz Baja Crystal," John mutters, gazing into her eyes.

"Do not change languages on me, John!" she says and lets out a growl of annoyance. "I am beyond pissed off with you."

"Crystal, can you please calm down?" John says, catching hold of her right hand, he moistens his full lips with his tongue. "I know I've been distant since you've been back, and I'm sorry. It wasn't my intention, I had a lot of work to do with my internship coming up, and things got a little hectic. Instead of jumping down my throat, maybe you should be more understanding."

Crystal's bottom lip quivers, and her shoulders drop in resignation. "Be more understanding? JP, you have never gone a week, not speaking to me. While I was in New York, all you could talk about was how happy you were that I was moving back, that you couldn't wait for us to start our lives together. How can you say these things to me, then ghost me out of the blue?"

"I'm not ghosting you, Crystal. Honestly, I didn't fully prepare myself for your return; I didn't prepare for us. Not just yet. Everything that has been happening in this town has been frightening and very overwhelming."

"You didn't prepare for us to start a life together? Is this the bullshit excuse that you are giving me, John?" she shrugs her shoulders, unable to fight back her tears any longer, "What about what happened between us for the past two years? Doesn't that mean anything to you?"

Reaching out with his arms extended, John pulls Crystal in a gentle embrace, his body firmly pressed against hers.

"Of course, it meant everything to me, Crystal. You know that I love you, right?" he says, staring adoringly at her.

"Well, you have a weird way of showing it," she says, giving him a side-eye.

"Crystal, you have to believe that I love you."

"If you love me, John, then what's your problem? Tell me the truth, did you meet someone else? Please, make me understand because none of this makes any sense."

"I didn't meet someone else, Crystal," John says huffing under his breath, "It's not you, it's me; I—" he takes a brief pause, a faint flush rises on his cheeks.

"I think we should take things slow."

"Slow? Are you breaking up with me, John?" Crystal asks, swiftly distancing herself from his embrace.

He shakes his head, watching her back away from him. "No, Crystal, I am not breaking up with you; I don't want what we have to ruin our friendship. That's all."

"Friendship?" Crystal wails with disbelief, "now you're friend-zoning me? Seriously, John, I cannot deal with this right now."

"Crystal," he sighs with a saddened expression, "I need some time to myself to figure this all out. I want to know what we have is the real thing."

"It is real, John! What is there to figure out? We're not in high school anymore; we are adults now, and what you are doing is ruining us. You are making a huge mistake."

"I missed you so much, and I don't want anything to taint our relationship, Crystal, just give me some space, that's all I'm asking you. Please."

John's words gradually seep in, causing Crystal to distance herself further from him; she didn't want to agree or accept what John asked of her. Her lips downturn into a sorrowful pout as she glares at him intensely.

"I can't believe this is happening; you were my best friend before we decided to take things to the next level. Now you're standing here telling me that you need time away from me," she says, struggling to keep her composure.

"You promised that you would never hurt me! You promised that we would be together forever, John."

John's lips trembles; he found that he could not meet her eyes; it is as if he betrayed her trust. "I don't want to hurt you, Crystal, I just need time."

"You know what, John? This conversation is over, and so are we. You can take all the time you need now; I don't care anymore."

"Crystal, it doesn't have to end like this; you don't have to break up with me," he pleads, desperately trying to change her mind.

"I'm not breaking up with you; you are the one that broke us up, John. If you didn't want to be in a relationship, then all you had to do was say it; you would have saved us both a lot of time and energy if you were honest from the start instead of acting like a damn coward."

"Is everything okay, Crystal?" Terrance asks, interrupting their conversation. He places his left hand upon her shoulders, giving John a sly smirk.

"Terrance, I thought you left already."

"I was getting into my car, and I heard you and John arguing. I thought I would come over and make sure that you are fine."

Before Crystal has a chance to respond to her ex-boyfriend, John becomes enraged. He inches towards Terrance, clenching his fist tightly. "She's fine, that means you can leave now, asshole!"

"John, that's rude," Crystal scowls at him, sensing jealousy.

"It's okay Crystal; I'll be the bigger man, I wouldn't want to waste my breath on a dumb jock like Johnny boy here."

"Dumb! Who the hell are you calling dumb, Johnson? Last time I checked, you weren't doing so well with that fraudulent karate business you brag about," John says, raising his voice until the veins on the top of his forehead bulge out.

"My business is better than what you are doing? Exactly what do you do, John?" Terrance asks, sarcastically, squinting his right eye, "Oh, that's right; you illustrate Barbie doll dream houses that serious architect companies will never invest in."

"You're a piece of shit, Terrance! You always were and always will be; I know for a fact that you've been struggling to get over Crystal since she dumped you and chose to be with me."

"Wow, is that your best shot Johnny? Is that all you got? The way I see it, it looks to me like Crystal has had enough of you and your wannabe prince charming act."

"Stop it!" Crystal shrieks. "That's enough!" she says and extends her hands out, keeping both Terrance and John away from each other.

"Why don't you shut your mouth, Terrance!"

"Tough guy Johnny boy is getting mad, boo hoo hoo," he taunts him in a whiny voice, "what are you going to do, huh? Fight me?"

"I'm not going to fight in a cemetery just to prove that you are a dick, Terrance."

"Can both of you just stop!" Crystal cries out, getting their attention. "Our friend is dead; you guys need to end this stupid rivalry. It's getting old."

A sigh of annoyance slips from Terrance's lips as he stares apologetically at Crystal. "You're right, Crystal, I'm sorry."

"I'm sorry too, Crystal," John apologizes, while reaching to grasp her hand but is quickly snubbed.

"Terrance, can you take me home, please?" she asks in a soft-spoken tone.

A smirk crosses his features, staring dead into John's eyes. "Of course Crystal," Terrance smiles, nodding his head as he strokes his hand along her back.

Showing silent attention to John, Crystal frowns, walking away with Terrance. Taking a few steps, Crystal hears John utter, "So that's it," John huffs, "you're going to leave without saying goodbye to me."

His facial expression grew long at Crystal; John's thoughts were muddled, conflicted with emotions that he didn't know how to control. Did he want to be Crystal? Or didn't he? In a confused state, John's eyes fixate on her, desperately waiting for a response.

Shrugging her shoulders with no care in the world, Crystal stops and turns around swiftly, giving him a long glare. "Goodbye John and good riddance."

"This isn't over, Crystal."

Disconnecting her eyes, Crystal mentally brushes off John's comment and exits the cemetery with Terrance, leaving him in the center of broken grey granite gravestones alone with only cries of the dead.

❊ ❊ ❊

KILLER CREEK LANE

Wind seeps through the open windows while Terrance presses his fingers deep into the steering wheel. Making a narrow turn onto Killer Creek Lane, he shifts his gaze to Crystal, sitting quietly in the passenger seat. Terrance found comfort in her presence; he knew Crystal needed someone to console her with the grief she has had over her parents passing away. Losing his mother as an infant, Terrance can relate to Crystal's pain.

Parking in front of her two-story beige and brown cottage home, Terrance turns off the ignition. The heavy silence inside the vehicle quickly diminishes when raindrops hits the car roof like an orchestra of percussion.

Crystal's soft brown eyes remain glassy for a moment while she watches the rain have a full-blown tantrum, thrashing around like an angry toddler, thumping the earth and snarling at the trees that bend to avoid its fury.

Gradually, the sound of the rain becomes more distinct, Terrance notices Crystal's gaze is into the far distance. "Hey, CJ, are you okay? You haven't said one word since we left the funeral."

Crystal draws in a steady breath. "I'm sorry, Terrance, it's been a long day for all of us, and I needed some quiet time to myself."

"Look, I know it's none of my business, but what happened back there with John? I mean, you looked pretty angry."

"With all due respect Terrance, I don't feel like discussing anything that has to do with John; it's private, and it's between him and me."

"I understand. I thought maybe you wanted to vent. Crystal, I know we haven't spoken much since we broke up and I know it's weird for you to talk to your ex-boyfriend about a new relationship you're in, but if you ever need to talk to someone, I am here for you. I hope that we can be friends because I still care about you, CJ."

Smiling with her mouth closed, Crystal nods her head slightly. "Thank you, Terrance; I think it's sweet that you care for me, and yes, we are still friends."

A delighted look stretches across Terrance's face. "How about we grab a bite to eat soon, catch up on old times? How does that sound?" he asks, capturing Crystal with his infectious smile.

"That would be nice, Terrance; I would love that. Thank you for taking me home."

Reaching over for a hug, Terrance leans in and kisses Crystal on her left cheek. "You're welcome, Crystal. You should hurry before the rain comes down harder, I'll see you soon."

Giving him a warm-hearted smile, Crystal extends her hands, pulling the latch on the passenger side door. Exiting the vehicle, a cascade of raindrops pummel in a mob-like roar towards the dry, unyielding ground. Opening her silver-grey parasol, Crystal shields herself quickly as her black suede pumps soils in a pool of water.

Waving goodbye to Terrance, she hears a distant rumble of thunder. Sprinting across her lawn towards the front porch, droplets from the sky bounce off the sprouting grass like the light springs off the gray clouds. She catches a drop on her tongue. One simple drop quenches her silent thirst.

Advancing towards her front door, Crystal turns around and sees Terrance speeding down the quiet lane. The smell of the heavy rain is electric to her senses. Taking in a deep breath, Crystal glances across the street at Mr. McGregor's house, where she sets eyes on a stunning shiny vintage black motorcycle parked in front of the rusty white garage door.

CHAPTER SIX

JASON

TWO DAYS BEFORE CRYSTAL RETURNS

The night descends on Killer Creek Lane as darkness sweeps in, eliminating the stars in the sky. A gust of wind engulfs the quiet neighborhood while Joseph McGregor relaxes inside his small townhouse cottage, seated comfortably on his brown leather reclining chair. A retired veteran and resident of Lakeview Falls for over twenty years, Joe McGregor is known as the introverted, middle-aged man who has always kept to himself, rarely socializing with his neighbors on the rural Lane.

Suffering from high anxiety for the past six years, Joe heavily medicates himself with high dosages of Ambien. Confining himself due to constant fear of being slain in his town that's plagued with mysterious murders, Joe steers clear from the outside world.

Taking small sips of Kentucky Wild Bourbon, Joe slumps in his recliner beside the warm undertones of his custom-built fireplace. The cozy living room gathered elements of vintage 18th-century paintings from different artists and styles to create a welcoming atmosphere. It was Joe's domain of voluntary quarantine.

❋ ❋ ❋

Tuning in to his regular evening game show, **"HOW FAST CAN YOU RUN?"** The game show known to tests people's limits to see how far they were willing to go for the chance at winning one million dollars. Joe excitedly anticipated another adrenaline episode of his favorite tv show that kept him entertained for three hours every Monday.

Intensely gazing at his high definition flatscreen television, Joe watched a young male contestant choose a sheepshead card that challenges him to walk barefooted, hands and knees across hot fiery charcoal and barbwires. Hooting and hollering at the screen, Joe cheered for the contestant who began to scream in agonizing pain.

Propping his foot on the glass coffee table for a better seating position, Joe is rudely interrupted by a sudden loud tapping noise to his front door. A sigh of annoyance escapes his thin lips while taking another sip of his alcoholic beverage, ignoring the uninvited visitor.

"Boom! Boom!" A thunderous pound to the door sends Joe jolting from his recliner chair, spilling his drink onto his camouflage wool sweater. "Shit!" he grunted.

The repeated sharp noise to his front door sounded like an explosion alarming him instantly; the reverberated sounds were like a pulse beating in his ears, triggering his anxiety to the highest level. Cautiously approaching the door with a silent step, Joe takes a few steady breaths to calm his panic.

Running his short stubby fingers through his coarse auburn hair, Joe leaned toward the side window. Brushing his nicotine scented curtains to the side, he stretched out his neck to see who it was in front of his house. Noticing a shadowy figure on his porch, Joe slowly opened the door and is startled by a young man holding up a wrench in his hand.

"Christ almighty!" Joe screeched, looking at him gripping the steel tool, "you scared me half to death, kid! What the hell is the matter with you? Why are you holding a goddamn wrench? You look like a maniac!"

JASON

The young man lowered his hand, quickly dropping the wrench to the ground. "I'm so sorry to have disturbed you, sir, my bike broke down, and I was wondering if you could help me," the young man said in a soft-spoken tone, stroking his short sleek dark brown hair.

Staring at the young man's apparel, which is a glossy black leather jacket, a white- t-shirt, fitted dark blue ripped denim jeans, and old sneakers that were falling apart, Joe thought to himself, it seemed strange; his clothing didn't "fit" his generation. The young man had a more oldies doo-wop kind of look.

Hooking a thumb in one of his belt loops, the man looked calm and remote. His hands unclenched from his fists at his sides. The muscles in his mouth twitched, and his fingers quivered, never letting his eyes off Mr. McGregor. Though he seemed unthreatening, his relaxed expression oddly frightened Joe.

"Are you Insane?" he exclaimed, glaring at the vintage black motorcycle parked on his clean-cut lawn," is that the best parking you could find? I just had my grass trimmed for Christ sakes!" Joe hollered with an irritated expression.

"The street is a bit rough, and I didn't want to scratch my tires; I do apologize."

"How can I help you? I'm busy and would like to get back to my show."

"I wanted to know if I can use your phone. It's an emergency; I promise It will not take long."

"Use my phone? Kid, this is the 21st century. They don't have cell phones where you come from?" Joe asked.

Shrugging his shoulders, the young man takes his cell phone out of his pocket. "My battery died, and I couldn't find a place to charge it."

Roughly rubbing his head, Joe reluctantly gave in, he opened the door wider, allowing the young man to enter his home. "Okay, you can use the kitchen phone in the back, but afterward, I need you to leave, is that clear?" Joe said sternly.

His facial features softens into a smile, entering the home. "Yes sir, thank you so much, you are very kind," the young man politely said, nodding enthusiastically.

Pointing towards the narrow dimly lit hallway, Joe guides the young man, directing him to the back kitchen. Swiftly closing his front door, he fastened the top lock when he was terrified by an unsettling heavy wheezing sound mixed with a low base groan.

Joe's body jerked to a sudden standstill, feeling the muscles of his heart tightening with incredible force. Slowly turning around, terror sucked the very breath from his mouth, horror-stricken by the sight of the young man transforming into a seven-foot-tall grotesque skinless demon. A menacing aura held Joe in a tightening grip, paralyzing him to the spot.

Mr. McGregor's olive tone color quickly drains from his face with the fear that immobilized his brain, holding him captive. Backing away, he stumbled; his calloused feet slip on the refurnished wood. Feeling the fine hairs in the back of his neck rise, Joe felt trapped like he was suffocating amid no escape.

The demon slowly opened its gaping mouth, breathing out a thick black air filled with a noxious odor. Scowling at Joe, the creature let out a whimper wickedly taunting him while milky substance egresses from its flesh.

As its enormous hands grapple Mr. McGregor's neck, lifting him in the air, it uttered, "Thank you for your hospitality, but I will no longer be needing to make that phone call. I will, however, need your face," he said, in a ghoulish tone, disturbing to one's ear.

Heavy silence enveloped Joe; the sudden shock made him tense while his ocean blue eyes peered into the demons fiery red orbs. A soft, somber escaped his lips, feeling the creatures dripping fork-shaped tongue slithering across his face. Unable to hold in his bowels, Joe defecated on himself. He felt the warmth of his feces seeping through his boxer briefs.

Joe felt helpless at the hands of the grotesque beast. Swinging his foot, struggling to release himself from the demon's grip, the incredible strength the devil possesses could not be defeated by a mere mortal like himself.

Clasping Joe's throat tightly with its left hand, the demon used his right talon claws, lodging them deep into his forehead. As blood trickle down Joe's nose dripping onto his polished wooden floor, the creature gradually pulls the skin off his face exposing raw organs and ligaments. The demon took its grey talon and plucked out Joe's eyes from its socket, Inserting them into its mouth. As it devoured them, the creature enjoyed the silky texture of each pupil melting at the top of its discolored tongue.

Swallowing Mr. McGregor's facial remains, noises seep out of the demon's mouth, creating a chaotic sound. Its limbs snapped, rearranging itself, altering into a new visage.

Walking away from Joe's lifeless body, the demon grabs the rocks glass, taking a swig of the Kentucky bourbon. A mischievous smirk surfaced upon its face while advancing towards the square-shaped crystal glass mirror in the living room.

The demon holds its gaze for a long moment, visually exploring its new identity. Now a replica of Mr. McGregor, the beast gently caresses his rugged face snickering, "This look will do the job," He said with a malevolent expression.

❉ ❉ ❉

PRESENT DAY

Lowering her black parasol, Crystal embraces the cleansing of mother nature, like crystals that drift down to the world. The midday fall showers soon clear, giving way to a glowing medallion in the sky. Upon entering her modern style two-story house, the sun's rays send a glossy gold sheen all around the foyer. Kicking off her black suede pumps that are soaked from the rain, Crystal removes her grey wool coat, placing it on the coat hanger by the front entrance.

Advancing towards her staircase, Crystal places her petite hands on the polished mahogany banister. She makes her way up to her bedroom when she hears a faint knock on her door without warning. Crystal glances over her shoulders; her eyes flash in confusion as she slowly goes down the steps to see who it is.

Walking towards the door, Crystal clasps the bronzed doorknob, turning it clockwise. She opens the door and is taken by surprise when a young man turns around. He catches her attention instantly, with his alluring smile and piercing emerald green eyes.

Her heart-shaped lips part into an O shape mesmerized by how handsome he is. He is tall, roughly six foot two, and well built; his muscles ripple underneath the fitted black leather jacket he is wearing. His dark brown short wavy hair face frames his face perfectly.

Fixated on his full round lips, firm jaw, and golden-tan skin that is as luscious as an amber sky in the mid-day of August, Crystal's heart takes off like a thief in the night. The young man returns Crystal's gaze, sending a startling jolt through her limbs. His eyes seem to bore into the depths of her soul.

Tucking an unruly lock of her curly hair behind her ear, Crystal clears her throat. "Hi, can I help you?"

Flashing Crystal a grin, the young man inches closer, leaning his hand against the door exterior. "Hi, I apologize if I'm interrupting you. I'm looking for someone by the name of Crystal Francois; does she live at this residence?" he asks in a formal tone, still keeping his gaze locked on hers.

"Yes, I am Crystal Francois, and you are?"

"My name is Jason," he says softly, extending his smooth broad hand. "Jason Warwick. I'm Joe McGregor's uncle—I mean Nephew—I'm Joe McGregor's, nephew," he stutters, letting out a snicker.

An odd expression stretches across Crystal's face as she struggles to suppress her laughter. "I'm sorry, what?"

"Let me start over; I'm a bit nervous," Jason says, staring bashfully into her dark brown eyes, "you are magnificent."

Hearing him utter the M-word, sends Crystal's heart racing. She could feel her cheeks getting warm. "Thank you, that's very nice of you to say."

JASON

Noticing Crystal dressed all in black, holding a memorial card in her left hand, Jason suspects that he might have caught her at the wrong time. "Did you just come from a funeral?" he asks hesitantly.

Gripping onto the side of her vintage pencil dress, Crystal tries to breathe slowly, telling her inner self to calm down and not burst into tears. Her legs seem like jelly as her knees were knocking together nervously.

"Yes, one of my good friends passed away a week ago," she sniffles, biting her bottom lip to keep from crying.

"Gosh, I —-I apologize, I shouldn't have asked you that question. I saw you holding the funeral card and——— gosh, I feel so stupid," Jason apologizes, displaying empathy for her.

His voice is so warm and comforting; even the stingiest of strangers will immediately warm up to him.

"Don't be; you didn't know—so, is there something that you needed?" Crystal asks calmly.

"Yes,—" he pauses briefly, taking in a deep breath. "My Uncle left his keys here for me to pick up. I'm house-sitting for a few weeks."

"Yes, of course, the keys; I was waiting for you—" Crystal quickly blurts out.

"Were you?" he asks while staring adoringly at her.

Embarrassed, she lets out a giggle nervously, shaking her head. "Oh, gosh no, I wasn't waiting for you—I meant, I was waiting for someone to come by and—-" she stutters. "I'm going to shut up now."

"It's okay, Crystal; I know what you meant."

"The keys are in my kitchen; let me grab them for you, stay here, and I will be back."

"Thank you, Crystal. I appreciate it."

Giving him a friendly nod, Crystal scurries to her kitchen to retrieve her neighbor's house keys. Returning the keychain with a dozen trinkets attached to it, Crystal hands it over to Jason.

"Here you go, there's an abundance of keys, and I'm not sure which one is for the front door, I hope you find the right one for the hole."

Jason's jaw drops with an awkward expression. "I'm sorry, I beg your pardon."

"Oh shit!" she mumbles under her breath, feeling a sense of awkwardness, "that came out so wrong. I meant the keyhole."

Bursting in laughter, Jason takes the keys from her. "You're very humorous, Crystal; I like that, thank you for the keys," he says in a playful tone.

"You're welcome, Jason," Crystal replies, smiling back. She notices the shiny black motorcycle in front of Joe McGregor's house, "Is that your motorcycle across the street?" She asks.

"Yes, it is! Do you like it?"

"It's a gorgeous bike," Crystal says to him.

His full lips flick up to a smirk, gazing at Crystal very seductively. "Maybe I can give you a ride sometime if you'd like?"

"I've never been on a motorcycle before; I think it would be a nice experience," she says shyly, breaking eye contact with him."

"I think you would enjoy it; once you get on, you will never want to get off."

"Sounds like a thrill ride."

"It's the best feeling Crystal," he says, shifting his gaze across the street, Jason fiddles with the keychain in the palm of his hands.

"I don't want to take up any more of your time Crystal. I'll see you around. And thanks again."

"You're welcome," she says, nodding her head a few times, waving her hands at him as he advances down her porch steps.

Slowly closing her door, Crystal brushes her cream laced curtains, peeking out the side window. As she looks at Jason crossing the lane transfixed by his presence, Crystal is startled when he suddenly turns around and pierces her with his gleaming emerald stare.

Falling too deep in the moment, butterflies come in full force as her heart does somersaults. Quickly backing away from the window, Crystal covers her face with both hands and mutters, "Nice job, Crystal. Could you be any creepier?"

CHAPTER SEVEN

CHOOSE WISELY

Sunlight shone through the sheer white curtains as Crystal awakens from a deep sleep. She opens one eye and quickly feels the burn in her shocked retinas before slamming it shut again. Moaning from the tapping ray of light against her face, Crystal slowly rises from her queen size bed. Rubbing the sleep from her eyes, she reaches for her wide-tooth comb to untangle the morning knots in her curly hair.

Glancing at her neon rainbow-colored LED alarm clock that reads **7:30 am**, Crystal is startled by a burst of laughter echoing downstairs. Quickly slipping on her off-pink ballerina slippers, she feels a sudden vibration from her cell phone tucked underneath her cream satin pillows. Slipping her hand under the pillow, Crystal pulls it out and sees in bold letters, **"JOHN: 10 Missed Calls: 7 New Messages."**

Crystal's eyes fixate on the screen, giving it a long glare; her curiosity heightens as she swiftly scrolls through her messages. In a pathetic attempt to win her affection back, John Pheiffer repeatedly begs Crystal to respond to his calls. Pleading for a response, John continued to profess his undying love for her and asked for a second chance. He didn't shy away from mentioning how much he loathes Terrance and is convinced that her ex-boyfriend wants to get back together with her.

Displeased by John's attitude, Crystal immediately deletes the messages and tosses her phone onto a pile of freshly washed clothes beside her bed. The emotions she felt for him is something that will not go away quickly. Crystal was madly in love with John and looked forward to a happy life with him. She always dreamed of a Romeo and Juliet love story minus them dying in a tragic event.

Her future with John seemed clear as day or so she envisioned in her mind for the past two years. Crystal hoped to one day get married and have children with him. John had always portrayed himself as a loyal partner who would risk his life to make sure she is safe. Now it seemed as if those dreams were fading away to nothing.

※ ※ ※

Rising to her feet, wearing only a pink crop top and white cotton panties, Crystal yawns, stretching out her arms. Stimulating her muscles in a circular motion, she hears a gentle tap on her bedroom door. "Come in," she says, grabbing, a ponytail holder from her nightstand.

Entering her bedroom, Alexandria flashes her a sly smirk, devouring a crisp bacon strip. "Good morning, big head. I thought you were going out with Trey this morning?"

Squinting her eyes at her sister, Crystal walks over to her pile of clothes. "Trey is coming to pick me up in an hour. He has been begging me to attend this demonology lecture since he signed up a few weeks ago."

"What is Trey's obsession with demons?" Alex asks with an awkward expression. "I mean guys like him are mostly into the drag queen life, but Trey is the opposite, like Aleister Crowley, don't you think?"

Shrugging her shoulders, Crystal exhales a deep breath. "Who knows, Trey is Trey, and I love him no matter what he's into, plus he wants to experience this course having me by his side. Trey mentioned the Professor who teaches the course is an advanced demonologist that has a lot of knowledge on ancient voodoo and demonic magic."

"Sounds interesting; maybe this professor can tell us who's killing guys in this town."

"What?" Crystal gasped in awe, "Alex, is this about what happened to Matt?"

"Jesus Crystal, how long have you been living under a rock?" Alexandria exclaims, raising her arms in the air, "Matt's murder was just one of many deaths that have been happening all over the state. This town is getting worse by the second, and no one knows who is behind it. It's scary Crystal, scary enough for us to start thinking about selling this house and leaving this god awful place."

"Sell the house? Why on earth would we do that? Mom and Dad left it to us."

"You're right. Our parents did leave us the house, Crystal, but only because they put it in their will."

"I'm not selling our parent's house, Alex; this is all we have of them."

"I know Crystal, but look what happened to them—someone killed our parents and that person is still out there, what if they come back to finish us off too?"

"My answer is still no, Alex."

"Crystal, please just think about it," Alexandria pleads, "if it's still a no in a few months, then I can sell my share of the house and move out with Derrick."

"Alex, that's not how it works. You can't sell your share of the house if I don't sell mine. Plus, where would you move to with Derrick?"

Pausing for a brief moment, Alexandria disconnects her gaze from Crystal. "We have been making plans to take a trip to his hometown in Singapore."

"Singapore? That's over nine thousand miles away from here, Alex! Are you thinking of moving there?"

"I've been thinking about it for a while, but that was before you came back home. Crystal, Derrick and I planned to visit his parents and get away for a few months. I wouldn't want to leave you here by yourself, well, unless Derrick and I get married, then you're screwed," Alex says, throwing her head back, releasing a burst of humorless laughter.

A smile tugs at the corner of Crystal's lips. "Alex, you don't have to worry about me, and just so you know, I wouldn't force you to stay here; you're an adult, and you have your own life. I've been the overprotective sister for so long that I forgot how much you've blossomed into a beautiful woman."

"Awww," Alexandria lips downturn into a pout, "why are you such a great sister?"

Walking over to her sister, Crystal extends her arms, giving Alexandria a long embrace. "Because I love you, and I couldn't ask for a better sister to annoy the crap out of me and call me big head all day. Now enough of our mushy talk, what do I owe the pleasure of your beautiful presence this morning?"

"I came to tell you that there's breakfast downstairs if you're hungry," Alex says, disconnecting from their embrace.

"Breakfast?" Crystal asks flabbergasted, "Alex, you don't cook. You only microwave."

"Haha!" a snicker escapes her lips, "you're right. I can't cook for shit; that's why Derrick is downstairs cooking for me."

"Well, that was very nice of Derrick; he is a keeper Alex, but remember he's your boyfriend, not a short-order cook," Crystal says, teasing her sister.

"I know, Crystal, Derrick means the world to me," Alex responds, placing her hand over her chest, flashing a warm-hearted smile.

Alexandria fell in love with Derrick Kuro Yin three years ago when they met at Lakeview Falls annual summer barbecue cookout. Her first interracial relationship with a guy of Asian American descent, Alex was mesmerized with his olive skin tone, hazel brown slanted eyes, and athletic physique. Derrick is not only handsome but extremely polite and well-mannered.

Derrick comes from a high-class family who owned real estate in Lakeview Falls but later sold them and moved back to Singapore. A scholar and honor student at Lakeview Falls University, Derrick was top-ranked as the best cadet at the local police academy in Michigan. Part-time grad student and part-time deputy, Derrick Yin has worked hard to get where he is, and now he is on a mission to hunt down who killed his best friend.

❆ ❆ ❆

"Are you coming downstairs or what Crystal?" Alexandria asks her in a whiny voice.

Rummaging through her clean pile of laundry beside her bed, Crystal grabs a pair of pink sweatpants and a grey cotton sweater with bold lettering in white **"LVFU"** logo written in the front. John had given her the shirt while she was away at college. The shirt still has the scent of his favorite musk cologne she once adored.

Crystal huffs in annoyance. "Yes, can you give me a few minutes to get ready, or would you rather I come down in my underwear?" she says, flashing her high waisted cotton briefs.

"No, my boyfriend doesn't need to see you in your underwear. By the way, you need to shave the sides," Alexandria says, pointing at the visible hair stubs on each side of Crystal's crotch.

Using her hands to shield her private area, Crystal sneers at her sister. "I have plans to touch it up a bit."

"Well, I would take care of that trim quickly because John is downstairs."

Crystal's eyes glint maliciously. "What!" she exclaims and throws her hands behind her head in disbelief.

"Oh my God, Alex! Why is he here?"

"Crystal, can you calm down?" Alex says, swiftly closing her bedroom door. "He came with Derrick; what was I supposed to do?"

"Tell his ass to leave!"

"Oh come on Crystal, If I tell John to leave, then Derrick is going to think I'm a mean bitch."

"Who cares Alex, Derrick has no idea what John did to me!"

"You might want to keep your voice down since they both can probably hear you. Now, what the hell happened between you two? Is he still acting like a dick?"

"He was when I saw him at Matt's funeral. We argued, and it didn't end well. I don't know what's going on with John, one minute, he's confused and ignoring me, then the next minute he is calling and texting me excessively begging for me to take him back."

"Did he break up with you, Crystal?" Alex asks.

Slipping on her sweatpants, Crystal puts on her sweater, advancing to her vanity to check herself in the mirror. "John said he wanted me to give him some space, so I told him he could take one indefinitely."

"So, you broke up with him?"

"Technically, yes, I love John, but if this is the kind of crap he's going to pull with me, then I don't want to be with him."

"Crystal, I'm surprised you would let John go that easy, I mean, you had all these plans with him, and now you are just going to throw that all away because he asked for a time out."

"Are you siding with him, Alex?"

"Of course not Crystal. I think John realizes what he did was wrong and wants to apologize to you. John loves you. His eyes are puffy; It's obvious that he's cried a lot. Look—you don't have to take him back, but at least listen to what he has to say. Let John explain himself before you give him the heave hoe."

"I don't have anything to say to him, Alex; maybe this is for the best. I mean, there are other fishes in the sea."

Confused by her sister's response, Alex stares awkwardly at her. "Other fishes in the sea? Where is all of this coming from Crystal? Are you talking about possibly dating other guys?"

Crystal shifts her gaze towards her mirror to admire her reflection. She sleeks her hair back with a clear gel putting it in a ponytail, letting her long curls flourish. Giving her sister a dazzling smile, Crystal walks up to her, placing her hand on her shoulder.

"There's something I need to tell you—I met someone."

"What do you mean you met someone? You just got home."

"The mystery house sitter came by to pick up Mr. McGregor's keys yesterday, and he is not old like Mr. McGregor. This guy is young; he's very handsome and super nice."

"Crystal you just met this guy. Are you seriously thinking of ending things with John for a stranger? He did one stupid thing."

"John made his bed, and now he will have to lay in it. I'm not sure there's anything to fix between us."

"Crystal, you don't mean that, do you?"

Making her way to her front window, Crystal peers outside where she glances across the street, directing her gaze at Mr. McGregor's house. "Something changed the moment I met this guy, I don't know what it is, but I want to know more about him."

CHAPTER EIGHT

WARNING SIGNS

Downstairs in the white cottage style kitchen, Derrick pulls out the prepped dough from the stainless steel refrigerator. At the same time, John sits comfortably, devouring a plate that consists of four grilled sausage links, scrambled eggs, butternut biscuits, and a side of assorted fresh fruits. As he watches Derrick unravel the raw pastry, John admires the natural wooden hues that warm up the white kitchen. The warm peachy tones and creamy white walls play nicely together, exuding warmth and comfort.

Noticing Derrick placing the leftover pan of eggs on the back burner, John quickly pushes his plate in his direction. "Hey, Derrick, can I have some more scrambled eggs?" John asks, taking a bite of his sausage link.

Reaching over to retrieve the pan, Derrick takes a metal spoon, scooping a portion of eggs. Adding the leftovers to John's plate, Derrick clicks his teeth. "You know JP, LVFU serves breakfast in the cafeteria. You might want to check it out sometime."

"They only serve food to students, Derrick," John responds, grabbing the plate.

"John you live on campus; you should be able to get something there."

"I rent on campus, Derrick. Since half of the school transferred out of LVFU because of these murders, I got lucky to get a low price on one of those dorm rooms. The only downside is that I can't eat there."

Preparing to make more biscuits, Derrick kneads the dough with his bare hands on the Oak kitchen island. Parting the soft textured pastry in sections, he molds them into a square shape.

"John, why can't you find another place to live?" Derrick says, lifting his darkly defined eyebrows over his squinty eyes in confusion.

"Because I'm broke, Derrick; ever since my dad had a stroke last year and my mom moved to Minnesota to be closer to his clinic, it has been rough handling things alone. I've been using my pell checks, and that's only covering my room and architectural supplies that I use when I am designing potential projects."

"Does Crystal know about this? I mean, maybe if you tell her what's been going on, she would understand."

"She knows about my dad; she doesn't know my financial problems. I don't want to burden her with it. It's not her problem; it's mine."

"Dude, she broke up with you because you told her you wanted a break. I'm still trying to figure out why you would do something so stupid. All you had to do is explain to her your situation. You guys have been so happy for the past two years. Why mess it all up? You two are great for each other."

"Derrick, I was scared that she would be disappointed in me, I promised Crystal this picture-perfect life, and now I might not be able to give it to her. I regret what I said to her; I wasn't thinking straight, Derrick."

"No shit; you better fix this, JP because I'm going to get my ass chewed for bringing you here."

"Don't worry, Derrick, I will talk to Crystal. There is no way I'm losing her."

"John, I know you are going through tough times. I wish I could help you out, but Alexandria spends a lot of time with me in my dorm."

"That's okay man, thanks anyway."

"Are you sure there isn't any other option as far as residence beside the dorm?"

"No, Derrick, I have to wait till my internship kicks in, and then I can figure things out from there. You know I might have to hire you to cook for me, Derrick," John says jokingly.

Walking over to the kitchen sink, Derrick repeatedly washes his hands to rinse off the dough in between his fingers. "Ha! Very funny JP, I only cook for my family and my girlfriend, well soon to be my wife one day."

Drying his wet hands on a red and white checker box kitchen towel, Derrick sees Alexandria enter the kitchen with a worried expression. He walks towards her, wrapping his long arms around her back. "Alex, are you okay?" he asks, kissing her softly on the lips.

"Yes, Derrick, I'm fine. I had a long chat with Crystal."

Feeling anxious, John rises from his seat. "Did you tell her that I'm here."

"Yes, John, and she is not happy about it. If I were you, I would try to come up with the best explanation as to why you wanted space from her because she doesn't look like she wants anything to do with you at the moment," Alex says to him with a stern expression.

"Alex, I love your sister. I'm going to fix this. Trust me."

※ ※ ※

The hissing of the teapot boiling on the stove releases steam that shoots out from the kettle. Alarmed by the whistling sound, Alexandria disconnects herself from Derrick. Walking over to the tea kettle, she turns the round steel knob, turning off the oven. Grabbing her mother's antique gold fern leaf teacup, Alexandria opens her oak wood cabinet and pulls out a chamomile tea bag.

Placing the tea bag into the cup, Alex grabs the kettle with a potholder and pours the hot content in it. Setting the tea kettle down on her wooden cutting board, she advances towards her small flatscreen television mounted above the kitchen counter. Her mother had it set up when she would cook and watch her daily soap operas.

Using the slim remote, Alex aims it at the screen, turning on the television. Switching channels, she stumbles upon the local news station where they are reporting in front of Lakeview Falls University. On a split-screen beside the female reporter is three photos of missing male students from the university.

In shock, Derrick's mouth widens, staring at the screen. "Holy shit, I know those guys. Matt and I had a physics class with Coltan Hayes. That guy was such an asshole."

"What is going on with this town? People are disappearing left and right. This entire situation is bizarre," Alex says, turning the volume to a higher level.

Standing in a grey pants suit and matching fall jacket, the female reporter grips her microphone, staring intensely at the camera while flocks of students walk pass her, flipping the bird at the cameraman.

"Good Morning, I am Serena Stoley with 999 KZG5 news. We are reporting live at Lakeview Falls University, where three varsity athletes went missing hours after a football game. Coltan Hayes, Brandon Thompson, and Gregory Bradford attended this local college before they were reported missing by their family late last night when they didn't return home. Some say it's a hoax orchestrated by the three who were known as notorious pranksters. Detectives are investigating the disappearances at the moment. The local sheriff's department is positive that the missing men link to the recent murders. The horrifying events are causing panic throughout this small town, and we can only hope and pray that these young men are found and returned home safely."

While the reporter continued speaking, Kyle Jackson walks pass the cameraman, flashing a sly grin. His ebony black coarse hair contrasts against his dark melanin skin. Kyle is an anti-white activist for the **All Black Lives** protection movement and is known as the university's biggest antagonizer. Standing beside the female reporter, Kyle acts with total disregard by making gang-related hand gestures, taunting the cameraman.

"Is that Kyle?" Alexandria exclaims, spitting out her tea, "what the hell is he doing?"

"Acting a fool like he normally does," John says, shaking his head in bewilderment.

"I don't know how you're friends with that dude, JP; he's a racist," Derrick sighs in frustration.

"Kyle is a cool guy; he just has minor flaws."

"Minor flaws?" Derrick's jaw drops, "John, he's a dickhead."

Making the volume higher, Alexandria clicks her teeth. "Can you both be quiet? I think that reporter is going to ask him a question."

"If Kyle Jackson opens his big mouth, this will be the end of him," Derrick mutters with agitation.

"I'm scared to hear what he's going to say because whatever it is, it's going to get his ass kicked out of school, and this time for good," John mutters.

Meanwhile, as Kyle glares at the overweight cameraman, his eyes seem sharp and cold, just like the rest of his facial features. The small curve to his lips indicates there's something funny.

Holding the microphone inches away from Kyle's face, the female reporter gives her cameraman a five-second countdown. Going live after taking a short break to put an end to Kyle's petty and disruptive antics, the reporter questions him on the missing men.

"Thank you for taking the time to answer some questions about the missing students. Can you state your name, young man?" she asks, signaling the cameraman with her index finger to focus the camera more on Kyle.

"Kyle Jackson," he says, licking his right index finger, stroking his left eyebrow, "excuse me, do I look good over here?" he asks, pointing to his left side. "Or should I move to a different angle?" he asks the cameraman, swaying his body from one side to the other, striking a pose with a cocky facial expression.

"Mr. Jackson, this isn't an audition for the Bachelor. Tragic events have been happening in your home town, and I would like to ask if you know the three male students that have been reported missing?"

Snatching the microphone from the reporter's hand, Kyle grips it firmly, staring into the camera lens. "If you are asking me about those white guys! Yes, I know those assholes! Not only were they vile pieces of shit, but they were also racist, racist to black people! And you know what I say? I say bravo to whoever took those scumbags! They just made the world a better place to live in for you and me. I'd like to say on behalf of the murderer, thank you, Mr. SERIAL KILLER, for sparing the lives of my black brothers in this town because there isn't much of us."

Clenching his fists, Kyle raises it in the air. "Power to my people, the colored ones. Shout out to my homies in Detroit."

Grasping the microphone, the reporter scowls at him. "Mr. Jackson, I think that will be all for today. Thank you, and please get some help."

Dismissing Kyle from her presence, the reporter apologizes on camera when she is suddenly interrupted by an alert coming from her network earpiece.

"I'm sorry, I'm getting an alert from the station; we have just received information that effective immediately, there will be a town curfew for Lakeview Falls and Deerfield, starting at 6 pm. All locals should return to their homes at sundown. I am Serena Stoley with 999 KZG5 news and now back to your regularly scheduled program."

❊ ❊ ❊

Shutting off the television, Alexandria stood in silence for a brief second before taking in a deep breath. "What the hell did we just watch? Has Kyle officially lost his mind?"

"I would say yes, he managed to get his ten-seconds of fame. What a prick," Derrick groans as he grabs everyone's plate to the kitchen sink.

Slowly coming down the staircase, Crystal advances to the kitchen, where she notices everyone staring at the blank television screen with an unpleasant expression. "Hey, what's going on? Why do you all look like you've seen a ghost?"

"Coltan, Brandon, and Gregory are missing," Alex replies, placing Crystal's food plate on the kitchen table.

"Oh my God! Are you serious? How? What happened?"

Eager to see Crystal, John rises from his seat. His face lights up as he catches sight of her. "We don't know what happened, Crystal. They went missing last night. No one knows where they are."

"I can't believe this."

A weird expression surface upon Alexandria's round face. "Geez Crystal, I thought you didn't like those guys."

"I'm not fond of them, but you know Coltan Hayes is Simone's boyfriend, and I'm sure she will be distraught when she hears about this."

Advancing towards her sister, Alexandria clasp both hands on each of her shoulders. "Crystal, we don't know if he's dead. Let's not get ourselves upset about the unknown, okay?"

"Okay, Alex, I won't. I'll try to get in touch with Simone and check up on her."

"That sounds like a great idea. Simone will be happy to hear from you."

Pulling out his cell phone from his pants pocket, Derrick receives a text message from his head chief. "Damn," he grunts, "that's Sheriff Mills, he needs me at the station; Alex we gotta go," Derrick says, grabbing his crossbody backpack and a biscuit.

"Okay, let me get my purse," Alex says, scurrying into the kitchen. Alex gathers her modern philosophy books swiftly, shoving them into her large brown satchel purse.

Walking up to Crystal, Derrick gives her a warm embrace and says, "Crystal, I'm sorry we didn't get to chat. I hope you enjoy the breakfast," kissing her on her forehead, he smiles, "it's so great to have you back home."

"Derrick, you are so sweet. Thank you for everything and for being my sister's rock. You have no idea what you mean to this family."

Releasing himself from their embrace, Derrick takes a slight pause and stares at Crystal, "I know things have been rough for you and Alex for the past year, and I just want you to know that I am here for you both. Through thick and thin."

"Thank you, Derrick, you are the best future brother-in-law a family could ever ask for," Crystal says, gently brushing her hand against his left arm.

"We will catch up soon, my future sister-in-law. Alex! Baby, we have to go!" he yells out, heading toward the front door. "JP, are you coming with us?" he asks.

"Yes, I will meet you guys outside. I need to speak to Crystal."

Brushing him off, Crystal keeps her distance as John slowly walks in her direction. "I don't have anything to say to you, John," Crystal says, giving him the side-eye.

"Hurry up, John, I gotta go," Derrick hollers.

"Oh shoot," Alexandria blurts out, searching for something inside her purse, "I forgot my keys in my bedroom, Derrick. I'll be right back," Alexandria says, racing up the staircase to her room.

Approaching Crystal, John's expression softens. "Crystal, can we talk?"

Her arms crossed over, Crystal's eyes pleadingly gaze up in his, trying to search for a reason why she shouldn't kick him out of her house.

"John, What are you doing here?"

"Crystal, I've been trying to reach you all morning," he says, pouting his lips, "you haven't been returning any of my calls or text messages."

Feeling no ounce of sympathy for John, Crystal looks away. "I guess now you see how I felt when I was trying to reach you."

"Fine, I deserved that, but two wrongs don't make a right."

"What makes you think it's okay to just show up to my house, uninvited."

"You gave me no choice, I needed to speak to you, and this was the only way."

"John, I don't get you at all; you're the one that wanted to have space and time to think, not me."

"Crystal, I was wrong for what I said; I've been stressed out and struggling to find a way to talk to you about it."

"I can't go through this merry go round you have me on, John. I'm not sure that I want to be with you. I don't know if I trust your intentions anymore."

A wave of emotions suffocates John, his eyes well up. "No, no, don't say that Crystal, please. I was wrong, and I'm so sorry. You have to let me make this up to you. I love you, Crystal; I can't lose you."

The expression in John's eyes is so remorseful that the air around Crystal seems to reciprocate, almost as if she weeps along with him.

Before she can respond, the sound of Alexandria's ankle boots echoes down the staircase like the rumbling of a diesel engine.

"I'm all set; let's go!" she says, advancing towards Derrick, kissing him on the lips.

Waving goodbye to her sister, Alexandria opens the front door and is startled by Jason, who stood there with a bright smile. Enthralled by his alluring eyes, Alex struggles to shift her gaze.

"Damn!" she mutters under her breath. "I mean damn," she quickly glances at her digital watch, realizing that Derrick was beside her, "we are going to be late, Derrick," she says, grinning at him.

Jason laughs. "I'm so sorry, I'm looking for Crystal. Is she home?"

"Yes, she is, and who are you?" Alexandria asks suspiciously.

"I'm Jason Warwick; I'm house-sitting across the street for my uncle Joe," he says, pointing across the street.

"Right, she did mention that you came by to pick up the keys. I'm Alex, her sister, and this is my boyfriend, Derrick."

Extending his arm, Derrick shakes Jason's hand. "Nice to meet you, Jason," Derrick says, directing his gaze at the black motorcycle in front of the garage. "Hey, that's a sweet ride you got there, Harley?"

"Yeah, it's a vintage 1946 Harley Knucklehead bobber," Jason says with a gleam in his eyes, admiring his motorcycle, "it's a family heirloom."

"Crystal! Jason, the neighbor, is here to see you!" Alexandria squeals.

In shock, Crystal stood silently, staring at John. Unable to hold in her excitement, her lips flick into a smirk. "Okay, Alex; I'll be right there."

"Who the hell is Jason?" John questions with an intense glare.

"He's Mr. McGregor's nephew; he's house-sitting while his Uncle is away on a trip."

"Oh, I see," John responds sarcastically.

"See what, John?"

"The reason why you haven't been answering my calls. It makes sense now. A new guy comes to town, throws himself at you, and you fall for him instantly. I mean, look at you, Crystal; you can't stop smiling. This guy comes over uninvited, and you don't seem upset, when I come over uninvited; you look at me like you want to cut my balls off!" John exclaims.

"I just met him, John! Nothing is going on between us."

"Not now," he huffs upsettingly.

"I can't believe you, John. I don't have time to deal with your shit! I would appreciate it if you would just leave! Now!"

"Come on, Crystal! Can you blame me for being just a tad bit upset?"

"Goodbye, John."

"Fine, Crystal, I will respect your wishes, but just so you know, I'm not giving up on us, not by a long shot," he says, walking past her with a heavy sigh.

❋ ❋ ❋

"Hey, John, let's go!" Derrick says, raising his voice from the outside porch.

"It was nice meeting you again, Jason," Alexandria says with a smile, advancing down the porch steps.

"Yeah, man, see you around. You gotta show me how that bike works one day," Derrick says, patting Jason on his back.

Nodding enthusiastically, Jason grins, waving at them. "Sure thing, sounds like a plan; see you both soon."

Observing Alex and Derrick as they enter his vehicle, Jason is snub instantly by John, who gives him a sinister glare. "Stay the hell away from my girlfriend," he threatens.

Looking away, Jason gives off a cocky smirk as John stomps towards Derricks' car. Watching them drive off, Jason is delighted to see Crystal standing by the door. "Hey Crystal, how are you?"

"Jason, what are you doing here?" she asks, staring adoringly at him.

"I'm sorry for just showing up, I would have called, but I didn't get a chance to ask for your number."

Listening to Jason's rich baritone voice sends shutters down her spine. His very presence is so enchanting and otherworldly that she remains motionless. "Here," she says, handing him her cell phone, "you can add your number and call me so I can save yours."

"Awesome," he smiles, typing his number on her phone, "can I call you tonight?"

"Sure."

Crystal's heart skips a beat. Her intuition tells her to take things slow, but her heart says otherwise. She could not stop smiling at him; it was as if he had her under a spell.

Retrieving her phone back, Crystal makes sure she saves his number. Placing it in her pants pocket, she notices Trey pull up in front of her house.

"Oh crap, my ride is here. I wish we had more time to talk, Jason, but my friend Trey is here, and I have to head out."

"No problem, I will call you later."

"Okay, I'll be waiting," Crystal says, grabbing her wool jacket from her coat hanger.

"Great, by the way, that guy that was here, was that your boyfriend?"

Hesitant, Crystal clears her throat. "We used to date, but not anymore."

"Hmm, that's what I thought," he says, flashing a grin.

"Can't wait to talk to you later, have a good day."

"You too," she replies, watching as Jason leaves her porch steps, walking across the street to his bike.

Noticing Trey perking his lips at her through the car window with a silly expression, Crystal quickly locks her front door. Scurrying to Trey's smart car, Crystal sees Jason drive pass them on his motorcycle.

Opening the passenger side door, Crystal takes a seat. "Hey, bestie."

"Hey, sweets, who is that fine piece of ass you were talking to?" Trey asks, batting his eye seductively.

"His name is Jason. He is house-sitting for my neighbor across the street."

"He's sexy; they need to make more of those in this town. I'm so tired of staring at the dried-up quacks at school. I want a man that looks just like that."

Blushing, Crystal becomes smitten. "He is pretty good looking, huh?"

"Too bad you're with John."

"I broke up with him."

"Oh no," Trey sighs, "that sucks. Guess that means I have no chance at snatching the new guy, huh?"

Letting out a short random laugh, Crystal gives Trey a goofy smile. "Trey, he's straight."

"Please, girl, I can have a straight man switching lanes very quickly," Trey says, flamboyantly snapping his fingers as he drives off down the lane.

CHAPTER NINE

DOOMSDAY

TOWN HALL CIRCLE

Heavy condensed clouds dominate the sky, ominously huddling together. Red and orange-colored autumn leaves fall from the trees, scattering like a divine intervention on the granite concrete pavement. Across from the Raven Bell Tower, squirrel's roam in the crisp fall morning through unkempt bushes in Fearman Street Park as citizens of the town keep themselves scarce, staying safe inside their homes.

Amid a new age, apocalypse, an eerie silence, engulfs the social center, creating darkness and hopelessness for residents that have nowhere else to escape. The Town Hall Circle is left abandoned by business owners who board up their stores, leaving the shopping center completely bare. With only a few brave retailers keeping their shops available to the public, the people of Lakeview Falls remain vigilant not to fall prey to a flesh-eating serial killer.

※ ※ ※

The rattling winds swim through Crystal's hair swaying directly over her shoulder as she gazes out the passenger side window while Trey cautiously drives up Fearman Street, never allowing his eyes off the road. Breathing in the clean cold air, Crystal scans the wilderness of the abandoned Town Hall Circle thriving with twisted rotten crabapples. Block after block; sidewalks are chipped and fractured due to many years of low maintenance and negligence.

Complete in its incompleteness, Fearman Street has a depressing and sad aura down the narrow road that resembles a black ribbon of slick asphalt. There were no words to express how broken the town has become.

While Trey makes a sharp turn into Hangman Lane, each streetlight post displays missing person flyers of boys ranging from ten to late twenties. The years dated on the stained color flyers stem from 2015 to 2025. The innocent lives of male youths targeted in Lakeview Falls have been a mystery which no one, not even the local authorities, can solve.

The sight of the images posted all over town causes Crystal to have a queasy feeling in her stomach. A murmur escapes her lips, shifting her eyes at Trey, who enters the back entrance of the parking lot of Lakeview Falls University.

Checking his rearview mirror, Trey leans forward and opens his compartment, pulling out a handicap placard. Placing the card on his dashboard, Trey parks into a vacant handicap spot near the school's side entrance.

"Someone needs to take down those flyers; it's been a decade," Trey sighs, taking his keys out of the ignition.

"Trey, why do you have a disable parking permit?" Crystal frowns, staring at the blue placard. "You know it's illegal to carry that when you're not handicapped, right?"

"Shit, I forgot my best friend is a law school graduate," he grits his teeth at her, "Crystal, please don't be mad at me. I found the card a few days ago, and to be honest, I'm not breaking the law. Well, not at this moment."

"That's no excuse, Trey." Crystal sighs with annoyance.

"Look around you, Crystal; no one cares in this town anymore. Plus, everyone that owned a handicap spot here disappeared."

"I don't understand why so many guys are disappearing from this town? None of this makes any sense Trey."

"Crystal, this isn't anything new. Don't you remember Lakeview Falls' urban legend story about the **Concrete Carols?**"

Instantly, Crystal's body jerks back. The very thought of Concrete Carols injects terror into her blood. As a child growing up in Lakeview Falls, terrifying tales had circulated about children kidnapped from their homes before sunrise. No one knew why children became a target during the early 1960s. Rumor spread that evil clothed men cursed the town due to betrayal and greed.

❋ ❋ ❋

Froshkada, an evil entity, known as the invisible soul snatcher, allegedly buried children alive in different hot spots all over the Town Hall Circle. Seeking to collect another group of fresh meat to torture, **Froshkada** hoped to successfully traumatize every child, forcing them never to take showers since it only captured the ones who were clean and smelled as sweet as blackberries harvested in the peak of August.

The children of Lakeview Falls would pay the ultimate price for what happened in the mid-1950s, starting with a family of six who made history as the most children in one family to disappear in one day. Fairuza, Toby, Alana, Harold, Jameson, and Stella Carol lived on Skinner Bone Lane in 1961. The children were one year apart from each other, ranging from eight to thirteen years old.

While reconstruction of the Town Hall Circle was in progress, all young residents of the town assembled in Fearman Street Park. A playground filled with swings, seesaws, and steel slides as fun entertainment. Each child had access to romp around the park until sunset, then was instructed to return home.

On a warm Sunday afternoon, the Carol siblings decided to play at Fearman Street park before supper. Alone with the entire playground to themselves, the Carol siblings mischievously entertained themselves chasing squirrels and possums with broken tree branches.

As the children dispersed throughout the park, they heard a low pitch whimper echoing from the golden leaf bushes. Fearful, the children called out to one another to regroup and leave the park together, when suddenly, an eerie wind whips around the bleak playground, causing the rotting seats of the swings to sway gently on their groaning chains, rattling and screeching as if making an announcement.

Finding themselves back together, the siblings quickly ran towards the gated exit. Extension twigs erupted from the bushes, wrapping itself violently around the children's ankles and wrist-twisting tightly around their limbs where they could no longer move.

Struggling to free their arms from the grip of the twigs, the children felt the burning sensation of the sharp branch piercing their skin, damaging blood vessels. The intense pain spread to the rest of their bodies, causing them to wail and scream, feeling the twigs dig deeper. Forceful winds circulated in a counterclockwise motion around the siblings with velocities of around 30 km/h until the children were swept away in thin air.

When the sun began to set, Henrietta and Gerard Carol became worried and searched for their six children. Upon entering Fearman Street Park, both parents were horror-stricken to see the disastrous sight inside the park. Large fragments of wood scattered around from the disintegrating wooden benches that surrounded the edge of the playground. A fishy odor assaulted their nostrils as they inched further into the park, listening to what sounded like cries from their youngest daughter Fairuza.

As Gerard and Henrietta walked pass a disturbing aluminum statue of a black raven that stood upside down, they realized that the cries they heard from a distance were now coming from beneath their feet. Looking down, they let out a bone-chilling scream, horrified to see each of their children's faces embedded into the cemented ground, displaying grisly smirks.

❄ ❄ ❄

"That's a horrible story, Trey!" Crystal exclaims, slapping him on the right side of his arm, "I can't believe you made me remember that. That story scared me for my entire adolescent life."

"But it was a true story, Crystal, and we don't know if Froshkada decided to come back and start eating guys this time. Maybe it lost its taste for kids."

Detaching her seatbelt, Crystal groans inwardly. "Give me a break Trey; There is no proof that the story is true. It's folklore made up sixty years ago to frighten children. I am certain our parents told us that story to make sure we would stay out of trouble."

Holding up his index finger, Trey moves it side to side, shaking his head. "No, Crystal, they told us that shit to warn us of all the bad things that have happened here. You know Gabby used to sleep at my house every time we went to play in that park. She was more traumatized than both of us put together. She would sleep with raw onions around her bed so that she wouldn't get kidnapped."

Laughing softly to herself, Crystal allows a weary smile to loosen her lips. "I miss her, Trey. I bet she still hates me even though I did nothing to her."

"Gabriela doesn't hate you, Crystal; she would never hate you. Her boyfriend's death brought out an ugly side of her; she had no right to act that way toward you; none of this was your fault. Matt's murder was a tragedy, and we don't know who did that to him. We might not ever know."

"Why can't this town be normal, Trey?"

"Girl-look where we are; Lakeview Falls is nothing close to normal; it never was and never will be," Trey says, lowering his driver's side window.

Suddenly, Trey feels a steel object touching the side of his temple; using his peripheral vision, he is terrified to see it's a pistol. His body didn't know how to react; it just shut down to a point where he was hardly breathing.

"Give me all your fucking money, bitches!" Kyle wails, waving around his silver Glock 17, frightening Trey and Crystal from inside the vehicle.

"Fack!" Trey squeals, jumping up from his seat, knocking his head against the car ceiling. "Kyle, what the hell is wrong with you! Stupid idiot!"

Unleashing a burst of wicked laughter, Kyle inserts the pistol inside the front of his cargo pants, backing away from the vehicle.

"Come on guys, I was just messing with you, have a sense of humor."

"Sense of humor?" Trey scowls, exiting his vehicle. "Putting a gun to someone's head isn't funny, Kyle, you could have killed me!"

Clenching her fist to her chest, Crystal blows open the door fuming. She immediately storms over to Kyle with an irritated expression. "Seriously, Kyle, you are such a jerk! What on earth are you doing with a gun? Are you crazy?"

"Relax, Crystal; I'm licensed to conceal a firearm, and trust me, at the rate this town is going, I will stay strapped and ready to bust a cap in someone's ass if they come after me."

"So now we're just entering schools with weapons? Kyle, haven't you watched enough school shootings on the news to know that this isn't the way to solve anything."

"You can't compare school shootings to what's happening in Lakeview Falls Crystal. They just found those douche bags Coltan, Brandon, and Gregory hanging upside down In the fields a few miles from here skinned down to the bone," Kyle replies with a smug smile.

A blank expression sweeps across Crystal's face, unable to react to the terrible news. Her lips turn into a pout. "How can you smile at something so horrid, Kyle? Are you that heartless?"

"Honestly, I don't give a shit about those guys. They were bullies; Karma is a bitch."

"Are you serious, Kyle? How can you say such a thing? You know, you could pretend that you have a shred of decency in you," Trey exclaims with disgust.

"Trey is right, Kyle; you know that could have happened to any of us."

"But it didn't Crystal," Kyle sarcastically snickers, placing his arms around Crystal and Trey. "If anything happened to you or Trey, I would be deeply saddened; I love you guys."

Brushing Kyle's hand off his shoulder, Trey gives him the side-eye. "I'm glad to know you care for us, Kyle. Now that you've made that clear, I can sleep better at night."

Leaving the parking lot, Trey, Crystal, and Kyle cut through Lakeview Falls football field towards the school's main entrance. The morning sunlight's beautiful intensity is like gold embroidery, flashing across the Kentucky bluegrass like a torch.

"Do you think that whoever killed them could be the same person that killed Matt?" Crystal asks with a saddened expression, reliving the night she saw Matt's mutilated corpse.

"Who knows," Kyle says, shrugging his shoulders with no remorse. "I'm sure one person isn't capable of killing multiple people in one shot. Instead of worrying about who the murderer is, we should care about the fact that we are still alive. Plus, I don't think whatever thing killed those guys eats black people. We should be fine."

"Are you kidding me, Kyle? That is the dumbest shit I've ever heard in my entire life," Crystal says, pushing the entrance gate open. "What does color have to do with this? I hardly doubt a murderer would waste time picking out a certain race to kill."

"Speak for yourself; these Edomites are scared for their lives," Kyle replies, pointing his index finger at a group of Caucasian male students in front of the university, huddled in a group, hugging while singing Martin Luther King's **"We Shall Overcome."**

An annoyed expression is painted on Crystal and Trey's face as they glare at Kyle, who finds comfort and pleasure in other people's fears. Kyle sinisterly grins as if he prayed for more torture towards who he calls his "Uncolored enemies."

Checking his digital watch, Kyle notices that he is late for his Biophysics class. "Damn, all this killing talk has me late for Dr. Fiacho's class. How about we all meet up at the diner later? It's Tuesday, which means all you can eat French fries."

"Sure, Kyle, whatever," Trey mutters, "will do me a favor? Can you refrain from the black and white talk? We still have friends from different ethnicities that will feel uncomfortable with your presence if you open your mouth."

"Fine, I promise I will not say a word," Kyle responds, stroking his index finger against his lower lip.

Pulling the bronze door handle, Trey, Crystal, and Kyle enter the university's main lobby, where Kyle bids farewell, making his way to the school's East wing section. Advancing down the corridor, Trey and Crystal walk towards the double brass doors, which leads to the demonology lecture hall in the West wing section.

Along the dark red west wing walls, Crystal eyes fixate on memorial photo plaques of alumni who had lost their lives from mysterious murders and disappearance throughout the years. The smiles of familiar faces she once knew are nothing more than a memory, which she will carry with her for as long as she lives.

Continuing her visual exploration, Crystal hears gut-wrenching sobs that tear through the halls. Bombarded by a few students who rush out of the corridor, Trey and Crystal see Gabriela consoling their friend Simone Carter.

Simone is Crystal's childhood friend from pre-school; born as bi-racial, Simone possesses unique goddess features, almost like a deity. Bonding from an early age, Crystal and Simone were inseparable until they graduated high school and decided to follow different paths in life. With college and their love life-consuming them, Crystal and Simone could not find the time to maintain their friendship. Upon learning of Crystal's parent's murder, Simone made it a priority to always keep in touch with Crystal, ensuring that she would stay in her life no matter what.

Known in Lakeview Falls for practicing advanced witchcraft "Le Shezantre" and starting a meditation group for rookie Wiccan practitioners called **"The Inner Spiritual self-guide to finding your inner energy."**

Facing demonic spirits from past seances, Simone knows what lies beneath the town's surface that hides wickedness. Informed earlier of her boyfriend's demise, Simone wishes she had received a warning sign that could have protected her partner.

Distraught by the news, Simone finds comfort in Gabriela. She holds Gabby in a firm embrace while resting her head on her shoulder. Hot torrents of grief course down Simone's soft cheekbones.

Deep emotions stir as Crystal and Trey rush over to Simone and Gabriela, standing beside them. Crystal's heart breaks, listening to Simone's long-lasting sobs. The trauma of losing someone in Lakeview Falls seemed like a never-ending story of torment and grief. Noticing Gabriela ignoring her and focusing solely on Simone, Crystal slightly taps Simone on her back. Swiveling around, Simone takes a step back, parting from her embrace with Gabriela.

"Crystal! You're back home," Simone whimpers, throwing herself into Crystal's arms.

Simone's round almond hazel brown eyes shed a solemn tear while Crystal pulls her head gently towards her chest. Simone felt hot as if singed by flaming coals while Crystal strokes her long black extensions that rest in the mid-back area.

"I am so sorry, Simone. I can't believe this happened," Crystal says, rubbing Simone's lower back softly, "I know how much Coltan meant to you."

"That bastard!" Simone wails in anger, "he was cheating on me for two years."

"What?" Crystal gasps with bewilderment, "when? How?"

"Coltan has been very busy fooling around with half of the girls on campus. I found out with the help of my spiritual sisters. We created the **"Male Ale Deception spell."** I was able to see every slut he's been sleeping with."

"Holy shit," Trey squeals in shock, cutting in on their conversation, "so—I take it that means you're not sad that he's dead."

"Of course I'm sad that he's dead, Trey. I can't believe he would do this to me."

"Simone, Coltan didn't deserve you. It's horrible what happened to him, but I know that there's someone out there that will love you and respect you for the wonderful person you are," Crystal says, caressing her face.

Hearing Crystal's comforting words to Simone, Gabriela can feel a searing pain in her heart. Making an effort to express the words that were bottled up inside, Gabby silently brushes her hand against Crystal's arms getting her attention. Her genuine expression indicates her true nature.

"Crystal, can we talk?" Gabriela asks as her voice fills with emotions.

"Of course, Gabby."

Excusing herself, Crystal leaves Trey and Simone alone to speak while she and Gabriela walk by the vending machine. Shaking off the tension in her muscles, Gabriela draws in a steady breath.

"Crystal, I want to apologize for how I treated you at Matt's funeral. I had no right to blame you for his death; I was hurting so much inside that I didn't even realize I was also hurting you in the process. You are my best friend, Crystal, and you didn't deserve that. It was wrong of me to act that way, and I'm sorry. I don't expect you to forgive me because I know I don't deserve your forgiveness," Gabby says quietly, wiping a stray tear from her eye.

"Gabby, I know you are still grieving, and sometimes people say things they don't mean in the heat of the moment. I wish that it didn't happen, but it did, and we can't go back and fix it, but we can always move forward and learn from our mistakes. I love you, Gabby. Nothing will ever change that."

"I've missed you so much, Crystal, and I never want to fight again with you."

"I don't want to fight either Gabby," accepting her apology, Crystal doesn't hold back, wrapping her arms around Gabriela.

The LVFU emergency alert system disrupts a moment of exceptional bonding between the two. The reverberating pitch of the microphone being handle sounds like a loud train crashing through a wall.

"Attention, all Lakeview Falls students, this is a PSA from your chief, Sheriff Mills. Due to an ongoing murder investigation, I will be canceling classes for the day. Courses and lectures will resume tomorrow morning. Be sure to check the university bulletin for curfew hours. Thank you for your compliance, stay safe, stay in your dorms, and stay alive."

After the announcement ends, Trey cries out in a fit, throwing his black portfolio binder onto the beige travertine tile. "FACK!"

"Trey, what's the matter with you?" Crystal asks him with uneasiness.

"Professor Baptist's class is canceled too. Crystal, we won't be able to attend his lecture today. I was looking forward to this demonology class."

"Trey, I'm sure the lecture will be back tomorrow. What is the deal with this course? I've never seen you so excited about anything."

"Crystal, this guy is the real deal. He knows his shit, plus I got the scoop from a few people that took his course last semester, and they said he keeps underground info about this town. It's pretty freaky. Trust me, this is a class you don't want to miss; you're going to love this guy," Trey says, flashing Crystal a crooked smile.

CHAPTER TEN

THE STONE

LAKEVIEW FALLS SHERIFF'S DEPARTMENT

Sliding his pen across his Oakwood desk, Sheriff Mills signs his signature on John Doe's case documents on murdered young men marked unidentifiable. A groan escapes his mouth as he places the papers into an almond-colored folder, inserting them into his second desk cabinet, locking it with a unique key. Seated in his mid-back leather swivel chair, Sheriff Mills spins himself clockwise in a circular motion when he is startled by a knock on his door.

Entering his office, Justin flashes half a smile at his father while gripping his deputy manual book in his right hand. "Dad, I mean, Sheriff, I mean Sir, I mean-" he repeatedly stutters, almost like he struggled to remember how to talk.

Annoyed by his son's idiotic behavior, Sheriff Mills clicks his tongue. "Oh, for Christ sakes, Justin, what do you want?"

Mentally brushing off his father's rude response, a sigh slips through Justin's lips. "Sorry for interrupting you, but there's a woman on line two that says she has an urgent message for you."

"A message? At noon?" he grunts, rolling his eyes in annoyance. "Did this woman say what the message is about?"

"No, she refuses to speak to me—she specifically asks for you. I think you should take the call. It sounds important."

"Jesus, for the love of God," he mutters, pursing his lips in annoyance.

Reaching over his desk, Sheriff Mills taps his touch screen office phone. Pressing the speakerphone option, he taps on line 2. He narrows his eyes, listening to muffling static accompanied by heavy, ragged breathing.

"Lakeview Falls Sheriff's Department, this is Sheriff Thomas Mills, who may I ask is speaking?" he asks, extending his feet above his desk.

"The blood of the people shall soak through your veins! The sons of the statue come forth to resurrect!"

Raising his nose in the air, Sheriff Mills abruptly takes his foot off his desk, listening to the raspy voice of an elderly woman on the other line. "Is this a cruel joke? Who the hell is this?"

"I warned that young man about the girl; I told him he would be first to die a horrible death. He didn't listen to me, and now it's too late for all of you. They are coming for her! And there's nothing you can do to stop them," the old lady growls wickedly.

Terrified by the old lady's disturbing revelations, Justin feels a sudden tightening in his throat. He stares long and hard at his father when suddenly his deputy manual guide slips from his hand, falling onto the polished tiled floor.

"Oh shit, is she talking about Matt, Dad?"

"Listen, I don't know who you are or what kind of game you are playing, but if you don't tell me who you are, I will track your number-"

"Games? Oh, Sheriff. I am the truth to the unknown, and if I were you, I would watch my back."

"Alright, you old goat! I've had just about enough of you; I don't have time for this crap! You are a sick woman, and I'm hanging up!" he groans inwardly, unable to contain his anger.

"You are all marked for death. You need to destroy it before it comes in contact with her! She who holds the stone!" the old lady belts out in a low pitch tone.

"Go to hell, Lady!" Sheriff Mills shouts, ending the call abruptly.

Breathing heavily, his pulse races almost as if he would burst. Slamming his palm repeatedly on his touch screen phone, Sheriff Mills slumps back in his chair. His muscles grow tense as he cracks his knuckles, trying to process what the old lady said to him. Taking a brief pause, he suddenly remembers the voice matching with the deranged woman he saw in Deerfield.

"That old hag," he whispers, biting his upper lip.

"Dad, who was that? Do you know her?"

"The day Matthew and I went to check out those dead bodies off Deerfield, that raggedy old woman came out from the bushes and began shouting something so bizarre."

"What did, she say, Dad?" Justin asks, advancing towards his desk.

Rising from his seat, Sheriff Mills hesitates for a moment before speaking. He let out a shaky breath. "She said the shifters have woken; I have not a damn clue what that means and I sure as hell don't want to find out either. Anyway, right after she approached Matthew, she whispered something in his ear; whatever it was, it scared the shit out of him."

"That woman said that she tried to warn him. She was talking about Matt, wasn't she?"

"Who the hell knows. She's a nutcase. I would take anything she says with a grain of salt. She is nothing but a crazy old woman from a hillbilly town."

"Dad, don't you think you should have let her explain what she said to Matt? She might know something that could help us. Maybe she knows who is killing these guys in town."

"Help us? That woman can't help us, Justin, she's babbling a bunch of bullshit that I don't understand! She who holds the stone? What in the hell does that mean?"

Walking over to his window, Sheriff Mills opens his deep burgundy curtains, drawing it to one side, allowing the sunlight from outside to brighten up the dull room. Looking over his shoulder, he glances at Justin with conviction in his eyes.

"Justin, I need you to search every last file cabinet in this department and find me all the cold case files dating back 2018 to now. I need to see if any of the past murders have any link to what's happening right now."

"Yes, Dad," he says, nodding enthusiastically, "I mean sir —I mean-"

Looking Justin dead in the eye, Sheriff Mills arches his thick eyebrow. "Get the hell out of my office before I have your brother replace you!"

Crossing his arms, Justin looks the other way. "Phillip would never take this job, Dad. There's no way he will ever take your place as a Sheriff of this town."

❄︎ ❄︎ ❄︎

KILLER CREEK LANE

Death lurks inside Mr. McGregor's cottage home, who's remaining rotting flesh decomposes on the hard wooden floor. Standing by the foyer door, Jason's icy breath stabs the inside of the stainless glass window while observing the Francois residence. The aroma of Crystal's French perfume lingering on his white t-shirt makes his nose twitch in disgust. Having no physical contact with her, Jason could not fathom how her pheromones could permeate his clothing.

Sickened by the odor, he quickly removes his shirt, leaving himself bare-chested. Breathing loudly, Jason hears the roaring sounds of a vehicle coming down the lane. From a distance, a yellow smart car pulls up to the curb. His emerald green eyes maliciously glint as he observes Crystal exiting the vehicle.

As he watches her petite frame walk up the cobblestone steps, Jason's daunting breath flows as he admires her firm ass twitch from one side to the other. Licking his plump lips in pleasure, he plots the next phase of his masterplan.

❄︎ ❄︎ ❄︎

Entering her humble abode, Crystal closes the door behind her and types the assigned code number to the home security system mounted on the main entrance wall. Removing her grey wool coat, she hangs it on the coat hanger and places her house keys on her copper grove console table. Advancing up the mahogany wood stairs, Crystal reaches the top of her steps where her eyes fixated on her parent's bedroom door.

Since their death, the room remains untouched. Neither she nor Alexandria wanted to face what was behind the polished brass door. They knew the moment they removed their parent's belongings; it would be saying goodbye to them all over again. Continuing her gaze, Crystal puts on a brave face and decides to face what she has been in denial about for over a year.

Giving the door a cautious push, Crystal steps into her parent's bedroom, instantly smelling the memorable fragrance of her mother's favorite perfume called "Angels Et Démons." The aroma is an intoxicating mixture of fresh roses and dandelions. Closing her eyes, Crystal takes in every single memory she had of her dear mother. From her soft angelic voice to her tall, slender figure, beautiful dark brown eyes, and silky dark brown hair that flowed so effortlessly.

Examining the room, Crystal gazes at the glass panel in the wall, which adds lively color to the soft-hued bedroom. The sun's reflection shines on the beautiful dresser and old-style mirror that her father Robert had built for her mother on their 19th wedding anniversary. Walking over to their king-sized bed, Crystal takes a seat on the soft, warm blue-colored comforter that contrasts with the midnight-colored flooring and vibrant wood centerpiece.

Noticing a photo frame lying face down on the drawer, Crystal reaches for it. Turning it around, she sees it's a family photo of her, Alex, and their parents at **"Wallios World Dream Park."** The old photo was taken in 2009 when Crystal was eight years old, and Alex was seven. The family had posed side by side with famous cartoon characters from Crystal's favorite children TV shows, including **Princess Amethyst** and **Ganthforth, The Flying Gargoyle,** the most powerful dragon in the universe.

Crystal's eyes well up with tears while she rests the picture against her chest. The Nostalgic feeling of her and her family, creating memorable moments throughout the years, will stay forever in her heart. Saddened that her parents are no longer with her, Crystal wishes nothing more than to have her mom and dad in her life one last time so she can tell them how much she loves and misses them.

Sitting in silence, Crystal hears a sudden creek down the hallway; her heart lifts when she is surprised to see her aunt Jacqueline approaching the bedroom door, holding a small turquoise blue gift bag in her right hand.

"Aunty J, I had no idea you were stopping by today?" she joyfully exclaims.

"Crystal, sweetheart," Jacqueline exclaims, rushing to her side.

A spitting image of Crystal's mother, Aunty J, has a smooth bronze skin tone. Her wavy bob hairstyle compliments her diamond-shaped face and hazel brown eyes. Taking a seat beside her niece, Aunty J caresses her face wiping, a teardrop on her cheek.

"What's the matter, Crystal? You know you can talk to me, right?"

"Yes, I know, Aunty J. I was looking at a family photo, and my emotions got the best of me."

"Crystal, it's okay to cry," Jacqueline responds, placing her hand over Crystal's knee." I know the death of your parents has been very traumatic for you and your sister; it hasn't been easy for me either. Crystal, I never thought in a million years that I would lose my older sister. Desiree was my better half, my rock. She and your father held this family together, and they both loved and adored you and Alex more than life itself."

"I should have stayed in Lakeview Falls, Aunty J; I shouldn't have gone away to school. Maybe if I made better choices, Mom and Dad would still be alive," Crystal sobs, grasping the tissue box from the nightstand.

"Better choices? Crystal, you went to law school; you studied hard and got good grades. Getting accepted to an Ivy League University with top honors is a huge achievement. Your mother and

THE STONE

father always encouraged you to follow your dreams. They would have never wanted you to sacrifice your education for them."

"Why did they have to die?" she whispers in a whimpering tone, "why does everything turn to shit in this town? I've been going through that night repeatedly in my head Aunty J, and I can't understand how someone could hurt them in such a horrific way. They didn't deserve that."

"Crystal, I spoke to Sheriff Mills a few minutes ago, and he said that he would be reopening your parent's case. Don't worry, sweetie, we will find the monster who did this to them. And when we do, they will pay for what they did."

"Everything feels like a nightmare, Aunty J. I don't know how I will manage everything. With owning the house and finding a job, it just feels like a huge weight has fallen on my shoulders."

"Crystal, I am here for you, and so is your sister. There's no way I would allow you to struggle. You are my niece, and I will always look out for your best interest," Aunty J smiles while running her fingers through Crystal's soft curly hair.

"Now, let's wipe those tears away and talk about your birthday," her aunt says, clasping the gift bag, placing it on her lap.

Examining the gift bag, Crystal is mesmerized by the diamond-encrusted pagan symbol in the center. "Aunty J, my birthday is in two weeks."

"I know, that's why I want to celebrate it a little early with you. Now I am fully aware that you are not a fan of surprises, but I'm sure you will let this one slide," Jacqueline says, handing Crystal the gift bag.

A warm-hearted smile surfaces on Jacqueline's face as she watches Crystal open the bag slowly. "Before your mom passed away, she stopped by my apartment and gave me this gift bag to give to you. I wasn't sure why, but all your mother said was she didn't want it getting into the wrong hands just in case something happened to her."

Baffled, Crystal couldn't believe her mother foresaw her imminent demise. "Aunty J, why would my mom say something like that?" she asks and squints her eyes, suspiciously, "do you think she knew something was going to happen to her?"

"I don't know Crystal," Jacqueline responds with a slight frown, "whatever is in this bag is something your mom wanted you to have. Why don't you open the bag and see what's inside."

A nervous chuckle escapes Crystal's lips. "I wonder what she bought me," she says, pulling out a grey jewelry box.

Crystal sees a small white card taped to the box with her mother's signature penmanship. The sealed envelope reads, "Happy Birthday to my firstborn."

Slowly opening the box, Crystal gasps at the sight of a stunning 18K white gold necklace with a purple crystal amethyst stone attached to it. Flawless to the naked eye, the elegant stone connects to three gold wire brackets. The cluster shaped stone had a vintage look to it, making Crystal value it more because her mother knew how much she loves antique jewelry.

"Wow, this is so beautiful," she shrieks, taking the necklace out of the box, "Aunty J! Isn't it beautiful? I can't believe my mom bought this for me; I mean the stone looks a little old but…"

"It is old," her aunt says, cutting her off, Jacqueline's thoughts race as she stares with a haunted expression at the necklace. "Your mother didn't buy that necklace. I can't believe she still had it for all these years."

"Aunty J, what's the matter? Is there something wrong with the necklace?"

"No sweetie, there's nothing wrong with the necklace, it belonged to your grandmother, Lucette. She passed it on to your mother, hoping she would pass it onto her future children. I'm just surprised to see it again, that's all."

"That's strange; I wonder why she passed it on to me and not Alex?"

"I don't know Crystal, I've asked myself the same question when your grandma gave it to your mother and not me."

"Oh wait, I completely forgot about the card," Crystal says, swiftly opening the envelope. Drawing out a small white card, Crystal reads it out loud.

THE STONE

To my dear Crystal,
This necklace holds importance to our family; it is what you inherit from our ancestors who crafted this precious jewel. Once you put it on, I ask that you keep it safe and never take it off, for she who wears the stone protects the good.
I Love you with all of my heart.

Happy Birthday
Love Mom

❈ ❈ ❈

Puzzled by the hidden message on the card, Crystal stares at it awkwardly. "I don't understand, what does she mean by protecting the good? Is this some kind of special healing stone?"

"The necklace is a family heirloom Crystal, and your mom has had it for many years; she wrote that letter to you because she doesn't want you to lose it."

"Well, it's gorgeous, and I will cherish this for the rest of my life," Crystal responds quickly, unlocking the necklace. " Can you help me put this on Aunty J?"

"Sure, sweetie."

Raising the necklace to Crystal's neck, her aunt secures the chain by clasping the lock. Turning her around to get a better view, Jacqueline forces a smile. "There you go, darling, all set."

Rising from the bed, Crystal gently kisses her aunt on the cheek. "Thank you, Aunty J, you are the best. So, how does it look?"

"It looks beautiful on you, Crystal; your mom would be so proud to see you wearing it."

"Thank you, Aunty J; I love it so much, this is the best birthday gif-" suddenly, her cell phone vibrates on the nightstand. Walking over to the stand, her smile widens, staring at a new message from Jason.

"Uh oh, I see that smile, must be someone special. I guess that's my cue to leave," Jacqueline snickers when she suddenly receives a text message from her cell phone.

"It's my guy friend; he's making me dinner tonight. It's taco Tuesday."

"Hmmm, the mystery boyfriend, huh? Aunty J, are you ever going to bring this guy over so we can meet him?"

"Yes, Crystal, I'm just waiting for the right time. I want to make sure that he is the one."

"Well, by the way, you're smiling, I can tell that he already is the one Aunty J."

"Don't worry; you will meet him very soon, I promise. I have to get going now; I will stop by in a few days to check up on you and Alex, be careful, if there's anything that you need do not hesitate to call me."

Bidding her aunt farewell, Crystal watches her leave and head down the mahogany steps. Taking a seat on the bed, Crystal is in awe as she reads Jason's message.

"Hello Beautiful, please meet me in front of your house as soon as you read this... Jason."

Not wanting to look desperate, Crystal waits five minutes before she replies to her handsome neighbor. Informing him that she will be heading out, Crystal takes one last look at herself in her mother's mirror before exiting the room.

※ ※ ※

Scurrying down the steps, she quickly opens the door and finds Jason standing beside his motorcycle, holding on to two polished black helmets. Wearing a black t-shirt, dark blue jeans, and his infamous black leather jacket, Jason's emerald green eyes bore into hers with a flare of heat, causing Crystal to blush and turn away in flustered embarrassment.

"Hi beautiful, I thought maybe we could take a ride."

As he stood there patiently waiting for her response, Crystal's heart takes off like a thief, unknowingly fleeing into the arms of a sociopath. Something about the way he smiles at her, the way his eyes shimmers, displaying an enchanting glow making her want to surrender to his every command willingly.

"Jason—I would love to go out with you, but I have plans to meet up with a few friends at Lakeside diner."

"Oh," he frowns, lowering his head in disappointment.

"Do you want to come?"

"Are you sure, Crystal?"

"Yes, Jason; I think it will be fun. I'm sure you've been dying to take a tour of the town. Why not let me be the one to show you around."

His gaze drops on her lips. "Here, let me put this on for you," he says, gently placing the bike helmet over her head.

Fastening the belt under her chin, Jason puts on his helmet and hops on his bike. Starting the engine, he notices Crystal frozen in one spot nervously staring at the motorcycle.

"Crystal, there's no need to be afraid. I have it all under control," he says, extending his palm out to her. "Hop on."

Feeling a sudden sickening sensation throughout her body, Crystal nervously hops on the bike. Positioning herself behind Jason, Crystal wraps her arms around his waist; trying to breathe slowly, she tells her inner self to calm down and enjoy the ride.

Hitting his foot on the pedal, Jason flashes a sly grin, hearing the roaring sound escapes from the exhaust pipe. "Just hold on to me real tight Crystal, and whatever you do, don't let go."

"Trust me, Jason, I won't," she mutters, holding onto him in a firm grip.

Closing her eyes tightly, Crystal leans her face against the back of Jason's leather jacket as he takes off down the lane at full speed.

CHAPTER ELEVEN

WHO'S NEXT

LAKESIDE DINER

Lakeside Diner is a family-owned eatery at the Town Hall Circle. Home of the famous Chuleta y Fritos, Juan Julio Santos, and his wife Consúela Marie Santos became the first Mexican immigrant couple to successfully build a multiethnic restaurant in Lakeview Falls. After the segregation ban lifted on minorities living in the small town, seventy years prior, the Santos family made themselves at home and into the resident's hearts with their delectable comfort food from their native country.

Keeping their establishment open for business in such troubling times, the Santos family has generously announced they will be serving free meals to all residents of Lakeview Falls for the remainder of the year.

❋ ❋ ❋

La familia Santos quiere agradecerles a todos por exceptuarnos como miembros de esta ciudad. Debido a muertes inexplicables, estamos aquí para apoyar a las familias que han perdido a sus seres queridos.

Translation:

The Santos Family would like to thank you all for excepting us as a member of this town. Due to unexplainable deaths, we are here to support every family that has lost loved ones. From our families to yours, we, the people of Lakeview Falls, will continue to stick together in this battle to stay alive.

Sincerely
The Santos Family

❈ ❈ ❈

Entering Lakeside Diner, the savory smell of pepper steak and sofrito rice and beans instantly entices Crystal's hunger. Shifting her gaze to Jason, she notices his nose scrunched in an unpleasant matter. Sensing her doe eyes fixated on him, Jason struggles to control his facial expression while trying to breathe.

The lingering fumes of freshly cut onions and fried bacon make him want to regurgitate the human remains of her neighbor onto the marble tile floors.

"Jason, are you okay? You look sick," Crystal asks, noticing how strangely pale his face had become.

"I'm fine, Crystal. It's just—" he pauses, swallowing a drop of bile stuck in his throat, "the smell of bacon makes me nauseous."

"Oh gosh, I'm sorry, Jason," she mutters, placing a hand over her mouth, "if you don't want to stay, we can always hang out some other time."

"No, Crystal," he says, revealing beautiful white teeth in a grin, "I want to hang out with you. Plus, you had plans already with your friends, and it would be rude of me to make you cancel. I was the one that excepted your invitation. Shall we grab a table?" he suggests gently grabbing her hand.

Adoringly gazing at her, Jason's affectionate gesture indicates an open heart. His thoughtfulness makes Crystal fall deeper for him each time she is in his presence. Lacing his fingers with hers, they proceed down the center of the aisle where all eyes are directing solely on them.

Drawing in attention, female students from LVFU stare at Jason with sparkles in their eyes. His unique style and demeanor set apart from everyone else in the town. His irresistible good looks can hold a person spellbound for long periods.

Approaching the red vinyl modular circled booth, Jason, like a gentleman, pulls out a white handkerchief from his back pocket and wipes the seat before letting Crystal sit down. "Ladies first," he said in a warm tone.

Taking a seat in the center of the booth, Jason slides over, throwing his arm around Crystal's shoulder. Their bodies are so close that Crystal can feel his warm breath on her soft cheek. The tingling sensation of his touch sends her heart fluttering like a hummingbird. Looking up at him, she sees his piercing green eyes glued on hers. His limbs go numb for several moments, staring directly at the antique necklace around her neck.

"That's a beautiful piece of jewelry you have. Where did you get it?"

"Oh, this?" she says with a delighted expression, gently touching the stone. "I just received it earlier. It's a birthday gift from my mom."

"It's your birthday?" Jason asks in awe.

"No, my birthday is in two weeks. It's on October 31st."

A snicker escapes his lips. "Your birthday is on Halloween?"

Crystal nods her head a few times in excitement. "Yes, it's on Halloween. I know, it's weird, right?"

"Not at all, Crystal. I think it's kind of cool. I'm sure you must throw costume parties on your special day, right?"

"Well, my parents did when I was a little kid, but as I got older, not so much. I'd prefer to stay at home nowadays; I'm quite superstitious when it comes to pagan holidays."

Making a funny face, Jason teases her. "What? Why? Are you scared of monsters or something?"

"Monsters?" she giggles, "there's no such thing as monsters Jason. I don't celebrate my birthday anymore because too many bad things have been happening in this town, and I would feel safer at home than to be around crazy people."

Cocking one eyebrow, Jason smirks. "I mean Crystal, we all have a little crazy in us, right?"

"I guess so, but either way, I refuse to associate myself with a day that celebrates demonic energy. It creeps me out."

"I understand, the world is full of creeps, and I don't blame you for taking caution. It's a cruel world we live in."

Fiddling with the straw dispenser, a smile tugs at the corner of her mouth. "Boy, you sure know all the right things to say, Jason."

"I can't help myself; I find your presence magnetic, Crystal. I want to know more about you. I hope you don't mind."

"of course not. I feel the same about you, Jason."

"If your birthday isn't for another two weeks, why did you open your gift so early? Was your mom that excited to give it to you?"

"My aunt gave me the necklace on behalf of my mom. Somebody murdered my parents last year," she replies. Suppressing her tears with a smile, Crystal bites the inner layer inside her mouth to stop herself from crying.

"Oh my gosh, Crystal," Jason grasps her hand, caressing it, "I am so sorry, what happened to them?"

"Their bodies were found dismembered in the trunk of their car."

"Holy shit!" he exclaims, covering his mouth in disbelief. "That's terrible. Did they find out who did it?"

"No, Jason."

Pulling her closer to him, Jason leans his head against hers. "I don't know what to say, Crystal. I am sorry that you had to endure such a tragedy."

"That's okay, Jason. Thank you for your kindness and sympathy. It's never easy for me to discuss my parent's death with anyone, but I think remembering the good times when they were alive is what keeps me going. And now that I have this precious necklace, I will always feel closer to my mom."

"Not for long," he whispers under his breath, glaring at the pendant deviously.

❈ ❈ ❈

Flipping through the lunch menu, Crystal deciphers whether she wants the all you can eat thin-cut French fries or the famous Santos Tuesdays platter of the day Plátanos y Camarones. She licks her lips at the mouth-watering photos of Latin cuisines on the front page.

"Welcome to Lakeside Diner," Gabriela says, greeting them.

Dressed in her black and red waitress uniform with a pair of white converse sneakers, Gabriela wears her wavy black locks up in a bun with a single loose curl dangling on the left side of her face.

"Crystal, you're here early, and you're not alone," she says, glancing at Jason.

"Gabriela, I didn't know you were working a shift today? I thought we were hanging out? Trey, Vicky, Phillip, and Kyle are coming soon."

"Kyle? Oh no," shaking her head, Gabriela scowls, clicking her teeth, "my father isn't going to be happy if he sees him here. Kyle causes so many problems, Crystal. Last night he was complaining that the food doesn't cater to urban residents. He's been petitioning for southern food, and he also threatened to call **333** and report us. What the hell is wrong with him? I've told Kyle numerous times that this is a Latin Diner that serves Mexican American Tapas cuisines. He said this isn't Mexico, and we should serve the customers what they want."

"Don't pay him any mind, Gabby, Kyle is Kyle. That will never change. Look, you don't have to worry. We spoke to him and asked him to be on his best behavior."

"He better, Crystal, because if Kyle acts up today, it will be his last day coming to my family's diner."

"Are you hanging with us today? Please say you are," Crystal asks, pouting her lips with a woeful expression.

Placing two cups of dark soda on the round table, Gabriela huffs under her breath. "Crystal, I'm sorry, my father is short staffed today; one of his cooks quit and left town. He stole two fucking aprons and twenty Porterhouse steaks. It took me an hour to calm my dad down."

"What the hell is he going to do with all those steaks?" Crystal asks, gritting her teeth, trying not to laugh.

Shrugging her shoulders, Gabby huffs in frustration. "Who knows, I hope that Hijo De Puta chokes on them. That jerk just cost my family to lose a lot of profit on grade A meat. Those steaks were part of the free meal assistance for the residents of this town."

"Gabby, if your family is tight with cash, why are you serving us free sodas?"

"Oh, those aren't free. The couple sitting behind you paid for it but never drank it."

"Ewww, Gabby," Crystal frowns in disgust, pushing the sodas away from her and Jason.

A delighted look stretches across Gabby's face while staring at Jason. "Aren't you going to introduce me to your new friend Crystal?"

Gently teasing Crystal, Gabriela takes a seat beside her in the booth giving her a good-natured nudging with her elbow.

"Jason, I would like to introduce you to my nosy best friend, Gabriela."

"But you can call me Gabby," Gabriela quickly cuts Crystal, extending her hand to shake Jason's.

"It's very nice to meet you, Gabby," he says, admiring her polite and down to earth personality.

"How did you and Crystal meet, Jason?"

"I'm house-sitting for my Uncle Joe, who lives right across the street from her house."

"Are you talking about Mr. McGregor? He left town?" she asks Jason feeling a bit concerned.

"Yes, my Uncle had some business stuff he needed to attend. Why do you ask?"

"That's strange," Gabby huffs, pulling out a post-it note from her black and red floral apron, "Mr. McGregor is on the free meal assistance plan for veterans. He called the diner last week to sign up for meal deliveries to his home. I'm surprised he didn't notify us that he was going away."

Jason remains silent while he maintains eye contact with Gabriela. Anger curls hot and unstoppable in his gut, like a blazing inferno that wants to burn inside out.

"You know what? My uncle hasn't been himself; he's been so stressed these days. I'm sorry that he didn't say anything to you. I guess he forgot."

"Hmmm, I guess so. Well, we have three weeks of pre-packed frozen meals for Mr. McGregor in the back kitchen. Since you will be residing in his home while he's away, is it possible you can take the meals for him?"

"Sure, Gabriela, I would be more than happy to take those meals off your hands. I can retrieve them when I'm leaving."

"Thank you, Jason, and if you hear from your uncle, please let him know that the Santos family is always here if he needs anything."

"That's very kind of you, thank you. It's nice to see that the residents care so much in this town."

"Of course, Jason, in tough times, we all stick together in Lakeview Falls, right, Crystal?"

"That's right, Gabby," Crystal responds, adjusting her necklace around her neck.

"Oh my God, Crystal!" Gabby gasps, catching her breath as she lays her eyes on the purple amethyst stone. "Where did you get that necklace?" she asks, stretching her hand out to touch the stone.

"Aunty J gave it to me; it was from my mom."

"It's beautiful, Crystal," caressing the cluster shaped pendant, Gabriela's index finger grazes the edge of the stone penetrating her skin, "ouch," she shrieks in pain.

A tiny droplet of blood seeps from the tip of her finger, landing on the menu. "Dammit," Gabriela winces uncontrollably, rising from the booth.

"Gabriela, are you okay? I'm so sorry," Crystal apologizes, grasping a napkin from the dispenser.

"Crystal, don't worry. It's a tiny cut; I'll be fine," Gabriela replies quickly, gathering both menus from the table. "I'm going to rinse my hands in the back, are you guys hungry?"

"Not right now; how about you, Jason?" Crystal asks, immediately gazing at him.

"I'm not hungry, either, thank you."

"Okay, well, I'll be back. Just in case you do want something, Anthony is on the floor. He can take your order," Gabriela says, excusing herself.

※ ※ ※

Strolling through the entrance door, Trey, Kyle, Victoria, and Phillip see Crystal and Jason from a distance, engaging in a deep conversation. They tread down the crowded aisle, with a smile plastered on their faces as they approach the booth. Ecstatic to see her friends, Crystal's smile widens but quickly fades when she glances in Kyle's direction.

Taking a seat beside Crystal, Trey and Victoria grab a menu from the empty booth behind them while Kyle and Phillip grab two chairs from a round table across, sitting next to Jason.

"Well, look who found a nice make-out spot with an ashen looking man. Have you been watching the Twilight series again, Crystal?" Kyle asks, teasing Crystal with a goofy smirk.

Giving Kyle the side-eye, an annoyed expression is painted on Crystal's face as she glares at him, hoping that Jason doesn't feed into his ignorance.

"Excuse our rude friend; he doesn't have any home training," Crystal apologizes to Jason for Kyle's insensitive remark.

"That's okay, I take it that's Kyle," Jason replies with an intensifying glare at the town's bigot.

"Yes, as a matter of fact, I am Kyle, and who are you?"

"I'm Jason Warwick."

"I'm Trey, Crystal's best friend in the entire world," he laughs, extending his hand, giving Jason a fist bump, "this is Victoria and her boyfriend, Phillip."

"It's a pleasure to meet you all," Jason says in a soft-spoken tone.

He quickly gazes at Crystal, grasping her hand from under the booth, "you have so many nice friends."

"Yeah, she does! Don't you?" Kyle asks sarcastically.

"Kyle! Quit being mean," Crystal scowls, feeling embarrassed by her friend's behavior.

"No, that's okay Crystal, as a matter of fact, Kyle, I don't have that many friends. And judging by your bigoted behavior, I have a feeling that everyone here pretends to like you when in actuality, you're nothing but a poor excuse for a human being," Jason snaps, unable to control his anger.

Elevating his chin, Kyle sits with his legs spread wide in his seat, fiddling with his freemason ring. "So, was there a shortage of Karen's around? Because I see you went straight for the melanin sister; didn't pass go once? Collect two hundred dollars?" Kyle wickedly glares at Jason, mocking him with his racist rant.

"I beg your pardon, did you say, Karen?" Jason exhales with a Pfft sound, "is that a racist term you call a white woman? If so, I'm sorry to disappoint you, Kyle, but I don't see color. I see the person within."

"You white dudes always have a fetish for our woman. Why is that? Do our Afro-centric sisters make you feel good when white woman treat you like shit?"

"Alright, that's enough, Kyle!" Phillip hollers, interrupting their bickering. "Chill the fuck out!"

Irritated by his surroundings, Jason's blood boils through his veins, fighting the urge to slay. His stay in Lakeview Falls has already proven to be challenging. His mission is to fulfill his diabolical duties and become a reckoning force alongside his father who's eternal entity is bound within a pendant possessed by a descendant of a **Courier.**

Focusing solely on Crystal, Jason sees no importance in her friends. Slowly getting up, Jason leans towards Crystal's ears. "I have to use the restroom," he whispers, caressing the back of Crystal's neck, "I'll be right back."

"Jason, I am so sorry about—"

"Shhh, you apologize too much, Crystal," his lips flick into an endearing simper peering into the deep depths of her iris.

"I'll be back," Jason says, giving Crystal one last gaze before heading to the men's bathroom.

THE BROTHER'S CURSE

"Nice going, Kyle! Why are you such a jerk?" Victoria angrily expresses while sucking on a cherry flavored lollipop.

"What?" Kyle shrugs his shoulders with no care in the world. "Oh, come on guys; I was only joking with him. Why is everyone so sensitive? You don't even know him."

"It doesn't matter, Kyle! You promised you wouldn't act like this; I think you should go and apologize to him," Crystal suggests.

"Right now?" Kyle squints his eyes confusingly at Crystal.

"Yes, now, Kyle!" Crystal exclaims. "He's been kind to me ever since he came to this town. The least you can do is say you're sorry and leave as such."

"He's in the bathroom, Crystal! I don't want to apologize to someone while their dick is sticking out," Kyle sighs with aggravation.

"Just fucking go already, Kyle! Get it over with," Phillip shouts while moving his seat away from him.

"Fine, whatever, I'll go apologize to -- what's his name?"

"Jason!" Crystal belts out with rage in her eyes.

"Right, Jason; you know what? Not for nothing, he kind of looks like that guy that played that **"IT"** clown in that movi——-" he says with a sarcastic smug, getting up from his chair.

Tossing a black plastic pepper shaker at Kyle, Trey grunts. "Would you go already!"

※ ※ ※

Making his way to the men's bathroom, Kyle feels a dread creep up from the pit of his stomach. Giving the etch glass door a cautious push, the door groans open, allowing Kyle to stretch out his neck. Without turning his head or appearing to communicate with Kyle, Jason whispers his words.

"Looking for me, Kyle?"

"Yeah, actually I am," he stutters, slowly approaching the empty urinal next to Jason.

Kyle stands beside him, unzipping his cargo pants. Sweat pours down his forehead as he stood still as possible. Excreting into the waterless urinal, Kyle clears his throat, accidentally aiming his phallus at the shiny white tiles.

"Hey man, I'm sorry about what happened out there; I was just busting your balls; no hard feelings, right?"

Turning his head over his shoulder, Jason snarls at Kyle, ignoring his apology. His eyes gleam with darkness as eerie silence envelopes the bathroom stalls with only echoes of thick water droplets colliding with the sink like loud cracks of thunder.

White lights above the ceiling warp into a dark, dingy red lighting with unseen dangers, painting an endless misery that adorns the slippery tile walls. The staleness of the air makes it harder for Kyle to breathe. His mind races faster than before with a terrible pressure entering his chest.

Induced by a shockwave that creates a slow rhythmic motion in the room, Kyle's vision becomes fuzzy. He instantly hears a slithering hiss coming from the urinal's left corner, which puts fear in his blood. Struggling with his eyesight, Kyle whimpers softly while the noise grows louder and louder, traveling around his head.

Gripping and rubbing his erect member, Jason watches as it shifts into an 8-inch black rattlesnake falling onto the tile flooring. The shuffling vermin claims its place. It slithers its way under Kyle's pants. Sensing something cold and clammy crawling up his legs, Kyle stood frozen in sheer horror, screaming to the top of his lungs as the rattlesnake pokes out from the crotch area hissing at him.

"What the FUCK!" Kyle wails, feeling the snake sink its sharp teeth into his manhood. Clenching his fist, Kyle immediately strikes the rattlesnake as hard as possible, sending it slithering back into Jason's pants.

Shapeshifting into Kyle's mirror image, Jason exposes his fiery red eyes and razor blade teeth, frightening him to his core. The color quickly drains from Kyle's face, staring at a demonic version of himself; it is as if the demon's eyes are burning down on his back like the heat of the sun.

Unleashing ungodly laughter from the very depths of hell, Jason uses his leverage to grip Kyle's throat. Lifting him in the air, he states, "I'm hungry now; time to eat!"

THE BROTHER'S CURSE

Attaching his lips to Kyle, Jason extracts his internal organs and other bodily fluids into his mouth. Choking on his intestines as it transfers into Jason, Kyle closes his eyes, wrestling to get out of Jason's grip; but his life was already flowing out of him.

Without warning, Kyle's cell phone jangles in his pocket. His eyes flash open to see Jason and two other male students from LVFU, awkwardly staring at him. Turning back and forth, panic-stricken, Kyle tries to push the images of himself as a demon out of my mind.

Terrified and shaking, Kyle points his index finger directly at Jason's face. "What did you do to me?" he questions. Streams of tears flow down his face faster than his heartbeat.

"Do what, Kyle?" Jason mockingly smirks at him.

Suddenly, the voices of Coltan, Brandon, and Gregory yelling **"White Power,"** mentally tug at Kyle's psyche. The neo-nazi chant sends jolts down his body. The sounds chorused with different tones and words like walking in a crowd of thousands.

"What's the matter, Kyle? You look like you've seen a demon," Jason moans, exposing his fork-shaped tongue.

"Aaaah!" Kyle wails, bolting towards the door. His screams are like a begging call from a wounded child who pleads for help. Sprinting so fast out of the men's bathroom, Kyle forgets to zip his fly.

Running past his friend's booth, Kyle flashes everyone with his penis before exiting the diner. Flabbergasted, Crystal, Trey, and Victoria stare at each other in complete shock while LVFU students start to laugh and applaud what they had just witnessed.

Throwing his head back, Phillip lets out a loud humorous laugh. "Is it me? Or did we just see Kyle's dick?"

CHAPTER TWELVE

HE DEVOURS YOU

LATER ON THAT NIGHT

A vast expanse of inky blackness darkens as the night goes on. A shade passes over the moon like an eclipse swallowing the light, never allowing it to escape. Cozied up on her off white chaise lounge chair in her spacious living room, Crystal snuggles under her faux fur throw blanket. Taking in the scattered soft lights that flicker from her modern style brick stone fireplace, Crystal enjoys the warm and relaxing atmosphere while watching the newest episode of the "Lakeview Falls Home Shopping Network" on her flat screen tv.

Tuning in for the 10 pm nightly segment, **"How 2 Keep Yourself Alive Another Day,"** Crystal listens to the ecstatic voice of the four foot eleven middle-aged Japanese billionaire false prophet Lana Cho. Lana is Lakeview Falls famous infomercial scam artist, pastor, and saleswoman. Preying on the vulnerable with her word of God, Lana Cho is the creator of gimmicky non-FDA approved self-defense gadgets and survival clothing lines for children and adults.

Advertising the newest heat protection gear called **"Protect Your Flesh,"** Lana and her stunt man assistant and husband Flamingo Bill demonstrate how to put on the suit safely. Carefully slipping on the composite material suit that consists of blended preserved human and python skin, Flamingo Bill puts on his glass hazmat helmet for safety purposes, just in case anything would go dangerously wrong on the live tv segment.

Wearing a black one-piece fitted suit and a white scientist lab coat, Lana Cho grasps hold of an X13 Flamethrower. The advanced mechanical device built with an acrid poisonous substance, cannot only burn a human to ashes in 0.2 seconds, but the pain is also equivalent to being torn apart by the sharp teeth of an exotic animal.

Standing nine feet away from her husband, Lana Cho turns to face the television studio camera, acknowledging her home audience with a bright smile. "Hello citizens of Lakeview Falls, are you afraid of being skinned off like a pig? Do you want to feel safe again and protect the soft layer that covers your bones? Well, look no further," she says, displaying the flamethrower to her live studio audience.

"OOH.......AHH...," the crowd exclaims in the background.

"For a limited time offer and from the makers of **"Spray The Killer and Runaway,"** I present to you my latest invention called **"Skin Savior: The Cure to not getting Devoured."** The newest outerwear protects yourself from being flayed alive by whoever is tormenting and torturing our residents. In Jesus's name, we ask you to save the precious skin of our beloved young men and boys of this town. Can I get an AMEN and a PRAISE JESUS!" Lana shouts with one hand, aiming at the ceiling.

"AMEN! PRAISE JESUS!" the crowd shouts with praise.

"This skin savior Hazmat suit is only a whopping $99.99; you heard right! It's only $99.99, and if you call now, you will receive a second set for free, including the safety helmet and a bottle of holy water. Order now."

"Show us how the Hazmat suit works, Sister Cho!" one male audience blurts out

"Yeah, show us!" a female says with a child-like tone to her voice, "we need to know if you are the miracle to saving the young men of this town!"

Quickly disapproving of the request from the audience, Flamingo Bill stares dead into Lana's ocean blue eyes. "Lana, don't you dare," he whispers with a distorted expression.

"Our word is what binds us, Bill," a devilish smile smears across her face, "we need to prove to our fans that we are the light and the way."

"Dammit, Lana, we haven't tested this suit," he groans, "I demand you go to a commercial this instant."

"HURRY UP! COME ON, WE WANT TO SEE!" an angry viewer says, rising from his seat, applauding, which leads to everyone else in the audience following the lead.

"Lana! You can't be serious! You have no idea how this......." Flamingo Bill stutters horror-stricken at the grisly smirk his wife gives him.

Flicking the **On** switch, Lana faces Flamingo Bill, adjusting her index finger on the trigger. Aiming the flamethrower at his suit, Lana cracks her neck from side to side. Slowly dragging in the humid air in the studio set, Lana exhales, discharging bright orange-colored flames at her husband.

Frozen to a point where he was hardly breathing, Flamingo Bill's eyes widen as the giant ball of fire hits his suit. The reaction of the audience is nothing more than amazement when they see the savior suit is indestructible. Booming cheers escape their mouths while flashing one hundred dollar bills shouting in sync, "Lana is God's chosen child."

As the crowd praises Lana, a bone-chilling scream silences the room when Flamingo Bill begins to convulse. A thick swarm of steam flows out of his mouth while a revolting stench of burning flesh erupts through the atmosphere.

Flamingo Bill drops to his knees as his eyes disgorge blood, "Oh my God, my Skin! My Skin! It didn't work you, stupid Bitch! I want a divorce!" Flamingo Bill screams as the savior hazmat suit disintegrates, melting his arms and legs before the tv cuts to a bright fuzzy screen that reads, **"PLEASE STAND BY."**

❆ ❆ ❆

"Holy Crap!" Crystal utters in disbelief while staring at the screen.

Shaking her head at the disturbing image of Flamingo Bill burning on live tv, Crystal quickly changes the channel to the local 12 o'clock news where the bold red letters **"SPECIAL BREAKING NEWS"** displays on the bottom of the screen. On a separate side of the screen shows four photos of a diverse group of men aging from 17 to 23.

A young male reporter stands in front of the **C** rated restaurant "UnLucky China Cuisine" while his hand trembles, holding a can of mace. He stares into the camera; his teeth chatters from the cold night.

"Hello, I'm Michael Ford, with 666 news, and we are coming to you live from Fearman Street, where four young delivery men have been reported missing since this afternoon."

"The young men displayed on top of your screen have been identified as Anthony Destefano, Sergio Ruiz Perez, Salim Muhammad, and Xiang Zhao Ming. If anyone hears any information about these young men, the Lakeview Falls sheriff's department urges you to please call the number at the bottom of your screen. The number is 1-999-FEAR, or you can go to the local Sheriff's department to make a report. There is a $400 reward for anyone that finds them. We will continue to update on these mystery disappearances when we have more information. Now we return you to your regularly scheduled program."

Suddenly reverberating sounds of her cell phone shudder on the foyer table beside her window sill. Uncovering herself, Crystal rises from the lounge chair and shuts off the television with a clap of her hands. Stretching her limbs, she advances towards the custom made bay window in her small sunroom. Clutching the cell phone in the palm of her hands, she is smitten to see it's Jason who is calling her. Taking a seat on the cushioned window bench, she answers the call.

"Hey, Jason," she softly says, brushing the bridal lace ivory curtains.

"Hello, Crystal, I hope you don't mind that I'm calling you so late. I know we saw each other earlier, but I couldn't stop thinking about you," Jason says with a rich deep tone to his voice that flows like a river.

Staring at Mr. McGregor's house from across the street, the disturbing reflection of the silver moonlight shines upon Crystal's face. The luminous celestial body of stars gleams like blades against the blackness of the sky.

"You were thinking about me?" she asks bashfully.

"Yes, you sound surprised, Crystal. I mean, I am quite fond of you. I don't know what it is, but the moment I met you, I knew there was something extraordinary about you."

Dressed in an off pink silk nightgown, Crystal rests her back against the wall. Her body curls up while hugging her vintage violet floral throw pillow, listening to Jason relish about seeing her earlier. His voice is sweet and velvety like chocolate, memorizing with each syllable.

"I enjoyed my time with you earlier, Crystal. I like your friends, they are very kind, well except for one of them."

"I enjoyed my time with you also Jason, and I apologize about Kyle. He can be quite offensive with the way he speaks to people."

"I can tell; he seemed off. I'm not quite sure why he flipped out at the diner."

"About that, Jason, what happened in the bathroom? You should have seen the way he ran out of the restaurant, he looked terrified."

"I have no clue, Crystal. All I know is that he came into the restroom and then freaked out for no reason. He kept staring at the mirror-like he saw something crazy. I did my best to calm him down, but he bolted out so quickly. Does he always act like that?" Jason asks.

"No, I've never seen Kyle scared like that, not since we were kids. Yes, he has racist views that I don't approve of; but something wasn't right with him this afternoon. It's almost like he was running away from a killer. I'm worried about him, Jason."

"Does he do drugs?" Jason asks, questioning Kyle's mental state.

"Drugs?" Crystal exclaims with an awkward expression, "no, I don't think he has ever done drugs."

"I know it's not my place to say this, Crystal, but I think your friend may have some serious mental issues. Have you or your friends ever thought about getting him some psychiatric help?"

"Jason, none of us have the time to fix Kyle. He doesn't need help, he needs Jesus," Crystal says, trying to suppress her laughter.

"Enough about Kyle, what are you doing up so late?" Crystal asks, staring at his shadow, sitting in the living room.

"Well, I was getting ready to have a midnight snack," Jason replies, fiddling with the remote control in his hand.

"Midnight snack, huh? Do you have the munchies?" Crystal asks jokingly.

"Actually, yes, I do," he chuckles, "I get these crazy cravings at night."

"Well, I wish I could join you. I have a sweet tooth."

"So come over? There's enough food to go around."

"I wish I could, Jason, but I can't; I have to be up early tomorrow. I'm meeting Trey at the university."

A deep sigh escapes his lips on the other line. "I guess that means you're kicking me off the phone, huh?"

"Trust me, I don't want to, but I promised Trey. He's been begging me to come to this lecture since I've been back, and I don't want to seem like a flake. It means so much to him that I go."

"How about I pick you up in the morning and take you to school, and maybe afterward, I can take you out on a real date, just the two of us. That's if you don't have plans."

"I don't have plans for tomorrow evening. I would love to go out with you again, Jason," she replies with a smile, gripping the throw pillow close to her chest.

"So, it's a date then?"

"It's a date, Jason."

"You just made my night, Crystal; I can't wait to see you. What time should I pick you up in the morning?"

"You can come around ten."

"Well, I guess I will see you tomorrow then, beautiful. Have a good night."

"Thank you, Jason, bye; oh, and enjoy that snack."

"I definitely will. Goodbye, Crystal," Jason responds with a sensual and smooth whisper before ending the call.

❊ ❊ ❊

After ending his conversation with Crystal, Jason's stomach begins to make painful growling moans. Even though he devoured a raw steak when he arrived home, he still feels famished. His craving for flesh becomes uncontainable. Rising from Mr. McGregor's favorite recliner chair, Jason makes his way over to the kitchen counter, where his eyes fixate on four large brown takeout bags aligned across the oak wood kitchen table.

Indecisive of what meal to eat first, Jason's hands transition, forming into a sickly grey complexion. Stroking his fingers across the countertop, it gradually begins to shift grotesquely into sharp claw nails that protrude from under his first layer of skin. As thick droplets of blood trickle down the hard wooden floor, Jason has a sudden urge to grasp hold of a pair of chopsticks and a fortune cookie, making his way over to the basement entrance.

The brass door grinds against its hinges as it is thrust open with a violent force. Walking down the damp rotted wooden staircase, the slew of cobwebs clings to the corners like untrimmed whiskers. Dim fluorescent lighting creates a chilling atmosphere while a foul odor from backed-up sewage pipes corrupts the air.

Reaching the bottom of the steps, Jason hears loud muffling sounds coming from the basement corner. Shapeshifting into his demonic visage, Jason grimaces as he advances towards the center of the room. Dangling from the ceiling, four delivery takeout guys hang naked, upside down by sharp silver barb wires. With each of the men's mouths sewn shut, Jason watches the young men's body shake savagely, defecating and urinating on themselves.

The sound of their warm urine, hitting the cold concrete ground, makes Jason more enticed and alarmingly aroused. With his frightening fiery red eyes, he walks past each man, twiddling the chopsticks in each of their faces.

Jason whispers sinisterly in the men's ears, "Who should I eat first?"

Staring directly at the Asian delivery guy, Jason points the chopsticks at him with a wicked sneer. "CHINESE?"

CHAPTER THIRTEEN

THE BROTHERS TALE

THE NEXT MORNING

Yellow rays of light claw their way upwards while the scarlet sun splashes across the horizon, displaying pink colors like a sea of cotton candy. Its brilliant rosy glow illuminates Killer Creek Lane, warming the air and ridding of everything dark. Placing her foot inside her stainless glass walk-in shower, Crystal turns the silver shower knob adjusting the temperature. The warm water slowly falls onto her skin, soothing the ache that claws at her limbs.

As the hot steam envelopes her body, Crystal reaches for her gentle scrub liquid body wash on the soap rack. Squeezing a few drops of the lavender-scented serum onto her bath sponge, she gently caresses it over her body. Circling under the shower, Crystal rinses the suds, sending them in a little stream down her back. Allowing her mind to wander off, Crystal closes her eyes and hums a classical tune while leaning her hands against the off white tiles.

Taking a deep breath, Crystal starts to sing her favorite love song, "How Deep Is Your Love," with a heavenly voice. The sweet vowels leave her mouth strong and powerful, which carries around the room in sound waves. Thoughts of Jason's handsome face run through her mind when suddenly, she is startled by a firm, masculine hand wrapping around her petite waist.

Swiftly turning around, Crystal belts out a high pitch scream. **"Aahhhh!** JOHN! What the hell! What are you doing here? How did you get into my bedroom?"

Seductively gazing into her dark brown eyes, John exposes himself in his raw form while the hot, warm water enshrouds his chiseled, tanned olive toned chest. His piercing amber, green eyes look at her curiously, his lips turn into a grin. "I found your bedroom window unlocked."

"So you thought that was an invitation to enter my home? John? What has gotten into you? If this is your way of courting me again, you have lost your damn mind. You know, in most states, this would be considered stalking as well as intruding."

Glaring at John, Crystal feels her face getting hot. She could not process what was happening at that moment; her thoughts run wild, thinking, "*How could her ex blatantly sneak into her house after the heated conversation they had a few days prior? Was this another attempt to win her back?*"

"Stalking, huh?" he smiles while his warm body embraces her in a comforting touch, "Well, if that's how you feel, Crystal, then all you have to do is tell me to leave. Is that what you want?" he asks sweetly, brushing a strand of her curly hair from her forehead.

John's eyes' intensity provokes Crystal into asking him to stay. With a yearning expression, they both gaze adoringly at each other. Each minute they are in each other's arms, it never seems to end.

"John—I—" Crystal stutters as emotions build up inside of her.

"Crystal," he quickly cuts her off, "I'm so sorry for the way I acted and for overreacting about that new guy. I love you so much, and I don't want to fight with you anymore. I'm in love with you, and that will never stop. All I want is you; All I want is us."

It was at that very moment, Crystal sees the hurt in John's eyes. Every time he said the words I love you, his tongue would glide beautifully over his perfect teeth and emit an adorable bit of air. John laces his fingers through her hair, feeling his body melt against Crystal's in the heat of fiery passion.

Slowly bringing his lips down to hers, his breath is hot as his soft kisses trail down her pulsating neck. John feels his heart pounding as he cups her face, capturing her full luscious lips. Leaning Crystal against the steamy white tiles, John stood between her legs and gently lifts them, wrapping them around his waist. His eyes resting solely on her beauty, John whispers.

"I belong to you, Crystal, and you belong to me."

"John—Please—" she whimpers breathlessly against his lips, feeling his erect member slip inside of her.

"Crystal," he cries out, twirling her hair around his fingers.

"CRYSTAL!" Alex hollers, thrusting the bathroom door open

Alarmed by her sister's voice, Crystal instantly jumps off of John. "Alex, you scared the shit out of me!" she says, slightly peeking out of the shower, "you could have at least knocked!"

"I heard screaming; I thought something happened to you. Are you okay?" Alex asks with a worried expression.

"Alex, I'm fine. The water was too hot," Crystal says, shivering from the cool breeze that lingers in the hallway entering the bathroom.

"Mmhmm, you know I could have sworn I heard a guy's voice too," Alex squints her eyes suspiciously at her sister.

"Nope, no guy in here... Is that all because I have to get ready."

Awkwardly glancing at the shadowy figure she sees behind Crystal, Alexandria gives her a sly grin. "You might want to hurry up, big head. Jason is out front waiting for you on his bike."

"Oh shit, I told him to come at 10. What time is it?"

"It's 9:30," Alex and John yell out at the same time.

"Oops," John mumbles in the background, staring at his waterproof wristwatch.

"Hi, John!" Alex snickers, giving her sister a long stare.

Peeking his head over Crystal's shoulders, John flashes her a smirk. "Hey, Alex."

Scrunching up her face, Alexandria clears her throat. "I'm going to pretend this never happened."

"Bye, Alex! Tell Jason that I will be down in fifteen minutes."

"Okay, I will let him know. Oh, and I'm staying with Derrick tonight at his dorm. The house is all yours just in case you are planning an adult sleepover."

"Get out, Alex!" Crystal says, chucking her bath sponge at her.

"Bye, big head," Alex says, exiting the bathroom.

Watching her sister close the door behind her, Crystal slaps John on the arm. "You could have at least kept quiet."

"I'm sorry, I slipped. What's the big deal anyway? Crystal, this is your house too, and you can do whatever you want..." Stroking the left side of her cheek, John leans in for a kiss. "So where were we?" he whispers.

"You were leaving," she says, connecting her index finger with his lips, "I have to get ready now. Playtime is over, John."

"You're kicking me out for this guy? What's going on, Crystal?"

Crystal grasps her towel, taking a step out of the shower. She wraps it around her like a lover draping itself about her sensual curves.

Grasping his navy blue boxer briefs from the tile flooring, Crystal hands them over to John. "Jason is giving me a ride to the university."

"So, you're going to choose this guy over me?" he asks her with a saddened expression.

"Bye, John."

"Fine! I'll go, but we will finish what we started; I promise you that!" he replies, advancing towards the bathroom entrance.

"No, no, no! Out the way you came in!" Crystal demands, pointing him directly towards the bedroom window.

He shrugs his shoulders with bewilderment. "Seriously, Crystal?"

"Goodbye, John," Crystal responds, giving him a friendly wave as he climbs out of her window.

❊ ❊ ❊

LAKEVIEW FALLS UNIVERSITY

Lakeview Falls University stood partially secluded due to many staff and faculty members taking refuge at community colleges outside of town. As murders and disappearances of young men continue to rise, the once prestigious university bravely keeps its doors open to the future alumni and class of 2025.

With only ten professors teaching on campus, small workshops and historical lectures are available for students who wish to complete their courses and receive their college credits for the fall and winter semesters.

The popular Demonology course is the most talked-about lecture ever in the history of Lakeview Falls University. It only permits twenty students per session. Anyone who wishes to participate in the curricular studies shall go through an assessment held by none other than Professor Jean-Baptist.

Entering the executive style lecture theater hall, Trey observes a few ecstatic students conversing amongst each other while waiting impatiently for the class to start. Noticing Phillip, Simone, Victoria, and Terrance seated in the front row, Trey sees the seats begin a quarter of the way to the middle of the room. Choosing two chairs located to the back, Trey makes himself comfortable while he waits for Crystal.

Adjusting his body in the upholstered posture support chair, Trey admires the vibrant red color of the seating and the connected desk that features the advanced K4 Hilkido tablet that bears 260 kg plus free Wi-Fi. Leaning over, sliding his black leather backpack under his seat, Trey instantly feels soft fingers stroking the back of his neck.

Ticklish, Trey unleashes a high pitch giggle, wiggling himself uncontrollably around in his chair. Swiftly jerking his head around, he sees that its Crystal, who is the tickling culprit.

"Dammit, Crystal, you know that's my weak spot. For a minute, I thought it was my knight and shining armor finally coming to sweep me off my feet and out of this evil ass town."

"Awww, sorry, Trey, but there are no knights in Lakeview Falls. I guess you will have to settle for me today instead."

Slumping back in his chair, Trey pouts his lips. "Thanks for putting a damper on my fantasy, Crys. Can't a sexy masculine diva such as myself dream a little dream?"

Taking a seat beside her best friend, Crystal hangs her cross-body bag behind her chair. Wrapping her arms around his back, Crystal kisses Trey on his cheek. "Sorry, I'm a few minutes late; I had a little early mishap."

"Well, it looks like that mishap was a good thing because you are glowing, Ms. Fabulous, beautiful necklace, by the way."

"Thank you, Trey."

"You're welcome, love, so what mishap did you have?" he says, glancing at his touch screen watch. "We've got five minutes till class starts."

"You will never guess what happened to me this morning."

"Judging by that small hickey on your neck," he points out with a silly smug expression, "I'm guessing something kinky?"

"Oh, Shit!" Crystal's mouth widens in an O shape, "oh my God, Jason." Crystal gasps, touching both sides of her neck with embarrassment.

"Jason?" Trey's head jerked to the side. "He gave you that hickey?"

"No, it was John," Crystal replies, scrunching her lip upward.

"JOHN!" Trey hollers in the classroom, accidentally dropping his cell phone on the marble flooring. "Bitch, what kind of party were you having this morning?"

"For crying out loud, Trey," she whispers, "John snuck into my shower this morning."

"He did what? How the hell did he do that?"

"He climbed into my bedroom window, then snuck into my bathroom while I was taking a shower. Things got a little hot and heavy and we kind of—fooled around."

"You can't kind of fool around Crystal, it's either you did, or you didn't."

"Fine, we almost had sex, Trey."

Fanning himself with his right hand, Trey puts on his dramatic act. "Well, I see you couldn't stay mad at your Latin lover for too long."

"I don't know what to do Trey, I still love John, but I'm starting to have feelings for Jason too. God I'm so confused."

"You're not confused, Crystal. You are stuck in a rough spot between two hot looking guys. In my opinion, I would just keep both."

Clicking her teeth, she replies, "No, Trey, I can't juggle two guys at the same time."

"So which one do you want, Crystal? Jason or John?" Trey asks with a grin pinned on his face.

A huff escapes Crystal's heart-shaped lips. "It's so hard to decide, Trey," she replies in a whiny tone.

"Crystal, you have to listen to your heart; you know what you want; you're just scared of the heart you will break," resting his head against her shoulders, Trey grasps hold of her hand.

"Look, I know you better than anyone Crystal, and when you love, you love with all your heart, and I know this from personal experience with you."

"Oh really, and how is that my handsome best friend?"

"Do you remember when we were in the first grade Crystal, and you told me that you had a massive crush on me and you saw us getting married one day, and then I told you that I only liked boys and then—"

"And then I shoved Play-Doh in your mouth," she lightly chuckles, "yes, I remember that, Trey."

Trey's eyes brim with glee and a smile tugs the left side of his face. "Crystal, that's the day I knew we would be best friends forever. Even though you were a kid, you always wore your heart on your sleeves."

"Awww, Trey, that is such a sweet thing to say."

"It's the truth, Crystal. You have a good heart, and honestly, I can't see a life without you in it. You have been my best friend since I was four years old, and I love you so much."

"Not as much as I love you, Trey."

THE BROTHER'S CURSE

❋ ❋ ❋

"Good morning everyone, please take your seats so we can start our session," Professor Baptist says, entering the side door of the lecture hall.

Laying his leather briefcase on his pinewood desk, Professor Baptist advances to his silver acrylic lectern. Appearing to be an ex-military man, Jean Baptist is tall, dark, and handsome. His light brown eyes are sharp and attentive, while his ebony black hair styled in a Caesar hair cut contrasts against his vibrant melanin skin.

Standing behind his podium, Professor Baptist wears a neatly pressed white button-down shirt, a brown blazer with a custom made dragon design on it, a brown fitted suit pants, and polished black oxford shoes. Glancing at the students, he reaches inside his suit pants and pulls out his light adjuster remote, which he uses to dim the theater's lighting. Professor Baptist clears his throat and proceeds to speak.

"Hello everyone! And welcome to the metaphysics of demonology. Today's workshop will not be on paranormal studies. Due to alarming recent events that have taken place in our town, I think it's time the class has an in-depth discussion about the dark history of Lakeview Falls. The urban legends and myths of a town filled with mystery, fear, and death date back decades upon decades. Some might believe that whoever resides here is forever cursed. Some would ask, why can't you just move someplace else?"

"Because we're broke!" Phillip hollers, causing half of the class to chuckle.

With a stern expression, Professor Baptist leaves the podium and walks up to the front row where Phillip is seated. "What is your name, young man?" he asks.

"My name is Phillip Mills, sir," he replies, sitting up in his seat, folding his hands.

"Mills, so you're the Sheriff's son, right?"

"Yes, sir."

"Well, that's unfortunate," Professor Baptist sarcastically sneers at Phillip, brushing him off, walking back to his podium. "If you wouldn't mind, Mr. Mills, I would appreciate it if you can keep your mouth shut for the rest of the time you are in my classroom."

Slouching in his chair, Phillip remains mum for the rest of the lecture, while Victoria, Simone, and Terrance give him an unpleasant stare.

"If anyone else wishes to make any comments feel free to do so after class. Now without any further interruptions, I will continue with my lecture. Before I decided to move to Lakeview Falls two years ago, I remember as a young boy growing up in my country Haiti; my grandmother Gertrude used to tell me urban legends about this town. As a curious child, I was surprised that she knew American folklore. To my surprise, my grandma told me that anyone who practices the black magic of the French gods knows every wicked story of demonic spirits that roam this earth and beyond."

Turning on his projector, Professor Baptist clicks to a photo that displays twelve old Wiccans surrounding an open cornfield, each holding a silver dagger in their hands ready to make a sacrifice, while a figure laid in the center of the circle. Then he clicks to another disturbing photo of a grotesque fleshless demon with sharp horns above its head and razor-sharp teeth that hung over its mouth.

"My grandmother told me a story that till this day still haunts me. It was **"The Tale of the First Coming Human Flesh-eating Shapeshifter Demons."** Before Lakeview Falls had ever existed, Wicker Lake Cove was the town's original name. It started as a small village, built In 1801 by a dark and powerful French Wiccan woman named Collette Francis Courier. The town was where she and her coven sought refuge until the year 1825 when a dangerous shapeshifter demon named MASTEMA and his twenty-four demonic soldiers entered their village in hopes of ruling over the coven. MASTEMA was a 17th-century flesh-eating demon whose powers could transform him into anything he desires, including any human form he wants by eating his victims' flesh. MASTEMA posed like a charming individual who manipulated and tricked people into doing his biddings in his human visage. Legend has it that he lured a beautiful young girl in the town by glamouring himself into a very handsome young man, irresistible to any woman's eyes. He impregnated the young woman for reproducing purposes. Instead of waiting for her to naturally give birth, MASTEMA violently ripped her cervix open with his sharp-clawed nails, killing her instantly, delivering his twin infant sons. When word got out that the young girl was carrying the demonic babies, Colette, and four Wiccans from her coven, quickly made a dangerous decision to destroy the demons once and for all. As Mastema and the twenty-four shifters went about slaughtering half of the village, Colette Frances Courier, cast a spellbound curse to damn MASTEMA and his soldiers into a unique rock an—"

Without warning, the emergency school bell rings. Interrupted in the middle of his lecture, Professor Baptist quickly announces his next session if anyone wishes to attend the day of Halloween. While everyone made their way out of the lecture hall, Crystal grabs her crossbody purse, putting it over her shoulders while Trey gathers his belongings.

Grunting in annoyance, Trey pulls his backpack from underneath his seat. "Damn, that class was getting good. Fack! I wanted to learn more about this MASTEMA demon. This school can never allow us to learn shit."

"Well, he's having another class in a week and a half Trey; you can always come back."

Slipping his backpack behind his back, Trey rises from his chair. "Do you have any plans for the rest of the day, Crystal?" Trey asks, brushing his hands over his head.

"I have a date with Jason this afternoon, but I was thinking of speaking to John first. I want to clear up what happened between us this morning."

"I think that's a great idea, Crystal. Just remember, John is your first love. Go easy on him."

"I will, Trey," Crystal says, quickly embracing him, "I'll call you later, okay."

"Okay, Crystal. I'm going to speak to Professor Baptist."

"Bye, Trey," Crystal smiles, exiting the room.

Making his way down the aisle, Trey walks over to the podium where Professor Baptist is arranging a few folders in his briefcase. "That was a fascinating lecture, Professor Baptist. I know you didn't get to finish the story, but I'm curious to know about Mastema's sons," Trey asks desperately, wanting to know more about the story of the demon.

Taking a brief pause, Professor Baptist looks up and stares intensely at Trey. "What do you mean, Mr. Delgado?"

"You said that the witch damned Mastema and the rest of the shifters into a rock. You never told us about what happened to the babies."

"Great question. I see you were paying attention. Well, the tale says that Mastema put a special curse on the boys. Before Mastema disappeared into the special rock for eternity, he carried out duties for both boys. They must live out the rest of their immortal lives, searching for the rock that was hidden by the witch that placed the spell."

"But how would they know where to find it, Professor Baptist?"

"Legend says that the last girl from the Wiccan generation will possess this rock, and this is the girl the brothers will hunt down and kill to resurrect their father and the twenty-four demons. The ritual would have to be implemented two hundred years from the day Francis cursed Mastema, which was October 31, 1825."

"Which would make it this year, this month, right?" Trey mutters with an eerie feeling in the pit of his stomach.

"Correct, Mr. Delgado."

"Wow, that is one crazy story Professor, I didn't know Lakeview Falls had that kind of dark history. Is there any proof that this is true? Is Mastema's sons still existing?"

"Mr. Delgado, the only way to know if this story is real is if that rock is still in existence. Sadly we might not even know if it is. There's a lot of things people don't know about this town. Lakeview Falls never stood a chance at being a happy and peaceful town where residents can feel safe. There are too many evil spirits lurking within. None of us will ever figure out why we keep having these horrible murders and disappearances. You know, I moved here because this town intrigued me, supernatural forces plaguing a small town in Michigan? It seemed fascinating at first, but now I'm starting to realize that everything my grandmother told me about Lakeview Falls could all be true, and none of us are safe here, not now, not ever."

※ ※ ※

MEANWHILE

Hordes of students from the east wing section of the university stream through the brass doors, while Gabriela exits her pre-med classroom that has ended for the day. Trying to get to the lady's room, Gabby feels stifled. Struggling to get away from the crowd, Gabby feels as though she is pushing against a current. Reaching the restroom by the registration office, Gabriela enters the bathroom to find it empty.

Walking over to the sink, Gabby checks her appearance in the mirror. Lacing her fingers through her long wavy jet black locks, a cool breeze from the side window nips at her neck. The winds from outside suddenly increase with intensity, causing Gabby to close the window quickly.

Turning on the faucet, Gabriela proceeds to wash her hands when she is startled by the eerie sounds of a male's voice whispering her name. Glancing over her shoulders, Gabriela sees strange shadows reflecting on the bathroom stalls.

"Gabrielaaaaa," the voice hauntingly whispers, sending chills up and down her spine.

"Who's there?" she says as her lips begin to quiver. Gabby feels eyes peering down her soul while her knees weaken beneath her.

"Gabrielaaaaa," the sound echoes again.

Shivering, the tiny hairs on her skin rises as she approaches each stall. Kicking them open one by one, Gabriela is relieved to see they are all unoccupied. A sigh of relief escapes her rosy lips as she slowly turns to face the mirror again. Closing her eyes, she whispers the "Santa Maria" prayer. Letting out a shaky breath, Gabby opens her eyes.

"AAahhh!" she releases a splintering scream as she stood frozen in terror.

Her eyes widen at the sight of Matt's reflection standing behind her. His eyes hang from its sockets while blood trickles down his face, holding up a frosted vanilla cake.

"Hey, Baby! Do you want a slice?" he asks with wicked laughter, echoing sharply into her ears, like claws scratching a blackboard.

Scurrying out of the bathroom as fast as she could, Gabriela's feet slap the glossy floors, sending her jetting past various figures that blur in her speed. Focusing on the main entrance ahead of her, she sprints quicker, bolting out of the exit door.

CHAPTER FOURTEEN

KILLER CREEK LANE

Multiple media outlets across the state continue to harass the local Sheriff's department in Lakeview Falls with endless phone calls demanding answers to recent murders. Assigning deputies to be watchmen at homes where young boys might be potential targets, Sheriff Mills remains vigilant. He continues his investigation on who is abducting only males in his town.

Walking out of the employee break room, taking a sip of his favorite French roast coffee, Sheriff Mills walks down the brightly lit hallway, passing his deputies' working station. Heading towards his office, he is Instantly taken aback by a sweet-savory aroma of pastries coming from Deputy William O'Brian's desk.

The newest rookie and member of the force, Deputy O'Brian is a twenty-nine-year-old transfer student and an officer from Toledo Ohio's number one ranking correctional department. His slightly pale skin tone exposes the quarter size birthmark on his right cheek. Deputy O'Brian oddball appearance sticks out like a sore thumb, from his short and stocky physique, red freckles, dirty blonde curly hair that looks hard to comb, and thin lips that look pinched together as if he was holding his words for dear life.

He slumps back in his adjustable chair, indulging in a double glazed sweet cream donut when Sheriff Mills suddenly snatches the sweet pastry from his hands with a devilish grin on his face.

THE BROTHER'S CURSE

"How did you know I loved glazed donuts, O'Brian?" Sheriff Mills asks, releasing a euphoric grunt before taking a bite out of the donut.

"I didn't," the young deputy's face set into a scowl, clearly irritated, "but thanks for eating my lunch," Deputy O'Brian sighs with annoyance, giving Sheriff Mills the side-eye.

"Anytime Deputy O'Brian; hey look on the bright side, you needed to shed a few pounds. My early Christmas gift to you," Sheriff Mills responds with a devilish smirk, waving the donut in his face as he walks away.

Whistling a tune while taking a whiff of the half bitten donut, Sheriff Mills enters his office, closing the door behind him. Walking over to his desk, he takes a seat on his black leather recliner chair. Propping his feet up, Sheriff Mills crosses one leg over the other, staring at the delicious sweetened dough.

While he munches on the double-glazed donut, crumbs spill over and onto his salt and pepper beard. Plucking it out, Sheriff Mills blows a string of hair off of it and inserts it back into his mouth. Closing his eyes while enjoying the last bite, he is startled by his office phone ring tone that sounds like birds chirping and wild hyenas.

Swallowing the remaining remnants of the donut, he quickly answers the phone. On the other end of the line is an older man with a rich Italian accent.

"Lakeview Falls Sheriff's Department, this is Sheriff Thomas Mills. How may I help you?"

"Good day Sheriff Mills, this is Bernard Castellón, and I have a friend that lives in your town that I would like to report missing," the man says as his voice fills with emotion.

"Oh, for Christ sakes, another one? God help me," Sheriff Mills mumbles to himself.

"I beg your pardon, Sheriff?"

"I'm sorry, I didn't mean for you to hear that," he replies with a slight cough, "who would you like to report missing Mr. Castellón?"

"I want to report my friend Joseph McGregor; he has been missing for over a week."

A puzzled expression surfaces on the Sheriff's face. "Joseph McGregor, the veteran who doesn't leave his house? That man keeps himself isolated. He's not missing."

"He is missing Sheriff! I can feel something isn't right," the man bellows angrily, "I need someone to go check his house as soon as possible."

"Mr. Castellón, with all due respect, Joe isn't one to accept visitors at his premises without an invitation, unless it's an emergency. The last time someone asked our department to check up on him, he had one of his PTSD episodes, and one of my deputies almost got shot by him. I suggest you should go check on your friend by yourself."

"I can't. I live in Alaska, plus, Joe never ignores my phone calls. I am his next of kin, and I take care of all his utility bills and mortgage."

"Maybe his phone isn't working... or he wants to be left alone as per usual."

Breaking down, Bernard's muffling sobs echoes on the end of the receiver. "I've known Joseph for twenty years, and he wouldn't just vanish without telling me. Joe emails me his electronic checkbook every first week of the month, along with his signature. Since his bills come to my house, I send the checks along with a bill slip to the utility companies."

"Mr. Castellón, emails get lost all the time; I'm sure those checkbooks will show up sooner or later."

"We are in the second week of October, and I have not received anything from him. I have a tracker from **Shashoo.com**, and it shows me the exact day and time it will arrive. Sheriff Mills, I've been taking care of Joe McGregor's finances for over ten years, and he has never been late sending those checkbooks, ever. Please, I'm begging you. I need to know if my friend is okay."

Listening to Bernard's frantic plead for help, beads of sweat rolls down Sheriff Mills' temple with fear of being reported to the media for declining on checking on a fragile veteran with PTSD.

Sitting back in his seat, Sheriff Mills calmly lets Bernard know that he will take a trip to Killer Creek Lane and check on Mr. McGregor.

He assures Bernard that he will contact him as soon as possible once he checks Joe's house. Ending their conversation, Sheriff Mills rises from his comfortable chair and leaves the station, making his way over to Killer Creek Lane.

❊ ❊ ❊

KILLER CREEK LANE

Dark clouds travel like sheep high in the sky, bringing gray and dull weather on the once beautiful day. Driving down the quiet suburban community, Sheriff Mills arrives at 468 Killer Creek Lane. Parking his patrol car in front of Mr. McGregor's home, he takes a good look at the unpainted dark wood exterior of the townhouse cottage that silhouettes against the rooted trees.

Scanning the twenty houses on the lane, a wave of fear hits Sheriff Mills as he stares down the lane. Drifting off in his thoughts, Sheriff Mills remembers all the cool neighbors he befriended over the years who died mysteriously. He enjoyed helping the older generation in the community instead of the young debased retards.

Since taking the throne as head chief, Sheriff Mills notices how deranged and eerie each neighborhood started to look as the years went on, especially Killer Creek Lane. The gated family community consists of brick stone townhouses. Ten homes displayed a wholesome look. The remaining ten showcases front yards with an overgrown mess of yellow grass and hollow trees, dispensing rotten tomatoes that fall onto the cracked pavements.

Stepping out of his patrol car, Sheriff Mills receives a good-hearted greeting from Joe's next-door neighbor Paul Stoller, who stood with his German Shepard by the **Curb Your Dog** grass patch in front of his home.

"Afternoon Sheriff," Paul smiles, freely waving his hands in the air.

"Good day Paul, taking good ole Busta Brown for a walk?"

"Yes," he replies, flagging an empty blue poop bag," I also needed the fresh air. I had to get out of the house, with all that racket going on next door, I'm grateful that someone finally got in touch with you. I was planning on making a complaint today."

In confusion, Sheriff Mills tilts his tinted shades, raising an eyebrow. "Complaint? What complaint?" he asks Paul.

"There's some guy that's been staying at Mr. McGregor's home for about a week and a half, and all I hear is non-stop drilling sounds coming from his basement. It feels like a damn earthquake. That racket goes on mostly at night. You have to do something, Sheriff."

"Don't worry, Paul; I'll get to the bottom of it. Thank you for informing me."

Paul's nose crinkles as he smiles. "Thank you, Sheriff Mills," he sighs in relief, nodding his head, "damn kids these days, they have no respect. Take care, Sheriff," Paul says, walking away with his dog down the lane.

Walking up the porch steps, Sheriff Mills is disturbed by the sight of a gothic style handbell beside the entrance door. The 6-inch cast-iron medieval dragon sculpture hangs above the bell, displaying its broad wings and stylized serpent body. Swiftly pulling the bell chain, Sheriff Mills groans in disgust while wiping his hands on the side of his uniform pants.

Taking off his sunglasses, Sheriff Mills hooks his shades' arms on the second to the top button of his brown uniform shirt. He hears the door groan open, revealing a tall young man dressed in fitted black jeans and a black v neck muscle shirt. His shoulders squared, and his back straight, Jason glares at the shiny gold badge attached to Sheriff Mills' uniform shirt.

"Good afternoon, Sheriff, may I help you?"

"Good afternoon, young man, is Joe McGregor home?"

Cocking his head to one side, Jason smirks. "No, Sheriff, he is not home."

THE BROTHER'S CURSE

"He's not home," Sheriff Mills whispers to himself, "what's your name, kid?" he asks with a stern expression, tapping his polish black oxford shoes on the deck tile.

"My name is Jason Warwick," he replies politely, extending his hand out to shake the Sheriff's hands.

Rudely brushing off Jason's kind gesture, Sheriff Mills pulls out his mini tablet from inside his jacket pocket. Pulling up the information on the checkbook tracking that Bernard sent to him through his email, Sheriff Mills rubs his throat hastily.

"Is there something I can help you with, Sheriff?"

"Yes, as a matter of fact, you can. What is your relationship with Joseph McGregor? And where is he at the moment?"

"Joseph McGregor is my uncle from my mother's side of the family. He took a trip out of state and asked me to house sit for him till he comes back."

Using his index finger, Sheriff Mills delicately types the young man's statement onto the touch tablet. "Do you know approximately how long your uncle will be out of town?"

"No, he left in such a hurry, I didn't get a chance to ask him. Why? Did something happen to him?"

"That's what I'm trying to find out, Mr. Warwick. A friend of your uncle's, called my station an hour ago, reporting him missing. He informed me that he receives a check from your uncle every first week of the month, and the check never arrived at his home. You wouldn't know anything about that, would you?"

Keeping his attention on what Sheriff Mills says, Jason seems attentive, but it was all an act. "I'm sorry, Sheriff, but I do not keep tabs on my uncle's finances. He is a little rough around the edges when it comes to his personal life, he does have some issues, you know, fighting in the Vietnam war will do that to most veterans."

Glaring at the young man, Sheriff Mills found that he couldn't stop staring into Jason's emerald green eyes. "I suppose you have a point, Mr. Warwick, and you're sure you have no idea where your uncle might have gone?"

Having a sharp intelligence, Jason is quick with his response. He is smart enough to persuade Sheriff Mills that he is Joe's nephew. Searching through Mr. McGregor's belongings, Jason found enough information to coax up a brilliant strategy to keep law enforcement astray. It wouldn't be long until they figured things out, but he would already be long gone with the purple amethyst stone by then.

A mocking smile crosses Jason's face while he slowly taps his fingers against the front door. "No Sheriff, I wish I could help you, but I don't have any information for his friend. If my uncle does contact me, I will be more than happy to relate the message to him, or you can give me his friend's contact number, and I can tell him myself."

"You know what, Mr. Warwick? That will not be necessary. Can you make sure to call the station and let me know if you hear from him?"

"I will be more than happy to do so, Sheriff. Now, if that is all, I will be going back inside. I do have other things to attend to," Jason replies, slowly closing the door.

"Not so fast," Sheriff Mills yells out as he blocks his hand between the door, "before you go inside, I was speaking to the neighbor next door, and it has come to my attention that there have been some loud drilling noises coming from your basement in the middle of the night. Can you explain that?"

"Oh gosh, my apologies. I had no idea I was disturbing the neighborhood. I've been remodeling parts of the house for my uncle. Since he is on anxiety medication, it's hard for him to keep up with his household duties."

"Right, right," Sheriff Mills says casually, removing his brown sheriff's hat. "Look, I don't like to tell people what to do in their homes, but I think it would be nice if you can try and keep the noise to a minimum, maybe do it during the day. Folks here in Killer Creek Lane do need their sleep."

"Will do, Sheriff, and don't worry, the neighbors will not hear a peep," he says firmly, staring directly at Paul's house.

"Thank you, oh, and before you go, Mr. Warwick."

A profound irritation surges inside Jason as he composes himself from yanking the sheriff into the house and having him as an early lunch.

"Yes, Sheriff, do you need something else?"

"I was just curious about this special bell you got here," Sheriff Mills says with a puzzled expression, pointing at the dragon statue.

"What about it, Sheriff?" Jason asks, clenching his teeth, irritated by the Sheriff's ongoing questioning.

"I've never seen this before; this doesn't look like Joe's style. Where did you get it?"

"It's an old family heirloom, my father's side of the family are collectors, and they have a fascination with dragons. The creatures are known to bring good luck. I thought it would be a nice touch to the house."

Fiddling with the bell chain, Sheriff Mills lets it go and watches it swing back and forth, releasing a chime-like tune. "Nice touch, huh? Well, it does stand out."

"I would love to stand here and chat, but I need to get back to some cleaning I was doing in the kitchen—So—"

"Of course, you have a great day, Mr. Warwick, and welcome to Lakeview Falls. I hope you enjoy your stay," he finishes, backing away from the door, Sheriff Mills heads down the porch steps.

A sinister smile appears on Jason's lips. "Take care, Sheriff," he waves before slamming the door shut.

Reaching the bottom of the steps, Sheriff Mils feels worrisome about his unusual exchange of words with Jason. Something about the young man didn't seem right. But then again, he was always a good judge of character when it comes to people.

Before heading to his patrol car, Sheriff Mills takes a walk around the house by the driveway. Approaching the ground floor windows, he notices the square shape glass frames painted shut as if it was not open in the past twenty years.

Inspecting the window, Sheriff Mills tries to see the basement inside but has no luck since it had a slight tint.

"Uggh," he grunts, "what the hell is that kid fixing down there?" Sheriff Mills mumbles, taking one look before he heads back to his vehicle.

In the meantime, peering out the kitchen window, Jason watches Sheriff Mills drive off down the lane. Famished, Jason heads over to the stainless steel refrigerator. Grasping the handle, he caught hold of it, opening the fridge widely. Pulling out a human lung, Jason cradles it in the palm of his hands. The organ is slightly soft but firm enough that it doesn't squish when he bites into it.

Indulging in his afternoon snack, Jason makes his way down the basement steps. A gleam shone in his fiery red eyes as he stares at the slabs of loose decomposing skin dangling off the silver barb-wires from the ceiling. Inching towards the room's left corner, Jason grabs a digging shovel, grinning at his victims' dismembered body parts in a six-foot homemade grave.

CHAPTER FIFTEEN

BOOGEYMAN

LAKEVIEW FALLS UNIVERSITY

An abundance of emotions circles through Crystal's body as her heart beats faster and faster until it reaches its climax. In her stomach, the swarm of butterflies comes in full force as she nervously stands in front of John's dorm, Room 204. She shakes off her uneasiness and double knocks on the gray oak door. Memorizing what she had rehearsed earlier, Crystal is numb. She didn't know what to say; she didn't know how to feel. Her heart yearns for John, but in some crazy way, her soul aches for Jason. Was that even possible? Could she be in love with two guys at the same time?

Hearing footsteps approaching the door from inside the room, Crystal can no longer control her hands that shake in an odd trembling rhythm. As the door slowly opens, Crystal suddenly loses the ability to speak when she locks eyes with John. The sparkle in his amber, green eyes, the way his lips curves in an alluring smile sends jolts of electricity through the molten core of her being.

Gazing at her youthful beauty, John tilts his to the side, mesmerized by her presence. "Crystal."

"Hello John," she gazes at him standing by the door with his arms crossed over one another, "can we talk?"

"Of course, Crystal, come in," he says in a soft tone, inviting her inside his dorm.

The generously proportioned bedroom gives off a cozy cabin feel. Ample light flows through the windows allowing a glossy gold sheen to shine on the wood-clad walls, giving the room a warm environment. Kicking dirty gym clothes to the corner of the room, John has little clusters of clutter here and there, including various packs of instant noodle soups crammed to the sides of the room.

Walking over to his king-size bed, John takes a seat at the edge, while Crystal advances towards the silver glass vision drafting table and custom made stool. In awe, Crystal is amazed at the sight of the sizeable architectural design sketch of a magnificent glasshouse drawn above a mountain surrounded by a valley of framed colors trees that appear in autumn.

"Wow, this is beautiful," she revels, gazing at the design. "Did you draw this, John?"

"Yes, Crystal, I've been handing out some new samples of my work to a few companies."

"John, this is amazing; I know that one of these companies will see the talent you have and hire you."

"Thank you, Crystal. That means a lot coming from you. It has always been a dream of mine to be a world-renowned architect."

"I do not doubt in my mind that you will John," she replies. Placing her hand over her chest, she takes a glimpse of the sketch then back at John. "What you have created is a masterpiece and also my dream home. I would love to live in a house like this, but for now, I guess a girl can dream, right?"

"Sit with me," John says, extending an open hand out to Crystal.

His voice, so warm, so comforting, how can she resist? Taking his hand, Crystal sits beside him, enjoying the soft feeling of his smokey-colored bedspread that brings a touch of elegance. Smiling at her with the utmost adoration, John leans in closer, placing his right hand over her left knee.

"So, what's going on, Crystal?" John asks nervously, gazing at her.

"Umm," Crystal hesitates, taking a deep breath.

"You know what?" he abruptly interrupts, "before you say anything, Crystal, I want you to know that I apologize for the way I've been acting towards you and accusing you of having something with your new neighbor. On my part, I should have been honest with you about my finances and struggles for the past year. I know that if I want us to grow and build a stronger connection in our relationship, then I need to communicate better with you."

"John," she whispers.

"Let me finish," grasping her hand, John gives her a knowing look. "I don't want to argue with you Crystal. I'm in love with you, and all I want is you, no one else," John says, expressing his undying love for her.

"John, I don't want to fight anymore either, that's why I wanted to speak to you; what happened between us this morning made me think about—"

"This morning?" he asks confusingly, "What about this morning?"

Searching his eyes for an explanation as to why he seems stupefied, a soft giggle escapes Crystal's lips. "What do you mean what about this morning? Come on, John, this isn't funny; you know what happened between us earlier. How can you forget that you snuck in my shower?"

"What?" John backs away, giving off a slight chuckle. "Crystal, what are you talking about? I wasn't in your shower this morning; I was here on campus trying to find Kyle."

"John, this isn't funny, now quit fucking around!" she hollers, rising from the bed angrily.

Feeling light-headed, Crystal is flabbergasted. Could she have been dreaming the entire thing? Impossible, of course, John was there. What they shared felt more real than anything. His kiss and his touch brought out so many unexplainable emotions.

"Crystal, are you okay?" John asks, grabbing her hands.

"Why are you playing this sick game with me? After what you just said, how can you forget what we did? It was five hours ago that we almost made love in the shower."

"What! Seriously, Crystal! Do you think if I had the opportunity to be naked with you, I would forget that in less than five hours? Look at me, does my face look like I'm lying?" John says with a saddened expression

"Crystal, I think you may have had an intense dream."

"I was not dreaming John, I was wide awake, and so were you!" Crystal says, staring at John's man region.

"Whatever or whoever you saw in that shower, Crystal, it wasn't me. I'm telling you the truth."

Having a meltdown, Crystal wails, "If it wasn't you, John, then who the hell was it?"

"I don't know, Crystal. Are you sure everything's okay with you? Because you don't seem like yourself."

Disconnecting her hands from his, Crystal moves further away. "What do you mean I don't seem like myself?" she says with a frustrating tone. "Are you trying to imply that I'm going crazy or something?"

"No! I don't think you're crazy, Crystal. I don't understand why you would think that I would do such a thing. I would never evade your privacy."

Turning away, Crystal struggles to keep herself together. Psychologically, she cannot comprehend why John would deny their intimate interaction earlier. The way he behaved in her shower shows that he is willing to screw with her head, a manipulative tactic to keep her chasing him.

Scurrying to the front door, Crystal sheds a tear with a sense of embarrassment. "I think I should go, John. I can't commit myself to someone who intends to play mind games with me."

Refusing to accept Crystal cutting him out of his life, John pleads with her, "Please, Crystal! Don't leave! Why can't we make this work?" he asks and follows her as she exits his room.

"I'm sorry, John, but I can't be with you; the quicker you forget about us, the better we both will be," Crystal sobs as she quickly sprints down the hallway, never looking back.

❆ ❆ ❆

Departing from the side entrance of the university, Crystal wraps around the football track where she stumbles upon Gabriela. Noticing her best friend sitting alone on an empty bench hunched over, wiping her eyes, Crystal walks over to her.

"Gabby," she says softly. "What's wrong?" Crystal asks, showing concern as she takes a seat next to her on the steel bench.

A solemn tear falls down her rosy round cheeks. "Something strange is happening to me, Crystal and, I don't know how to make it go away," she utters with suppressed sounds of hiccups.

Gently caressing Gabriela's back, Crystal pushes a strand of hair away from her face. "Make what go away, Gabby? What is it? Please talk to me."

"Crystal," her bloodshot eyes bore into hers, "you're going to think I'm losing my mind, but I saw Matt in the girl's bathroom."

Crystal's eyes widen, trying to absorb what her friend was telling her. She asked herself, how could Gabby have possibly seen Matt when he's dead? But then again, she thought she took a shower with John. Maybe they were both losing their minds.

"Gabby, what do you mean you saw Matt?"

"When I went to use the bathroom a while ago, I heard a voice call out my name. At first, I thought it was someone messing with me, but then I checked all the stalls, and they were empty. When I turned around to face the mirror, that's when I saw Matt. Only, it wasn't a friendly version of him; it was much more sinister. His eyes were dangling out of the sockets, and he was holding a frosted vanilla cake, and do you know what he asked me?"

"What did he ask you, Gabby?"

Her lips tremble, "He asked me if I wanted a slice." Gabriela whimpers.

A burst of untamable laughter escapes Crystal's lips, followed by a snort reverberating from her nostrils. "Shut up, that did not happen, Gabby."

"Oh my God, Crystal, that's not funny. I almost had a stroke," she says, jokingly, pushing Crystal away from her.

"Come on, Gabby, your subconscious is playing tricks on you. You're still grieving over Matt's death, and sometimes spirits come to visit to have closure."

"Closure? He looked demented. I'm telling you, Crystal, I've never seen anything so real in my life."

"You're serious about this? Gabby, do you think he's haunting you?"

"Crystal, I don't know what's happening to me. I miss him so much."

Wrapping her friend in a tight embrace, Crystal coddles her. "I know how much you miss Matt, Gabby, but you have to try to keep it together. Matt wouldn't want to see you like this."

"How am I supposed to go on without him, Crystal?" letting out a deep sigh Gabby buries her head deep into Crystal's chest. "We planned our future together; we were going to secretly elope in a few months. Matt and I wanted to move out of this god awful town and buy a house in the country so we could start a family."

"I'm so sorry Gabby, I know how much you are hurting, and I'm here for you no matter what, always," Crystal says, giving Gabby a kiss above her forehead, cradling her.

※ ※ ※

Elated for his date with Crystal, Jason heads over to the Francois residence, carrying a single red rose in his hand. Salvaging whatever was still intact in Mr. McGregor's garden, Jason prepares to woo the damsel in distress with his good ole fashion charm. Standing with perfect posture, he gently knocks on the door, taking a slight whiff of the flower's sweet nectar scent.

Opening the door, Crystal's aunt greets Jason. She takes a step back, enthralled by his dashing good looks. "Good afternoon," she bashfully says, giving Jason a friendly smile. "May I help you?"

"Hello, you must be another gorgeous sister to Crystal," he smirks innocently at her.

"Well, aren't you a charmer," she chuckles, waving her hands to the side playfully. "Thank you for the compliment, but I'm Crystal's, Aunt Jaqueline."

"It's a pleasure to meet you, Ms. Jaqueline," he bows at her feet like a gentleman. "My name is Jason Warwick, I am Joe McGregor's nephew."

"Oh, of course, your house-sitting, right?"

"Yes, just for a short time till he gets back from his trip."

"It's nice to meet you, Jason."

"Likewise, so—I am here to pick up Crystal; we have a date. Is she home?"

"No, Crystal isn't home yet, but you're more than welcome to come in and wait for her if you'd like?"

"Oh, I wouldn't want to impose. I can come back in a little while."

"Nonsense, you're not imposing Jason. Come in," she replies, kindly inviting him inside.

"Thank you, Ms. Jaqueline," he says, walking into the foyer section of the house.

Upon entering, Jason immediately senses a warm and homely ambiance that surrounds the house. Graciously escorting Jason into their spacious living room, Jaqueline kindly directs him to the L-shape turquoise leather couch. Before having a seat, Jason's eyes scan the well-decorated room, and notices a beautiful fireplace with family photos propped up on the mantle.

Walking up to the fireplace, Jason comes across Crystal's vintage photo as a young girl standing next to a Christmas tree. She wore her hair in two pigtails and was dressed in a multi-colored stripe sweater with pink corduroy pants. He snickers under his breath while gazing at her infectious smile; for some strange reason, Jason thought Crystal looked adorable as a child. It wasn't like him to have human emotions since he had blocked it out for two hundred years.

At the other end of the mantle, his eyes fixate on a family portrait of Crystal, her sister Alexandria, and their parents sitting on the front porch. He picks up the photo gazing at it, flashing a warm-hearted smile. "Is this her parents?" he asks, looking over at Jacqueline.

"Yes, Jason, it is. It's a lovely photo of them."

"She told me they passed away; it's awful what happened to them."

"It was a terrible loss for all of us, especially for the girls. Crystal was very close to her mother, and her death hit her pretty hard. Not to mention that she decided to leave school in New York to move back here to be closer to her sister. Crystal is very overprotective when it comes to Alexandria," Jaqueline says, trying to refrain herself from crying.

"Family always comes first," Jason says, sounding sympathetic as he places the picture back on the mantel.

"You're right, Jason, and how about you? Where is your family?"

Before he could respond to Jaqueline's question, Crystal walks into the house, surprised to see them engaging in conversation. "Hey, what's going on?"

"I had the pleasure of meeting Jason," Aunty J says, advancing towards Crystal, leaving Jason alone in the living room.

Embracing her niece, Jaqueline kisses Crystal on the cheek. "He's so cute and such a gentleman," she whispers in Crystal's ear, "I think he likes you."

Looking over at Jason standing by the fireplace, Jaqueline withdrawals from the embrace, displaying a silly smirk. "Well, I will give you and Jason some privacy. I'll be upstairs. It was nice meeting you, Jason. Hopefully, I'll see you again," she says with a quick smile, walking up the staircase.

"It was a pleasure meeting you too, Ms. Jaqueline. Take care," Jason says, waving goodbye to her.

Standing by the staircase, Crystal is met by Jason, who keeps his hand behind his back, slowly inching closer to her. "I'm so happy to see you, Crystal."

"I'm happy to see you too, Jason. I hope my aunt didn't talk your ears off."

"No, not at all; I like your aunt. She's a nice lady."

"I didn't know you were coming by so early, Jason."

"Yes, I'm sorry, I know you said to come in the evening. I just got so excited about our date, oh here," Jason says, removing his hand from behind his back, presenting her the red rose.

"Awww, thank you, it's beautiful," Crystal says, gently taking the rose from him.

"Not as beautiful as you, Crystal. So, your aunt was telling me the reason why you moved back home."

"Oh, did she?"

"Yes, and I think you're an amazing person for sacrificing your future for your sister."

"I wouldn't call what I did a sacrifice, Jason; it's something that I had to do. She's my baby sister, and it didn't seem fair to let her live here by herself. I mean, yes, she's an adult and can take care of herself, but she's my sister. I needed to be here for her."

"Crystal, I have to admit, I wish I had a chance to know my real family. My biological parents died when I was just a baby."

"Oh my God, Jason, I'm sorry."

"It's okay. A family adopted me when I was toddler. Somehow living with strangers who wanted to love me wasn't enough. I was always thinking of what life could have been if I knew my real mother and father. As I grew older, I felt like a loner; always trying to fit in to make people like me. And then I met you, this kind and compassionate woman that I didn't think existed. Crystal, you have been so generous and welcoming since I've been here, and I think you're gorgeous," he looks away, feeling his face flush.

"I guess there's something about you, Jason. Something extraordinary."

Gazing deep into her dark brown eyes, Jason stood numb. His human side takes over his entire body, exposing a vulnerable side he never wanted to show. Stroking his hand on the side of her cheek, Jason caresses her smooth skin. "Ever since I met you, Crystal, I've been yearning for my lips to touch yours," Jason says boldly, clasping the front of her denim jeans, pulling her closer to him.

"So what's stopping you, Jason," Crystal says, lustfully gazing at him as she reaches up on her tip-toes.

Leaning towards Crystal, Jason's head touches hers, eye to eye. Slowly, he brought his lips down to hers in a soft sensual kiss.

THE BROTHER'S CURSE

Wrapping her arms around his waist, Crystal tugs on his black leather jacket as he grasps the back of her blouse aggressively.

Their tongues entwine endlessly, leaving Crystal breathless; Jason's olive toned skin turns bright red, indulging in the sweetness of her mouth. Their kissing becomes so intense and so orgasmic that Crystal pulls away from him before things get out of hand.

"What's wrong, Crystal? Did I do something? Was I too rough?"

"No, no, of course not," she touches her swollen lips, longing for more, "You caught me by surprise; Thats all. I have never had anyone kiss me like that before," she says, looking at him with her doe eyes.

Jason looks at her, his emerald green eyes squinting, and his mouth smirks in a smile that sends chills down her spine. "So, why did you push me away, Crystal?"

"It's because—my aunt is still here. Maybe we can continue our kiss when we leave," she snickers, smitten by him.

"Oh, right. I forgot your aunt is still here. I'm sorry," Jason whispers.

"Since we didn't plan out what we're doing yet, is it okay if we stop by the diner before we start our date?"

"You want to go to the diner? Why?" Jason asks with an odd expression.

"I want to check on Gabby. She was a bit out of it at school; Matt's death still shakes her up, and I need to make sure she's fine. I promise we won't stay long."

"We can go wherever you want, Crystal; I think that's nice of you to check on your friend. Can you promise me one thing?"

"And what is that, Jason?"

"That I can have you all to myself tonight," Jason's responds, lacing his fingers through Crystal's curly black hair.

Feeling a tingling sensation whenever she touches him, Crystal presses her body against his. "I promise Jason, you will."

CHAPTER SIXTEEN

EVIL LURKED WITHIN

LAKESIDE DINER

"**MISSING: Kyle Jackson,**" the off white flyer reads with Kyle's photo displayed in the center. Fleeing out of the diner a few days prior, Kyle Jackson never returned home. Clueless to where he might have gone, Chantelle and Kwai Jackson reported their son missing. They created homemade flyers to get the word out to residents. Most citizens of the town ignored the disappearance of the young man due to his unruly racist attitude.

Although the town is diverse, the senior community that survived the town's evil presence in the late 60s did not want to associate themselves with the younger generation nor help find them if they ever mysteriously disappeared. In a declaration signed six decades ago, the seniors of Lakeview Falls who were once youths themselves in the horrid town vowed to keep quiet in a written statement.

Our parents' sins to live the American Dream have brought great pain to every child that steps foot on the sinful soil. We, the youths of Lakeview Falls, shall vow that if we survive and continue in life, we will dismiss ourselves from saving or helping any future youths who consume the evil aura in the town. The myth says that if you live in Lakeview Falls and have hate in your heart and wish wickedness onto others, the evil entities shall damn you without any sympathy.

Declaration from the Youths of the Falls "1969"

❋ ❋ ❋

Sunlight shines through the branches and sparkles on the flower dewdrop, creating various colors as the autumn leaves fall to the ground. It is lifted by a burst of wind, floating further away into the distance while the afternoon air is still and foreboding. Riding into Lakeside Diner's parking lot, Jason and Crystal pull up into an empty spot. As the two-hop off the motorcycle, crunches of dead leaves and a flyer stick under Crystal's suede boots.

Lifting her foot, she pulls off the half ripped paper and gasps at the sight of the missing person's flyer. "OH my God!" she exclaims horror-stricken, holding onto the dirt-filled paper she shows it to Jason. "Its Kyle! Jason, he's missing."

Sweeping the kickstand out to keep his bike still, Jason grabs hold of the flyer, staring at Kyle's photo. Kyle's haunted facial expression is pure anger, his teeth clenched so tightly, and his top lip scrunched up, nearly touching the tip of his nose. Kyle resembles someone who suffers from ongoing constipation.

Showing no remorse for Kyle's sudden disappearance, Jason lets out a wicked snicker. "Wow, this picture sure does him justice. He looks like a racist prick."

Walking side by side towards the restaurant's main entrance, Crystal is shocked by Jason's reaction. She stops midway, snatching the flyer from his hands. "Jason, that's not funny; what if something bad happened to him?"

Wrapping his arms around her shoulders, Jason caresses her arms with soft strokes. "Crystal, I'm sorry I upset you, I didn't mean for it to come out so harsh, but in all honesty, Kyle doesn't come across as a nice person. I'm not saying that I wish anything bad upon him. I'm saying that the way he presents himself to people makes him a target. For all we know, he could have pissed off the wrong person."

"I understand that you are not fond of him, and I don't blame you, Jason. He was very nasty and out of line. I just hope that nothing bad happened to him. If something awful happened to Kyle, then anything can happen to all of us," she frowns at Jason as they enter the diner.

Searching for Gabriela in the crowded restaurant, Crystal's eyes stumble on Trey, who's sitting alone at a small booth by the window devouring a cheeseburger. Looking up, displaying a ketchup stain on the side of his mouth, Trey ecstatically waves in Crystal's direction, gesturing her to come over. Unaware he had the cheeseburger in his hand, a drop of meat sauce splashes onto his white button-down silk shirt.

"Oh, Fack!" he exclaims, dropping the burger onto the white oval plate.

Walking over to the booth, Crystal and Jason take a seat across from him. Grabbing a wet wipe, Crystal quickly opens it, handing it over to Trey. "Hey, Trey, need some help?"

"Hey, guys! excuse my mess; I'm terrible at eating fast food," Trey says, using the wet wipe to clean the rose color sauce on his button-down blouse. "

"That's not the only thing you're terrible at eating, Trey," Crystal says, sarcastically winking at him.

"Oh, I see. Are you a comedian now?" Trey smirks, tossing the dirty wipe at her.

"Isn't that the expensive Moschino shirt you just bought for your birthday?" Crystal asks, gazing at the now ruined shirt.

"Ugh, girl! Please don't remind me; I saved up three paychecks to buy this top," Trey says, desperately trying to remove the stain with a wet napkin. "So what brings you two lovebirds here?"

"We're not staying long; I wanted to check on Gabby. She was a little upset earlier. Is she here?"

"Yeah," Trey points to the kitchen entrance, "she went to the back to check on an order."

Nauseous by the smell of the half-eaten cheeseburger on the table, Jason groans inwardly, trying not to stare at the plate of cooked meat.

"Are you hungry?" Trey asks, noticing Jason's unpleasant stare towards his meal.

"No, I don't eat red meat; it makes me sick," he says, turning his face away from the plate of food.

Taking a bit of his French fry, Trey gives Jason a seductive grin. "Okay, if you don't like red meat, maybe you would enjoy a nice tossed salad?"

Giving Trey a swift kick in his shin from underneath the booth table, Crystal scowls at him. "Trey, cut it out."

"Ouch!" he squeals in agonizing pain.

She shrugs her shoulders. "I'm sorry, Trey, my foot slipped," Crystal says, clenching her teeth.

Rubbing his ankle, Trey groans, "Uggh, is this what happens when a new penis comes in contact with my best friend?"

Not amused by Trey's sexual humor, Jason snickers sarcastically while grabbing the diner menu. Opening it, Jason puts it up to his face, blocking Trey from his view. "Crystal," he whispers in her ears, "how long are we going to be here?"

"Oh my God, what a surprise," Gabriela says, excitedly, approaching the table. "Crystal, I didn't know you were stopping by."

"I wanted to see how you were feeling. I was a little worried after I saw you at the university."

"Aww, Crystal, you didn't have to come all the way here just to do that. I'm fine now. You don't have to worry, okay?" Gabby says, reassuring Crystal that there was nothing wrong with her.

"It's my job to worry about my best friends," she says, reaching out to hold her hand, "I can't help it."

"You are too sweet Crystal, what would I do without you?" she asks, fluttering her eyes with a widening smile.

"I don't know, but you will have me around till we are old and brittle," Crystal giggles. "By the way, what the hell happened to Kyle?" Crystal asks.

"You saw the flyer, huh? Crazy shit, just before you guys came in, Kyle's parents were here handing them out. His mom and dad were hysterical; they haven't seen him in two days," Trey replies, adding more ketchup to his fried potatoes.

"Two days ago? That was the last time we saw him right before he ran out of the bathroom like a crazy maniac," glancing at Jason, Gabby stares dead in his eyes, "you were in there with him, Jason, what happened?"

Irritated by Gabriela's constant interrogation, Jason's eyes calmly search hers. "I have no idea Gabby, I am as clueless as you are," he replies, turning his gaze towards the window.

"It's not like Kyle to just disappear into thin air."

"Exactly," Trey says, agreeing with Gabby, "it doesn't make any sense. Kyle has never left this town, and even if he did, why now? And without saying anything to anyone, even to his parents. This whole shit sounds sketchy to me."

"Excuse me, Miss! Yoo Hoo, we need more coffee," an elderly woman shouts, flagging Gabriela from across the diner.

"Shit, it's Mrs. Coppercorn. That lady is a pain in my ass," clicking her teeth, Gabby sighs with frustration, "let me grab her a cup of coffee before she starts screaming at me. The last time that old woman got anxious, she pressed her life alert by accident, and then came drama. I'll be right back," Gabby says, heading back to the kitchen.

Checking his wristwatch, Jason rises from his seat. "Maybe we should head out now, Crystal."

Clutching her crossbody purse in her hand, Crystal gets up, fixing the pleats on her wide-leg denim pants. "Okay. Sure, sounds good; Trey, can you let Gabby know that we are leaving."

"Wait, you're leaving; so soon?" Trey asks, pouting his lips," you guys just got here."

"We have a date, Trey," Crystal says, holding onto Jason's hand.

"Ooo, a date, huh? Well, I think you guys should hang out for a few more minutes. Gabby told me an hour ago that she has something important to tell you. I think you should wait for her."

"Oh God, I hope it's not another surprise. I think I'm good for the rest of the year."

A deep huff escapes Jason's lip. "I guess we should have a seat again."

"So, Crystal, did you hear? LVFU is throwing a huge Halloween party for the town. I figured since it's on your birthday, we can celebrate it there. I mean, we always have a good time on your born day," Trey says, flashing her a dazzling smile.

Full of malice, Jason defensively lashes out. "Trey! Crystal doesn't always have to do the same thing on her birthday! Maybe this year she can do something different, perhaps I can take her somewhere nice. Right, Crystal?" he asks in a softer tone of voice, grabbing hold of her hand kissing it.

Trey gives Jason a bitter stare. "No offense, Jason, but I think it's up to Crystal to decide what she wants to do! I guarantee you she will choose her family and friends over you. A new guy that we know absolutely nothing about!"

"Come on, you two. Chill out; this isn't a competition," Crystal calmly intervenes, "we can all celebrate my birthday together, including Jason." She says, gazing into Jason's piercing green eyes.

"I'm sorry, Crystal, I don't know what came over me," Jason says, apologizing for his behavior.

Extending his arms, Jason politely gestures for a handshake. "No hard feelings Trey."

"Yeah, sure, Jason, no hard feelings," Trey responds with uncertainty.

Reciprocating the handshake, Trey senses a weird vibe about Crystal's new love interest. From Jason's controlling behavior to his split personality. Trey knew what a mentally abusive relationship looks like, and it seems as though his best friend might be falling into one, dangerously quick.

Coming out of the kitchen, holding two cups of freshly brewed coffee, Gabriela glances out the diner window where she is horrified to see Matt standing in the middle of the parking lot. Terror sucks the very air that she breathes. Fear cripples her as she stares

EVIL LURKED WITHIN

at him, wearing a blood-stained deputy uniform, sneering at her holding a frosted vanilla cake.

"No, No, Nooo!" Gabriela releases a high pitch scream, "It's happening again!"

Suddenly, the restaurant's atmosphere slowly shifts in slow motion; feeling a sudden pressure in her chest, Gabriela sees the room circle in a rapid movement. Trapped in a bizarre time warp, she hears the jukebox play Latin music in reverse. Immediately shuffling backward, Gabby's trembling hands drop the two cups of coffee beside Mrs. Coppercorn and her companion.

"Ahhhh!" the older woman hollers, jumping out of her seat. She knocks down her walker. "You stupid little twit! Look what you've done!"

While everyone awkwardly stares at Gabriela, Crystal gets up from her seat, rushing to assist her friend, who stood distraught, still gazing at the window.

"Gabby! What's wrong?" Crystal grabs her hand, staring directly at the window where she sees a few patrons getting into their cars, leaving the parking lot.

Gabriela shakes her head slowly, pointing at the window. "You don't see him?"

"See who, Gabby?"

Her chin trembles. "Matt!" she mutters as a single drop of grief wells up from the corner of her eye.

"Matt? Gabriela!" Crystal cries out, gripping her friend's arm, spinning her around. "Look at me Gabby, Matt is not out there! He's gone! Okay? Now you have to calm down because you're freaking me out!"

"It's Matt! He's right there with that fucking cake!" she yells out, causing patrons to flee the diner due to her erratic behavior.

"What's wrong with her?" Jason asks Trey while staring at Crystal, trying to calm her friend.

"How the hell should I know! I've never seen Gabby like this."

Trying to make sense of what is happening, Crystal realizes that she could not get through to Gabby. It was like she tuned everything and everyone out, including her. Observing Matt getting into a silver sedan, Gabby swiftly removes her apron and darts out of the diner, shouting his name like a madwoman. Chasing after her, Crystal, Trey, and Jason watch Gabby get into her black ford Chrysler and drive off, following the vehicle.

"What the hell was that?" Jason asks Crystal.

"We have to go after her, Jason!" Crystal says, frantically running towards his motorcycle.

Flabbergasted, Jason runs after Crystal. "Wait! What? Why?" Jason asks her.

"Because she thinks she saw Matt!"

"Matt? You mean her dead boyfriend?"

"Yes, Jason! She's not making any sense. We have to go now!" Crystal says in a panic.

"All right, Crystal, let's go!" he says, hopping on his bike. "There goes our date," he angrily mumbles to himself.

"Don't leave me! I'm coming too! I'll follow behind you guys!" Trey shouts, hopping in his smart car.

※ ※ ※

Speeding down Fearman Street, Gabriela chases the silver sedan. Gripping her steering wheel, she guns the car down the lane, pushing every bit of horsepower from her Chrysler. Narrowly avoiding a pole, Gabriela pivots and turns blindly onto Cobbleton Parkway. Tailgating the silver sedan, Gabriela hits the car's bumper, making the driver struggle to switch lanes.

Reaching Hunters Point interstate, both vehicles heads towards the highway, where traffic starts to pile up, leaving them at a standstill. Breaking down, an onslaught of sobs escapes Gabby's mouth as she watches a middle-aged Caucasian man exit the sedan, storming towards her with rage.

Catching up to Gabby on the highway, Jason, Crystal, and Trey notice the man coming closer to Gabriela. At the same time, a toddler sits in the backseat of the vehicle, crying hysterically for his father.

"What the hell is the matter with you, lady? Are you fucking nuts!" the man wails, banging on Gabriela's car door.

"I'm so sorry," she cries out, "I thought you were someone else!"

Kicking her front tires, the man points his index finger at her. "Sorry? You could have killed my kid and me driving like that!"

Getting out of his car, Trey runs over to Gabriela. "Jesus! What the fuck is your problem, man," he says, glaring at the older man, "can't you see she's sorry."

"Is this, your friend? Because she almost killed my kid and me!"

"Sir, I'm am awfully sorry. My friend is going through a terrible loss, and she didn't mean to hurt you!"

Looking out of touch with the world, Gabriela feels her head spinning. As traffic starts to move quickly north, the highway clears, leaving the four of them, including the man and his child, alone on the main road. Hopping off the motorcycle, Crystal sprints over to Gabriela while Jason stood by his bike, staring from a distance.

Kneeling on the ground, Gabriela stares at Trey and Crystal, feeling helpless. "I could have sworn it was Matt. What's the matter with me?"

"Do yourself a favor! Keep your friend off the road before she kills someone!" the man angrily shouts before walking back to his car, leaving the four alone on the road.

As more tears trickle down Gabriela's cheeks, more thoughts whirl through her head. "He's dead because of me!" she cries out in pain, "he's dead because of me!"

Firmly holding her in his arms, Trey cradles her. "Gabriela, it's not your fault that Matt is dead. Your grief is causing you to become paranoid; you need to calm down. What you saw was not real; it was probably an illusion because you can't let him go."

"Maybe you're right, Trey, maybe I need to go home and rest. I haven't taken a break since he died."

"Listen, I can take you back home, and Crystal can drive your car back to the diner. How does that sound?" Trey calmly asks Gabby, helping her up from the granite ground.

"No, Trey, I want to drive back alone."

"Gabriela, after what just happened, it's too dangerous for you to drive. Please let me give you a ride back to town," Trey pleads with her.

"Trey, let me go," Gabby whimpers, disconnecting herself from him, "I'll meet you guys at my house that way; you know I got home safe."

Caressing her back, Crystal still feels worrisome, leaving her best friend by herself. "Are you sure, Gabby?"

"Yes, Crystal," she wipes her tear-stained eyes, "now, give me a hug so we can get out of here," Gabriela says, hugging both Trey and Crystal at the same time.

After their long embrace, Gabriela gets into her vehicle, locking her door. Inserting her keys into the ignition, she turns it counterclockwise and is frightened by a spark that strikes the tip of her finger. Groaning from intense pain, Gabriela takes her hands off the steering wheel, instantly placing her index finger in her mouth to soothe the ache.

Afraid to drive, Gabriela decides to take Trey's offer and exit her car. Pulling the latch to open the door, Gabriela comes to a horrifying realization that she cannot get out. Trapped inside the vehicle, Gabriela is startled by an abundance of fiery sparks coming from under the glove compartment. Leaning toward the back seat, Gabriela repeatedly bangs on the rear window, desperately trying to get Trey and Crystal's attention.

Without warning, a cloud of black smoke seeps through the air condition and begins to fill the inside of the vehicle, leaving Gabriela gasping for air. A splintering scream escapes her mouth as she continues to bang her fist, causing the window to crack.

"Help Me! Get me out of here, please!"

Hearing the echoes of someone screaming from a distance, Jason, Crystal, and Trey see smoke coming out of the vehicle's engine. At high speed, both Trey and Crystal run towards the car while Jason stood beside his bike, emotionless. Adrenaline coursing through their veins, they can barely see a few feet ahead of them. As the smoke intensifies, Trey and Crystal stood on each side of Gabby's car, desperately attempting to open the door. Jerking the handle, they pull away because of the severe heat burning the palms of their hands.

Shifting her body frantically from one side to the other, Gabriela feels another spark hitting the back of her neck. Trying to kick the inside of the car door, Gabriela screams as fire breaks out from the car's back seat. Unable to shield herself, Gabriela's clothes and hair quickly catch on fire melting, into her skin.

Flagging his coat to put out the fire, Trey is sickened at the sight of Jason standing by his bike with a heartless expression on his face. "Why the fuck are you just standing there! Help us for Christ sakes!"

Running over to the car, Jason extends his long legs and kicks the passenger side window with his leather boots. Shattering the glass, Jason is thrown instantly to the ground by a massive fireball.

Removing his navy blue t-shirt, Trey wraps it over his hands and arms to try as hard as possible to break the other side of the window.

Horror-stricken, he screams, backing away from the car when he sees a badly burnt Gabriela slam her head against the window. Slowly her face glides smoothly down the window, causing her burnt skin to fall off the bone, sticking to the glass.

Grappling Crystal, Jason forcefully pulls her away from the vehicle. As she fights to get him off, her body jolts when the trunk of the car explodes, sending Trey flying to the side of the road.

"Let me go, Jason! Gabby is going to die if I don't save her, she's going to die!"

Pulling Crystal further away, Jason shields her from witnessing the chaotic sight of the car going up in flames. "Crystal! She's gone! We have to get away from the car. It's going to blow up!"

Before Jason can utter another word, the car explodes, sending steel metal particles scattering all over the road. The bank of thick smoke fills the air along with the horrid stench of burnt flesh while everyone stood numb, staring at the charred remains of Gabriela's car.

Laying on the ground, Jason holds Crystal tightly in his arms as hot torrents of grief courses down her face. Pulling her deeper into his chest, Jason is caught off guard by a silver sedan, driving slowly past them. Grimacing at Jason, Matt nods his head at him before leaving the scene.

Jason's eyes gleam with darkness as he whispers with a vengeance, "Game on, Brother."

CHAPTER SEVENTEEN

GONE

CRYSTAL NARRATES

The rain slows to a gentle tap as I stood by my windowsill, listening to the trickling water beat a soft, solemn tattoo on the shallow glass. I asked myself how many more deaths can I endure in my life? First, the murder of my beloved parents, then Matt and now Gabby. The grieving process has left me completely distraught. I couldn't bear the thought of something happening to anyone else, especially my sister, Alexandria.

A week has passed since that fateful day that I lost my best friend, and I've found myself staying up countless nights afraid to go to sleep, fearful that I might relive that horrible day I watched her burn alive in her car. Those painful and horrific screams are embedded in my head and might not ever go away.

After Gabriela's passing, her parents opted out of having a traditional funeral for her. Instead, the town's pastor held a heartfelt eulogy at their home. Only immediate family, and close friends attended.

Unable to have an open-casket viewing, Gabriela's body was cremated and buried in Lakeview Falls Cemetery next to Matt's burial plot; that way, their souls would be together for eternity.

Since Gabby's death, Trey has been distant to everyone, including me. At the memorial, he was upset that I brought Jason with me to pay our respects. Making a scene, Trey had a meltdown and forced Jason to leave the memorial. Still upset by Jason's selfish behavior, Trey made it clear that he had no place or right to be at the funeral since he barely did anything to save Gabriela from the fire.

I kept thinking to myself, What if Gabby didn't see Matt's image? Would she still be alive? Or was this fate by the powers that be. Wrapped up in my thoughts, I hear the doorbell ring. I leave my bedroom and rush down the stairs. Slowly opening the door; I am surprised to see that it is Jason.

He was standing there in the pouring rain, stroking his hand through his short brown hair, slicking it back. His emerald green eyes, beautiful and haunting, displays sadness and pain. I hadn't seen or spoken to him since the memorial, and now he is here. Why? I ask myself, what is his reason for showing up at my house? What are his real intentions?

CHAPTER EIGHTEEN

SKIN DEEP

KILLER CREEK LANE

Raindrops continue their ravage on the earth, ripping cruelly at the ground and whistling angrily through the crimson king maple trees. Flashes of lightning look like skeletal fingers reaching down to strike the incandescent earth, while boiling clouds grumble in the distance, complaining of the heavyweight they bore.

Slow drips of rain descend from the sky, trickling on Jason as he stood face to face with Crystal. What seemingly felt like an innocent blooming romance soon turns into something far worse. It didn't take long for Crystal to see Jason in a different light. Although he portrays himself as someone trustworthy and kind-hearted, his actions speak the opposite.

Abandoned without so much as a phone call, Crystal felt heartbroken once again by a man who snaked his way into her life and her heart, and for that, she knew she couldn't forgive him.

❈ ❈ ❈

Crystal feels her heart sink as Jason's piercing eyes bore into hers. Searching his face for hidden signs of deception, she stood numb, infuriated by his presence. A deep groan escapes her soft lips. "I have nothing to say to you, Jason, now, please go."

As Crystal slowly pushes the door forward, Jason swiftly puts one foot in between it, blocking her from closing it. Shooting warm air out of his mouth with each breath he exhales, Jason leans in towards Crystal, shielding himself under the portico roof as the torrents of rain continue to fall upon him.

"Crystal, I know that I'm the last person you want to see right now, and I don't blame you," he tells her. His lips quiver as water droplets enter his mouth. "I'm so sorry about disappearing on you; I had no right to treat you that way, especially how kind you have always been to me. And most of all, I am deeply sorry for what happened to Gabby. There's no excuse for the way I stormed out of her memorial. It's just that Trey was so upset with me—" He pauses. "Crystal, you have to believe that I didn't mean to hurt you."

"It doesn't matter, Jason; There is nothing I can do to bring my best friend back. So, stop wasting my time. Take your sorry ass back across the street and continue counting the remaining days you have left in this town."

"I'm not leaving," he mutters, inching closer to her, smelling his scent still lingering on her sweater.

She clicks her tongue. "I beg your pardon?" she hisses with one hand on her hip.

"I will leave you alone if you allow me to take you out, just this once."

"Take me out? Are you insane? You don't just ghost me and decide you want to return when it's convenient for you, Jason."

"There's a place that I want to show you."

Crystal takes two steps back, shaking her head with disapproval. "I'm not going anywhere with you, Jason, so if you would kindly leave!"

"Please, Crystal," he pleads, extending his cold, wet palms, "come with me; that's all I ask of you. And after today, I will understand if you don't want to see me again."

"I don't believe you, Jason."

"Crystal, I promise to leave you alone and never step foot in front of your house, I swear."

The dreadful lightning is evil and haunting as Crystal's tiring eyes glances at the dark grey clouds. "Jason, how can we go anywhere? It's pouring outside."

He tilts his head up while the raindrops trickle down his nose, then direct his gaze back at Crystal. "It's only water, Crystal. It won't hurt you," he says, pulling her into his charming gaze.

Jason's approach seems genuine and sincere; it is evident that he feels guilty about Gabby's death, and he wanted to gain Crystal's trust again. Of course, that is the only way he can get what he came for: **the Stone.**

Accepting his invitation, Crystal decides to take a ride with Jason. Clueless about where he is taking her, Crystal keeps her guard up. It wasn't that she was afraid he would cause harm to her; she is more afraid of losing herself in him. The uncontrollable urge to surrender her every being without being forced is the most dangerous action a woman can ever do when in the presence of any man. Every minute spent with Jason is like playing with fire. As soon as the flame ignites, she'll burn.

TOWN HALL CIRCLE

Rain drums the ground like a hundred marching soldiers as Trey scurries down Fearman Street, running past empty stores in the deserted shopping center. Quickly trying to find a place of refuge until the storm ends, he arrives in front of a vintage witchcraft bookshop named **"Flokatraté Coven Box."**

Trey's eyes widen with gleam while staring at the old voodoo dolls and enchanted spell books displayed behind the glass window. Upon entering the shop, Trey accidentally knocks his head over the antique satin brass shopkeepers bell above the door. Staring at him with incredulous eyes, the bookkeeper continues cashing out a female customer who purchased handmade brown leather-bound journals that look old and worn out.

Flashing a grin, Trey wanders around the small shop, gazing at the variety of mixed potions displayed on an off-white shelf. From healing stones and sages to mason jars filled with distinctive colorful liquids resembling old magic serums. On the opposite side of the wall is a tall glass case cabinet dedicated to only special herbs and spices used for incantation spells and ancient curses.

Trey's mesmerized as his eyes stumble upon a renaissance carved oak bookcase that holds over one hundred demonology and pagan books. His mouth creates excess saliva that begins to trickle down the side of his lips. Using his forearm to wipe the drool off his mouth, Trey continues his gaze. The two twin glazed cabinet doors display a carved image of a half-man, half-dragon. Inching closer to the bookshelf, Trey senses a warm breath assaulting the back of his neck.

"Excuse me, can I help you, sir?" she asks in a husky tone, nervously tapping her dirty metallic colored boots on the hickory wood floor.

In her late forties, the heavyset woman, displays unattractive features that would scare off anyone who stares at her for an extended period. Her wild curly red elbow-length hair, long crooked nose, and black moles mix with freckles covering her round milky white chubby face.

Turning around, Trey is frightened by the bookkeeper's silver-grey eyes. "Fack! You scared me half to death," he exclaims, backing away with his hand over his chest, gasping for air.

"I see you are admiring my bookshelf," she says, walking over to the exquisite carved wood, gently stroking her hands, softly singing a song in Yiddish.

"Is there something that I can help you with?"

"Yes," Trey replies, observing the large black books with pagan symbols on a separate bronze shelf. "I'm looking for a book on shapeshifter demons."

Tilting her head to the side, her right eyebrow arches, curiously. "shapeshifter demons? Why would a nice youth like you want with a book like that?"

"I'm taking a workshop class on demonology at Lakeview Falls University, and I'm doing a research paper. My professor teaches a course about a shapeshifter demon that resided in Lakeview Falls centuries ago. I am curious to learn more about this story. I've had it stuck in my head for a week."

"Interesting," she twiddles her fingers across her chin, "weren't you told as a child that curiosity kills the cat?" the bookkeeper says with a wicked tone in her voice.

"I'm pretty sure I've heard that phrase many times, but I'm more curious than a cat, " he lets out an awkward chuckle.

The bookkeeper glares over her shoulders. Her eyes stalk the back door to the secret sanctuary. "Well—I do have one rare book on shapeshifter demons, but it's not for sale," she scoffs.

She brushes Trey aside and returns to her register counter. "Sorry young man, but you're out of luck."

Trey pleads, following the bookkeeper, "Please, I need to borrow that book. I will pay you any price."

Arranging small jars of black **"Banjuloloa"** across the counter, she maintains no eye contact with Trey. "I told you already, the book is not for borrowing nor to purchase. I suggest looking for another shop that will cater to your needs."

"Mam, please, I'm begging you. This research paper is due in less than a week. I can't miss this deadline. Can you at least let me read the book at the shop? It would mean the world to me."

Bringing her index finger to her top lip, she taps twice and groans. "Fine, come with me."

In dire need of finding out more about Mastema, Trey successfully talks his way into getting his hands on the shapeshifter demon book. Leading Trey to the back of the shop, the bookkeeper shows him an ancient cedar antique chest with a symbol of a creature half-man, half-devil with ten serpents protruding out its head engraved on it.

Scanning the rusted dark cherry chest, Trey stood impatiently while the bookkeeper kneels, grasping the tortoise padlock. Swiftly unlocking it, the woman opens the wooden crate and takes out an ancient and dusty brown embroidered book with a carving image of what looks like a demon with a lion's head and serpents surrounding its body. The devil holds up two baby gargoyles on each hand.

With caution, the bookkeeper carefully takes the book out of the chest and slowly hands it over to Trey. "Take heed to the advice I give you and read with caution. You should not take shifter demon stories lightly. The information stated in every page is true and never say any of these demon's names out loud; it can cause unwanted summoning. Never under any circumstances allow this book into someone else's hands, except the chosen."

"The chosen? What does that mean?" Trey asks suspiciously.

"Can I trust that you will follow my instructions?"

Clenching the book against his chest, Trey excitedly shakes his head. "Of course! Absolutely. I promise I will return this book to you once I am done reading it."

"No need to return it; I will let you have the book but under one condition. In return, you shall never tell anyone where you got this from, agreed?"

"Agreed!" Trey says in a triumphant voice. "Thank you so much; I will guard this book with my life."

Elated, Trey dances his way out of the coven shop, bidding farewell to the bookkeeper. As he heads back outside in the pouring rain, the woman immediately closes the door. Peering through the small window by the entrance door, she watches Trey from a distance before hanging a sign on the main door entrance that reads, **"OUT OF BUSINESS."**

LAKEVIEW FALLS UNIVERSITY

Soaked from head to toe, Trey enters his dorm room. Eagerly awaiting to find out what's in the book, Trey takes off his wet grey wool jacket and places it across a small folded chair he has in the corner of his room. Walking over to his espresso colored computer desk, Trey takes a seat and places the book beside his rose gold laptop. Using his **TVOX** voice command, he turns on his small flatscreen television and switches to the four o'clock news.

Before indulging in the demon world, Trey takes looks at an 8x11 photo on his desk of him, Crystal, and Gabriela at their homecoming dance in high school. A tear trickles down his cheeks, still distraught over Gabby's passing. Sniffling quietly, he wipes his face and takes a deep breath opening the Shapeshifting Demon book named, **"First coming Human Shapeshifters."**

Flipping through each page, Trey suddenly felt a sickening urge to regurgitate as he stares at disturbing black and white sketches of creatures from the 18th century. Continuing his search on the demon Professor Baptist had discussed, Trey finally comes across **Chapter** 66, "Flesh-eating Shapeshifter demon."

Carefully reading each paragraph, Trey is horrified to learn how these crafty half-human creatures skin their victims, ultimately disguising themselves with their visage. It says that the shifter demon can change their appearance in two ways to look like their victims.

#1 - The Demon consumes the skin of their victims.

or

#2 - The Demon can get acquainted with the victim, such as befriending them or having close interaction, which mimics their personality and characteristics.

Also, the flesh-eating shapeshifter demon only eats the flesh of little boys and young adult males. This way, they can preserve their human form and existence; eating their uncircumcised genitals and feces is also a considerable delicacy for the demons.

Feeling nausea in the pit of his stomach, Trey continues searching for the story on Mastema when he is distracted by a male reporter's voice on TV.

"This is the four o' clock news, and I am Bo Fleming. Reporting live at 478 Turtle Hill Grove in Portal-Cam Omaha, Nebraska, I am interviewing lone survivor ten-year-old Mikaila Holliston. The Holliston's, a family of five, were brutally butchered and skinned alive four weeks ago. Luckily little Mikalia's life was spared by this maniac killer."

Holding up a college graduation photo of her older brother Jason Holliston, little Mikalia lets out a gut-wrenching sob, pleading with the media to find who killed her family, including her brother, whom she adored with all of her heart.

Horror stricken, Trey's jaw drops as he stares at the handsome man's piercing emerald green eyes in the photo. How could it be possible? How can the same guy who has been in his town for two weeks be the same person that died in that photo?

Looking back at the book, Trey gasps covering his mouth. "Holy Shit! Jason is a Shapeshifter. FACK!" he hollers while he continues listening to the reporter.

"As investigators check every house surveillance, we ask everyone in the gated community of Portal Cam to contact your local police department if you saw anyone suspicious around the Holliston home on September 9th around 3:30 in the afternoon. If you have any information, please call the number at the bottom of your screen. The number is 1-900-666- 6000. This is Bo Flemming with 666 news, now back to your regular schedule program, **The Brother's Curse.**"

Opening his laptop, Trey searches the Holliston murder on Shashoo.com. Finding the article and a family photo of the Omaha family, Trey immediately prints out the picture on his copying machine. Like the rumbling of thunder, Trey's heart pounds like a jackhammer as he clasps his cell phone, calling Crystal on speed dial. Listening to her voicemail go off, Trey decides not to take a chance going over her house just in case Jason sees him.

Instead, Trey takes matter into his own hands and sends out a mass forward text on his cell phone that reads, **"Meet me tonight at the University Library Hall as soon as you get this message. It's a matter of life and death! Trey..."**

CHAPTER NINETEEN

TOUCH OF THE BEAST

RURAL MAPLETON ROAD

Gripping Jason tightly around his waist, Crystal is startled by flashes of lightning and thunder that rumble as the rainstorm cleanses the world. The sprinkles turn to blankets of raindrops, pouring onto the winter ground. At the same time, Mother Nature releases her feminine force, unleashing thick sheets of icy water that covers the rich soil and replenishes it with blossoming life.

Arriving at Rural Mapleton Road, Crystal sets eyes on an abandoned 17th-century chapel that lies in the middle of an open field that stretches out for miles. The old sanctuary was built in 1798 and used by spiritual practitioners called **The Womb for Sacred Sorcière**. The chapel stood untouched and unwanted for thirty-six years by citizens of Lakeview Falls due to its ungodly history.

Deemed hazardous to the public's spiritual safety, Sherman Wexler and the "Devine Psalms Ministry" enforced restrictions in 1988, where citizens could no longer attend prayer services at the chapel. Due to witnesses reporting bodies of missing children appearing in the rural forest pathway, Lakeview Falls former Com-

THE BROTHER'S CURSE

missioner permanently closed the area and the church in October of 1989.

❋ ❋ ❋

The loud cries of black ravens fill the air while flying high, pounding its wings, warning one another of any visitor's invasive presence. Stepping off Jason's motorcycle, Crystal smells the wet earth's scent while staring at the old chapel's haunting exterior. Mostly built out of stone, the two-story country style cathedral displays moss coverings that trails around the archway and above the tall double oak doors. Its iron hinges and fierce metal bolts scare away intruders.

Grasping Crystal's hand, Jason quickly leads her inside the chapel. The cold stone rustic walls seem to draw inwards as they descend upon the room. The structure inside the church is far from holy. "Were spirits trapped in this place?" Crystal questions herself, glaring at the partially shattered stain glass windows, molded interior walls and wooden cedar pews chipped off and deteriorated.

Walking further down the aisle, Crystal notices a distinctive pagan design carved into the cold faded marble floor that frightens her to the core. She can smell the fear that had been haunting the inhabitants of the old chapel for many years.

The entire scenery gives Crystal the creeps, which makes her question what Jason's motives are for bringing her there. Inhaling the dampness in the air, Crystal sighs. "So this is where you so desperately wanted to take me?" she asks, mockingly, glaring at him.

Inching closer to her, Jason stands beside Crystal, gazing at the abundance of cobwebs that hangs over a bizarre metal wall sculpture of a serpent nailed to a silver dagger.

"Yes, Crystal," he replies, "this is exactly the place I wanted you to see."

"Why on earth would you bring me here, Jason? How do you even know about this place?"

"For the past week, I've been riding to different parts of this town and two days ago, I stumbled upon this old yet intriguing chapel. I don't know what it was, but something about it made me want to bring you here."

"Why?" shrugging her shoulders, Crystal turns to face him, searching for a better answer, "this is an abandoned church that hasn't seen walks of life in decades. It's out in the middle of nowhere, Jason—now, why did you bring me to this old church?"

"It's not just an old church, Crystal; there's something about this place, something peaceful. Isn't that what you've been searching for, is peace?"

"If I needed peace, I could have stayed home, Jason, not standing in some creepy building that looks like it can come tumbling down at any second."

"Stop worrying about what it looks like and take a minute to enjoy the pure silence, listen to the rainfall. Think of the last time you felt some form of peace in your life Crystal," Jason says, brushing up against her arm.

"Peace doesn't exist in my world, Jason."

"It does if you allow it to Crystal, close your eyes and take in this moment."

Closing her eyes, Crystal drowns out everything around her. The pain and guilt that corrupts her very soul fights its way out. Taking a deep breath, Crystal exhales, opening her eyes, realizing that Jason is staring at her with his illuminating eyes.

"Aren't you scared?"

"Of what, Jason?"

"Living in a town where people die or go missing every single day?"

"I got used to it for a very long time; it is scary, but there's nothing I can do to stop bad things from happening. I choose to live here because of my family; we all have choices in life Jason, just like you chose to sit on your bike and watch my best friend violently burn to death," she says quietly, breaking eye contact with him.

"Gabriela's death was not my fault, Crystal, you have to believe that. There was nothing any of us could have done to save her. I did what I could to help you and Trey. I broke the window, remember?"

"The only reason why you helped us was because Trey yelled at you."

"You say that as if I did it on purpose. What was I supposed to do, Crystal? You don't understand how that affected me," Jason says, defending himself.

"In what way did Gabby's death affect you?" Crystal angrily asks.

"It effects me because I almost died in a fire, Crystal!"

Lowering his head as if the feelings of sympathy override his sinister nature, Jason's saddened expression takes Crystal by surprise.

"What?" she exclaims, "what are you talking about, Jason?"

"When I was an infant, a woman rescued me from a burning building. It's a painful feeling every time I think about it. Most days, I choose to block it out. Crystal, when I saw Gabriela locked in that car, everything I went through came rushing back. So, yes, I stood there not because I wanted to but because I couldn't process what was going on. It was as if I was reliving my demise."

Pulling up his right sleeve, Jason exposes a large scar on his arm, stretching from his wrist to his elbow. Showing Crystal the first-degree burn that covers his skin, Jason quickly pulls down his sleeve.

"I don't expect you to feel sorry for me, Crystal, and I'm not trying to make excuses either. I want you to know that I've never shared my personal life with anyone except you."

"Why didn't you say something to me before you decided to vanish for a week? I would have understood Jason."

"Don't you think that I wanted to be the one to comfort you, to let you know I was here for you? But instead, I acted like a damn coward, and for that, I am very ashamed of myself."

Shifting his gaze to Crystal, Jason pulls her closer to him. He wanted her trust; he wanted her forgiveness. He wanted her. Facing Crystal, Jason brings his hand up to cup her cheek; his thumb runs along the curve of her cheekbone. Nestling into his hand, Crystal feels Jason's warmth seep into hers. It is magic, the way their lips connected.

As Crystal falls into a world of passion, she suddenly feels a sharp pain in her chest, causing her knees to weaken. She collapses to the marble floor as an acute pain erupts through her head.

Her surroundings become a blur as she sees a vision of four middle-aged African American women in the middle of the fields repeatedly chanting a spell while they sacrifice a young girl.

Overwhelmed with excruciating pain, Crystal clutches onto her amethyst stone necklace tightly, forcing the vision to disappear instantly. A strange feeling washes over Crystal as Jason grabs hold of her hand, bringing her to her feet. Shaken by what she has just experienced, Crystal kindly asks him to take her home.

❄ ❄ ❄

KILLER CREEK LANE

Thunderous clouds gather, choking out the light of life while Crystal's arms tighten around Jason's waist. Leaning her face against his back, Crystal feels a sense of adrenaline rushing through her body. Observing Jason's hands clutching on the handlebars while the rain pours on his dark brown hair, Crystal finds him incredibly sexy, and the very touch of him leaves her feeling exuberant.

Arriving in front of her home, Crystal finds it hard to disconnect herself from Jason. Enjoying her hands gripping his back, Jason's obsession for Crystal takes his breath away, not from the intense squeeze but from the realization that her arms were around him and not letting go.

"Thank you for coming with me," Jason says in a soft-spoken tone, glancing over his shoulders, pressing his side cheek against hers.

"Thank you for taking me, Jason; I guess we both needed a place to vent."

Closing his eyes, Jason has a sudden rush of raw emotions pulsing through his veins as her smooth skin lays against his. Crystal's sweet nectar breath makes him want to grab her and kiss her at that moment.

"Would you like me to walk you to your door?" he asks nervously, not knowing what her response will be.

"I don't want you to walk me to my door," her pouty lips tremble, "I want you to come inside and stay with me for a while. I don't want to be alone, Jason; I want to be with you."

"Are you sure you want that, Crystal? If I come with you, I don't think I will be able to control my urges."

She whispers in his ears, "I don't want you to."

❈ ❈ ❈

Thrusting Crystal against the wall, Jason grabs both her legs and wraps them around his torso. Kissing Jason aggressively, she wraps her arms around his neck and laces her fingers through his hair, pulling on it. The harder she pulls, the harder he kisses her. Cutting her bottom lip with his razor-sharp tooth, Jason watches a single drop of blood run down her chin. Her tone legs still fastened around his waist, Jason takes Crystal into the living room. Raising Jason's shirt, she slowly starts to feel his body as he undresses her. His gaze lingers down her chest before their lips touch again.

Making Crystal's heart rate go faster than he can ever imagine, Jason leans in to enjoy the moment. While his body fills with endless passion, Jason wraps his hand around Crystal's head and strokes her jet black locks while the back of her body faces the Venetian mirror. Gazing at Crystal's alluring reflection, Jason admires her naked body. Aroused by their intimacy, Jason transitions to his demonic form, causing his manhood to shift into a serpent, slithering itself around her hips, moving up her back.

Jason's pure form does not affect Crystal; the purple amethyst stone's powerful force of energy glamour's her to only see Jason as who he is and not a grotesque beast. Therefore, in Crystal's eyes, she's making love to Jason in his human form.

❈ ❈ ❈

LATER IN THE EVENING

Moonlight trickles from the bleeding sky and plays on the windowsill while the crackling sounds of wood burn fiercely in the fireplace. For a moment, there is a peaceful silence as Crystal and Jason lay naked on the camel-colored faux sheepskin rug. Sound asleep, Jason has a brief moment of clarity, watching how innocent Crystal looks. Gazing at the purple amethyst stone necklace, Jason touches it with his index finger, whispering, "I will not let you down, father; I will get you out."

Awaken by the feel of Jason's touch; Crystal opens her eyes to find him gazing at her with a magnetic smile. "How long was I passed out?"

"Not long; I enjoyed watching you sleep. You are the most peaceful, most beautiful sight to see."

Unable to resist the emotions he starts to feel for Crystal, Jason struggles as half-demon, half-human. He is forbidden by his father to express any feelings towards the chosen. Embracing Crystal, Jason decides to open up to her.

Feeling his face flush, Jason gently grabs her hand. "Crystal, there's something I need to tell you,"

"What is it, Jason?" she asks, gazing into his emerald green eyes.

Before he could utter out the next words, Alexandria enters the house mortified at the sight of her sister and Jason naked on the living room floor.

"Oh, my God!" she exclaims, covering her eyes, "I didn't see anything, I swear!" she shrieks, racing up the staircase.

Rising from the floor, Jason quickly gets himself dressed. "I'm sorry, Crystal, but I should go; it's getting late."

"Go?" she gets up, wrapping her naked body with a faux fur blanket, "didn't you say you had something to tell me?"

"Don't worry, it's not important," he whispers, kissing her on the forehead, "I'll call you, okay?"

Nodding her head, unable to utter a word to him, Crystal watches Jason grab his leather jacket from her couch before exiting her home.

A deep sigh escapes Crystal's lips with a saddened expression, confused as to why Jason left her house in such a hurry. Feeling a sudden burning sensation on her back, she walks over to her mirror. Slightly shifting her body to the right side, Crystal is alarmed to see claw marks across her back.

"What the hell is this?" She mutters, while gently stroking her skin.

❋ ❋ ❋

MEANWHILE

Once Jason arrives back at Mr. McGregor's house, he storms into the living room and stares at the fireplace for a few minutes. Disgusted at himself for engaging in sexual intimacy with Crystal, Jason's anger spirals out of control. Even though it felt orgasmic, it wasn't part of his mission; he couldn't possibly ever feel love for her. Jason knew Crystal had to die, no matter what.

In a psychopathic rage, Jason punches the mirror, shattering it to pieces. His hands start to bleed as he proceeds to destroy the living room, throwing glass vases at the walls and ripping apart furniture until nothing is left. Noticing the next-door security lights go on unexpectedly, exposing a bright light; Jason fears the neighbors will report him to the Sheriff's Department for making a loud disturbance. Grabbing his keys, Jason runs out of the house and hops on his motorcycle, fleeing Killer Creek Lane.

CHAPTER TWENTY

DEADLY PILEUP

LAKEVIEW FALLS LIBRARY

The moment Trey enters the library hall, not a word is said, but he can feel all eyes glaring at him while he grips onto the shapeshifter demon book tightly under his arm. Approaching the front desk, he scans his access card and greets the librarian. The sweet old woman sits in a diagonal position combing through her long matted grey hair while reading **"The Older you are, The Dryer you get."**

Giving him clearance to enter the library hall, Trey slowly makes his way down the narrow aisle. The scent of rosy carpet freshener mix with the burning smell of hot fluorescent light fixtures causes Trey to become nauseous. His eyes dart around the room, scanning everything and everyone, from the sound of people turning a page in their books to people sneaking food in their backpacks even though there is a sign that clearly says: **No Food or Drinks.**

Walking past rows upon rows of bookshelves, Trey finds a secluded spot towards the back of the library. Taking a seat at the neatly arranged steel round table, he awaits his party of three to arrive. Trey's legs begin to quiver with anxiety while his hand trembles, checking his cell phone to see if Crystal received any of his text messages.

'No New Messages 12:30 am' displays on his front screen. "Come on, Crystal, where the hell are you?" Trey whispers to himself.

Trey sits impatiently while his eyes dart around restlessly. Feeling his heartbeat race, Trey focuses on the urgent message that he sent Crystal an hour ago, begging her to call him. As he rubs his eyebrow against his sleeve, Trey looks up and notices Simone, Victoria, and Terrance coming towards his direction.

Beckoning for them to quicken their pace, Trey becomes paranoid about Jason finding out what he knows. Thinking about it made a shudder from his feet, traveling to his head. For a second, he prays that the beast has not followed his friends. Reading the book word for word, Trey learns more than he should about shapeshifters. He knows how they manipulate, their quick senses, and their craftiness to prey on their targets.

Approaching the steel table, Terrance gently places his brown backpack on the table. "Hey Trey, what's going on? We got your text message. Is everything okay?" he asks with a worried expression, taking a seat beside him.

"Oh God, you have no idea how happy I am to see you guys," Trey says breathlessly.

"Trey, whatever you have to say to us, it better be good because it's almost 1 a.m.," Victoria clicks her teeth while twiddling a grape flavored lollipop in her mouth.

Excessive sweat falls from his forehead. "Sit down, please," Trey says. Under pressure, his voice shakes, becoming almost inaudible. He starts to shiver, but it isn't from the air conditioner in the library. It is the thought of losing Crystal to a demonic skin-walker.

"Trey, you look like you haven't slept in days," Terrance says, observing the dark circles under his eyes.

"Maybe it's because my friend just fucking died!" Trey shouts angrily.

A few students, including the librarian, oddly glances over at their table, signaling Trey to keep the noise down. Slumped over in his seat, Trey notices all eyes in the room were on him.

Walking over to Trey, Simone takes a seat across from him. Grasping his hand, she caresses it. "Trey, you have to calm down, we are all grieving Gabriela's death, and we know that this has not been easy for you, but it's clear that you need to take care of yourself. We haven't heard from you in days, Trey."

"What is this big emergency you called us here for Trey? I was in the middle of helping Phillip move to one of those rented dorm rooms on campus."

"Why is Phillip moving?" Terrance interrupts her, "I thought you guys were staying at his dad's house."

"Sheriff Mills is an old fart, and he doesn't like my cooking."

"Shhhhhh!" a female student from across the table whispers to Victoria.

Giving the student the side-eye, Victoria flips her the middle finger. "Shhhh, my ass!"

"Victoria, can you sit down, please? I don't want to attract any more attention," Trey says, scooting his chair closer to the table. "So, I asked you guys to come here because I don't know who else to show this to," he says, chewing his fingernail to the end.

"Show us what, Trey?" Simone asks, watching Trey pull out an article from his leather backpack.

Scanning the library to make sure no one is watching them, he shows his friends the article he printed up online. "Check this out," he mumbles, pushing the paper in their direction.

"What the hell? Is that Jason?" Victoria exclaims, staring at the family photo of the slaughtered family.

"Yes, it is Jason, Jason Holliston."

"Who?" Terrance squints his eye with a puzzled expression.

"There's a family that was murdered in Omaha, Nebraska four weeks ago. One child survived. She was on the four o'clock news today, holding up this photo of her older brother, Jason Holliston. His sister found him in his room skinned from head to toe," Trey says.

Irritated, Victoria makes slurpy sounds with her lollipop. "So what are you trying to say, Trey?" she asks him.

"I'm trying to say that the guy that's walking around Lakeview Falls sweet-talking our friend is wearing this guy's face."

"Trey, you sound crazy, man." Terrance sighs with annoyance, "How can you expect us to believe thats true? Maybe this Jason Holliston guy is his doppelgänger. I mean, there's no way someone can steal another person's face and wear it. Unless your leather face from the chainsaw movies," Terrance says, glancing at the photo then back at Trey.

"Terrance, this asshole has been lying to Crystal this entire time. Don't you find it strange that ever since he came to Lakeview Falls, bad shit has been happening to our friends? Look at what happened to Gabby. Jason was with Crystal and me that day; he didn't give a shit about helping us. It's like he wanted Gabby to die."

"Trey! Listen to yourself," Simone says in a worried tone, "you're not making any sense right now. There is no way Jason is walking around wearing another guy's face?"

"Simone is right, Trey," Terrance agrees with a quick nod, "you've been watching way too many Stephen King movies."

"I am telling you that something is not right about Jason Warwick. At first, he seemed like a cool guy, but now I am having second thoughts about him. He is the reason behind everything going wrong in this town. All the young guys going missing and getting skinned and hung. Hello?" he raises his voice, waving his hands by his ears, "this is no coincidence."

"Trey, weird shit has been happening in this town for decades!" Victoria blurts out, "and yes, what happened to Gabby was horrible, but Jason coming to our town couldn't possibly have anything to do with that or the murders that have occurred. You have no proof, Trey; you sound like a basket case."

"Remember when Kyle freaked out at the diner after he went to the bathroom to apologize to Jason. Well, no one has heard or seen him since then; there are flyers of him all over town."

"Trey has a point; we don't know what happened in there. You know Kyle doesn't get scared of anything," Victoria replies, agreeing with Trey.

"I think Kyle is dead, and I think Jason killed him," Trey says as sweat trickles down his forehead to the tip of his nose.

"Trey, seriously, I think you need to take a Xanax," Terrance suggests, gently patting him on the back, "you need to get some sleep asap. I haven't seen you in class for two days; you look like shit, no offense."

"I don't need sleep Terrance," giving him an uneasy glance, Trey snatches the article from the table, "I need you guys to believe me. I know this sounds crazy, but—what if all of this connects to the story Professor Baptist was telling us in class."

"What story?" Victoria asks in confusion.

"The story about the shapeshifter demons that lived in Lakeview Falls in the 18th century."

"Trey, that was an old witches tale. Professor Baptist was trying to scare us. That story is bullshit," Terrance says, slumping back in his seat, crossing his arms.

"Come on, Terrance, think about it; ever since Jason moved here, he hasn't left Crystal's side once. He's always with her." Trey replies with a side-eye.

"So what, Trey," Victoria huffs in annoyance, "that doesn't mean anything; it doesn't prove that he's a demon. "

"Bullshit! He is a demon. No one knows where he's from. All we know is that he's Mr. McGregor's nephew," tapping his fingers on the article, Trey stares directly at Jason Holliston, "Jason Warwick shape-shifted into this guy."

"Now that's crazy talk, Shapeshifters? Come on, Trey; this is insane. I think you are exaggerating this entire situation. I'm leaving; I got Kimberly Moore upstairs in my room. I don't have time for this shit!" Terrance scowls, rising from his seat.

Trey's breathing grows faster as he contemplates his actions. His knees fidget while his fingers drum loudly on the table. "Terrance, wait," a sigh slips through his lips as he pulls out the shapeshifter demon book from his backpack.

Taken aback, Terrance's eyes widen by the sight of the disturbing book. "Whoa! Where the hell did you get that?"

"Don't worry; it's not important."

"Not important," he exclaims, inching closer to see the engraved image on the front cover, "that shit looks creepy; is it a spell book?"

"No, it's not a spell book. It's a demonology book with a similar story that Professor Baptist told us a week ago. Don't you remember the story about the demon named Mastema that came to Lakeview Falls two hundred years ago to wreak havoc, killing most of the Wiccans that built this town? Well, it says that after Mastema's sons were born, he put a curse on them to live immortally in hopes of hunting down the girl that holds this."

Turning to page 25, Trey points at the photo of the purple amethyst stone pendant. "If the brothers find this stone and the girl that has possession of it, they will have to kill her to release their father and the twenty-four shapeshifter demons locked inside the pendant."

"So, what does this all mean, Trey?" Terrance asks, sitting back in his seat.

"It means that our friend is the girl that possesses this stone. You guys, this is the same necklace that Crystal's wearing; her mom left it for her before she died," Trey frowns, staring at his friends.

"Oh my God!" Simone gasps. "You're right Trey, it is the same necklace; I saw Crystal wearing it too."

Leaning towards Trey, Terrance grabs the book flipping the pages. "Okay, so let's say that this story is real and shapeshifter demons do exist. Are you telling us this Jason Warwick guy could be one of the brothers? And if so. Why hasn't he killed Crystal yet?"

"I'm glad you asked that, Terrance," Trey smirks sarcastically, "Jason can't kill Crystal until the 25th birth year, which is her birthday."

"You're saying that these demons are supposed to kill our friend on her birthday? Trey, that's the day after tomorrow!" Terrance bellows angrily, placing his hands behind his head. "How do we stop it from happening, Trey?"

"I don't know, Terrance. I've read every page in that book, and there's nothing that says how to destroy these brothers."

"You said that their father Mastema cursed them; if so, shouldn't there be something in that book about breaking the curse?" Victoria asks, snatching the book away from Terrance with a smug smile.

"Maybe, I think Professor Baptist might have the answers to that. He has a lot of knowledge about the history of this town. I think he can help us save Crystal from these demons."

"Look at the time Trey," Terrance says, pointing at the LED wall clock mounted on the wall near the librarian station, "it's too late to ask him now; he left school hours ago."

"Quick question, why are you telling us all of this and not Crystal? If this guy is after her and wants to get this necklace, shouldn't she know what she's up against?" Victoria asks Trey, handing him over the book.

"Victoria, I tried to call Crystal all evening, and she hasn't answered her phone, which only means one thing."

"She's probably with Jason," Simone replies with a worried expression.

"Correct, Simone. I think Jason is trying to pluck us off one by one. The fewer people around Crystal, the better chance he has at hurting her. I am positive that he will come after me, and If I'm going to die, then all of you are going to die too," Trey points at each of them, looking dead into their eyes. "I'm not going down by myself; we're all going to leave this shit together."

"Wait a minute," Victoria says backing away from the table, "if you think Jason is after us, then what about his brother. Isn't he after Crystal too?" she asks suspiciously.

"He is after her, Victoria, but the question is who the hell is he?" Trey says while rising from his seat, grabbing the shifter book and his backpack.

"Trey, where are you going?" Simone asks, grasping hold of his hand.

"I should go to Crystal's house. Since she's not answering her phone, it makes no sense to continue calling her. I have to tell her what's going on; she has to know who Jason is. Once I show her the photo, she will have no choice but to believe that Jason is a monster."

"I think it's safer if we go with you, Trey," Simone suggests, getting up from her chair.

Glancing at Simone, Trey flashes a half smile, walking past her. "No Simone, she's my best friend, and she should hear this from me, okay? Don't worry. I'll call you later if something comes up."

"Trey, please be careful," Simone says, watching Trey throwing his backpack over his shoulders.

"I'll see you guys tomorrow, be safe out there," Trey says, bidding farewell to his friends as he leaves the library hall gripping the book tightly in his hand.

❄ ❄ ❄

Eerie sounds echo loud and clear as Trey walks through the cold dark hallway. The wind chills coming from the open window creeps onto his spine like a thousand needles pinning him down to his last breath. Trey's knees weaken beneath him as he finally makes it to his room **307**. Before heading over to Crystal's house to warn her about Jason, Trey decided to go back to his dorm to retrieve his mini laptop and car keys.

Entering his room, he turns on his night light beside his bed and places the shapeshifter book on his computer desk. Pulling his cell phone out of his pocket, Trey sends Crystal one last text message, letting her know he is on his way to her home. Placing his phone back into his jean pocket, he is startled by a loud knock on his door, followed by a mellow tapping of fingernails against the wooden surface.

With thoughts racing in his head, Trey is frightened as the door suddenly creaks open like the cell bars of a dark prison. The wind sucks through the slightly open door as if it is waiting for a chance to swallow up a person who hugs a wall too tightly in fear.

Slowly taking a few steps back, the doors groan open. The grotesque beast reveals itself, glaring at Trey. Horror stricken, Trey stood numb as the demon charges at him, clenching its hand around his throat. Puncturing tiny holes into Trey's skin with its talon claws, the demon moans as blood trickles down the back of his neck.

Electrifying pain crushes every nerve in Trey's body while he desperately tries to fight the beast off. Smothering his hands over the creature's face, Trey feels the grinding of razor-sharp teeth gnawing his index finger clean off. He attempts to scream, but his effort rendered useless as the demon takes its claws, forcing his mouth open. The beast gradually regurgitates a yellow, rich liquid serum into Trey, immobilizing him from the chest up.

The demon paralyzes Trey's vocal cords and watches his body wobble before falling onto his back, almost cracking his neck. Powerless, Trey is dragged out of his room and down the dormitory hall in the middle of the night.

❈ ❈ ❈

KILLER CREEK LANE

The moon exposes half of its face glowing dimly like a cream disc suspending in the velvet sky. The wind gently blows the sickly smell of rotting garbage from the abandoned homes that even the homeless were afraid to pass. Killer Creek Lane is devoid of all happiness while street light strikes on the shadow of the grotesque beast dragging Trey through the driveway and into Joe McGregor's backyard.

The demon enters the kitchen and opens the basement door. It drags Trey by his left leg down the steep, cracked wooden staircase. Trey's body hits each step harder than the first as if treated like an animal in a butcher house. His head's impact hitting the edge of the steps causes an immense amount of blood to flow down his forehead as he is thrown violently onto the cold concrete ground.

Lifting Trey from the floor, the demon throws him over its shoulders and heads over to a heavy metal fisherman hook nailed to the wall. Immobile, Trey is hooked from the back of his shirt, dangling like a slaughtered pig. After a few minutes, Trey slowly regains consciousness to feel sharp claws slicing his chest repeatedly.

Panic-stricken, Trey swings himself from side to side, begging for the pain to stop. Slapping its clawed hand across Trey's face, the

THE BROTHER'S CURSE

beast walks behind him and proceeds to tie his wrist together with barbed wires. Unhooking Trey from the metal device, the demon places him on an old wooden chair where he waits for his next inflicted torture.

Unraveling silver wires from a steel roller, the demon inches closer to Trey's face and begins to sew his mouth shut slowly. Each incision through his lips feels like a knife digging deep into his temple. Whimpering softly, Trey feels his eyes slowly give away to the darkness. The thought of dying alone in a basement scares him. Never again would he see Crystal, nor hear her call him Trey Trey, a name he grew to love.

Sensing his soul drifting away from his body, Trey defecates on himself. Aroused by the warm urine hitting the ground, the demon unleashes wicked laughter, taunting Trey. With his lips sewn tightly, the beast finally reveals its human form to Trey, causing him to fall backward in his seat. With fear in his eyes, Trey realizes his life is over.

Picking Trey up, the beast walks over to the corner of the room and throws Trey into a rotting corpses pile buried in the homemade grave. Unable to free himself, Trey is left alone in a six-foot underground hole until the demon returns to finish him off. Throwing a few severed limbs over Trey's face, the beast slowly walks up the stairs singing a riddle. It exits the basement, slamming the door shut, leaving Trey in complete darkness.

CHAPTER TWENTY-ONE

LAZURKISMURMA

LAKEVIEW FALLS UNIVERSITY

Clouds drift across the morning sky, like white beds of cotton swaying back and forth, hauntingly. The wind chimes blow in the breeze, rattling the cone-shaped campus bell as a thick fog rapidly disperses over Lakeview Falls University. An aura of gloom surrounds the campus as morning classes are canceled unexpectedly due to the sudden disappearance of Trey Delgado.

Sorrowful sobs from students reverberate up and down the third-floor dormitory hallway while deputies close off the west wing section with a yellow **"DO NOT CROSS"** tape as the forensic team investigates the scene. Sheriff Mills, Deputy Derrick Yin, and Deputy Justin Mills question Humphrey Nicols who resides across Trey. The peculiar hippie has a track record around campus selling non-traceable credit cards to make extra cash on the side.

His hands clutched firmly at his hips; Sheriff Mills' dark eyebrows crinkle together. "Mr. Nicols, did you hear any noises or any violent altercation coming from Mr. Delgado's room between the hours of 1 and 3 a.m. this morning?"

Shuffling through his pants pocket, Humphrey pulls out a used condom wrapper. Raising it towards his nostril, he takes a whiff, scrunching his face. "Well Sheriff, last night I was hanging out with my girlfriend, and she was going to let me get to third base, finally—and I've been so lonely without—"

"Hey, Dick! That's not what he asked you!" Justin bellows, pointing his finger at Humphrey's face.

"Whoa, Justin!" Derrick exclaims, grappling his left arm, taking him aside, "you have to calm down, man. You can't let your emotions get in the way of your professional work."

"This is bullshit, Derrick!" Justin's temper and voice both rising in utter rage, "Trey is our friend! He wouldn't hurt a soul! Why! Why him?"

"Justin, we are going to find him, okay?" Derrick says, stroking his hand against his friend's back, comforting him.

Clicking his teeth, Justin petulantly shakes his head. "Dammit! It's not fair, Derrick!"

Breaking down, Justin is unable to grasp that his friend has vanished. Trey's loyalty to his friends is what sets him apart from anyone he's ever met. He was a friend that would put his life on the line for the ones he loved, no matter what. In his thoughts, Justin questions: "Whoever attacked and kidnapped Trey knew of him, and his disappearance wasn't random like the other missing young guys in town; this looked like it was personal."

Breathing heavily, Sheriff Mills' pulse races, his muscles grow tense as Humphrey continues to rant about his date the night before. "Listen, Mr. Nicols, this is a serious matter; if you saw or heard something across from your room, we need to know!"

Loudly smacking the gum in his mouth, Humphrey cracks his knuckles. "I didn't see anything, but I heard some banging and muffling sounds," he replies, scratching the top of his head.

A long sigh escapes Sheriff Mills' lips. "You heard muffling sounds and banging? And you never thought that maybe someone was possibly being attacked? Why didn't you check it out?" he questions with a brow raised.

"It's a huge campus, Sheriff Mills. The noise I heard could have been a couple of drunks trying to find their way back to their room; it's happened so many times before. One night there was screaming in the hallway, and I did check it out. And guess what? I got a beer bottle smashed over my head by some dirty drunk chick that thought she saw a leprechaun."

A mad glint lingers in the Sheriff's eyes while he fixes his sheriff's hat. "Thank you, Mr. Nicols, that will be all," he says, walking pass the young man, releasing a grunt.

"I'm sorry I couldn't help you, Sheriff Mills. I hope you do find Trey; he's a good guy," Humphrey responds, slowly walking back inside his room.

Scanning the hallway, Sheriff Mills looks left, then right, making a mental note of everything, when his eyes come across a yellow slimy substance on the marble floor by the doorway. Bending over, he withdraws a silver pen from his shirt pocket and carefully dips it into the content. Instantly It disbands, forming an acidic goo.

"What in God's name is this?" Sheriff Mills mutters, backing away from the liquified toxin.

Meanwhile, inside Trey's dorm room, a female forensic analyst collects blood droplets samples on the hard wooden floor beside the computer desk. Extracting the blood and inserting it into a glass tube vial, the analyst notices a severed index finger lying on a slant beside Trey's twin size bed.

She carefully picks up the forefinger with a special tweezer and inspects a small tattoo with the initials **T&C** slightly above the knuckle. Placing the index finger in the clear evidence bag, the forensic specialist marks it off as Victim **T. Delgado Evidence #2.**

Reluctantly tearing his eyes away from Trey's dorm room, Sheriff Mills paces back and forth down the hall, waiting to speak to the forensic specialist. Nervously glancing sideways every minute, he notices something from the corner of his eye. Exiting Trey's room, the forensic analysts approach Sheriff Mills with an evidence bag containing Trey's finger.

"Jesus Christ!" he squirms in disgust, "is that what I think it is?"

"Yes, Sheriff Mills, I collected the finger right beside the missing victim's bed."

"Is that all you found?" Sheriff Mills asks the analyst, hoping that there weren't any other body parts lying around.

"Yes, Sheriff, I've taken samples of Mr. Delgado's blood also. It looks mixed with some sticky substance. I'll take it back to my laboratory and do more testing. For now, I think you should seal off this room, so there's no unwanted tampering," the female analyst says sternly, placing the evidence in a small carry-on ice cooler box.

With a polite gesture, Sheriff Mills tips his hat to the female specialist as he watches her remove her purple latex gloves, throwing them in the trash can before heading down the hall.

Simone, Phillip, and Victoria notice deputies evacuating frantic dorm residents from their west wing rooms as they shove their way through a horde of students. Quickly sliding under the caution tape, they sprint over to Sheriff Mills, who was in the middle of sealing off Trey's room.

"Dad!" Phillip cries out with a worried expression. "What's going on? We heard something happened to Trey. Is he dead?" he asks, putting his hand on his waist, arms crooked like sugar bowl handles.

"For the love of God! What are you three doing here?" Sheriff Mills asks, stomping his feet down-hard enough to create new callouses on top of the preexisting ones. "You have no authority to come in this section; it's closed off for the day, now go home!"

"Come on, Dad, just tell us what happened."

"Phillip, how did you get pass the security?"

"I showed them the sheriff card you have at home, and I told them I was your son."

"Oh, so you broke into my safe? That's just fucking beautiful, so now I have a son who's a kleptomaniac!" Sheriff Mills scowls, yanking Phillip by the back of his neck.

Leaning his lips against Phillip's ears, Sheriff Mills nestles his nose on the tip of his lobe. "Listen to me you little ass hat, just because I'm your father and the sheriff of this goddamn town doesn't give you a get a free pass to a crime scene. Next time you pull that shit, I will have you arrested. Do you understand me?" he grits his teeth, whispering to Phillip?

"Yes, sir," Phillip replies, nodding his head slightly, before being released from his father's forceful grip.

"Now leave! All of you!" Sheriff Mills orders, pointing towards the exit door.

"Dad, please, we need to know what happened to Trey. He's our friend," Phillip pleads with his father.

"I know Trey is your friend, he's a good kid. But in all honesty, I have no idea what happened to him. He's missing; it looks like there was a physical altercation between him and someone else. I have deputies questioning every student that resides on this floor. As of right now, I don't know if Trey is alive or if he's dead. I don't know shit! But since you three are so concerned, did any of you see or speak to Trey yesterday?"

"We saw—We saw him—" Victoria hesitates, thinking of what to tell Sheriff Mills.

Clearing her throat, Simone cuts Victoria off. "We saw him yesterday afternoon at the town hall circle grabbing lunch, but that's it."

"Hmmm," he scratches his chin, staring at Victoria, "did he mention anything about meeting up with anyone after lunch?"

"No, Trey didn't say anything to us. I mean, I don't understand why anyone would want to hurt him," Victoria replies, breaking eye contact with him.

❆ ❆ ❆

While Sheriff Mills continues to converse with Victoria and Phillip, Simone's hazel brown eyes stalk Trey's dorm room that is yet to be closed off to the public. Noticing the door halfway open, Simone sneaks inside the room unnoticed. Her senses are on high alert while glancing around the room—Simone's eyes darts to every spot, stumbling upon the shapeshifter demon book on Trey's computer desk.

Edging a cautious inch closer, Simone grabs hold of the book and places it into her black satchel bag. Taking one last look around the room, she exits the dorm and is startled by Victoria standing by the door, glaring at her with a shady expression.

"Simone, what are you doing?" Victoria asks, looking over Simone's shoulder.

On guard, Simone holds her purse close to her side. "Nothing, I thought I saw something in Trey's room," she says, walking pass Victoria with an intense stare.

"Simone, I think we should tell Sheriff Mills about what Trey told us at the library."

"No, out of the question," Simone shakes her head, disagreeing with Victoria, "we can't say anything to Sheriff Mills. I swear to God Victoria, if you open your big mouth, I will come for you."

"What's your problem Simone," she scowls, "Crystal is my friend too. I don't want anything to happen to her."

"Bullshit Victoria, we all know you pretend to be her friend because of Phillip. You don't give a shit about Crystal or any of us."

Taken aback by Simone's comment, Victoria shakes off the uneasiness that overtakes her. "That's not true Simone. I care about Crystal as much as I do for Trey, and I want to help."

"Fine, you can help by not mentioning what Trey told us."

"What if Trey's dead, Simone? Do you think we're next?" Victoria asks as her hands begin to tremble.

"I don't know Victoria; look, I have to find Crystal. If you hear anything on Trey, tell Phillip to text me."

"Good luck, because whoever is after Crystal will go after you too," Victoria mutters, walking away from her.

❉ ❉ ❉

KILLER CREEK LANE

Opening her white windows inwardly in her sunroom, Crystal allows the sunlight and gentle morning breeze to enter through her sheer cream curtains while she gazes across the street at Mr. McGregor's house. Smitten, love slowly invades her heart as she thinks of the intimate moment she had with Jason. Burying her nose in her pink cashmere sweater, Crystal smells Jason's intoxicating scent devour her every being.

Searching for her cell phone in the living room, Crystal stumbles upon her rose gold device, sitting face down on the foyer table. Turning the phone over, she sees the low battery image display in red. Placing the device on the cordless charger, she notices the phone light up with a **"Doop Da Doop Da Dee"** melody going off before it shows **20** missed calls and text messages from Trey.

"Oh shit!" she shrieks, scrolling through her message box. One message stood out in all capitalized letters **"PLEASE ANSWER ME CRYSTAL! PLEASE! I NEED TO SEE YOU!"** Calling Trey immediately after reading his urgent text, Crystal hears his voicemail go off after one ring.

"The number you have dialed is disconnected, message 4678."

Slowly dragging in air, Crystal eases it out of her lungs. A sickening feeling takes over her entire body as she listens to the busy signal on the other end of the line. What if something happened to him? What if he called her because he was hurt? Crystal asked herself.

Scurrying over to the coat hanger, Crystal grabs her jacket, scarf, and crossbody purse. Unplugging her cell phone, she decides to go to Lakeview Falls University to find him. Grasping the brass knob, Crystal opens the door and is surprised to see Simone standing on her front porch.

Her eyes widen with fear as negative thoughts race through her mind about Trey. "Simone? What are you doing here?" Crystal asks.

"Crystal, there's something I need to tell you," Simone says softly, brushing a strand of hair matter from her face.

Throwing her crossbody purse over her shoulders, Crystal becomes irritated. "Can it wait, Simone? I have to head over to the university to find Trey; I received twenty missed calls from him."

Simone heaves a sigh, her brown eyes are serious, staring intensely at Crystal. "So that means Trey never showed up to your house last night."

"What are you talking about, Simone? Did something happened to Trey?"

"Trey is missing, Crystal."

"What do you mean he's missing?" Crystal cries out frantically. Clamping her hands over her mouth, Crystal quickly lets her gaze drop; her eyes do not lift, not even for a second.

"No one knows what happened to him. There are deputies all over campus. Right now, they think someone kidnapped him."

"Oh my God! No, not Trey, this can't be happening," Crystal sobs uncontrollably. The essence of misery swirl through her with a broken heart and a battered soul. Oblivious to the world around her, a wave of pain crushes every part of Crystal. It's as if she has fallen into a dark abyss.

Glancing over her shoulders, Simone thinks she sees a dark shadow staring at her from Mr. McGregor's townhouse cottage window. She shakes her head as if to chase away such thoughts.

"Crystal, there's something important that I have to tell you, but we can't stay here."

A frown falls upon Crystal's lips. "Where do you want to go, Simone?"

"The Town Hall Cafe might be the safest place at this point. We can take my car," Simone suggests, reaching out to take Crystal's hand.

CHAPTER TWENTY-TWO

THE BOOK

TOWN HALL CAFE

Bakery air steams through the chimney, and buttery fumes travel outside the Town Hall Cafe and Bakery doors. Built-in 1963, the wholesome mom and pop bakery shop has catered to Lakeview Falls residents for sixty-two years. Now owned by Sierra Melonmock and her daughter Carmella, the mother and daughter duo maintains their family's business by serving homemade coffee grown from their famous vanilla velvet bean farm in the town of Hunters Point Lane.

Welcoming all those who visit the cafe, the Melonmocks create a never-ending warm and inviting embrace. Each morning, the bakery-cafe fills with the distinct aroma of rising dough transforming into a delicious tray of oatmeal cookies and donuts, with mystery fillings gleam in their luminous frosting to tame the worst sweet-tooth.

The savory goodies are packed and delivered every week to children in the town. Homeschooled by their parents, the little boys and girls of Lakeview Falls are kept safe from the evil that lurks within while enjoying warm pastries from the town hall cafe—committing themselves to support the locals during the scariest time in Lakeview Falls history. The Melonmocks promise as long as they are still alive, they will continue serving the great citizens of the most wicked town in the state of Michigan.

※ ※ ※

Ordering a coffee, Simone and Crystal sit at a square shape table by an open window. Slumped back in her chair, Crystal's bleary eyes fixate on Simone, who sits nervously waiting for the barista to bring her the hot beverage. Watching the sunset over the branches, scraping the windowpane, she sighs in frustration.

"Simone, you have to say something to me. We can't sit here staring at each other all day. What happened to Trey?" she whimpers, grasping a table napkin to dry her teary eye.

Removing the book from her lap, Simone lays it softly on the table. Withering away with guilt for Trey's disappearance, Simone decides to reveal the truth to Crystal on what Trey discovered about Jason and what he is.

As the female barista approaches their table, she places two cups of coffee in front of Crystal and Simone. She reaches inside her neatly pressed apron and pulls out six sweetener packets, and hands three to each of them. With a warm-hearted smile, the barista walks away to attend to another table.

Sipping her coffee slowly, Simone withdraws the off white mug from her lips. "Trey messaged me, Victoria, and Terrance last night to meet him at the school library. He tried numerous times to reach you, but the calls were going straight to voicemail. So, in desperation, Trey decided to tell us what he discovered."

"What did Trey tell you, Simone? If you know something, then tell me already."

Extending her hands, Simone then pushes the shapeshifter demon book directly at her. "Take a look."

Crystal stares intensely at the disturbing image on the cover of the book. Her eyes lock on the engraved baby gargoyles before opening to the first page. "What is this, Simone?"

"Trey found this book; there's something that he desperately wanted you to see, Crystal. I'm not sure how you will react, but you must know the truth."

"The truth about what, Simone?" Crystal asks while glancing at the images of 18th-century demons. "This is an old demonology book. What does this have to do with me?"

"Crystal, Trey thinks that you're in grave danger. He is positive that Jason Warwick is out to kill you."

"Danger? Jason is out to kil—What?" Crystal backs away from the table with a distorted expression, "I'm so confused right now. I know that Trey isn't a fan of Jason since Gabby's death but to accuse him of wanting to hurt me. That's not Trey— he would never come up with something so silly like that. You must have heard wrong."

"Crystal, last night Trey was watching the news and saw a little girl holding up a photo of her brother that was flayed alive along with her parents. The photo was a picture of a guy named Jason Holliston. He looks identical to the guy that you're dating. Trey thinks he killed Jason Holliston and stole his skin."

"Stole his skin!" Crystal belts out in disbelief, swiftly pushing the book back to Simone, "Do you have any idea how crazy you sound right now?"

"I know it sounds crazy, Crystal, but it's true; after Trey spoke to us, he was supposed to head over to your house last night to show this book and an article he printed out from an online site that has the full story of that slain family."

"So, this is why Trey was trying to contact me?" Crystal sniffles, "what's so important about this book and that murdered family?"

"Crystal, Trey believes that Jason might be a shapeshifter demon."

"A what?" she shakes her head in bewilderment, "you cannot be serious? Is this a joke?"

"No, it's not a joke, Crystal? Trey is missing now, all because he found this book. I believe him."

"Why would you think that Jason is a Shapeshifter, Simone? They don't exist. Those are mystical creatures from books like this one in front of us."

"Crystal, mystical creatures have surfaced for decades in our town. Most have been a myth, but some have been true. You are smarter than this Crystal; whatever this guy is doing to you, it seems to be clouding your judgment."

"You don't know him, Simone."

"Neither do you, Crystal. Jason is too good to be true; he moves to Lakeview Falls, and in two weeks, he has you in the palm of his hands. Do you know anything about him? Have you asked him about his life, his family, where he comes from?" Simone asks with an intense gaze.

"Yes, Simone. Jason has spoken to me about a few things in his past, and frankly, I don't feel comfortable disclosing his personal life to you. It's not my place."

"Well, whatever Jason told you, might all be a big lie; I want you to take a look at this," Simone says, flipping the page to **Chapter 66**. Shifting the book towards Crystal, Simone points at the grotesque images of a half-human, half-demon creature devouring body parts, including young males' hearts.

Horror stricken, Crystal's stomach turns icy. She feels as though something has walked through her, leaving her limbs numb and shaky. "Are you saying that Jason is this demon?"

"I think so, Crystal. The recent murders that have been happening in Lakeview Falls have a clear pattern. Only men are being attacked, eaten, or skinned. The only thing that can kill this way is **Lazurkismurma Demons.** They are the first half-human and first flesh-eating shapeshifter demons from the late 1700s. These demons prey on young males' flesh to preserve their appearance and existence; also, they can shape-shift into anyone they kill or get into contact with at any time."

"This is a lot to process, Simone," Crystal sighs, "how can Jason be a demon?" she mutters softly.

"Lazurkismurma's can glamour a person into not seeing their real identity, that's unless they want to reveal themselves to you, but it's rare. What's creepy about them is that they can also put you in a terrible sexual trance. This demon can shift into a very nasty looking creature with an erect serpent, causing their partner to hallucinate and see illusions. Check this out," Simone says, turning the page to **Chapter 75,** pointing at the photo of the amethyst stone necklace.

"When I noticed your necklace, I was amazed at how beautiful and rare it is, but when Trey saw it in this book, he put two and two together. These demons and that necklace are part of a prophecy. The story Professor Baptist told us in class is true, and if this is the same stone that locked up those Shapeshifters, then that means that Mastema's sons will come back to take what's theirs."

"And what would that be, Simone? How can a necklace that my mom left for me be a target for two brothers?"

"Mastema's sons need that necklace, Crystal. The brothers have to retrieve it on your birthday, and they need your blood in return for their father and other demonic spirits. Girl, you are wearing some bad juju. That pendant around your neck holds twenty-five demons. If anyone gets in the brother's way in the process of them trying to resurrect their father, they will kill them. And it only gets worse if you break the cycle."

"What cycle? What does that mean, Simone?"

"When you received the necklace, did anyone touch it?"

The walls close in on Crystal when she remembers how mesmerized Gabby was when she saw the amethyst stone necklace. "Oh my God! Gabby," she gasps.

"Crystal, did Gabby touch the necklace?"

Hearing her phone vibrate, Crystal takes it out of her pants pocket. Staring intensely at the screen, she sees that it's a message from her Aunt Jaqueline. "Simone, I have to go," Crystal says, quickly rising from her seat, grasping her coat and purse.

"Wait, Trey put the article inside the book; it has the photo of Jason Holliston," Simone says, shuffling through the pages of the book. "Shit, it's not in here," she groans inwardly, realizing that the article is missing.

"Can I take this book, Simone?"

"Yeah, sure. What are you going to do with it, Crystal?"

Grasping the book, Crystal firmly grips it in her right hand. "I'm going to get some answers about where this necklace came from," she says to Simone, storming out of the cafe.

KILLER CREEK LANE

Thrusting her front door like a destructive force of nature, Crystal is ready to destroy everything in her path. Placing her coat and purse on the foyer table, she smells an aroma of ground beef mixed with sweet onions coming from the kitchen.

"Crystal, is that you?" Jaqueline calls out from the back room.

Taking deep breaths, Crystal walks down the hall, advancing towards the kitchen entrance. Observing her aunt facing the stove while lining taco shells on a baking tray, Crystal remains silent. A boiling fury surges inside of her as she violently slams the shape-shifter book on the dining table, startling her aunt.

"Crystal!" she presses her hand over her chest in shock, "you scared the crap out of me! I was preparing you and Alex some dinner. What's going on?"

"I'm not hungry, Aunty J."

"Crystal, where did you get that?" Jaqueline asks, glancing at the brown embroidered book. She moves away from the stove, distancing herself from Crystal with a frightened expression.

"I take it you've seen this before?" Crystal replies, opening the book to page 205, showing her the photo of the purple pendant.

An eerie silence takes over the room while Crystal glares at her aunt. "I'm going to ask you where this came from, and I swear to God you better not lie to me."

"What do you want to know, Crystal?"

"Where did Grandma get this necklace? Why did she give it to my mom to pass it on to me?"

Before her aunt can respond to the question, Alexandria enters the kitchen, interrupting her sister and aunt in a heated conversation. "Hey, what's going on? I heard a loud noise from upstairs, is everything okay?" she asks them.

Walking over to her niece, Jaqueline places her hand on Alexandria's back. She escorts her out of the kitchen. "Alexandria, I think you should go to your room. Your sister and I have important matters to discuss."

"No!" Crystal hollers, grabbing her sister's hand, pulling her back into the kitchen, "Alex stays here. She has every right to hear this too. My sister is not going to get shunned out of what you've been keeping from me. Alex deserves to know what's going on. Now, why did Mom give me this necklace?" Crystal asks, pulling the chain from under her sweater.

"Holy shit! Mom left that for you, Crystal? Why do you always have to get the good stuff?" Alex whines, taking a seat at the kitchen table.

"Trust me, Alex, you don't want this necklace."

"Crystal, what the hell is going on? Why are you so pissed with Aunty J?"

"How about we let our favorite aunt explain that!" Crystal directs her gaze at Jaqueline, "so, what are you waiting for, aunty J? Tell me where the necklace came from!"

"Your mom was given that necklace on her fifteenth birthday. Grandma took her into a private room, where she told her something in secrecy. Of course, as a thirteen-year-old, I was nosy and tried to listen behind the door. After about fifteen minutes, I heard your mother burst into tears. When she came out of that room, she looked distraught."

"What did Grandma tell my mom, Aunty J?" Crystal asks while streams of tears flow down from her eyes. "It must have been something horrible if it caused her to cry."

"Crystal, the moment your mom wore the amethyst pendant, she began to have terrible nightmares. Her dreams were severely tormenting her to the point that she took it off and hid it. I never saw that necklace again, not until your mom brought it to my house to give it to you on your 25th birthday. Even though the necklace did things to my sister, she had no choice but to pass it on to you, Crystal. She had to follow the rules that were made by our ancestors. Every firstborn female must receive the necklace and protect it from the shifters without breaking the cycle. Your grandmother told your mom that no one outside the family could touch the stone."

Charging at her aunt, Crystal pushes her against the kitchen wall. "Oh my God! You knew this, and you still let me put it on? So what, are we witches?"

"No, our ancestors were. But we all hold a special force not as strong as you; you're the last generation to receive the necklace," Jaqueline confesses.

"Do you have any idea what this thing is doing to me?"

"I'm sure it isn't pleasant," Jaqueline whispers.

"My best friend is dead because of this stone! Gabby touched it!" Crystal shouts, kicking one of the kitchen chairs to the marble floor.

"What else do you know about this, Aunty J? What happens to me?"

"I swear to God I don't know anything else, Crystal."

"There are two monsters after this stone, and they're killing off my friends, and you're telling me that you don't know anything else?"

"I'm so sorry, Crystal! But there's nothing I or anyone else can do. Your fate is sealed, and unfortunately, this is your destiny."

"My destiny for what?"

"For the brother's to find you and kill you."

"Kill her!" Alexandria jolts up from her seat, "what? No, this isn't true!" Alexandria exclaims, running over to her aunt.

"Are you saying that my mom left this for me, knowing that I was going to die? She wrote on the card that the necklace would save me."

"She said that because that was the only way to get you to put it on, Crystal. Your mother didn't have a choice; this killed her inside for many years, knowing what would happen to you. Our ancestors predicted the prophecy centuries ago; this was going to happen whether you liked it or not."

Crystal feels a gut-wrenching pain that pierces her very soul as she listens to her aunt confess their family secrets. She grabs a coffee mug from the kitchen sink and throws it in her aunts direction.

"You bitch!"

"Crystal, take it easy," Alex says, clasping her sister's arm, "you know aunty j wouldn't lie to us, right? Right aunty, J?" she tilts her head to the side, waiting for her aunt to respond.

"That's why you were acting funny when I opened that box; I can't believe you! I don't deserve this shit! I was happy where I was until I moved back here!"

"Don't you get it, Crystal! It doesn't matter if you were still away at school. Those brothers would still hunt you down regardless. I'm so sorry that this is the way you had to find out, Crystal."

"I hate you! Get out!" Crystal says, pointing towards the front door.

"What? Crystal, please, you don't want to do this. Let me help you."

"It's too late for help! Now get the fuck out of our house! You're no family to me. Get out! Don't you ever come back to my house!"

"Crystal, please!" her aunt pleads, clasping her hands together.

Snatching her aunt by her forearm, Crystal drags her out of the kitchen towards the front door. Struggling to unleash herself, Jacqueline sobs while Alexandria tries to pull Crystal away from her. Betrayed by a woman who vowed to protect her and her sister, Crystal throws her aunt onto the porch slamming the door shut.

"Oh my God, Crystal, what has gotten into you?" Alexandria says, horrified by her sister's actions.

"Alex, you have no idea what she and Mom have been hiding from us. There are two guys after me! After this!" she points to her necklace. "I never want to see that bitch again!"

"Crystal! Do you think Jason is one of those guys?"

Biting her lip to keep herself from crying, Crystal collapses on the floor, dejected, swollen with emotions realizing her chosen fate. "I don't know Alex, but if Jason is, I have to find a way to stop him."

CHAPTER TWENTY-THREE

BODY COUNT

PIKE HILL LANE

Paralyzed by the painful feeling of isolation, hot torrents of grief stream down Jaqueline's round face as she drives up Pike Hill Lane. Her lips begin to tremble as she tries to focus on the main road. Clasping one hand on the steering wheel, Jaqueline uses her free hand to straighten her tilted rearview mirror. Shifting it to a better angle, Jaqueline takes a glance at the puffiness under her eyes. She never cried so much in her life, as much as she did at that moment. Betraying her niece to protect the secret of her family's coven comes with a price, and it's the body and soul of her beloved niece Crystal.

Wanting to be as far away as possible from Lakeview Falls, Jaqueline decides to pay a visit to her significant other, whom she's been intimately involved with for a year and a half. Entering the private residential area, Jaqueline drives up the steep hill. From a distance, she sees the magnificent 17th-century brick stone Victorian house.

Surrounded by neatly trimmed trees and the greenest grass, the three-story house has large pointed towers that rise from the roof, accentuating above the front entrance. The exquisite stained-glass window imported from France covers the stone lintels and sills at the very ends.

Parking her SUV in the open-spaced driveway, Jaqueline checks her appearance one last time before exiting her vehicle. Her high heel boots slap against the pavement as she makes her way up the cobblestone steps. With a sad whimper, Jaqueline heaves a sigh while running her manicured fingers through her silk pressed locks.

Taking in a deep breath to relax her tense muscles, she slowly exhales, fixing her black blazer jacket. Approaching the door with a silent step, Jaqueline extends her index finger, pressing down on the solid brass doorbell button. A sense of loneliness plagues her as she listens to the creaking sounds of the door opening.

Revealing himself to Jaqueline, Professor Baptist stands beside his door with an alluring smile. "Jaqueline, mon chéri, is everything okay? You look upset," he says with a rich and deep creole accent, pulling her into a warm embrace.

Sobbing, Jaqueline looks at Jean extremely dazed with discontent in her eyes. "Oh Jean, I'm sorry for coming so late, I've been driving around for a while, and I didn't know where else to go."

"Shhh, Shhh, mon amor," he whispers, wrapping his broad arms comfortably around her petite body. "There's no need to apologize, Jackie. Come inside, I will pour you a glass of wine," he says in a sensual tone.

Glancing at the dim street lights along the road, barely managing to keep themselves alive, Professor Baptist escorts Jaqueline inside his home, and slowly shuts his front door.

❊ ❊ ❊

LAKEVIEW FALLS SHERIFF'S DEPARTMENT

While the heavy winds blow across Fearman Street, the sky becomes dark. Like an iceberg, the misty cold night seems to harden around Simone as she hurries up the granite steps towards the front door of Lakeview Falls Sheriff's department. Florescent lights glare on the marble tile floors as Simone strolls down the lobby wearing black faded, ripped jeans, a crop beige sweater, and thigh-high leather boots that hug her tone legs.

Approaching the visitor's waiting room, Simone glances inside and notices distraught parents showing each other photos of their missing children. While deputies spent their morning investigating Trey's disappearance, five teenage boys were kidnapped at Fearman Street Park while playing basketball.

Local shop owners at the Town Hall Circle agreed to cooperate with the Sheriff's department by handing in all video footage recorded from outside their stores in hopes of catching the maniac that has been terrorizing their town and killing the youths. Listening to the onslaught of sobs of mothers weeping while burying their faces on their husbands' chest, Simone walks away and heads over to the main deputies' section **DP678**.

Observing Justin banging his pen on his desk to release ink, Simone approaches his station. The sweet apple scent of her perfume assaults his nostrils instantly catching his attention. Deputy Mills has fancied the spiritual enchantress since their high school years but never pursued her romantically due to her toxic relationship with the late Coltan Hayes.

Justin feels flustered, having Simone in his presence. His hands become clammy, and his face flushes a crimson red. He loses himself in her beauty as a smile tugs at the corner of his lips.

"Simone, what are you doing here so late? Shouldn't you be back at the dorm?"

"Justin, I came here because I wanted to know if you've heard anything on Trey?" she asks, taking a seat at his desk.

"No, not yet, Simone," he sits back in his seat, twiddling his pen between his fingers, "we are doing everything we can to find him. For now, we have deputies patrolling each lane and questioning anyone that might have saw him earlier that day. If I do hear anything, you will be the first to know."

For a second, Simone stood quiet. Still, she wasn't ready to back down from finding Trey, not just yet. Lost in her thought, Simone had to solve the mystery of Jason's other half.

His eyes fixed on hers, Justin's head cocks to one side. "Is there something else that you needed, Simone?"

"Justin, I need your help. I have to get into Trey's dorm room."

"What? Why?"

"Trey might have left something in there that can help with his disappearance."

"Like what, Simone? We checked every inch of that room. Besides the severed finger the analysts found, there's nothing else in that room."

"Listen to me, Justin, Trey has something important in that dorm. If I don't find it, then our lives are on the line."

"Simone, what's going on? If you knew something was in his room that could have helped us, then why didn't you tell my father or me earlier when you were at the university?"

"It's complicated, Justin; I had something that I had to take care of earlier."

"So you're telling me that there were more important things to attend to then helping us find our friend that could be hurt or worse killed?" Laying back in his seat, Justin huffs under his breath.

"I'm sorry, Justin. I know that I should have told you before, but I need you to help me get in that room now."

"Simone, I can't. It's closed off. Only law enforcement is allowed in there."

"Duh, that's why I need you to come with me," she says, squinting at him.

"Can you at least tell me what we are looking for, Simone?" he asks, shuffling through his paperwork on his desk in search of his car keys.

"I'll explain everything to you once we get to the university. Please, you have to trust me, Justin."

The chair squeaks as Justin gets up from my seat. "I do trust you, Simone. I hope that you find whatever it is you are looking for in that room because if you don't, it's my ass on the line."

Grabbing his deputy jacket, Justin and Simone sneak out the station's back door and drive to Lakeview Falls University.

❈ ❈ ❈

PIKE HILL LANE

Seated comfortably on the leather sofa in the elegant Victorian living room, Jaqueline observes Jean's perfect posture as he walks towards her with two glasses of French red wine. Taking a seat beside her, Jean hands her the drink.

"Cheri, talk to me, what happened?" he asks, gently placing his hand on her left leg.

Resting her head on Jean's shoulders, an involuntary whimper escapes Jaqueline's lips. "I had a terrible fight with my niece, Crystal. She kicked me out of her house."

Stroking his fingers behind the back of her neck, Jean nestles his nose against Jaqueline's ear. "Mon amor, I am so sad to hear that. Why would she do that to you? I thought you were very close with Crystal."

"It's all my fault, Jean; I kept a secret from her for many years—," she stutters, "I've lost her for good— she will never forgive me," Jaqueline wails, reaching into her purse for a Kleenex.

"Do you want to talk about it, my love?"

Wiping a tear from her eye, Jean cradles Jaqueline in his arms. His loving touch helps her forget the pain. The corner of Jaqueline's lips twitches before spreading into a smile.

"I do Jean, but I'm not supposed to share my family history with anyone."

"Well, I'm not just anyone, Jackie. I am your partner, and you can trust me, so please tell me, why is Crystal so upset with you?"

"I don't know how to explain this to you, but here it goes," she says, letting out a shaky breath. "Before my sister's murder, she gave me a necklace to give to Crystal for her 25th birthday. The only problem is that this is not an ordinary pendant. It holds Twenty-five demons inside. And it gets worse; two 18th century shapeshifter brothers are after Crystal to retrieve the stone."

In shock, Jean tries to open his mouth to speak, but no words seem to flow out. A bitter taste of bile mix with wine rise from the back of his mouth. Clearing his throat, he tries to make sense of what he was hearing.

Her eyes fixed on his, Jaqueline gently places her hands on each side of his face. "Jean," she whispers," please say something."

"Jackie, I was not expecting a story like that."

"You think that I am crazy, right? I'm sure you will be running for the hills after tonight."

A chuckle escapes his lips. "Nonsense Jackie, I am not running anywhere. I believe you."

"You do?"

"Yes, I do, mon amour. I know a lot of old spirits. Most practitioners of the voodoo decent believe in entities magically placed in antique jewels. Maybe it would be best for Crystal to take it off," Jean suggests.

"Jean!" she exclaims, "she cannot take it off. Crystal must keep the necklace on at all times."

"Cheri, I want to help you. Do you think Crystal would speak to me?"

"Speak to you?" she asks with a puzzled expression, backing away from him, "do you know Crystal?"

"She came to one of my workshops at the university; I'm sure I can be of some help. If you believe that Crystal is in danger, then we should go to her house and speak to her."

"No!" she extends her trembling hands, placing them on Jean's chest. "You don't understand Jean, that necklace is powerful and dangerous. The two men that are after it are no match for neither one of us. If we try to get in their way, we could be next to die."

"Jaqueline, please relax, my love; whatever is going on, I can help you, okay? You are safe with me."

"Thank you, Jean, but It's too late; the brothers are here already. I don't even know how Crystal can kill them."

"Jackie, you mustn't give up on family. We all have loved ones we want to save. Don't worry mon amour; you will find the answers you're looking for."

"I love you so much, Jean. What would I do without you?" Jaqueline says softly, moving her hands to his face and caressing his cheeks.

Locking his eyes onto hers, Jean gazes upon Jaqueline's lips. Leaning in, he possesses her inner soul. It's gentle like cotton, melting her heart. Licking the bottom of her lips, Jean kisses her passionately. Slowly closing her eyes, Jaqueline takes in his warm breath in her mouth.

Clasping her hand on the back of Jean's head, Jaqueline suddenly feels a burning sensation in her esophagus. Like hot lava ejecting out of a volcano, an explosion of pain erupts inside Jaqueline's throat, causing it to swell up. Desperately trying to pull herself away from Jean, Jaqueline is grappled by him in a tight hold. Punching him repeatedly with her fist, Jaqueline is terror-stricken to see Jean's beautiful brown eyes display an awful red glow from the pits of hell. His pupils form instantly into a diamond shape that resembles a feline.

Digging her acrylic nails deep into his arms as hard as she could, Jaqueline's cuticles tear, trickling blood onto the mahogany wooden floor. She feels Jean regurgitate a thick clear fluid into her mouth. The acidic liquid slowly burns off her bottom lips, leaving a massive hole above her chin. The reaction to the volatile fluid sends her entire body into a violent convulsive state.

Withdrawing himself from Jaqueline, Jean rises from the couch and watches her body engulf with smoke from the acidic reaction. Jaqueline's body brutally twitches back and forth while her eyes melt into her face, causing her smooth melanin skin to bubble, forming boils the size of golf balls.

Gradually liquefying into an orange-colored glop, Jaqueline dissolves into the leather couch. The smell of burning flesh ferments the oval-shaped living room, releasing a pungent odor similar to rotting eggs. Observing the dissolved organs dripping off the sofa, Jean props up his shirt collar while sneering at the remains of Jaqueline.

"Tsk, tsk, remember when I said you would get the answer, mon amour? Well, guess what?" a burst of wicked laughter escapes his lips, "I do have the answer. Drumroll—please!" he says, making a drum base sound with his mouth.

"And the answer is—I am going to get my amethyst stone and gut your fucking niece till there's nothing left of her," he says with a harsh tone to his voice.

Strolling over to the kitchen counter, Jean glares at the remains of the real Professor Baptist half-eaten torso lying on the tile floor. With a wicked expression smeared across his face, he takes a sip of the red wine before chucking the glass at the stainless steel refrigerator. Releasing a sardonic snicker, Jean walks towards the patio door. He slowly turns the knob, letting himself out while whistling a classical tune.

CHAPTER TWENTY-FOUR

DARKNESS

LAKEVIEW FALLS UNIVERSITY

The far end of the West Wing section had been closed off for the entire day, while forensic analysts collected all samples and evidence from Trey's room. Restricting students from entering their residential apartments, Sheriff Mills blocked off the third-floor dormitory with orange and white retractable cones from one end to the other. Temporarily locked down for the next seven days, the west wing dorms will be adequately cleaned and disinfected for students who still reside on campus.

Sliding under the **Do Not Cross** strip, Simone and Justin quietly make their way towards Trey's dorm room. The low lighting in the hall gives the impression of an insane asylum. The bitter, cruel air coming from the open window forces Simone to pull her leather jacket's edges together. While the gelid winds nip at Simone's neck, chilling her to the bone, her attention focuses on capturing the villain that has caused nothing but pain and torment to her peers, including her childhood friend Crystal.

Being both brave and foolish, Simone cannot withstand the prolonged torture of not-knowing where Trey is. Not knowing whether he is dead or alive, she tries to convince herself that she can find a way to piece the rest of the puzzle and finish what he started. Putting her life on the line to save Crystal, Simone's loyalty is unquestioned.

Approaching Trey's dorm room, Simone and Justin stare at the yellow and black **CAUTION** Barricade tape attached to the front door. Withdrawing dark blue latex gloves from his deputy jacket, Justin carefully detaches the sign. Turning the knob counter-clockwise, Justin opens the door.

The smell of danger lingers in the musty air as they both enter Trey's room. Shielding her mouth, Simone is taken back by the disgusting odor coming from the brown area rug by Trey's full-sized bed located by the cream-colored wall.

"Uggh," her nose twitches in disgust, "I don't remember the room smelling like this earlier."

"Earlier? Simone? Were you in Trey's room before?" Justin asks, lowering his eyebrow in confusion.

"I might have taken a peak," Simone says nervously, scrunching her top lip.

"A peak?" Justin groans, his shoulders rise and fall before he speaks again, "Jesus Sim, you know if you got caught-"

"Don't worry, Justin. Sheriff Mills didn't see me—"

A sudden sigh escapes Justin's lips as he looks around the room. "So what exactly are you looking for, Simone?" he asks, noticing a group photo hung on the wall above the computer desk of him, Trey, John, Simone, Phillip, Terrance, and Crystal on their graduation day six years prior.

"I'm looking for an article Trey printed out from his computer of a murdered family from Omaha Nebraska," Simone replies, scanning every section of Trey's room. Nearing his oak wood dresser, Simone pulls each drawer open. "Dammit, where did he put it?" she mutters to herself while shuffling through Trey's rainbow-colored boxer briefs.

"Is this why you dragged me out of the station Simone? You needed to find a news article?" he shakes his head in frustration while staring at the clutter of clothes scattered on the wooden floor. "What's so important about this article Simone?"

"Justin, there's a family that was slain four weeks ago in their home, and one of them was a college graduate named Jason Holliston. He was the oldest son of three, that was found dead."

For a moment, Justin stood still; it was never easy for him to process the murder of an innocent family. His hands clutched to his hips; he lets out a breath of exhaustion. "Simone, don't you think that searching for our friend is more important than looking for an article on a deceased family? I thought you said there was something in this room that can help us find Trey."

"There is Justin; the only way to find Trey Is to find the asshole that is responsible for his disappearance. And that's why I need to find that damn article, Justin!" she cries out, unable to keep calm.

"Simone, please calm down. If you can't find the article here, then maybe we can go back to the station and look it up on my computer," Justin suggests, removing his deputy hat, revealing his short wavy brown locks.

"I checked the computer already, Justin; the article disappeared from every online site. I don't know how that happened. I've searched multiple websites, from **Shazoo** to **Loople**. It's like someone made it vanish into thin air."

Closing the dresser drawers, Simone turns around. Her lips downturned into a pout as she gazes at Justin. "You have to trust me, this is important. If I don't find that article, then we are screwed," a groan escapes her lips while she stares around the room again. Glancing towards the end of Trey's bed, Simone notices a porn magazine.

Advancing a step closer, she sees the glossy erotic mag under the leg of the bed. Titled **"Grab Em by the Balls,"** the latest issue of *Men Loves Men*, displays a shirtless male exotic dancer sitting on a leopard print fur rug, wearing a diamond-encrusted thong with his legs spread open.

Staring awkwardly at the magazine, Simone stops herself from judging Trey's distasteful collection of entertainment. Instead, she continues to scan around the bed. In shock, she sees a grey paper with lettering sticking out from underneath the mattress. "Holy shit! I think I found it?" Simone exclaims.

"Be careful, Simone; try not to get your fingerprint on that," Justin says, pointing at the paper with his small flashlight.

Kneeling, Simone bends her neck in an awkward position to get a better view. Relieved; she realizes that it's the same article folded in two. Extending her left hand, she takes hold, pulling it towards her. Stained with a yellow substance, Simone carefully handles the material, grasping the paper from the corner.

Taking a seat on Trey's bed, Simone takes a deep breath while staring at the folded paper. "This is it, Justin, this is what will help us find Trey."

Walking over to the bed, Justin sits beside Simone. "So— are you going to explain to me what's going on?" he asks, watching Simone unravel the article.

"It's a long story, Justin."

"Well, we don't have much time Simone, my dad schedule deputies to patrol this area in the next half hour. Now, if there's something that can help us find Trey, then this would be a great time to tell me."

"Okay," she says softly, handing him the article, "yesterday, Trey was watching the news, and he saw a special broadcast on the slain family. Their murder is similar to the deaths that have been happening here in Lakeview Falls."

Listening to Simone, Justin's eyes dart to the photo of Jason Holliston. "Hold on," he gulps, glancing at Simone before looking back at the picture. Rubbing his eyes, Justin clears his throat.

"Isn't this the same guy that Crystal brought to Gabriela's funeral? I remember him; he's the guy Trey was arguing with, right?"

"Yes, and no, Justin," shifting her body towards Justin, Simone brushes her hands over her knees. "This guy is the real Jason, not the one we saw with Crystal."

"I'm sorry, what? What do you mean, the real Jason, Simone?"

"Justin, Trey discovered that Jason Warwick is not the person he says he is. Jason is a shapeshifter demon."

"Shapeshifter demon?" Justin shrieks, scratching the side of his neck. "Here in Lakeview Falls? Is that even possible? I mean— Shapeshifters?"

"Yes, Justin—" she clicks her teeth, "Trey found a demonology book that explains what they are and how they can transform into any human being they come in contact with."

"I—I," he repeatedly stutters, "I don't know what to say, Simone."

"I knew you wouldn't believe me," she says, burying her face in her hands.

"Hey," he whispers, grabbing hold of her hand, "I never said I didn't believe you, Simone. Lakeview Falls has seen a lot of crazy shit—from ghost sightings to paranormal stuff. Let's not forget about Froshkada," he says hesitantly, looking away with fear in his eyes. "Jesus— so you think this Jason Warwick killed the guy in Nebraska?"

"I do—I know this all seems bizarre, Justin, but it makes sense. The minute Trey saw this article and read the demonology book, he knew he was in danger. Everything that is occurring is because of a necklace Crystal received from her late mother."

"A necklace? What necklace, Simone?"

"That's another long story, Justin. Listen, all you need to know is that Jason, along with his mystery brother, is out to kill Crystal. They are after that necklace, and they have to retrieve it on her birthday. I want to help her, Justin, but It looks like whoever tries to get in their way are either dying or disappearing."

"Did you say that Jason wants to kill Crystal?— Simone, you need to tell me everything that you know— you are not alone. I can talk to my dad and—"

"Justin, No! You can't tell Sheriff Mills anything. No one else can know."

"No one else? Simone? Who else knows about this?"

"Besides you? Victoria, Phillip, Terrance, and of course, Crystal."

"Crystal knows? Shit— how is she handling this?"

"Not very well, Justin. It would be hard for anyone to process something like this."

"So now that we know, does this mean we can potentially become targets also— just like Trey?"

"It's possible, Justin."

"So? Now what, Simone? What are we supposed to do with this kind of information?"

"You have to arrest Jason!"

"Arrest him?" his eyes widen, bewildered by her suggestion. "On what grounds, Simone? I can't arrest this guy, not based solely on a photo or an assumption that he's a shapeshifter. I need proof that he killed that family. All I can do is run a background check on him once I get back to the station."

"He's dangerous, Justin; I feel it in my gut. What if Jason knew Trey was on to him, and he decided to hurt him?" Simone asks, folding the article and placing it in her purse.

"I'll take that," Justin says, extending his right palm out to her.

"What? Justin, I need to show this to Crystal."

"Simone, the forensic team took photos of every item in this room. Each one, as you can see, is marked off with a number card."

"But Justin, this was underneath the bed. They couldn't have noticed it," she pleads while hesitating to hand over the article.

"I think you should let me have it, Simone. That way, if anyone questions why it's missing, I will take the blame for it."

"But you can lose your job for that, Justin."

"I don't care, Simone, I wouldn't allow you to get arrested for this," Justin responds, taking possession of the article.

Allowing a weary smile to loosen her heart-shaped lips, Simone inches closer to him. "You would do that for me, Justin?"

"Of course Sim," he replies, throwing his muscular arms around her in a genuine embrace.

Justin's deep blue eyes hold her fast in a surprisingly intense connection. "Anything you need, I'm always here for you, Sim. I know that you have been through a lot this past couple of weeks, and I'm sorry about what happened to Coltan."

Hair strands bordering Simone's face hides the solemn tear that streams from her eyes. She exposes her vulnerable side while emotions within stir, revealing a connection she once shared between her and Justin.

"Thank you, Justin, but you don't have to say something you don't mean. I know you weren't fond of Coltan. It's my fault. I knew how you felt about me, and I still chose to be with him instead of you."

Within a split second, Justin quickly realizes how sincere and beautiful a human being Simone is. Like a moth to a flame, he looks at her, stroking her soft sun-kissed cheeks. "That's all in the past Sim. I respected your decision to stay with Coltan even though he was a jerk and didn't deserve you—I don't regret expressing my feelings to you. I still have you as my friend and that means more to me than anything else."

"Justin, if you feel that way, then will you help me take down Jason? Please; You are all I have."

"Simone, I want to help as much as I can, but we can't do anything without solid proof. We don't know if Jason did something to Trey, and the forensic analyst won't have the result of his blood sample until tomorrow. I wish there were a way that we can apprehend him without it looking like we know anything about Crystal or this mystery necklace."

Simone sits in silence for a moment, unhappiness etched deeply upon her face. "Justin, I'm afraid tomorrow might be too late. By the time you receive those results, we will find Trey dangling dead from a pole. What if Jason comes after you or me, Justin?"

Embracing her tightly, Justin whispers in her ears, saying, "Don't worry, Sim, whatever Jason is, I will not let him hurt you or Crystal. We will find a way to stop him."

❉ ❉ ❉

KILLER CREEK LANE

Long moments passes as Crystal's eyes rapidly scan **Chapter 25,** titled in French **"L'histoire des frères."** Translation: **The Brother's Tale**. The first page of the long chapter displays the imagery of the amethyst stone pendant in different angles. The 18th century stone, sculpted to perfection, is shaped similar to a spade.

Overwhelmed by the information presented in front of her, Crystal's thoughts run wild with questions on who could have created the stone and the shapeshifter book. "Where did it originate?" she questions as she continues to scan each page from top to bottom.

Betrayed by her mother, the one person she loved with all her heart, Crystal must now figure out how to save herself without anyone's help. How can a woman who birthed her inflict this type of pain to her flesh and blood? Holding on to a secret that would cause her daughter to lose her life at the tender age of twenty-five is beyond an execrable act. It's the last nail in her coffin.

Crystal Imagined a fairy tale ending with the perfect husband, a beautiful home, and adoring children to love. But alas, a life once dreamt will never come true. Instead, cursed with the touch of a demon, Crystal will choose whether to live or die by the amethyst stone.

Hoodwinked, Crystal must come to terms with her demise in less than twenty-four hours. Now a sacrificial lamb for two sadistic brothers, she must face Jason and possibly his other half, who is also after her.

Long moments pass as Crystal's eyes rapidly inspect each page of **Chapter 25**. She bit her bottom lip halfway through and held it tightly until she reaches the end of the horrid tale and prophecy of wearing the purple amethyst stone.

Laying on her bed, Crystal takes a deep breath reading the last page, which states what the mission of the brothers is and the fate of the chosen holder of the stone. In bold ink, medieval lettering, Crystal absorbs each word as if it is the last time she will see it.

❦The Sons of The Great Mastema must successfully remove the amethyst stone necklace off the chosen girl before they kill her. Once she dies, only one brother shall proceed in dipping the amethyst stone In her blood. The ritual is the only way all twenty-five shifters can successfully set themselves free to roam the earth and cause havoc entering any human vessel they desire. The

chosen girl cannot wear the amethyst stone necklace during the ritual under any circumstances.

She mutters under her breath, "Is this why you wrote not to take it off, Mom? So what the hell happens to me if I keep it on? Dammit!" she scowls, closing the book.

Suddenly, she remembers the vision she had at the old church where witches sacrificed a young woman in the middle of a large field. "Could this be a sign or revelation of what might happen to her?" Crystal questions herself, brushing a strand of her curls behind her ears. Writhing in mindless distress, Crystal senses a throbbing pain erupting in her head. Feeling as though it will split in two, she gently rubs her temples.

"I know you're upset, but I think what you did to Aunty J was wrong, Crystal," Alexandria says, standing beside the bedroom door.

Crystal's dark brown eyes flash in annoyance, "I asked you to give me some time alone, Alex."

Scratching below her earlobe, Alex flares at her sister, "I just received a text message from Aunty J; she said she's leaving town before sunrise."

"Good riddance," Crystal mutters, giving her sister the side-eye while sitting up on her bed.

Alex slams her hand against the door. "That's all you have to say, Crystal? You're going to let her leave like this?" Alex cries out.

"I can't believe you! You've made a huge mistake, Crystal! You could have at least let her explain why she did this to you; she's still our aunt and the only family we have."

Crystal rises from her bed with cold eyes darting at her sister, "So if you love her so much, then why don't you leave town with her to, Alex!"

Deeply upset by Crystal's outburst, Alexandria gives her sister a long stare of disappointment before charging out of her room, slamming the door behind her.

"Alex! Wait! I'm sorry!" Crystal wails in tears.

Hearing Alex shut her bedroom door; A searing pain gradually seeps in, strangling Crystal's heart. Heaving a sigh, she walks over to her nightstand and grabs her cell phone. Searching through her contact numbers, Crystal sends a text message to a friend asking to meet her at the Town Hall Cafe for a cup of coffee. Slipping on her black suede ankle boots, Crystal grasps her crossbody purse and leaves her bedroom.

❊ ❊ ❊

TOWN HALL CAFE/BAKERY

As Crystal enters the warm bakery cafe, the tremendously soothing atmosphere gives her a sense of peace and tranquility. The sweet smell of fresh cinnamon bun cakes and richly brewed roasted coffee feels like she just stepped into heaven. Scanning the cafe section, Crystal notices him sitting in the center booth by the window.

She gives a hint of a smile, waving at Terrance. A delighted look stretches across his handsome face as he watches Crystal approach the red velvet colored booth. Rising from his seat, Terrance greets Crystal with a heartfelt embrace and a kiss on her left cheek.

"Hey Terrance, thank you for meeting me here," She breathes a sigh of relief, "I know it's late," Crystal says, taking a seat by the window.

"That's okay, Crystal," he smiles, gently touching her hand. "I didn't think we would get a chance to spend some quality time together. I'm happy that you texted me."

"Were friends, right?" Crystal asks, squeezing his hand, unable to let go.

"Of course we are friends, Crystal, always," Terrance replies, glancing at a slightly saddened expression on her face.

"Simone told me that she informed you about Trey," He hung his head low, "I'm so sorry Crystal. Somehow I feel as if this is all of our faults—we should have listened to him. We should have—-"

Gently placing her right hand over his, Crystal caresses his fingertips, "This was not your fault Terrance, there was no way we could have known that Trey would go missing."

"That's not the point, Crystal; Trey has been one of the most loyal friends that I've known since high school, and I feel terrible about how I acted at the library. I thought he was just fucking around with us. It's not every day that someone tells you a shape-shifter is after your friend. I don't know how to process this—I don't even know how you're processing this. You seem so calm."

Crystal's lips tremble while her eyes filled to the brim with tears, "Trust me, Terrance, I might seem calm, but I'm scared. I'm scared of what might happen to me after tonight; I'm so worried about Trey. I wish he didn't have to suffer because of me."

"Crystal, Trey was worried about you last night. He wanted to be the one to tell you what he found. I didn't want to believe what he was saying, but I should have. Crystal, we should have never let him go alone to see you with all that information. Shit! Whoever took him probably found that book too."

"I have it."

"You do? Did you find anything about how to destroy the stone or the psychopaths that are looking for it?"

"No, Terrance. I skimmed through a few chapters, but there's nothing on how to destroy it. At this point, I'm not sure there's anything anyone can do to help me."

"You're not dying on us, Crystal; we are going to find a way to stop this, okay?" He says, leaning over, wiping a teardrop trickling from her chin

"How? How can any of you help me when your lives are in danger because of me?"

"Honestly, I don't know, Crystal. I'm still trying to grasp all of this information," Terrance responds, biting his inner top lip, gazing into her eyes, "Whatever happens, Crystal, know that none of us will let these assholes hurt you."

"I miss Trey."

"I know you do, Crystal; Trey cares about you so much. He would do anything for you."

"He's my best friend, Terrance."

"He's mine too, and we are going to find him, Crystal. We have to believe that; If not, then he'll know we gave up on him."

Looking over his shoulder, Terrance stares at the men's restroom, "Hey," he shifts his gaze back to her, "may I excuse myself; the little boy's room is calling me. Oh, and in the meantime, you can check out the late-night menu so we can order something to eat when I come back. How does that sound?"

"That sounds good," Crystal responds with a warm-hearted smile, watching Terrance head over to the men's restroom.

Flipping through the menu, Crystal deciphers whether she wanted a cinnamon bun or a red velvet cupcake, which was her favorite dessert. Noticing the lights in the cafe dim into more romantic lighting, Crystal gazes downwards and sees the reflection of lights flickering in a rhythmic motion from the mahogany floor. Her eyes gleam as Terrance slowly makes his way towards her holding a candlelit red velvet cupcake with buttercream frosting.

Singing happy birthday to Crystal, Terrance's voice is feathery, sounding vulnerable but strong at the same time. The vintage clock strikes midnight, and Crystal officially turns twenty-five years old. Placing the cupcake in front of Crystal, Terrance smiles with his mouth closed.

"Terrance, you remembered."

"How could I forget Crystal? I have been the first person to wish a happy birthday since you were sixteen. And I have also successfully beaten your sister eight years in a row and counting," he simpers.

"Happy birthday, CJ! Go ahead, make a wish," Terrance softly says, staring at the pink candle burning slowly.

While Crystal observes the tiny droplets of wax trickling over the delectable creation, she sniffles quietly, gazing at the single candle that might be her last. Closing her eyes for a brief moment, Crystal opens them and swiftly blows it out, "Happy Birthday to me," She whispers reflecting on her life, knowing that it would all be gone soon.

CHAPTER TWENTY-FIVE

THE BROTHER'S CURSE

LAKEVIEW FALLS SHERIFF'S DEPARTMENT

The sky changes from light yellow, mixing in with purples, and breaking up the blue's deeper shades from the previous night. The sun's brilliant rays peek out of its horizon, warming the crisp air while deputies stand outside the Sheriff's department, posting missing flyers of Trey Delgado on the lamp post. Seated at his desk, Sheriff Mills searches through his stack of papers of unsolved cases when he hears his office phone go off. Placing the documents in a black folder, he swiftly answers the call.

"Lakeview Falls Sheriff's department, this is Sheriff Thomas Mills; how may I help you."

"Good morning, Sheriff Mills. It's Bernard Castellón."

Adjusting himself in his seat, Sheriff Mills groans inwardly, "Mr. Castellón, how may I help you this morning?"

"Sheriff Mills, I have been waiting for you to call me back about my friend Joseph McGregor. I still have not heard from him since the last time we spoke. I'm worried sick about him."

Opening his top draw, Sheriff Mills retrieves his tweezers. Slumping back in his seat, he begins to pluck his nose hairs, "Mr. Castellón, there's no need to worry. I went over to Joe's house, and I met his nephew Jason. The young man explained to me that Joe left town for a few weeks. The kid has been watching over his place."

"Jason?" Bernard asked with a shaky tone to his voice, "Sheriff Mills, Joe doesn't have a nephew."

Jolting up from his chair knocking it to the floor, Sheriff Mills drops his tweezers, "What do you mean he doesn't have a nephew?" He grunts angrily, leaning his feet against his file cabinet beside his desk.

"I mean, Joe doesn't have any siblings. Sheriff Mills, Joe, is an only child. His mediate family died many years ago in an airplane crash. I'm the only family he has."

"GODDAMMIT!" Sheriff Mills scowls, kicking the cabinet.

"Sheriff Mills!" Bernard bellows from the other line, "Whoever is in Joseph's house is no family to him. Something happened to my friend, and if you don't go out there and find him, I'm going to sue the shit out of your entire department! You will be hearing from my lawyers!" Bernard hollers, ending the phone call.

Fuming, Sheriff Mills slams his fist down onto his desk. Rising from his chair, he throws his paperwork onto the floor. His voice grows louder as he stomps out of his office, "Son of a Bitch! I knew something wasn't right with that kid!"

"Listen up, boys!" he whistles, getting the attention of his deputies, "we need to search for a man who is now the suspect in the disappearance of Joseph McGregor. His description is; Caucasian male, mid-twenties, six-foot-four, short dark brown hair, slender physique, green eyes. He owns a black vintage motorcycle and goes by the name Jason Warwick. He is considered possibly armed and extremely dangerous. I want you all to go out there and find this scumbag! If he tries anything, use excessive force but don't kill him. I want you to bring that Son of a bitch back to this station alive!"

❋ ❋ ❋

KILLER CREEK LANE

Buried in her mattress, Crystal looks kinder in her sleep, almost like a child. Her body curls up while hugging a fuzzy pink pillow tightly. Awaken by a swift knock on her door, Crystal moans for more sleep. Entering her room, Alex slowly walks towards Crystal's bed, holding a breakfast tray. Taking a deep breath, Alex started to sing, with a heavenly voice.

"Happy birthday to you, Happy birthday to you, Happy birthday dear, Bighead—Happy birthday to you."

Easing herself up in a sitting position, Crystal suppresses her laughter as her sister places the tray on her lap. Amused at her sister's attempt to cook her a meal, Crystal quirks her eyebrow while she glances at her breakfast. The tray consists of a glass of freshly squeezed orange juice with a few visible pits, a crystal vase with a single sunflower, a plate of fluffed scrambled eggs and one burnt toast spread with extra butter.

"Wow!" Crystal exclaims joyously, "I can't believe you made me breakfast," She grits her teeth staring at the very charred toast," Well, at least you didn't burn the eggs," Crystal says sarcastically, snickering.

Sitting beside her, Alexandria gives Crystal a gentle touch on the back, "Crystal, I apologize about sticking up for Aunty J last night. When I was in my room, I had time to think about what she said to you, and if I were in your shoes, I would be upset too. I can't imagine what you're going through; this whole situation scares the shit out of me, so I know that you must be terrified."

Sipping her glass of orange juice, Crystal swallows the content spitting a pit into her hand. Placing it on her napkin, Crystal rests the drink on her nightstand. "Alex, I'm sorry for what I said to you. It's just hard knowing that Mom and Aunty J kept a secret from me; from— you" she pauses, taking a deep breath, "I don't know what to do, Alex," she sniffles fighting to hold back tears.

"I know how much Mom loved us, Crystal, but it's not right that she hid this secret from you for all these years."

"Alex, I don't understand why Mom would do this to me; all I know is that I have to face whatever this is. As Aunty J said, it's my destiny."

"Crystal, doesn't it frighten you that there is a chance you might die?" Alexandria asks timidly.

"Alex, I'm not going to die, okay?" Crystal says, placing the breakfast tray on the vacant side of her bed. Tenderly taking her sister's hand, Crystal holds onto it, not wanting to let go.

"Listen to me, Alex; I'm going to figure this out. I don't know how, but I will. There has to be a way to stop this; to stop them. I won't let those brothers hurt me."

"I hope so, Crystal, because I don't know what I would do without you," Alex says, firmly gripping her sister's hands. "Oh my God," she jolts up from the bed with an elated expression, "I forgot. There's a gift that came for you."

"What gift?" Crystal asks suspiciously.

"You'll see," Alex replies as her eyes darts towards the door, "hey, you can come in now."

Approaching the door, John reveals himself with a bouquet of two dozen white roses, gazing at Crystal with his piercing amber, green eyes. John's sharp facial features soften into a smile that warms Crystal's heart.

"Oh my God, John?" she says, surprised by his presence. Lacing her fingers through her curly hair, Crystal felt embarrassed by her unkempt morning look.

"Happy birthday Crystal, I'm sorry I didn't call first. I hope it's okay that I showed up," he says with an uncertainty of whether he should approach her or not.

"Oh John, I'm so happy to see you," she waves, gesturing for him to enter her room, "come in, come in."

Placing the white roses on her small cushioned couch across from her bed, John pulls one rose out of the neat decor bouquet and walks over to Crystal. Sitting on the edge of her bed, he hands her the single white rose while Alexandria excuses herself, giving them time alone.

Nervously rubbing his hands together, John bashfully looks away. "I hope you like the bouquet Crystal, I know how much you love white roses."

"There beautiful John, I love them," she says, inhaling the delectable nectar scent of the spring flower.

Noticing how distant John was from her, Crystal pats her hands against her quilt. "You know, you don't have to be so far away from me John. I'm not going to beat you up," she says, teasing him.

"Haha!" he chuckles, inching closer to her, "very funny, Crystal. You can never kick my ass unless I let you," he smirks.

"I know we haven't seen each other since Gabby's funeral, and maybe I should have reached out," Crystal sighs, pouting her lips. "I'm sorry for what happened between us in your dorm room, John. I shouldn't have left the way that I did; I should have—"

John takes hold of Crystal's hand and gives her a knowing look. "You don't have to apologize, Crystal. There are things that have happened to us and our friends that are unexplainable. I'm more worried about you; I heard about Trey, and—I can't tell you how horrible I feel that he's missing."

"Trey meant everything to me; he was my best friend. Now that he is gone, I don't think I can take losing another person that I love, John."

"I know, Crystal; I feel the same way. I don't want to lose you either. Look, it's still your birthday, and I think you should at least celebrate that. It's a special day for you. I know Trey and Gabriela would want you to enjoy it to the fullest."

"To be honest, I wasn't planning on doing anything today, John."

"Let me guess because it is Halloween?"

Distressed, Crystal shrugs her shoulders. "I don't think it's safe for me to leave the house, John," she says, not knowing how to explain her troubles to him.

Crystal's anxiety takes hold of her petite frame while the amethyst pendant dangles innocently from her neck. The terrifying thought of twenty-five demons lurking in something small yet so diabolical injects terror into her blood.

"Crystal, you shouldn't stay home on your birthday. How about I take you out after I speak to my intern advisor at the University. I can swing by around 1 pm, and we can bypass the whole trick or treaters and enjoy a peaceful lunch at the cafe. What do you say?"

Observing the gleam in John's eyes as he waits for her to respond, Crystal didn't know how much time she has left before the brothers hunt her down. A time to reconcile and forgive John's endeavors is needed. Crystal did not want to leave the world with guilt nor regrets.

"I would love to celebrate my birthday with you, John," she softly says, gently brushing her hands against his, "but first I need your help."

The tender touch of Crystal's hands feels warm and inviting. A sense of uneasiness envelopes John as he stares into the eyes of an empty soul. "I'll do anything for you, Crystal. Tell me what you want me to do."

"I want you to take me to the university. I have to speak to a professor named Jean Baptist; he said he would be on campus today teaching a lecture. I need to find him, John. It may be the last chance I have at saving my life."

❉ ❉ ❉

RURAL MAPLETON ROAD

Rays of the morning sunlight filter past the rafters and dances across the old oak hollow trees, while the leaves change to a golden hue, and the prairie grasses turn brown. The harvesting of corn in Rural Mapleton Road is soon to commence. The senior residents who wished to stay away from Lakeview Falls found comfort in owning land and shared crops to make a decent living while keeping themselves hidden from becoming carnage to the unknown entities.

Driving through the fields on his yellow tractor, an old grey-haired man comes across Jason lying in the middle of the large acre of land by Wicker Cove Sanctuary. Bringing the rusty machinery to a halt, the older man turns off his ignition.

Slowly hopping off the vehicle, he grunts, "Damn, arthritis will be the death of me." Rubbing the side of his right hip, the older man grabs his wooden cane and limps his way towards Jason. Using his rod, the old man begins to poke Jason's back.

Feeling a sharp pain, Jason awakens, irritated by the painful jabs to his spine. **"OUCH!"** Jason growls ferociously, slapping the cane away from him. "What the fuck are you doing, old man?" he says, glaring up at him with a furious scowl.

Stumbling backward, the older man loses his balance. Quickly using the cane to prevent a fall, he wails, waving the rod in the air. He angrily hisses at Jason. "Do you speak to your mother with that foul mouth?" the man says, frowning at Jason.

"Do you want that cane shoved up your ass?" Jason grunts, flipping him the middle finger.

"You are one rude little bastard!"

"What do you want, old man?"

"You're trespassing on private property, you punk! Now get the hell out of here before I call the Sheriff's department!"

Rising from the grassy field, Jason brushes a few brown leaves and dirt off of his faded black jeans and leather jacket. "No need for that, I'm leaving old skunk," Jason huffs, walking past him.

The old man's wrinkled skin sags down his face as he firmly clasps his old walking stick, with carvings of snakes painted along the sides. "Don't you ever show your pale face in these neck of woods or next time I will shoot your ass!"

Hurtling past the man, Jason flies through the fields, heading over to his motorcycle. The muffled sunlight gleams like gold as Jason races on the main road, hopping quickly on his bike. Grabbing his keys from his back pocket, Jason stood still, realizing that he didn't have the urge to devour the old man. His limbs spasmodically move, and in an instant, Jason's mind feels like it's taken a fistful of tranquilizers.

A mad glint lingers as he looks up at the sun. Like an unblinking eye, the sky feels complete with emptiness. An unnerving shrill howling escapes Jason's lips, **"CRYSTAL!"** Jason bellows as he starts his motorcycle. He drives off down the rural road, leaving tire marks on the pavement.

❋ ❋ ❋

AT LAKEVIEW FALLS UNIVERSITY

Waiting for John in front of the administration office, Crystal decides to take a walk to the lecture hall down the hallway. With less than twelve hours, Crystal is in dire need of finding a way to destroy the amethyst stone. She thought to herself, *If anyone can help her, it's Professor Baptist.*

Approaching the lecture room, Crystal notices a white letter taped to the double mahogany polished door that reads: **Classes canceled until further notice.** Giving the note a long stare, Crystal shakes her head, unable to process that her only hope ceases to exist.

"Oh God, What am I going to do now?" she whimpers as a male student walks pass her, clicking his teeth at the sign.

"Damn, I was looking forward to Professor Baptist's class today. He was going to continue that story on those shifters and witches," a heavy sigh escapes his mouth, scratching the back of his head, "I guess we will never know how the rest of the story goes."

"Do you know why he canceled classes ?" Crystal asks him.

"No. Not a clue."

"I heard Professor Baptist booked lectures and workshops for the rest of the semester. Why would he suddenly not show up to school?" Crystal asks, pacing around in a circle.

"When I went to the admissions office a few minutes ago, they said Professor Baptist never showed up this morning, not a phone call, not a text message. It's like he disappeared, but I guess that's been happening a lot in this town, right?"

"Right," Crystal responds, feeling dazed and confused.

"I hope they don't find him skinned or hanging off a tree or something. That would be so tragic," he says, lifting his shoulders, he shrugs. "Well, good luck finding another interesting class. There's not much left," the student says, walking away.

Massaging her neck, Crystal feels a sudden itch in her throat. Searching for a way to quench her thirst, she sees a water fountain by the auditorium. Quickening her pace, Crystal reaches the stainless steel cooler. Leaning forward, she touches the base part and swallows the water from the stream.

Meanwhile, outside the campus, Justin stands by the side entrance waiting to see if Simone's shows up for her class. Receiving the results on Trey's blood sample, Justin is eager to let her know what he found. Treading back and forth, Justin hears the roaring sounds of a motorcycle coming down the road.

Removing his shades, Justin is infuriated to see Jason Warwick parking up on the campus lawn. Noticing Jason's dirty, unkempt look and unpleasant expression, Justin keeps himself hidden behind a few students conversing by the side entrance.

❋ ❋ ❋

Entering the university, Jason storms down the hallway, where he sees Crystal from a distance, taking a sip of water. Looking up, Crystal sees Jason coming towards her in an aggressive matter. Wiping the side of her mouth with the back of her left hand, she mutters, "Jason?"

Advancing towards Crystal, Jason grasps her by the throat with one hand, lifting her from the ground and slamming her against the off white wall. The frightening sound sends students to their feet, running towards the classroom door. Clawing her fingers at his hands uselessly, Crystal uses her last breath to scream for help while Jason's emerald green eyes burn with emptiness and anger as he glares at her.

"Do you have any idea what you've done, Crystal? I was all you had and you've ruined everything! You bitch!" he yells out, gripping her throat tighter.

As Crystal's lungs burn with pain, the desperation to breathe overtakes her as she kicks her legs in the air, struggling to release herself from Jason's demonic hold. Hearing the chaotic disturbance from inside the administration office, John runs out to find Jason choking Crystal to death.

"What the fuck are you doing? Let her go!" John screams in rage, clasping the back of Jason's jacket.

Yanking him off Crystal, John flings Jason across the hall, where he slams into a classroom door. Hearing a loud commotion from outside the university, Justin runs inside, where he sees Crystal holding her neck and Jason lying on the floor with a bloody lip. At great speed, Justin sprints towards them while listening to his walkie talkie go off.

"Attention all Lakeview Falls deputies, there is a warrant out for the arrest of Jason Warwick, I repeat, there is a warrant out for the arrest of Jason Warwick. He is wanted for the disappearance of veteran Joseph R. McGregor. If you see a young man standing six-foot-four, dark brown hair, green eyes, and rides a motorcycle, apprehend him immediately."

Approaching Jason, Justin grabs his handcuffs from the back of his pants pocket. Gripping Jason by his forearm, Justin forcefully pulls him up and turns him around. "Jason Warwick, you are under arrest."

"For what?" he yells out, struggling to unleash himself from Justin's grip.

"For the disappearance of Mr. Joe McGregor."

"What?" Crystal exclaims.

While Justin reads Jason's rights, John runs over to Crystal. Embracing her, John holds onto Crystal as tight as possible while they both stare at Justin, handcuffing Jason.

"Don't worry, Crystal. Jason will never hurt you again," John whispers in her ear.

Crystal's eyes glare at Jason in disgust. "Oh my God, Trey was right. You're one of them."

Snapping out of a trance, Jason stares directly at her. "Crystal! I'm so sorry; I don't know what's happening to me," he mutters, realizing the pain he has just caused her.

Pulling Jason by his arms, Justin drags him down the hallway. From a distance, Jason's green eyes still fixates on her.

"Crystal, Please!" he shouts from the top of his lungs, "You have to forgive me! I love you!"

Listening to Jason plea for forgiveness, Crystal sees the despair in his eyes as Justin drags him out of the school. The words Jason utters couldn't have possibly been real, Crystal thought. *How could he love someone that he wanted to kill?*

While students whispered among themselves, John cradles Crystal in his arms as she sobs uncontrollably. "Shh, Shh, Crystal, don't cry; I'm here, and I will always protect you."

"What if Jason comes back, John?" she whimpers, burying her face in his chest, " I know he will find a way to hunt me down."

"I won't let him, Crystal. You're staying with me at my dorm. There's no way I'm letting you out of my sight," John says, caressing the back of her head while glaring at students staring at them.

CHAPTER TWENTY-SIX

THE END IS NEAR

LAKEVIEW FALLS SHERIFF'S DEPARTMENT

Controlled air systems swallow all the moisture in the cellblock, where Jason is being held captive. The walls of concrete surround him like a caged barbaric savage that he is. Fingerprinted and strip-searched, Jason stands beside the dirty porcelain sink clogged with different-colored hair strand textures. Brief moments of terror strikes Sheriff Mills and Justin as Jason's eyes gleam with utter darkness. A stare that can pierce through your heart like a sharp, unapologetic dagger, both father and son keep their distance while continuing their interrogation.

"I'm going to ask you again, Mr. Warwick, what happened to Joseph McGregor?"

Taking a seat on the cold steel bench beside a filthy urinal, Jason glares at Sheriff Mills with a villainous smirk. "I told you already that my uncle went away."

Banging on the cell bars with his black baton, Sheriff Mills groans. "Cut the shit, Warwick! The jig is up! We know Mr. McGregor is not your uncle. So what the hell did you do to him? How did you get into his house?"

THE BROTHER'S CURSE

"I don't know what you're talking about, Sheriff!" Jason says, eyeballing the bruise on his fingers from strangling Crystal.

"Oh yeah," Sheriff Mills scoffs, pulling out his .40 caliber pistol from his gun belt, "so you're telling me that if we take a little trip up Killer Creek Lane, we're not going to find anything in Mr. McGregor's house that's incriminating?" Sheriff Mills asks, sneering at him.

Remaining silent, Jason reaches behind his back; his bound hands scratch the irking itch. "Sorry, Sheriff, I think you've got the wrong guy."

"Wrong guy, my ass," Justin mumbles.

"Alright, you little shit bag! Since you don't want to answer that question, how about you try answering this."

His right foot impatiently tapping, Jason snarks at him. "I'm all ears, Sheriff Mills," he responds with sarcasm in his voice.

"Why on earth did you attack Crystal Francois at the university?"

"I didn't mean to do that; I blacked out."

"You blacked out? Am I supposed to believe that crap, Mr. Warwick?"

"Sheriff Mills, I don't care what you believe. I snapped for a second," Jason admits with a shrug to his shoulders, "I would never intentionally hurt my girlfriend."

"Your girlfriend?" Sheriff Mills bursts out in high pitch laughter. "Hmm, I had no idea that you two were an item."

"Yeah, well, I'm sure after what I did to Crystal, we won't be anymore," Jason says with his head hung low.

"You think?" Sheriff Mills sarcastically responds.

"Attacking your girlfriend on her birthday in broad daylight was not a smart move Jason," Justin says, watching Jason pace back and forth in the cell block.

"So you have two things over your head right now, Mr. Warwick. A missing veteran and domestic violence on my goddaughter. Is there anything else you want to add to that?"

"Crystal is your goddaughter?" Jason asks with a shocking expression, nervously folding his hands together.

"Yes, she is, and I'm very overprotective when it comes to her. You've messed with the wrong family boy."

"So, does this mean that I'm stuck in this shit hole?"

"That all depends on you, Mr. Warwick; you can make my life a whole lot easier if you admit that you did something to Joe. Or maybe you can explain the murders and disappearances that's been happening all over town."

A snicker escapes Jason's lips as he rises from the bench. "Why would I know anything about that, Sheriff Mills?"

"Do you think this is funny, huh?" Sheriff Mills grips onto the weapon in his hands.

He feels the tightness against his rough skin while cocking his gun, aiming it directly at Jason. "Do I fucking amuse you, jerk-off? Well, do I ?"

"Jesus, Dad, what are you doing?" Justin asks, swiftly pulling his father away from the cell, "Maybe you should take a break. Let's leave Jason alone for a little bit; I'm sure he will get tired of lying and tell us the truth. Okay?"

Sequestered in his thoughts, Sheriff Mills slowly lowers his gun. Nodding directly at his son, he places his pistol back into his gun belt. "I'll be back, you little prick," he says, giving Jason a side-eye.

Gripping onto the cold metal bars, Jason watches Justin lead his father out of the room. "Take your time, Sheriff, take your time," Jason says, saluting Sheriff Mills.

❋ ❋ ❋

LAKEVIEW FALLS UNIVERSITY

The moon sends a slightly silver mist upon Lakeview Falls. Its shimmering, dancing light looks like bridal organza cascading with a romantic glow. Scattered soft lights create an intimate atmosphere while John holds Crystal tightly in his arms. She nestles herself against his chest, feeling her body ache from Jason's brutal hands.

Softly rubbing her lower back, John moves his hands towards her head and gently runs his fingers through her hair. Completely lost in his warmth, Crystal informs John about the purple amethyst stone and the prophecy written about two brother's sacrificing her life to resurrect a two-hundred-year-old demon.

Horror-stricken by the revelation of his only love in danger, John feels an abundance of guilt. His heart sinks while leaning his head against Crystal. "Crystal, why didn't you tell me?" he exhales a deep breath, nuzzling in her curly hair.

Caressing his toned arms, curved around her, Crystal sighs. "I didn't know how to John. I mean, it's not every day someone tells you that two demon shapeshifters want to kill you."

"This is all my fault, Crystal."

"No— " she softly whimpers, cocking her chin up, "John, you didn't do anything."

"Yes, I did Crystal. If I had only been honest with you from the beginning—you would have never been with Jason. My selfish act and poor communication led you into another man's heart."

"John, I'm so sorry about how I've been acting towards you. I know that you have been trying so hard to make things work between us, and it's not fair that I never gave you a second chance."

A charming expression locked onto John's face. "Crystal, you don't have to apologize."

"I should have never been with Jason; I didn't even know who he was or why he was here in the first place."

"Don't blame yourself, Crystal. Jason was manipulating you. I knew something was off the day I met him in front of your house."

"John, I think Jason came here to kill me. I think he might be one of the brothers from the prophecy."

"What?" he shrieks, raising himself from the bed, "Is that why he attacked you, Crystal? Was Jason after the necklace?"

"Yes, but I'm not sure he was after it today. Jason could have easily snatched it off my neck, but he didn't. John, I have to keep the necklace on no matter what. I can't let Jason nor his mystery brother take it; it will cause harm to this whole town."

"Don't worry, Crystal; I'm not going to let anyone hurt you," John whispers, brushing his hand across her cheeks.

Suddenly withdrawing himself from their romantic embrace, John gets up from his bed and walks towards his dresser. "There's something I have to tell you, Crystal," with a saddened expression, John slowly opens the top draw.

"What's wrong, John?" Crystal asks, clenching onto his silk pillow.

"I'm leaving Lakeview Falls."

Like a shock to her fragile heart, Crystal gasps, "What?" she replies, suddenly feeling the world crashing down on her, "where are you going, JP?"

"I am moving to New York."

"Wha—" she shakes her head with confusion, propping herself up on the bed, "when did you make this decision, John?" Crystal asks, taken aback by John's news.

"I received a letter two days ago from Stratsford University in Catskills, New York; I got accepted to an internship for an architect position at Birch Hill and Rowe. I want you to come with me, Crystal."

Pulling out two plane tickets, John presents one to Crystal. "The company has an apartment set up for me. You and I can stay there for two years till I complete the internship."

In shock, Crystal put her hands over her mouth and starts to sob. Inching towards her, John wraps his arms around her waist, kissing her softly on her forehead. "I love you, Crystal, this is our chance to be together and do things the right way."

"Do you mean that, John? Do you want me to come with you?" she asks hesitantly.

"Of course, Crystal," a smile crosses his face, "after what you just told me; it's obvious that someone has to get you the hell out of Lakeview Falls. A second chance for us to live a life together would mean the world to me."

In awe, Crystal fixates on his handsome face. "Oh, John, I can't believe you would go through all of this so that we can be together."

"Crystal, It's not safe anymore for you to live in Lakeview Falls, not after what Jason did to you. Even though your parents left you the deed to the house, this is the best course of action. And I know that you don't want to leave your sister, but you have to think about your safety."

"I'm not sure how Alex will handle this, John."

"Alex will be fine, Crystal, she's with Derrick. He loves her very much; he will never let anything happen to her. Plus, now that they've locked up that psychopath Jason, he will not be able to hurt you. Not while I'm still breathing."

Tenderly stroking the side of John's face, Crystal's emotional connection for him entices as if they had never broken up. It was easy to fall head over heels with a man who masqueraded himself as a genuinely loving person. A web of lies and destructive deception spiraling out of control has led Crystal to see Jason for what he is.

Now eyes wide open, Crystal realizes that the adoring man standing in front of her is her one true love. John Pheiffer has proven himself more than once that he is Crystal's soulmate. Treasuring every minute with him, Crystal gazes at John while she hears the whispers of his breath as he exhales.

"Crystal, I love you with all of my heart, and I would want nothing more than to start fresh with you in a place where we fell in love. So what do you say? Will you do me the honor of accompanying me to New York?"

Unable to contain her happiness, Crystal squeals, "Yes! Yes, of course, I will go with you, John."

Elated, John sweeps Crystal off her feet and spins her around while joyous laughter escapes his lips. Being in John's arms feels familiar to Crystal; It brings back so many keen memories. With a sense of safety and comfort in each other's arms, their romantic moment is suddenly interrupted by a knock on John's door.

Lowering Crystal, John exclaims while staring at the door, "Who is it?"

"It's Wes!" a young man answers loudly on the opposite side of the door.

"Come in!"

THE END IS NEAR

Opening the door halfway, Wesley York sees John and Crystal in an affectionate bond. "Hey, John—oh, I'm sorry, I didn't know you——" he apologizes.

"It's ok Wes. What's up?"

"I wanted to know if you and Crystal are coming to the Halloween party?" he asks with a delightful grin smeared across his face.

"Ummm—" John pauses while quickly glancing at Crystal, "you know what, Wes? I'm not sure we are going. Crystal and I might stay the rest of the night in my room."

"Okay, John. If you do change your mind, I'll be downstairs with Nina. Oh, and Happy Birthday, Crystal," Wesley says with a kind-hearted smile before closing the door behind him.

Staring at the door, Crystal then directs her gaze back to John. "Wait," her right eyebrow arches curiously, "how does Wes know it's my birthday?"

"I'm sorry, Crystal, with everything going on, I forgot to tell you about your birthday party."

"Birthday party? What birthday party? What's going on, John?" she asks him with a suspicious glare.

"Crystal, before Gabriela passed away, she planned this Halloween party for you. She said she was going to tell you in advance; that way, it wasn't a surprise."

"Oh my God, I remember Gabby said she had something to tell me at the diner before she died. I guess that's what it was."

"I know Gabby's death is still fresh, and you don't have to go if you're not up for it, Crystal. We can sleep here, and in the morning, we can go back to your house to pack a few of your belongings. You can also speak to Alex and let her know that you will be staying with me in New York. How does that sound?" he says, kissing her softly on her right cheek.

"That sounds like a good plan, John."

"Great, so— do you want to go to the party? If not—we can——"

"I want to go to the party, John. I miss Gabby so much, and since she planned this special gathering for me, I want to be part of it."

❅ ❅ ❅

KILLER CREEK LANE

Adjusting Derrick's collar, Alexandria started buttoning his white tuxedo shirt. Preparing for Crystal's surprise birthday party, Alexandria dresses as a sexy burlesque dancer. The red sequence costume reaches the floor and reveals a vertical cut in the front to show off her slender legs.

A big fan of the **"Tough Guy: Fuggedaboutit"** series, Derrick decides to take on his alter ego and pose as the notorious mobster of the 1950s Giovanni Cuchiano, from the Manfiscado crime family. He decks out in a three-piece black and white stripe suit with black oxford shoes and a black top hat with a red feather on the right side. Excited about the celebration, Derrick is ready for the best night of his life alongside his beautiful girlfriend.

Fixing his cufflinks, Derrick hears his work phone go off on the foyer table. He leaves Alexandria in the living room, and walks over to the hallway to retrieve his device. Scanning the light blue screen, Derrick notices the call marked private. Hesitating to see who it is, a sigh of annoyance escapes his mouth before he finally answers the call.

"Deputy Derrick Yin. Who is this?"

"Derrick! It's Sheriff Mills. Are you home?" he asks breathlessly.

"Sheriff Mills? Why are you calling me on a private number?"

"Listen, Yin; I don't have time to go back and forth, playing twenty questions with you. Now where the hell are you right now?"

"I'm with Alexandria, at her house. Why? Is everything okay?" Derrick asks, covering his left ear to hear better.

"So that means you're near Joe McGregor's house, right?"

"Yes, Sheriff. What's going on?"

"Derrick, I need you to go over to that house," Sheriff Mills asks with a demanding tone to his voice.

"But—but—Sheriff—" Derrick stutters, "I'm getting ready to go to the Halloween party. Can't this wait until tomorrow?"

"No! It can't wait till tomorrow!" Sheriff Mills groans in extreme rage, "listen to me very carefully, Yin, I had Jason Warwick arrested earlier. I have reason to believe that he might have murdered Mr. McGregor."

"What? Murdered Mr. McGregor?" Derrick shouts.

"Mr. McGregor is dead?" Alexandria shrieks, placing her hand over her chest.

"Shhh," Derrick whispers, quickly getting Alexandria's attention to keep silent.

"Derrick, Jason Warwick assaulted Crystal this morning at the campus. But don't worry, she's okay."

"Holy shit!" Derrick exclaims.

"Derrick, I need you to go over to that house right now! Do you hear me? Go this instant."

"But, Sheriff—"

"Hold on one minute, Yin," Sheriff Mills cuts him off on the other line.

At the Sheriff's Department, one female deputy enters Sheriff Mill's office and informs him that an anonymous call just came in from a resident complaining about a terrible odor coming from 468 Killer Creek Lane. Immediately Sheriff Mills realizes the address is Joe's house.

"Get the fuck over to that house, Yin!" he grunts, ending the call.

"Derrick! What the hell is going on?"

Suddenly throwing his arms around Alex, Derrick rocks her gently. Shaking his head in bewilderment, Derrick draws in a deep breath, letting it back out with a loud sigh. "It's about Crystal. Jason attacked her at the school earlier."

"What!" she bellows, withdrawing herself from Derricks hold. "Oh my God, is my sister, okay?"

"Crystal is okay, Alex."

"What about Jason?"

"Jason is in jail, which is a great thing. But his arrest isn't only for assaulting Crystal. Sheriff Mills thinks Jason has something to do with the disappearance of your neighbor."

"Oh no, Derrick." Her eyes shift to the side, unable to shield a glassy layer of teardrops falling from her rosy cheeks.

"I knew something was strange about Mr. McGregor going away. He has never left his house to go anywhere since the murders started," Alex says, frantically pacing back and forth. "As much as I feel bad for the disappearance of my neighbor even though he hated me, I still have to find my sister Derrick, I can't stay here—"

"Wait— Alex, we don't even know where she —" interrupted by a text alert, Derrick taps his phone screen and sees that it's a message from John. He informs him that he's with Crystal and they will meet them at the Halloween party.

"That was John," Derrick says, placing his phone in his pocket, "he's with Crystal; They want us to meet them at the auditorium."

"Thank god she's with John. I think we should head over there right now, Derrick," Alex exclaims, grasping her long wool coat and her diamond-studded purse from the coat hanger.

"Alex, we can't go right now. I have to check your neighbor's house first," Derrick replies, grabbing his 9 mm pistol off the coffee table.

"What?" Alex wails with an irritated expression."Derrick, you can't be serious! You're not on duty."

"Alex, I'm a man of the law. Sheriff Mills ordered me to go there; If he thinks that something bad happened to Mr. McGregor, then I need to see if there is evidence in that house that can help us find him."

"No, Derrick! You can't go to that house alone without any backup."

Grasping his black double-breasted fur overcoat, Derrick heads towards the front door, "Alex, if I don't go, Sheriff Mills will fire me then kick my ass."

"Well, if you're going, then I'm coming with you," she insists, following him outside.

"Alex, I think you should stay home and wait for me. It might be dangerous."

Her lips tremble with each outlet of air, "I'm not staying here alone, Derrick! I'm coming with you!"

"Okay, Alex," Derrick replies, calmly taking hold of her hand, "don't say I didn't warn you."

❅ ❅ ❅

The bitterly cold air bites into their lungs as they sprint towards Mr. McGregor's home. Advancing up the bluestone porch steps, Derrick makes his way to the front door while Alexandria stands behind him, clenching onto his coat. Double knocking on the door, Derrick notices it slightly cracked open. Extending his right hand, Derrick fastens it around the doorknob, turning it clockwise. A low beacon of light filters through the dust riddled air as Derrick reluctantly steps in, peering at the tattered wallpaper that droops on the cracked walls.

Without warning, a pungent odor hits Alexandria while a swarm of flies attacks her from behind. Trying to prevent bile from rising in her throat, she covers her mouth as the putrid scent invades her nostrils. Clasping onto Derrick for dear life, they walk past the living room where they see every piece of furniture destroyed.

As they enter the kitchen, thousands of baby maggots saturate the hard wooden floor, trailing towards the basement entrance. Nearing the door, Derrick shields his mouth as he opens it. The vile stench grows stronger as they tread softly down the staircase. Turning on the flashlight on his cell phone, Derrick hears a loud thud echoing behind them as the wooden steps creaks and moans.

With their hearts beating fast as if some unforeseen circumstance was about to arise, Derrick and Alexandria reach the bottom steps, where brown rats scurry across the floor, making them gasp each time they disappear through the gaps in the wall.

Dust motes float in the thin shaft of light from the broken window in the room's far left corner. Noticing a light switch dangling above his head, Derrick pulls the string and is horrified by the dried blood and intestines scattered all over the granite ground.

"OH, God! Is that?— Are those?——" Alexandria cries out panic-stricken as she points at the gaping hole filled with dead bodies and severed limbs.

Fear in his eyes, Derrick quickly grabs Alexandria's hand. "Jesus, there's a dozen body parts in there. I think we should get the fuck out of here," he stutters, darting towards the staircase with Alexandria.

As they reach the top of the steps, Derrick opens the door when he suddenly hears a croaking sound. Stopping abruptly, he looks over his shoulders. "Did you hear that, Alex?" he asks, cocking a brow.

"Hear what, Derrick?"

Swiftly turning around, Derrick runs down the staircase. "I think I heard something; I gotta go back down there."

"What! Are you crazy? There are body parts all over the place. We have to get out of here, Derrick! Now!" she screams, tugging on his arm.

"I have to see where that sound is coming from."

Straining his ears, Derrick hears the wheezing sound again. He pays close attention as the sound directs him back to the six-feet grave. "It's coming from the hole."

Forcing her eyes shut, Alexandria hopes their circumstances will change, but like before, doom and gloom were what they encounter. Opening her eyes, Alexandria glances around the infested basement when she releases a bone-chilling scream, **"Aahhhh!"** Numb with fear in her blood, she stares directly at Kyle's face nailed to the wall with his testicles hanging outside of his mouth.

"Oh my God! Kyle?" Alex says, quickly spewing chunks on the ground.

Grabbing Alexandria's hand, Derrick gives her an intense gaze. "Alex, look at me. We have dig to this out!" he says, pointing at the severed limbs.

"What? No, I'm not touching that!" Alexandria belts out, trying to flee.

Clasping her by the arm, Derrick pulls her back towards him. "Alex, there's something in that hole. We have to find out what's in there; we have no choice. Now come with me."

Walking towards the pit, Derrick and Alexandria gradually pull out the human limbs one after the other. In disbelief, they discover Trey lying down in the hole with his eyes wide open, staring at them with tears in his eyes. A great tremor overtakes both Derrick and Alexandria as they observe the barbwire stitching inflicted on Trey's lips. Covered with human remains and feces, Trey looks frail and dehydrated. Using his arm muscles, Derrick pulls Trey's body out of the human debris. Picking Trey up, Derrick throws him over his shoulders and heads up the staircase with Alexandria.

Swiftly exiting the house of horrors, Derrick rests Trey's frail body on the porch swing. He quickly calls Sheriff Mills and tells him that he has found Trey alive at Joe McGregor's home. Ending the conversation, Derrick wraps his suit jacket around Trey's shoulders and immediately calls the ambulance.

CHAPTER TWENTY-SEVEN

HER LAST WISH

LAKEVIEW FALLS AUDITORIUM

Vintage light fixtures illuminate the white concrete walls while dancing bodies tangle together like waves on a vast ocean. Eclectic sounds of hip hop music intensify Lakeview Falls Wexler House auditorium as Crystal and John enter the crowded venue. It gleams with extravagance while Crystal's eyes fixate on the shimmering pink and black custom made birthday banner above the performance stage that displays her name written in bold gold lettering. On the left side of the stage, exhibits an 86 inch flat screen presenting memorable photos of Crystal and her friends throughout her adolescent and high school years. The night could not have been any more perfect; From the school alumni and faculty, wearing unique and scary Halloween costumes to the infamous Lakeview Falls music disk jockey, also known as DJ Butcher playing multiple genres.

    Thrusting themselves into the writhing mass of sweating bodies, Crystal and John channel the exhilaration of strobe lights and blaring bass booming in their ears. They make their way to the custom made crystal glass booth called **"Vexatron Virtual Birthday Card,"** with an LED lettering scroll above that reads, **"25 Is The Best Year To Be Alive."** The newest invention from New

Age Hologram coming to stores in the year 2045 made a unique creation for the Santos Family as a gift to Crystal.

Using her trust funds, Gabriela spent an exceptional amount of money for her best friend to experience the best birthday party of 2025. After feeling incredibly guilty about their argument at Matts' funeral, Gabby wanted to make up for her bad behavior, by proving her loyalty to such a loving and selfless friend like Crystal.

In high school, Gabriela fell ill with severe high blood pressure and needed a kidney transplant. Hospitalized for almost a year, Gabriela's family deem no match for her, leading to her diminishing state. Quickly signing up for an evaluation at a top-notch transplant center, Crystal went for extensive screening and was a perfect match for Gabriela. Donating one of her kidneys to her best friend at the age of sixteen, Crystal shared an emotional bond with Gabriela.

❅ ❅ ❅

Awestruck by the hologram, Crystal watches as every student's virtual faces pop up in random order wishing her a happy birthday. Some sang a song; some read poetry, and some said best wishes with a warm-hearted smile. The thought of human imagery displayed in a high tech fashion like the crystal glass hologram booth made Crystal wonder what other devices were in store for the future. As the LED lighting changes from pink to purple to shimmery gold, every wish she hears from her friends feels like her last.

Wrapping his arms around Crystal's waist, John nestles his lips against her neck. "Wow, Gabby outdid herself with this party. It's a shame she isn't here to experience this with you, babe."

"I can't believe she did this for me; I mean, all the high tech stuff must have cost Gabby a fortune," Crystal softly says, shifting her body around to face John.

"I'm sure it did cost Gabby a lot of money to set this up, Crystal. But remember it also cost a fortune for an organ, and you gave her yours for free."

She tilts her head to the side with a puzzled expression. "What is that supposed to mean, John?"

"I'm sorry, Crystal. I didn't want it to come out in that way. I want you to see that even though Gabby spent her savings on you, don't forget that you almost lost your life to save hers. Even though Gabby knew she didn't owe you anything for that transplant, she still found ways to show how thankful she was for what you did years ago."

"Dammit," Crystal mutters as a tear forms, trickling down her cheeks. "It's not fair that she died because of me."

"Crystal, you had no idea that she would have been in danger by touching that necklace."

"She was my best friend, and now she's gone."

"Please don't cry, Crystal," John whispers, claiming her tightly in his arms. "Let's try and enjoy the night. Gabby wouldn't have wanted you to cry on your birthday."

Crystal wipes the droplets of grief from her eyes, "You're right, John, no more crying."

"That's my girl," John says, jerking her closer with the adrenaline pumping through his veins, "why don't we dance."

"Dance? Me?" she asks with a silly expression, "I haven't danced in a long time, John."

"Until tonight," he extends his hands like a gentleman, "care to join me on the dance floor?"

A smile tugs at the corner of Crystal's lips as she takes John's hand. While they sway to the complex beat, her body moves to the rhythm of the music. John's arms feel like a calm blanket shifting over her skin. *Dancing with him is next to perfect,* Crystal thought to herself. Her dynamic expressions blend easily with his inner soul.

In a matter of minutes, intermingled smells of smoke and sweat assault her nostrils as she inhales deeply. Clearing her throat, Crystal suddenly withdraws herself from John.

"What's the matter, Crystal?" he asks, caressing her hand. "Are you okay?"

Rubbing her throat hastily, Crystal scrunches her face. "I have an itch in my throat. Can you get me a glass a water John? Please."

"Yes, of course, Crystal. Stay here; I'll be right back," John says, kissing her right hand before walking away.

As John made his way through the crowd, he notices Simone standing by the bar holding a rocks glass filled with an amber-colored liquid. Gesturing for the female bartender to come over, John repeatedly waves his hand for her attention.

"Excuse me! Can I have a glass of water and a Jameson on the rocks?"

"John?" Simone says in a soft tone, approaching him.

"Simone, just the person I wanted to see."

"I beg your pardon?" she snickers, taking a sip of her rum and coke.

"I meant to say that I am glad to see you."

"It's great to see you too, John; Have you seen the birthday girl? I've been looking all over the place for her."

Yes, Crystal is here. I brought her to the party, hoping that it would relieve the stress that has consumed her from the chaos with Jason. She's had a rough day, Simone, and I'm worried about her. Crystal told me that you are aware of the stone situation—and——"

"John——there's more to the stone that you dont know. I think it would be wise if we didn't have this conversation in a crowded place."

John takes a deep breath. He feels a wave of emotions stir from within, "Simone, I am trying to figure out why anyone would want to hurt Crystal. I want to protect her."

"I know you do, John." Simone says placing her hand over his arm. "We all want to make sure that Crystal survives tonight. Speaking of——Where is she?" Simone asks, shifting her gaze at the dance floor.

"Crystal is by the virtual glass booth." He says with a shaky voice. "Would you mind keeping her company while I get her a drink?"

"You're scared, aren't you, John? I'm scared too; don't worry, I'll watch over Crystal till you get back."

"Thank you, Simone."

Taking her drink, Simone leaves John at the bar and quickly walks over to Crystal, who gazes at the virtual card that displays Trey wishing her a Happy Birthday.

"I didn't know Trey had a chance to record this," Simone says, staring at Trey's infectious smile.

"I miss Trey so much," Crystal simpers, releasing a long sigh. "I wish we knew what happened to him."

"We will find Trey, Crystal. I don't know how, but we will."

"I'm happy you came to the party, Simone. It means a lot to have close friends around."

"Of course, Crystal—I've been looking for you; I heard what happened earlier with Jason."

A sudden pressure strangles Crystal as she exhales, trying to forget the moment Jason laid his hand on her. She sighs, feeling the throbbing ache in her chest. "I still can't believe he attacked me, Simone. You should have seen the hate that Jason had in his eyes when he clenched his hands around my throat."

"Crystal, I know that you wanted to believe that Jason was a good person, but he's not. Trey was right about him; he wants to kill you."

"You're right, Simone, but there's one thing that I don't understand."

"And that's what Crystal?"

"He didn't take the necklace— Isn't that what he's been after this entire time? I don't get it, Simone. If Jason wants to end my life, then why did he share those moments with me?— He told me things that I don't think a liar would even be able to make up. Jason was so kind and gentle the last time I saw him. We even——never mind," she sobs, looking away with embarrassment.

"Oh my God, Crystal, did you and Jason —?" Simone pauses with an expression of disbelief. "You know what—? Don't answer that; I think I know the answer. Eww," she squints her face with disgust.

"Something is different about Jason, Simone. I can feel it."

"I'm sure you can, Crystal. Whatever magnetic potency Jason has invoked will surely affect you in more ways than one. I hope for your sake that it wasn't the sexual trance we read in the shifter book. Sleeping with a Lazurkismurma demon can be quite traumatizing to your mental state and your body."

"Simone, Jason told me he loves me."

"Was that before or after he tried to strangle you?"

"After, Simone. I don't understand what is happening to Jason. It's like he has a split personality. He also said that he was the only one that I had and that I've ruined everything."

"What? Crystal, you know that Jason is messing with your head, right? There is no way that he could have changed in less than 48 hours. Unless—"

"Unless what, Simone?"

"Did you read anything in that book about shifter demons absorbing emotional feelings?"

"No, I didn't. Why?"

"I don't know," Simone shakes her head in confusion. "Crystal, I have this funny feeling about the tale of brother's story. I mean, in less than two hours, your birthday will end, and now that Jason is in jail, there's no way he can come after you or get the necklace. Which is a relief, but we still have another problem to worry about, and that's—"

"Ahem," Terrance coughs, getting their attention, "excuse me, ladies. I apologize for interrupting your conversation, but I was hoping to see the birthday girl," he grins, staring at Crystal.

Ecstatic to see Terrance, Crystal quickly embraces him. "Terrance, what a surprise! I am happy that you came. I mean, even though we saw each other last night."

"Wait, you two hung out? Without me?" Simone asks, sarcastically, placing her hands over her chest with a jaw-dropped expression.

Wrapping his arms around Crystal, Terrance gives Simone a sly smirk. "Well, we didn't plan it Simone. But I'm happy that it happened. Crystal and I enjoyed a fun pre-game birthday hang out at the cafe."

"Ahhh, I see after all these years you're still the 12 o' clock wish master, huh Terrance?" Simone teases him with a snicker.

"Yup, eight years and counting, Simone. Hey, maybe next year you can try and beat me to it."

"You know, listening to you two go back and forth reminds me of your childish banter in high school. I think I should go and find John," Crystal says, patting Simone and Terrance on the back.

"John is here?" Terrance asks, displaying a frown.

Giving him the side-eye, Crystal clicks her teeth. "Terrance, I hope you're not going to start anything with him."

"No, of course not, Crystal. I'm glad you two made up. You know what? Before you get John, maybe this would be a good time to give you your birthday gift."

"A gift?" Crystal's eyes beam with excitement, "Terrance, you didn't have to do that."

"Come on. It's your birthday, Crystal. Everyone deserves a birthday gift, and don't worry, it's nothing crazy; it's not like that oversized phantom clown I bought you six years ago."

"I still have nightmares because of that clown Terrance."

With sweet, joyful laughter, Terrance slithers a smirk, "It wasn't the best gift, Crystal. I promise that this one is much better. I have it in my car. I thought maybe we could go outside so I can give it to you."

"I think I should wait for John."

"It will only take a second, CJ; I have to get it out of my trunk," he says, shuffling in his pocket for his car keys, "hey, Simone can come with us too if she wants."

"Sure, I can tag along," Simone tilts her head to the side with a silly grin smeared across her face. "I needed a cigarette break anyway. Also, I can't wait to see the hunk of junk you got Crystal for her birthday."

"Haha! Very funny, Imone," Terrance mockingly says, sticking out his tongue.

"I hate when you call me that, Tayrance," Simone says, laughing her way towards the entrance door, "let's go before John gets back."

❊ ❊ ❊

As they exit the auditorium, the biting cold air sends everyone's body shivering. Every breath exhaled shows a plume of white steam displaying into the form of a cotton ball. As Crystal and Simone follow Terrance to his vehicle, branches silhouettes against the slate-grey sky, creating an enchanting yet mystical aura.

"It's freezing out here," Crystal says, quivering while blowing her warm breath into her hands.

"I need a cigarette," Simone mutters, reaching into her small purse and pulling out a pack of Sunny Milds.

Approaching the back of his car, Terrance opens the trunk. Lowering his head, he rummages through a few shopping bags, searching for Crystal's gift.

While Simone takes a drag of her cigarette, a coughing fit erupts in her lungs as she blows out another puff of smoke. Searching in her purse for her cell phone, Simone realizes that she left it charging in the coat check room.

"Shit," she hisses, "umm, you guys! I left my phone inside! I have to make a call to someone; I'll be right back!" Simone says, rushing back inside the auditorium.

Soaking up the enchanting atmosphere, Crystal gazes at the stars gleaming like shiny blades high above in the freezing air. Wrapping her slender arms around herself, she becomes impatient. "Did you find it yet, Terrance?" she asks him.

Lifting his head, Terrance closes the trunk lid, sighing with disappointment. "I'm sorry, Crystal; I could have sworn I brought it with me."

"That's okay, Terrance; you can give it to me tomorrow," she suggests, looking at the time on her watch.

Walking to the driver's side, Terrance pulls the latch on his car door. "You know what, Crystal? How about I drive back to my house and get it? It's only ten minutes away."

Incapacitated with fear, Crystal approaches the passenger side door, "Terrance, you don't have to do that. What if you go and something happens to you? It's too dangerous. There's a chance you might not come back, like Trey."

"You have nothing to worry about, CJ. Look at me," he says, flexing his biceps, "No one's hurting the undefeated black belt Jiu-Jitsu champion of Lakeview Falls."

"Okay tough guy, if so, then I'll come with you."

"No way, CJ! You're better off staying here. I'll be fine. Enjoy your birthday party. I'll be back as soon as possible," he says, placing one foot inside his vehicle.

"But—Terrance!"

With a stern expression, Terrance gives her a long stare. "Crystal, this isn't up for discussion. I'm not in the mood to hear John's bullshit. So please, go back to the party!"

Turning on the ignition, Terrance jerks his stick shift into first gear when he suddenly sees Crystal enter his vehicle. "Crystal! What the hell are you doing? I told you to stay here!"

"I'm coming with you, Terrance, end of discussion. Now shut up and drive," she smirks, pulling the seat belt over her shoulder.

"You are such a pain in the ass, CJ," Terrance says, shaking his head with a chuckle as he drives off down the road.

❅ ❅ ❅

LAKEVIEW FALLS MEMORIAL HOSPITAL

Someone yells, "Code Blue" from a distance, alerting doctors, nurses, and assistants that there's an emergency in room 333. Frantic with anxiety, Derrick and Alexandria sit impatiently in the visitor's room, waiting for news on Trey's condition. Patrons sitting across from them observe the two covered in blood and what looks like human membranes on their costumes.

Fear of the coming drains out of them as the smell of antiseptics and medicine fills their nostrils. Nervously tapping his foot on the marble tile, Derrick grits his teeth trying to tune out medical equipment in a symphony of sounds- buzzing in his ears.

Silently staring at the mounted television displaying a fuzzy screen, a wave of pain engulfs Alexandria to her very core. Haunted by the grisly scene in the basement, she repeatedly replays the moment she saw Kyle's mutilated face pinned to a dirty wooden wall like a tact animal.

Sensing Alexandria's trembling legs rubbing against his, Derrick wraps his arms tightly around her. "It's okay, Alex," he says, kissing her forehead, "Trey will get through this. He has to."

Comforting his girlfriend, Derrick sees a female doctor walk past the nurse' station, speaking to a nurse before approaching the waiting room. Holding a medical chart, the doctor advances towards them.

"Excuse me," she says with a shaky voice, "are you the one that brought Mr. Delgado here?"

"Yes, we are," Derrick stutters, rising from his chair, "Trey is our friend."

"My name is Dr. Emily Vastin," she says softly, introducing herself. "I am monitoring Mr. Delgado at the moment."

"Nice to meet you, Dr. Vastin. I'm Deputy Derrick Yin, and this is my girlfriend, Alexandria Francois. How is Trey? Is he going to be okay?" he asks with uncertainty.

"Deputy Yin, your friend, is fortunate to be alive; considering the injuries he has sustained on top of being extremely dehydrated. He has lost a significant amount of blood. I will have to administer a blood transfusion when he's more stable. He's extremely exhausted and comes in and out of a daze. I also removed the wire stitches from his mouth."

"Can we see him?" Derrick asks, grabbing hold of Alexandria's hand.

"I—I don't see any problem with that; I do want to inform you that Trey is having some difficulty speaking due to the deep puncture wounds to his lips. I just gave him a sedative, so he should be fast asleep very soon. You both have approximately ten minutes to see him, and then he needs to rest."

"Thank you, doctor Vastin—thank you so much for saving our friend," Derrick says, fighting back his tears.

"We, the people of Lakeview Falls, should be thanking you, Deputy Yin. Trey is one of many men in this town that survived.

You are a hero for finding your friend. By the way, where exactly did you find Mr. Delgado?"

Trying to process what had happened, Derrick softly sighs, releasing tension from his broad shoulders. "He was buried in a hole under human remains in a neighbor's basement."

"Oh, dear—Oh, dear," Dr. Vastin mutters. A disturbed expression surfaced on her face before she walks away, writing down information on her chart.

Watching Doctor Vastin leave the waiting room, Derrick and Alexandria quickly make their way down the dimly lit hallway. Quietly entering Trey's hospital room, they hear his heart monitor signal a steady beep. Staring at Trey lying peacefully in his bed, Alexandria begins to weep as her eyes fixate on the IV attached to his arms and a white bandage wrapped around his head.

Taking a cautious step towards his bed, Derrick sits at the edge. A deep sigh of sadness escapes his lips as he glances at Trey's engorged and bruised mouth from the wired stitches. Brushing his hand across Trey's hand, Derrick sees movement in both eyelids. "Trey, Trey—It's Derrick. Can you hear me?"

Trey's eyes flutter before slowly opening. "Derr—Derri—" he stutters with a hoarse tone to his voice.

"Hey Trey, everything is going to be okay. You're safe now. That piece of shit Jason is in jail; he's not going to hurt you or anyone else again."

Without warning, Trey's eyes widen with fright. Slowly dragging in air, he screams, releasing a splintering noise from his welted lips. Shifting his body from left to right, Trey

clasps onto is IV violently, trying to rip it out of his arm. "CR—YS—TAL! HE—LP."

"Trey! No! What's wrong?" Derrick shouts, struggling to restrain Trey. "Hey, you have to calm down! Calm down, Trey!"

Kicking his legs out, Trey weakly tries to push Derrick's hands while gasping for air. "It wasn't Jason—that did this to me."

CHAPTER TWENTY-EIGHT

FRIGHT NIGHT

LAKEVIEW FALLS SHERIFF'S DEPARTMENT

An absence of overhead lighting casts shadows into the main lobby's corners, spilling under the desk and over the top framed black-and-white police academy pictures on the wall. While two male deputies guard Jason's cellblock for the remainder of the night, Justin gathers multiple case files from his desk. Inserting the Holliston murders' article into a separate folder, he quickly makes his way down the lobby.

Hastily walking towards his father's office, Justin receives a text message from Simone asking if he will attend Crystal's birthday party. Standing beside a deputies cubical, Justin taps on his touch screen, replying to Simone when he is startled by a wailing sound from inside his father's office. Saving the text message in a draft box, Justin storms into the office and sees his father kneeling on the ground with his hands folded in prayer formation.

"Dad! Are you okay?" he exclaims, closing the door behind him. "I heard yelling. What are you doing?" Justin asks awkwardly, staring at his father, singing a sacred song.

"God answered our prayers, son," he simpers ecstatically, rising from the hard wooden floor. "They found Trey!"

"Wha—" dropping the files on the floor, Justin froze; quickly letting his gaze drop, he releases a deep sigh of relief before lifting his head, "oh my God, who found him, Dad?"

"Derrick and Alexandria," Sheriff Mills replies, walking towards the pile of documents scattered on the floor.

"Jesus, that's the best news I've heard all damn day, Dad," Justin nervously chuckles aloud, running his hands through his dirty blonde hair. "Where did they find him?"

"I asked Derrick to check Mr. McGregor's house for any clues that might help us with Trey's disappearance. At the same time, a complaint came in about a terrible odor coming from his house."

"And—" he blinks owlishly.

"And what do you think? Derrick went over there, found the poor kid buried under decomposing corpses in a goddamn grave in the middle of the basement floor."

"Holy Shit!—Is Trey going to be okay?" Justin asks breathlessly.

"Yes, Justin. He's at the hospital in stable condition, thank God," Sheriff Mill's responds, picking up the files off the floor.

Rushing to aid his father, Justin grabs a few black folders from his father's hand and places them on his desk. "I'm sorry about that, Dad."

Feeling stiff like a soldier, Sheriff Mills stretches his back to ease the aches and pain as he walks over to his desk. Gradually taking a seat, he does a range of motion with his neck rotating it from right to left, working the kinks he's suffered since last week due to sleeping in a wrong position.

Staring at the multiple files on his desk, Sheriff Mills scans the black and brown folders that are labeled the **Property of United States Government: Michigan State: Unsolved Murders 2009 to 2017.**

"Are these the files I asked you for two weeks ago, Justin?" Sheriff Mills asks while arranging the folders in order according to the date and year.

"Yes, Sir, I'm sorry it took me a long time to retrieve the files. There were minor mishaps. We have faxed copies of old unsolved

FRIGHT NIGHT

cases, but we didn't have the original copies of missing youths due to a freeze on their files. Every document on Lakeview Falls had been marked private by Mr. Wexler when he was in charge."

"That old bastard!" Sheriff Mills grunts, shaking his head with an annoyed expression, "Even though that man gave me the authority of this town and appointed me Sheriff, he was always a sneaky son of a bitch."

"I had to call a few people at the commissioner's office Dad. It was a pain in the ass."

"You wanted to become a cop, right?" he smirks at his son while putting on his reading glasses. "Well, welcome to my world, kid. You did a great job."

Opening the files starting from A through K, Sheriff Mills begins to skim through the murder cases. "Now that we have an official crime scene at Mr. McGregor's house, we can charge that hunk of shit with manslaughter. That basement has enough dead bodies to give that kid the gas chamber."

Anxiously pacing back and forth in front of his father's desk, Justin breathes heavily, resting the weight of his hands on each side of his hips. "Dad, do you think that Jason is capable of killing a dozen guys all by himself? I mean, that kind of carnage is not a one man's job."

Tilting his glasses below his eyes, Sheriff Mills looks dead into his son's blue eyes. "Are you suggesting that Warwick had an accomplice?"

"Maybe—Dad, there's something I need to tell you."

Laying the folder flat on his desk, Sheriff Mills leans back in his chair, stretching his arms behind his head. "What is it, Justin? Is this about the case?"

"Sheriff Mills," Deputy O' Brian says, peeking his head inside the office, "do you still need me to go over to Lakeview memorial hospital?"

"Yes—Deputy Yin needs a break from watching Mr. Delgado's room. Make sure you report to me every hour on Trey's condition."

"You got it, Sheriff Mills," Deputy O' Brian agrees, quickly closing the office door.

"I'm sorry, son. Can you give me a few minutes to skim through these files?"

"Sure, Dad. I have to use the restroom anyway," he replies.

Turning away, Justin tries to hold himself together. He breathes in slowly and shakes off his nerves. "When I get back, we need to talk Dad," Justin says with a stern expression.

"Yeah, yeah, yeah, you know the last time you looked like a nervous wreck was when that Carter girl turned you down. It's a shame a crazed killer murdered her boyfriend. Hell, maybe this time, you might have a shot with her after all," Sheriff Mills chuckles.

Justin's face turns paper-white at the thought of losing Simone to Jason's other half that is still out on the loose. "I'll be back; I have to make a phone call," Justin says, exiting the office, slamming the door.

"Jesus Christ," Sheriff Mills angrily throws his arms up, "easy on the door!"

A deep huff slowly slips from Sheriff's Mills' mouth as he makes himself comfortable in his lounge chair. Sorting through each file, he opens murder case file #2038. The folder holds information on young males slaughtered in a small town in Michigan named Cambelton Maine.

Massive article clips displayed families slain in the urban city from March 2014 to July 2015. Each brutal killings matched the murders in Lakeview Falls. Every murder in Cambelton Maine, had one thing in common; the oldest son in the family was flayed and eaten while the rest of the victims were gutted and dismembered.

Flipping through additional family photos attached to the articles, Sheriff Mills immediately stumbles upon one that alarms him. He takes a long hard stare at the photo with an unsettling feeling in the pit of his stomach. For a moment, Sheriff Mills thought he was losing his mind, but as he continued eyeballing the article, he knew something was off.

"What the hell is this? No way, this can't be right," he utters, quickly shifting his body directly to his silver laptop.

Turning on his computer, Sheriff Mills impatiently waits for the screen to load. As a result of slow internet service, he presses his fingers on the keyboards out of frustration, hoping to search for the article on the website www.Loople.com. When the internet finally launches, the screen displays "**Loople the way of the World: Enter your search with love.**"

Gently caressing the keyboard, Sheriff Mills sighs with relief, "Bless your heart Loople for having mercy on us middle-aged folks that can't work these goddamn gadgets."

Cracking his knuckles, Sheriff Mills proceeds to type the article information number he had in his case file displayed in front of him. Scrolling down the page, he finds the same article that contains a disturbing story on an African American family massacred in their home nine years ago in Cambelton, Maine.

Enlarging the family photo, Sheriff Mills sees both mother and father seated on a turquoise cushioned couch next to their two daughters and their teenage son. The family was dressed in formal church attire, wearing warm-hearted smiles on their faces.

Disconcerted, a sudden rush of nausea creeps within Sheriff Mills. Time stood still like never before. His face becomes pale; his heart sinks to his feet as if he just saw a ghost. Jolting up from his chair, Sheriff Mills cries out, "This can't be real!"

Frozen in one spot, Sheriff Mills shakes off the ominous feeling and slowly reads off each family member's name. Reaching the last family member who was the deceased teenage boy, Sheriff Mills sees the name **Travis Darnell** written in a bold font.

"Son of a bitch! Justin! Justin, Goddammit, get your ass in here!" he shouts, banging the palm of his hand against his desk.

Thrusting the door open, Justin sees his father in a frenzy pacing around the room, talking to himself, "Dad! I was on the phone with—"

Grasping the black folder, Sheriff Mills charges at his son, waving the file in his face. "I don't give a shit who you were on the phone with," his voice cracks as he tries to steady his breath, "I need you to do a background check for me right now! It's vital!" he says firmly, clasping onto Justin's shoulders.

"What the hell is going on with you, Dad?"

"Dammit, kid! Listen to me! I need you to search for someone right this instant."

"Okay, okay—-calm down, Dad! Who do you want me to search?"

"Terrance Johnson!" Sheriff Mills scowls, staring at the family photo on the computer screen.

❅ ❅ ❅

Silvery lightning conjures up in the clouds, unleashing a rising growl from the distant sky that comes down like violence upon souls. Driving down the one way street In Hangman Hill, Terrance makes a swift left turn into the quiet main road of Cobbleton Lane. Tapping his fingers on the steering wheel, he glances adoringly at Crystal while she gazes out the window.

Shifting his eyes back on the rural road, Terrance turns on an urban R&B station to create a relaxing atmosphere. Lost in her thoughts, Crystal observes the quiet townhomes while tuning out the explicit lustful song playing on the radio.

Noticing the interstate section on the main road that reads **Left Exit 25 Rural Mapleton Road 1/2 Mile,** Crystal's curly locks dance as her head swivels around, realizing that they had passed Terrance's house.

"I think we passed your house, Terrance," she says, glancing at the interstate entrance sign.

"Oh, shit did we?" he smirks, scanning his rearview mirror. "I'm sorry, my attention span is quite off tonight. I think it's because of your beauty, Crystal. You have a way of distracting a man with your presence," Terrance professes in a sensual tone.

"Terrance, cut it out; those smooth words do not work on me anymore," Crystal says, trying to suppress her laughter while keeping a straight face. "Look, we've been driving around for twenty minutes. It's getting late. Maybe we should forget about the gift and go back to the party."

Ignoring Crystal's plea, Terrance continues driving northbound towards the interstate. Swaying his head to the sultry song **Tear My Body Apart**, he purses his lips. "You know CJ; lately, I've been thinking about what you and I could have been if you had not broken up with me after we graduated high school. In fact, why did you break up with me?"

Crystal feels her stomach knotting up as nervous laughter emits from her lips. "Terrance, what happened between us is in the past. You and I both know how important it was for me to take that scholarship in New York."

"Yes, I know Crystal, but we could have maintained a long-distance relationship. That shouldn't be a reason to dump your boyfriend."

"Terrance, I didn't break up with you because I had to move to New York," she frowns, disconnecting her gaze from him, "I—we—" a sigh escapes her lips, "Terrance, I wasn't happy in our relationship."

Hearing Crystal's words felt painful, piercing through his heart. His gaze turns into a lethal stare as he accelerates, driving past the speed limit. "You weren't happy with me, huh?"

"Terrance, we lost that spark we had in the beginning. I tried to make things work, but It was hard to get those feelings back. Even though we didn't make it as a couple doesn't mean that we can't be friends, right?"

"Wrong, Crystal!" he shouts full of malice. "How could I be so stupid? he mutters, connecting the palm of his hand violently against his forehead, "I only had six years!"

Frightened by Terrance's expression, Crystal distance herself a few inches away from him. "What are you talking about, Terrance?" She asks, quickly extending her arms behind her back, cautiously trying to open the passenger door. "What do you mean you only had six years?"

Digging his fingers into the leather steering wheel, Terrance groans aloud. "I knew I shouldn't have trusted that he would get the job done! I can't believe he fell in love with you! I bet he screwed you real good too, huh? Huh, Crystal?"

Blindsided by Terrance's violent outburst, darkness envelopes Crystal, making every part of her body quiver. Her mind races while a terrible pressure enters her chest, suffocating the short breaths escaping her mouth. Everything goes blank as Crystal stares into

Terrance's cold-blooded eyes. It is as though she is looking at a vicious shark, waiting to gorge down anyone that passes.

"Terrence, what—what— why are you acting like this?" Crystal cries out, unable to contain the streams of salty tears coursing down her warm cheeks. "Who the hell are you talking about?"

His iris glowers with a final glance. "Jason! My brother!"

CHAPTER TWENTY-NINE

BLOODY BIRTHDAY

RURAL MAPLETON ROAD

Immediately shuffling away from Terrance, terror sucks the very breath from Crystal's mouth as she leans the right side of her body against the passenger door. "No, no— that's impossible, there's no way you can be—how can you? You're—you're—"

"Black?" he arrogantly responds with a disparaging sneer. "Well CJ, that's the best part about being a shapeshifter, I can be whatever and whomever I want. And melanin goes so well with me, don't you think?"

Horror retains its full glory the moment Terrance reveals himself as Jason's brother. In for the fight of her life, Crystal's panic fades into numbness; her heartbeat slows down increasingly while everything around her sounds muffled. Quickly clasping her hand on the door handle to flee, Crystal realizes the lock's jammed shut.

An egregious titter escapes Terrance's plump lips. "Tsk, tsk, I'm sorry, I forgot to tell you, the door is childproof," he says mockingly, tilting his head to the side.

Wanting to be suddenly small and crawl into someone's lap, Crystal closes her eyes and takes a deep breath, inhaling all the strength within her. In her moment of clarity, she realizes that she is on her own; there's no way to escape, nowhere to hide, and no one to save her but herself.

She rests her hands against her chest as fear settles deeper, causing the cold air from the cracked window to seep into her lungs. "Why are you doing this to me, Terrance?"

Terrance's eyebrows tighten with burning animosity. "I think you already know the answer to that question, CJ."

"What do you want?"

"I want the amethyst stone to bring back my father."

"You bastard! You tricked me!" Crystal whispers sinisterly.

"I didn't trick you, CJ. It was all part of my father's master plan. You see, I have been hunting you down since the day you were born. For many years, I searched for you with no success. But then I finally found you ten years ago. Of course, it was too early to kill you, so I decided to make myself at home; getting to know your friends and your family was my only hope of finding that precious amethyst stone necklace."

Without warning, Terrance grapples Crystal violently by the back of her neck, forcing her to maintain eye contact with him. "Everything would have worked out fine until you broke up with me and left town. You are nothing but a cheap slut that dumped me to go away to New York and fall in love with John! You know, the worst part was that after you left, I had to deal with that bitch you call a mother finding out my true identity. Desiree had no idea who she was up against."

"My mo- mother——" her eyes bleed with pain listening to her mother's name eject from the mouth of a horrendous monster. "What did you do to my mother?"

"Oh, my darling, Desiree. She was a tough cookie, an aggressive one, I must say. That woman put up a damn good fight, not telling me where she hid that necklace. Unfortunately, because she wouldn't surrender the stone, I had no choice but to kill her and your father too. Oh, he was a bonus. I could have eaten them, but I wanted to see your folks suffer, so I slowly chopped their bodies to bits," he says, snarling at Crystal, attempting to flee from his grip.

As more tears trickle down Crystal's face at lightning speed, more thoughts whirl through her head on how crafty Terrance was at deceiving her and the horrendous way he murdered her beloved parents who adored him. She feels electrifying pains traveling down her spinal cord, causing a rise to her body temperature. An ill, distressed moan slips from her parched lips as the infernal touch of Terrance scorches her skin.

While he jerks Crystal's head back, every breath drags more and more nausea from the pit of her stomach. Gut-wrenching sobs tore through her chest. "My parents treated you like family, Terrance! How could you do that to them? How can you be so disgustingly evil?"

"I did it because I needed you back in Lakeview Falls; I knew killing them would have you home in no time. Then, I thought to myself, how perfect of a plan that was? It's way better than trying to get back together with you! Trying to win your affections is too much hard work and not to mention a complete waste of my precious time. So instead of swooning you, I summoned my dear old brother; I gave him the quick scoop on that sad old neighbor and you and presto, you were eating in the palm of his hand. I see it didn't take long for you to get suckered into those piercing emerald green eyes, huh? He is quite a looker; it does run In the family."

"You're a sick coward! How dare you use your brother to get to me! Why Terrance? I trusted you!"

"The purpose of all of this was for Jason to come to Lakeview Falls and kill you. Then after he successfully put you down like the dog you are, we could retrieve the stone. All he had to do was free our father and the rest of our family to destroy this entire town with everyone in it. But my brother couldn't follow simple rules. It's a shame I have to find him and kill him too, but first I have to kill you, Crystal."

Brushing his lips against her forehead, Terrance licks salty beads of sweat that roll down her warm cheeks. "By the way, did you enjoy that steamy shower we had together?" he whispers with shrill malice in his tone.

The edges of reason blur, and fear lurch deep within Crystal. As panic fades into numbness, her heartbeat slows down, increasingly listening to him groan perversely in her ears.

"Mmmmm, you smell like cherries."

With full force, Crystal goes blank and smashes Terrance's nose with the back of her head. Unleashing herself from his monstrous grip, Crystal swings her left fist and slams it into his jaw, knocking out his front tooth. In a rage, Terrance shape-shifts into his demonic visage.

Ferociously glaring at Crystal with his fiery red orbs, two distinctive horns protrude from Terrance's enlarged head. His silky melanin skin sheds into a slimy grey substance splashing on the rearview mirror. Opening his gaping mouth, he reveals his razor-sharp teeth shaped as wooden stakes, snarling at Crystal. Raising his hand, he claws Crystal on the left side of her face with his talon fingers.

Crystal's head bobbles back from the ripple effect of his claws slicing through her flesh like a knife. Gushes of blood run down her face causing a deep wave of throbbing pain mixed with sharp, stabbing agony.

Unconscious of the abundance of fear, Crystal screams with great exertion as Terrance clenches her left arm and pulls her closer to him. "Let me go!" She yells, feeling the muscles around her bone contract painfully.

"You stupid, bitch! I'm going to kill you!"

"Fuck you, Terrance!"

Grasping the steering wheel, Crystal uses the palm of her hands to beat down on the horn pad signaling a black vehicle driving in front of them to stop. She desperately pleas for help, pounding on the steering wheel repeatedly until deep gashes become visible on her hand.

Watching the car drive further away from them, Terrance leans over and punctures Crystal's hand with his razor-sharp teeth, forcing her to release her hands off the wheel. Taking over the vehicle, Terrance speeds up to get closer to the car, trying to cut in front of it. He watches the black vehicle swivel, struggling to regain control of their wheel.

Driving at 80mph, Terrance rams into the side of the car, sending it swerving to the opposite side of the road where it collides with a highway truck, demolishing it on impact. While three innocent bystanders, including a two-year-old child, are violently ejected from the vehicle, the highway truck flips over to its side, skidding down the road.

The caterwauling of the metal plates touching the granite ground causes two bare wheel rims to spark, igniting an explosion blowing up the truck. As an enormous fireball shoots up in the air, Terrance's fiery eyes widen as he cheers on the catastrophic scene.

"Whooooo! Now that's what I call a big bang!"

Jolting from her seat, Crystal screams in distress, attempting to kick the passenger door open and flee. Injuring her left toe, she suddenly feels a hand full of her hair tugging her back. Veering in Terrance's direction, Crystal digs her index finger into his right eye- gouging out an eyeball.

Clashing like thunder in the night, Terrance back slaps Crystal, throwing her against the passenger side window. Shielding his wounded cranial socket with his free hand, Terrance presses down on the gas pedal, speeding at 100mph. Disoriented, Crystal regains her strength and bravely takes another chance at grabbing the steering wheel.

Fighting to get Crystal's hands off, Terrance releases both hands from the steering wheel. As the car swerves uncontrollably, it finally hits a side rail and flips over, heading down a wooden hill, tumbling at high speed. Falling backward against Terrance, Crystal kicks the side door and breaks it open, quickly ejecting herself from the vehicle.

Rolling down a dirt-filled slope, Crystal manages to grab hold of a sturdy tree branch and clasp on to it as tightly as possible. Positioning herself in an upright position, she looks down to see Terrance's vehicle continue to plummet down the hill, smashing into a boulder rock.

Crystal slowly steady's her balance with each plodding step as she progresses up the hill.

Her breath becomes labored as she continues to get higher. It felt like someone was pushing on her chest, not allowing her full breaths. Refusing to give up, Crystal uses all her senses and continues, making everyone moment count. Finally making it to the top of the hill, she gradually makes her way back to the main road.

Crystal's bloody and bruised body aches with excruciating pain while she climbs slowly over the side rail. Limping half a mile down Rural Mapleton Road, a sigh of relief escapes her lips when she sees the old chapel from a distance. Breathing heavily, Crystal heads towards the church to seek refuge.

❀ ❀ ❀

LAKEVIEW FALLS AUDITORIUM

Cries of thirsty patrons crowd around John as he finally retrieves his beverages. Enlivened with striking touches of red and white LED lighting, John pushes his way through dancing bodies tangled together. Advancing towards the virtual glass booth, John panics when he doesn't see Crystal nor Simone. Shuffling around in a frenzy, John drops his drinks on the refreshment table and searches for Crystal.

Heading over to the admissions booth, John sees Simone standing beside the coat check room staring at her cell phone. "Simone," he calls out, approaching her with a worried expression, "where is Crystal? I thought you were keeping her company."

"She's not here, John," Simone replies while her hands tremble, "I've been trying to call her—and—"

"What do you mean she's not here? Simone, where did Crystal go?"

Tensing up, Simone appears uneasy while she stares at her phone then directing her gaze back to him. "John—while you were at the bar, we stepped outside with Terrance."

With a shaky breath, John throws his arms behind his neck, gasping for air. "Why? What did he want?"

"He said he had a birthday gift for Crystal in his car—so we went to see what he got her and—"

"AND? And what Simone?"

"I left Crystal outside with Terrance and came here to grab my phone that was charging in the coatroom. By the time I went back outside, they were gone."

"Gone!" he bellows in frustration, pacing in a circle. His voice rises high like a piccolo but louder than a trumpet, startling party-goers who begin to whisper.

"You left her alone with him? After knowing what could happen to her tonight!"

"John, I left Crystal for five minutes. I didn't know she would take off with him."

"Dammit, Simone! What if something happened to her?" John scowls like a mad man storming towards the exit door.

Chasing after him, Simone follows John to the school parking lot, "John!" she cries out as she watches him walk over to his car, "where are you going?"

"To find Crystal and Terrance!" he exclaims, getting into his vehicle.

"But John! Wait!" Simone's breath quickens; she uses every muscle in her body to stifle a whimper before she begs John to reconsider his decision to go alone.

"You don't know where they went, John! How are you going to find Crystal if you don't know where to go? You shouldn't go there by yourself!" she yells out.

Willing to risk everything to save the woman he loves, John ignores Simone's pleas and drives out of the school parking lot. Swiftly making a left turn, John speeds down Fearman Street like a violently destructive windstorm racing across lands.

CHAPTER THIRTY

THE SHERIFF

LAKEVIEW FALLS SHERIFF'S DEPARTMENT

As time passes, the shadow grows more significant, and the light coming from the moon vanishes. The surrounding darkness sweeps over Lakeview Falls Sheriff's department like a plague, leaving every deputy on edge as they go off into the night warning residents and their children not to leave their homes. Meanwhile, in his office, Sheriff Mills glares at the computer screen in disbelief. He rocks back and forth in his leather recliner seat while his son stands beside the file cabinet going through a thick beige folder.

Flipping through Terrance's records in an LVF Town Resident binding folder, Justin comes across a copy of Mr. Johnson's Michigan State identification card. He notices a missing silver Decagram symbol on the card's bottom left corner. The unique stamp identifies all Lakeview Falls citizens and proves they have gone through the surreal ID scanning and are not a threat to the town nor residents.

Examining a photocopy of the card's backside, Justin sees an unknown state document number, 18252025200 that doesn't match Michigan's required state code. He then concludes that Terrance's identity is falsified when he notices in small print above the card, **Shadyshanker Inc. Corp,** which was an underground scam company in Concado Springs that produces fake state ID cards to drifters and ex-convicts.

Slamming the folder on his father's desk with great force rattling the wooden legs that support it, Justin scoffs in disbelief. "That piece of shit played us," he whispers, rubbing his chin hastily.

"Jesus Christ!" backing away from his mahogany desk, Sheriff Mills throws his arms up in a disgusting gesture, "would you please try to compose yourself and not break my goddamn desk! Now, what the hell did you find on Johnson?"

"Terrance's information on file is all fabricated, Dad. The state ID has the wrong code in the back of the card," turning the folder in his father's direction, Justin points out the fraudulent numbers.

"To hell with the ID card! What about the article Justin? How on earth can Terrance Johnson be dead and alive at the same time, huh? Am I losing my mind?" Sheriff Mills asks his son while scanning all articles on the Cambelton Maine family slaughterings, which was approximately the same time Terrance arrived at Lakeview Falls.

"Dad—You're not losing your mind; Terrance Johnson doesn't exist, but Travis Darnell did. Somehow Terrance killed that boy in the photo; I'm almost positive he did."

"What? Wait—" Sheriff takes a long hard stare at his son with a quizzical expression, "what?"

"Remember, when I said I had something important to tell you, Dad?" Justin says, reaching into his pants pocket and pulling out the wrinkled article with the Holliston family.

"This is an article that Trey printed from his computer right before he went missing. It's a slain family from Omaha Nebraska. Now tell me, who does this guy resemble?" Justin asks, handing his father the article and taking two steps away from him.

"He looks like that scum!"

"Correct, Dad. Jason Warwick is one of them."

"What the hell are you talking about, Justin? He's one of who?" Sheriff Mills hollers, rising from his seat with agitation. "Justin!

If you know something more about this Warwick guy, you better open your goddamn mouth right now!"

Positioning both articles side by side in front of his father, Justin stares with empathy towards Travis Darnell and Jason Holliston, who lost their lives to two ungodly creatures. The heavy heartedness of young males' dying in Lakeview Falls forces Justin to reveal to his father what has been causing great cataclysm to their town.

"Dad, you're going to think I'm crazy, but Terrance Johnson and Jason Warwick are shapeshifter demons."

"You're right; you are crazy!" Sheriff Mills clicks his teeth and grunts while opening a small bottle of Pepto Bismol to relieve his stomach ache. Taking a swig of the thick pink substance, Sheriff Mills swallows the liquid. He clears his throat.

"Shapeshifter demons? What in the hell are you talking about, Justin?" he asks, twisting the cap on the bottle.

"Dad, last night, I found this article in Trey's room."

"What the hell were you doing in that dorm, Justin? I have it closed off! You had no business going there."

"I had to go, Dad. Simone came to the station last night frantic about Trey. She told me about the article that might help us with his disappearance, so I decided to go back to the room and check it out. Simone needed my help; I couldn't let her down."

"Jesus Justin! You're not even dating this girl, and she already has you pussy whipped!"

Reasonably ambitious, Justin makes no reply to his father's inappropriate remark and maintains a calm, professional demeanor while pleading his case to him.

"Look, Dad, I took an oath as deputy to this town; you of all people taught me that a cop isn't a real cop until he solves crimes. Please, pay attention."

"Okay, son I'm all ears."

"You have two articles in front of you. Theres one with Travis Darnell, who died eight years ago, and one with Jason Holliston, who died four weeks ago. Both men killed the same way in two separate towns. Terrance came to this town eight years ago and Jason Warwick arrived here two weeks ago, which means he had enough time to kill the real Jason, shift into him and murder Joseph McGregor."

Not ready to back down on solving every murder of young boys in Lakeview Falls, Justin uses every resource he has to prove to his father that shapeshifters exist and are in their presence.

"Now that we know Jason is behind Mr. McGregor's disappearance, Terrance, on the other hand, seems a bit more complex. He moved to our town exactly one year after Travis Darnell's slaughtering. Dad, this is our big break! I am positive that Terrance Johnson murdered Mr. Darnell along with every young guy in Lakeview Falls for the past eight years. With proof of this article at hand and the fact that he fabricated his identity, we can catch Johnson and make him pay for what he has done."

"So let me get this straight——Jason Warwick and Terrance Johnson are posing as Mr. Holliston and Mr. Darnell, right?" Sheriff Mills asks with a baffled expression, grasping the news articles in his hands.

"Right Dad."

"I have to say I am proud of you and how quickly you pieced together this mystery, Justin. I have one slight problem with all of this; I'm having a hard time with the whole demon part. I know that this town has had a supernatural aura for many decades, but how the hell can we prove that demons live here? The United States government has already made us sworn not to blame any killings on creatures that were never proven to be real. Hell, we know this town is the scariest place to live, and no one wants to come here, but we have to face the fact that there's no way people out of this state will believe we have shapeshifters."

"Dad, you have to believe me. The longer we prolong finding Terrance, the worst things might get!"

"Justin, I need more proof! Shapeshifters are not going to cut it! Now I've come up with my theory of why Johnson looks like Mr. Darnell. You know people have a history of using facial latex to disguise themselves as someone else, right?"

"Oh, come on, Dad! You have got to be kidding me!" he scowls, walking away from his father's desk.

"It's true, Justin; we've all seen it in movies, especially those *Mission Impossible* ones. Maybe Warwick and Johnson knew the victims and found a damn good makeup artist or the best plastic surgeon to make them look identical to them."

"NO, DAD! FUCK—Dammit!" Justin curses his father with a dreadful imprecation.

Kicking over a mini garbage pail beside the desk, he throws his arms up with an exasperating gesture. "Dad, can you please listen to me? Jason and Terrance are Shapeshifters. At first, I thought maybe Jason had a twin or something, but then Simone told me that Trey found a demonology book with an old prophecy on Lakeview Falls. That book dates back to the 18th century. It's hard to explain at the moment, but to make a long story short, two shapeshifter brothers are on a hunt for a purple amethyst stone necklace that holds twenty-five ancient demons."

Sheriff Mills gulps. "Purple amethyst stone necklace?" he utters, feeling a hard substance lodged in his throat, but quickly realizes it is his breath suffocating him as he is breathing.

"Oh God, I hope it's not what I think it is-" Sheriff Mills mouths the words instead of saying them aloud.

He draws out his semi-automatic pistol and a new box of ammunition. "Jesus Christ, how could she give it to her? After everything her father said," he mumbles incoherently.

Staring at his father, forcefully shoving bullets into his pistol, Justin clicks his fingers to snap his father out of a daze. "Dad! Dad! Hello—Earth to Dad!"

"Goddamit, Justin! That necklace belonged to Desiree Francois! I can't believe she gave it to Crystal!"

Justin's heart collapses as if all of his energy had diminished. "You knew about the necklace this the whole time, Dad? How could you not tell me?"

"I don't know what you think I know, but I'll be real clear with you, Justin; if you are saying that demons are in that necklace, then this isn't good at all. Jesus, I remember overhearing Robert arguing with Desiree about not giving that necklace to Crystal. I wanted to know more about why this argument occurred, but it was not my place to question her parents, even though I am Crystal's godfather. All I know is that it put a wrench in their marriage for a very long time."

"Crystal's parents always seemed happy together," Justin says, grasping his firm chin with one hand.

"They were happy, Justin, it's just—" Sheriff Mills' voice cracks with grief, causing him to disconnect his eyes away from his son.

"Crystal's parents didn't agree on everything, like most married couples. Unfortunately, Desiree's childhood life and her family secrets began to bother Robert, especially that necklace. I was the only friend he confided in when it came to his raw emotions for his family, and I guess he must have known something was going to happen to him in the long run. Geez, I remember how bad that man cried, and I've never seen Robert Francois cry like that before. He begged, he cursed, he busted holes in the damn walls, pleading with his wife to not give Crystal that necklace. She was only five years old at the time, and I kept asking myself, why were they fussing over a small piece of jewelry to give her twenty years later? But it makes sense why her father didn't want it near her. Oh God, poor Crystal. I wonder if she knows what's happening?" Sheriff Mills utters with fear in his eyes.

"Crystal knows more than you think, Dad, and that's why Jason can't escape from our custody. He came to Lakeview Falls to kill her and take that necklace. Why do you think Mr. McGregor went missing? Jason concocted a perfect setup to be close to Crystal."

"I would strangle that son of a bitch if he took my goddaughter away from me, but thanks to your hard work son, Jason Warwick will never see the light of day. Speaking of, do you know that this entire time we've been speaking, he has been in that jail cell?"

"Well, where else would he be if not in his cell, Dad? Where is this coming from, and what's your point?"

"My point is, if Jason Warwick is a shapeshifter like you're saying, then why hasn't he shifted out of his jail cell?"

"What? That's a ridiculous question, Dad."

"No, it's not ridiculous, Justin. Shapeshifters can change into anything—like dogs— birds—I mean shit! He could shapeshift

THE SHERIFF

into a goddamn fruit fly if he wanted to," Sheriff Mills sternly says as he walks over to his coat rack, grabbing his olive green Sheriff's Jacket.

"This isn't a joke, Dad! Jason is a shifter. All we have to do is force him to shift."

"Listen, Justin, we can sit in my office all night going back and forth about Jason. It won't help us catch that bastard Johnson," he says, checking the clock, wondering how much time they have. "We need to put an APB on Terrance, and then we have to find Crystal immediately. Grab your jacket; we are going to———"

"BOOM!" Solid shattered glass pieces from the office window blasts out in a chaotic eruption, sending both Justin and Sheriff Mills to the ground.

CHAPTER THIRTY-ONE

TILLY

LAKEVIEW FALLS SHERIFF'S DEPARTMENT

An unpredictable force of nature blows through the local Sheriff's department's front entrance, leaving a dense cloud of darkness rotating in the sky like an oceanic wave. Impacted by remnants of debris, deputies in their cubicles swiftly pull out their weapons, aiming it at a curvy figure silhouetting with the flickering street lights. Celestial energies increase as an older woman resembling a spellbound harridan saunters towards the center of the room barefooted.

Glaring at each deputy shuddering with angst, the woman elevates her powerful arms allowing the cold, wintery breeze to pass through her light brown wavy locks to her ankle-length black chiffon dress.

Her delicate bronze skin and golden hazel brown eyes shimmer under the dim fluorescent lighting, stimulating a sense of calm to every deputy restraining their armed weapons pointed at her. Placing their pistols back in their gun belt, each officer returns to their station, walking in a zombified movement.

Disoriented by the explosive blasts, Sheriff Mills and Justin manage to drag themselves off the floor and exit the office. Both father and son notice deputies are sitting in a perfect posture as if they were mechanical robots from a cyborg science fiction movie. Slowly dragging in cold air from his heaving chest, Sheriff Mills' eyes widen by the sight of the crazy old lady he saw at the crime scene in Deerfield two weeks prior.

Clenching his fists, Sheriff Mills lets out a loud growl of annoyance. Fuming in utter disbelief, he marches directly at the woman who stood grazing her long hairy toes against the cold marble floor.

"You have some nerve showing up to my department! What In the hell are you doing here, lady?"

Caressing her orb-shaped breast seductively, the old woman wraps her hands around her curvy figure and begins to sway her hips from side to side. "Where is the young man? I can feel his aura seeping through the essence of my bosoms."

Disturbed by the woman's unhinged behavior, Justin distances himself. Standing behind his father, he clenches the back of his olive-green Sheriff's jacket as if he was a little boy, scared of the unknown creatures that hid under his bed at night.

Flashing an expression of pure disgust, Sheriff Mills stomps his black leather boots so loudly against the floor, an intense shock jolts from his feet up to his hips. "For Christ sakes lady," extending his index finger at her pointed nose, "what do you think you're doing? Does this look like your local neighborhood brothel? No! It's a Goddamn Sheriff's department!"

"Watch your tone, you silvered hair simpleton! My name is not lady, it's Tilly Rice, and this is how I channel my energy," she says as she continues swaying her slinky hips. "I need to know where he is right this minute."

Perplexed to whom the woman is referring too, Sheriff barks in frustration. "Jesus Christ! Where is who?"

Ghoulishly sneering, she answers, "The very, very bad boy!" Tilly mockingly clicks her crooked teeth, motioning her fingers in the Sheriff's face. "Where is he?"

"Dad, I think she means Jason," Justin whispers in his father's ears while shielding his eyes from the woman's eccentric intimidation.

A deep huff escapes Sheriff Mills' thin lips; he looks over his shoulders, giving his son the side-eye. "No shit Sherlock."

"How do you know we have who you are looking for in custody? What are you some goddamn psychic?" Sheriff Mills asks, crossing his arms over his broad chest.

"Dad, she sounds exactly like the woman that called two weeks ago?"

"That's because she is, son, and she owes me six new GODDAMN windows!"

As Tilly advances nearer and nearer, a tingling sensation spreads across Justin's body as if he is being attacked by an acute case of shingles. "You should let her see him, Dad."

"The hell I will! Are you out of your damn mind Justin? Who knows what she will do—She could sodomize him for all we know."

"Dad, she might be all we have in proving that Jason is a shifter. She knew about Matt's death, and you didn't listen to her. Maybe she can get something out of Jason. Dad, please let her go in just for a few minutes," Justin pleads with his father.

Staring at Tilly suspiciously, Sheriff Mills inwardly groans. "I don't like the sound of this, but if it helps get that bastard to show who he is, I guess I have nothing to lose."

❈ ❈ ❈

Escorting Tilly to the cell block, Sheriff Mills slowly opens the steel door. As they enter the musty-filled room, both Sheriff Mills and Justin see Jason lying on a thin worn-out mattress, tossing and turning in an uncomfortable position. Raising his black baton, Sheriff Mills bangs it against the steel bar with great force.

"WAKE UP SLEEPING BEAST! Today is your unlucky day, Warwick! You have a visitor."

He rises from the stained fill mattress with thoughts running through his brain, forbidding him to go to sleep. "Is it Crystal?" Jason asks.

Bursting out in an enormous snicker, an irritating smug tugs from the corner of Sheriff Mills' thin lips while glaring at him. "You have to be kidding me! After what you did to her, she will never want to see you, especially what we found back at Mr. Mc-Gregor's house. Scattered corpses and human remains buried in the basement ground; you will get the gas chamber without a doubt."

"Come on in, Ms. Rice!" Sheriff Mills says, flagging Tilly from outside the cell room.

Casually strolling in the room, Tilly senses powerful energy coming from Jason. "Just who I wanted to see," she softly says, gazing at him. "Can you both please give me some privacy with your prisoner?" Tilly asks, staring at Sheriff Mills with ferocity in her eyes.

"No way!" Sheriff Mills angrily blurts while nodding with disapproval. "This Thing is too dangerous to be left alone with you. Now I already am not happy with having you here. Don't push my kindness."

"Dad, maybe we should leave her with Jason just for a few minutes," Justin suggests, gently patting his father on his back.

"Fine," he half shrugs as a sigh of annoyance slips from his agitated lips.

Wasting no energy on fighting a battle, he knew he couldn't win, Sheriff Mills, and Justin quietly exits the room, leaving Tilly and Jason alone together.

❊ ❊ ❊

Inching closer to the cell bars, Tilly gazes at Jason, mesmerized by his alluring human form. She smiles mischievously, grazing each rusted bar with her copper Maklteriah rings.

"My oh my, I finally found you," She says, placing her right hand over her bosoms.

A stone glare carves into Jason's emerald green eyes. "What do you want from me?"

"More than you know. I've waited my whole life for this special moment. All I've ever wanted was to see what one of you look like in person. It's—it's quite astonishing that you've lived two hundred years on this earth and not one wrinkle has tarnished your visage. Although, I do feel sorry for the guy you killed to gain that precious face."

Ignoring her lecherous gaze, Jason walks towards Tilly with a wicked smirk plastered on his face. "Your sexual leering does not appeal to my kind; I have nothing to discuss with you or your coven. I do, however, admit that my deceiving and treacherous ways have not helped me at retrieving the stone you bitches hid for many decades."

"So, I take it that you know what I am?" Tilly asks.

"Yes, I do."

"Hmmm, so that means you found the chosen, huh?"

"Yes, I did, and her name is Crystal."

"I know what her name is but thank you for acknowledging her as if you care," Tilly grimaces while tapping her long almond-shaped nails against the off white walls in unison with the rhythmic tune she hums in her head.

"Judging by your indefinite imprisonment, I'd say you failed horribly at retrieving the necklace, and that's a win for Crystal. By the way, how exactly did you end up in jail? Holding the kind of power you have, especially being a shifter demon, I would have expected that you would have slaughtered this entire department by now. Why haven't you? Are you teasing these poor officers?"

Eerie howls and harrowing grunts fill Jason's loneliness. He takes a step back, unable to respond to Tilly's question; instead, he continues to examine each tiny hair follicle protruding from her chin.

"Oh my God," she gasps, leaning in closer to see the iris of his emerald green eyes changing in odd shapes, "my goodness—it can't be. Could it? She broke the curse, didn't she? But how?"

"What do you think?" he responds with impassion in his eyes.

"So that means that you chose Crystal over your father. Why?"

"Because I love her!" he yells in a high-pitched tone, slamming his fist against the wall.

"Loving Crystal has caused more pain than you will ever know, and you're paying the price for that now. It's clear why you can't set yourself free from this prison; your—your—"

"I'm mortal," Jason says with a raspy voice.

Revealing that he is now a full human, Tilly knew what she had to do. Stepping away from the cell bars, she opens the entrance door. Catcalling one of the deputies guarding the hallway, Tilly gestures for help. Luring the male officer into the cell block, Tilly instantly places her delicate hands above the deputies' forehead and begins to chant.

"Je ten garláremos mos letales solettrites inferías te, Je ten garláremos mos letales solettrites inferías te!"

As the dark waves churn threateningly around the deputy, the room echoes out the sounds of dead souls crying while mystical energy envelopes the department, leaving everyone paralyzed from the neck up. Releasing her hands from the deputy's head, Tilly backs away, watching the officer's ocean blue eyes convert to milky white, leaving him temporarily blind. In distress, the deputy begins to have seizures from the spell. Convulsing violently, the male officer smashes his body into the door before dropping to the ground with a single thud, knocking him out cold.

"It doesn't matter what you do! My brother will come for me," Jason whimpers.

Bending over the deputy, Tilly grasps his cell keys from the hook of his belt and walks over to Jason. "It is my duty to free you from this imprisonment. You have exactly one minute to get the hell out of here before everyone in this station regains their sight back!" Tilly says, unlocking the cell door and releasing Jason.

"What about Crystal? I have to find her!"

Clasping Jason by his arms, Tilly grips him firmly. "You will do no such thing! You need to leave Lakeview Falls right this instant and never come back! I swear if you stay here, you will regret it, I promise you."

Withdrawing himself from her grip, Jason groans with frustration. "I can't leave Crystal! She will die!"

"I don't give a shit how you feel you useless half breed! Now leave! Get out of here and never come back!"

Without turning his head or appearing to communicate with her, Jason whispers, exiting the cell room. "This isn't over."

Making his way down the hallway, Jason notices Sheriff Mills, Justin, and a few deputies frozen in one spot. Staring into their all-white eyes, Jason realizes Tilly's powerful spell disables everyone from seeing him.

"Crazy witch," Jason mutters, exiting the station. As he races down the concrete steps, Jason quickly walks up the lane and discovers his motorcycle parked on the corner.

He gets on his bike, and takes in a deep breath. His eyes fixate on the clouds that expand, resembling an arena football stadium. Feeling a forceful wind tunneling in his direction, Jason kicks the clutch and presses his foot on the pedal, fleeing down the road.

❆ ❆ ❆

Meanwhile, while everyone regains consciousness inside the sheriff's department, Justin and Sheriff Mill's hurry to the holding cell where they witness Tilly dragging the unconscious male officer by his collar. In a rage, Sheriff Mills grabs hold of Tilly, forcing her to release his deputy.

"What the— what did you do to my deputy, you old bat?"

"Dad! Jason is gone!" Justin cries out, staring at the empty cell room.

"Where is Jason?" Sheriff Mills says, shaking Tilly by her forearm, "I demand you tell me what you did or else I will have you arrested for harboring a fugitive!"

"I set him free, buffoon!" she exclaims, spreading her arms like a bald eagle.

"You set him free?" he stares dead into her cold eyes, "you set him free? How the hell is that possible? We were outside the whole time; there's no way he could have passed by us without being noticed."

"Maybe the boy used magic," Tilly says, flashing a sly grin.

"You worthless Cun—-"

"BEEP!" An alert goes off in Justin's pants pocket.

He pulls out his cellular device and sees an urgent text message from Simone. She informs him that Crystal left the party with Terrance. In a grip of silent panic, Justin's heart races. His fingers shake like a leaf while he responds to Simone's message letting her know that he will be at the university as soon as possible.

"Dad, we have to go to the Halloween party now! It's about Crystal and Terrance!" Justin says, walking out of the room.

"I need to find Warwick!"

"We will find him, but right now, we have to track down Terrance! He has Crystal! We have to leave now, Dad!"

"DAMMIT TO HELL!" Sheriff Mills scowls without turning around. Clenching his fists around Tilly's skinny arms, he clicks his tongue. "We are going for a ride Ms. Rice!" he says, turning her around and placing handcuffs on her wrist.

Frowning at him, Tilly narrows her eyes with disgust. "It's Mrs. Rice, and what in the world do you think you're doing, Sheriff? Maltreating a poor old woman, have you no shame?"

"Shame? You have some nerve coming into my station! You knock out one of my men and release a sociopathic serial killer into the streets! If you think that I am letting you out of my sight, you have another thing coming, lady. You're taking a ride with us!" Sheriff Mills says, escorting her out of the room, whistling Old Yeller.

CHAPTER THIRTY-TWO

THE CHOSEN

LAKEVIEW FALLS UNIVERSITY

Clenching her cigarette between her fingers, Simone fully inhales, blowing a cloud of smoke into the crisped air. She stares at the night sky like a cocktail of deep indigo's while a chill sets, forming tiny goosebumps up and down her spine. Like an iceberg, the bitter winds seem to harden around Simone as she shivers, tightening her leather jacket that snugs over her shoulders.

Standing outside the Wexler auditorium impatiently waiting for Justin to arrive, Simone's body jolts with a single twitch to the back of her neck. Sensing a higher connection from the unknown, Simone reacts, fearing what might happen to Crystal if they do not find her in time before the ritual.

Numb to the thought of losing her best friend, Simone recites in her head the last paragraph from the diabolical book of demons.

> *The blood of the girl. The oath of the beast. The father of all that is great. The ungodly creatures of the night. Set forth to become one; embrace a new world of skin-walkers, a world of human death, destruction, power, and rebirth. For all that is wicked shall shift in the twenty-five phase of the moon. In his name, the powerful MASTEMA set forth to kill the chosen.*

> *The forewarnings engraved holds such significance of what shall be and what's to come—casting a never-ending mystery above the head of an innocent woman who does not know how to destroy the master of all evil.*

※ ※ ※

Beaming headlights flash slowly, followed by patrol sirens echoing down the main road. From a distance, Simone notices Sheriff Mills' patrol car speeding like a rage of thunder in her direction. Flicking the cigarette butt onto the pavement, she leaves the school's front entrance and heads down the bluestone steps.

Upon exiting the vehicle, Justin's breath becomes sharp and frantic. His blue eyes widen with infinite fear washing over him as he thinks of the possibility of Crystal's life being cut short. A thin layer of sweat covers the nape of his neck as his shoes pound heavily across the granite ground approaching Simone.

A yearning gaze sweeps across Justin's flushed face as he gently slides his hand over Simone's soft cheeks. "Sim, are you okay?" he pants heavily. "If Terrance tried to hurt you—I will kill him!"

His breathing becomes a wheezing sound interspersed with sudden trembling of his body. As Simone laced her fingers through Justin's dirty blonde locks, her face softens. His thoughtful and selfless gesture towards her well-being feels warm and comforting. Justin's willingness to go through great lengths to protect her and their friends attract her more and more to him.

How could she not have seen this before? Simone asks herself. An immediate thought of regret runs through her mind, regret of not being with a man who expresses more than once how special she is in his eyes.

Gently placing her hand on Justin's arm, Simone gazes at him with a worried expression. "I'm fine, Justin, it's about Crystal. I think she is in grave danger."

"What happened, Simone? Where is she?" he questions with a brow raised.

"I don't know Justin—John brought her to the party, and then he went to get her a drink at the bar——that's when he ran into me and asked me to keep Crystal company, which I did until Terrance showed up. He told Crystal that he had a birthday gift for her in his car. He even asked me to come outside with them."

Fear engulfs Justin's conscience as he scratches the back of his broad neck. "A gift, huh? Simone, what kind of gift did Terrance give Crystal?"

"I never had the chance to see what it was, Justin. Shit!" she curses under her breath with guilt in her almond-shaped eyes. "This is my fault. I promised I would watch over her. If I had not gone back into the school to retrieve my phone —Crystal would be here."

Taking hold of Simone's hand, Justin strokes it gently, gazing at her with admiration. "Sim—this wasn't—"

"It is my fault, Justin. A few minutes alone on a day where she was supposed to be free from harm's way, and I left her. Oh, God—and John. God knows if he will find Crystal. We don't even know where she is—he doesn't know where she is. What if something goes wrong, Justin? What if John—"

Grasping her arms, Justin pulls Simone into his chest. He holds her for a brief moment, caressing the back of her soft black extensions. "It's not your fault Sim," he whispers with tenderness in his voice. Basking in the floral fragrance that intoxicates her entire jacket, Justin leans his face against hers. "Sim, there's something you need to know about Terrance. He's—"

"He's what?— what is it, Justin?" she asks while nestling her nose against his frigid neck to give him warmth.

"Get out of my car, you rotten prude!" Sheriff Mills hollers at Mrs. Rice, opening the backseat door, letting her out.

"Jesus Christ!" Justin barks with agitation, withdrawing himself from Simone. "What the hell is wrong with him?" Justin asks, startled by his father's random outburst.

Closing the door behind her, Sheriff Mills uncuffs Tilly. Placing the cuffs in his back pocket, Sheriff Mills grapples the old woman by her left arm and proceeds to walk with her towards Justin and Simone.

From a distance, Simone's eyes fixate on Sheriff Mills, escorting a woman in their direction. As if she has just seen a ghost, Simone stood still like a porcelain doll. Her head jerks to the side. "Oh my God, it can't be—" she gasps, staring at the old woman walking up to them.

"Grandma Tilly?" Simone exclaims, placing her hand over her mouth.

Tilly's hazel brown eyes gleam into Simone's with an intense connection. "Hello, my dear Simone," she says, giving her granddaughter an endearing smile.

Flabbergasted, Sheriff Mills cuts in between the two with a furious scowl. "Grandma?" he groans, throwing his arms in the air, unable to contain his temper.

"Are you kidding me? You're telling me this crazy old hag is related to you?" he asks, gritting his teeth at Simone.

"Yes, Sheriff Mills, this is Tilly Mae Rice, my grandmother," she replies, gazing at how enchanting Tilly looks.

Raising his foot, Sheriff Mills stomps down hard on the concrete floor, unleashing a deep exasperating growl. "Goddammit to HELL! Do you know what your nutty grandmama did? Huh? She just let a murderer run loose. If I were you, I would lock her up in a nursing home!"

Unaware of Sheriff Mills' accusation, Simone glares over at Tilly. "What is Sheriff Mills talking about, Grandma? What did you do?"

"Oh, I'll tell you what she did!" cocking an eyebrow, Sheriff Mills huffs. "Granny here decided to make an explosive grand entrance into my department. She danced around as if she was auditioning for showgirls and demanded to speak to Jason Warwick, whom we had in custody for murder. Then Mrs. Rice lets him go free and knocks out one of my deputies. How did she do it? No fucking clue!"

"Grandma Tilly, are you insane?" she cuts in front of Sheriff Mills angrily, snubbing him aside, "do you have any idea what you've done? Jason is going to kill my friend Crystal!"

"No, he's not. Relax," Tilly clicks her teeth with an eye roll. Crossing one arm over the other, she stares coldly at Sheriff Mills and Justin. "The half breed is not a threat to any of us."

THE CHOSEN

"Wha—? Not a threat? How? Grandma Tilly, do you know something? If you do, this would be the best time to speak up."

"Young lady, I do not answer to you. I'm the adult, and you answer to me, is that clear? I let him go because he can't harm your friend or anyone else, not anymore."

Tilly whispers, "Crystal broke his curse permanently; he's a full human now."

"Wait a minute," Simone says, gripping her sweaty hands around her grandmother's forearm, "how do you know? Holy shit, of course, you would know about this; that's why you left Lakeview Falls years ago to move to Deerfield. You knew this was going to happen, didn't you?"

"It's complicated, Simone. I left decades ago, and that was because my energy is not in sync with what lingers in this town. Plus, this is not about me; this is about the girl."

"How did Crystal break the curse, Grandma? How is Jason a full human now when she is still wearing the stone?"

Tugging Simone by the back of her leather jacket, Tilly quickly distances them from Sheriff Mills. "There's a lot that you don't know Simone, and we must not speak of this in front of them," she hints a nod at Justin and his father, "we need to talk right now, it's crucial."

"Grandma Tilly, what are you hiding? Whatever it is, you can trust Justin and Sheriff Mills. They will help us."

"Nonsense," she hisses ferociously at her granddaughter, tucking her pagan necklace between her bosoms. "They can't help us, Simone. If you were smart, you would tell them to forget about searching for that Jason guy? Hmmm, what a peculiar name. It sounds like a suburban white bread name. I would think a master of disguise would come up with something better."

A slight cough interrupts their conversation. Both women turn around noticing Sheriff Mills' nostrils flare in annoyance, glaring at them. "Excuse me, ladies, I don't want to interrupt your little family reunion, but I need to find Jason Warwick and Terrance Johnson!"

THE BROTHER'S CURSE

"Terrance is gone, Dad!" Justin scurries over, grappling his gun, hooked over his belt, "He's with Crystal, and we don't know exactly where they went!" Justin says with uncertainty, shifting his gaze down the misty roadway.

"Terrance? Of course, he must be the other brother," Tilly mutters with suspicion, "he has to be the second shifter."

"The other brother? No!" Simone shakes her head in disbelief. Terror washes over her, leaving the fine hairs rising in the back of her neck.

"That can't be possible. How could Terrance be? If he is Jason's brother, then he knew everything that night at the library," placing her hand over her mouth, Simone struggles to keep herself from regurgitating.

"Simone, that's what I needed to tell, you," Justin says, sneaking up behind her, "I figured it out; my father and I found an article of a slain family with a photo of Terrance, but it was-"

"Another guy? Terrance killed him, right?" a deep sigh escapes Simone's trembling lips. "So this is why Terrance lured Crystal and me outside. He didn't have a gift for her. He knew what he was doing. Poor Crystal, I can't even imagine what is happening to her." Simone sobs.

"Enough of the sorrowful weeping Simone, your boy toy needs to find Crystal right now. Come on, blonde boy, get to it! And take Archie Bunker along with you!" Tilly says mockingly at Justin.

"Get to what?" Justin squints his eyes with confusion, "we don't know where Terrance took her unless you know?"

"Must I tell you everything? What, do I look like a gypsy?" Tilly sarcastically asks as she runs her fingers through her hair in irritation.

"Tell him, Grandma Tilly! We don't have time for games!"

"Fine, If my intuitions are correct, I would say she is at the old Wicker Cove Church."

"The church? Do you mean that old chapel in Rural Mapleton Road? It hasn't been open for years," Simone gasps, "I have to make a phone call."

Panic-stricken, Simone feels a vast, mournful place of emptiness in her heart as she pulls out her cell phone from her leather jacket. Searching in her contact numbers, Simone calls Alex. Listening to a click on the other line, Simone hears a shaky breath. Alexandria's voice sounds lost and disoriented. Waves of fear circled her when Trey revealed to her and Derrick that Terrance kidnapped him and brought him to her neighbor's basement.

She Informs Simone about Trey's rescue and is taken back by the horrifying news that the same person who tried to kill their friend is with her sister. Letting out a splintering scream, Alexandria immediately notifies Derrick about Crystal and lets Simone know that they will leave the hospital and go straight to the church.

"Ms. Carter, who may I ask are you speaking to over the phone?" Sheriff Mills asks, walking towards her with his hands firmly secured on his hips.

"That is none of your damn business, Mr. Sheriff," Tilly says, cutting him off rudely, "if I were you, I would get in your car with your son and drive to that church before it's too late."

"If you are talking about the Wicker church, there is no way anyone would go there. That despicable cult chamber has been closed off for many years, and it is off-limits. Anyone that goes to that god awful place won't come out alive."

"My Grandma thinks Terrance could have brought Crystal there, Sheriff Mills."

"Why In the hell would Johnson take her there?" he asks, raising the curiosity in his head. "Oh, for heavens sakes! Justin! Let's go!" Sheriff Mills shouts angrily, turning quickly, locking eyes with his son.

Staring at his father flagging him to get in the patrol car, Justin suddenly looks at the sky with a sense of eternity that takes over his mind. Not knowing what the night holds for him and his father as they go off into unknown territory to rescue Crystal, Justin sees the sadness enveloping Simone's face.

Striding to the patrol car, Justin instantly turns around and rushes over to Simone. His steps pound in time with her heart as she stood, not knowing what he was going to do.

He Inches closer to her; his eyes gaze upon hers. Taking Simone's chin in his hand, Justin kisses her. His lips are soft, warm, and inviting to the touch, capturing every beat of Simone's heart.

As their lips part, Simone's hand brushes against his cheeks. "What was that for?"

Justin's eyes rest solely on hers with a fiery passion. "Just in case I don't make it back to you, Sim, I want you to remember this, always," Justin says with a smile that struck her in places she never knew was possible.

Holding on to one last gaze, Justin walks away and heads towards the vehicle where his father repeatedly honks his horn in irritation. Watching both men drive off, Tilly stares at how blissful Simone looks. Her face flushed by the intimate kiss she shared with Justin, Simone is brought back to reality, feeling an ache as her grandmother grapples her by her wrist.

"Grandma Tilly! Why are you grabbing me like this? Let go! We need to follow Justin and Sheriff Mills."

"You need to follow my lead Simone," looking at her sharply, Tilly walks away from the front entrance of the university. "We need to get to a safe place. Do you have a car?"

"Yes, Grandma, it's in the school parking lot? What do you mean we need a safe place?" she asks, baffled by her grandmother's erratic behavior.

"Simone, we need to leave Lakeview Falls immediately, before hell breaks loose!" Tilly says with an unsettling expression.

❄❄❄

RURAL MAPLETON ROAD

Grasping the dangling tree branch, Terrance's hands glide along the rough bark, causing much painful friction to his deteriorated human skin. Placing one foot on a rock beneath him for leverage, Terrance gives a good push, hoisting himself up. Finally, reaching the top of the forest hill, Terrance grabs the iron rail and eases himself over it effortlessly. His ragged breath heaves rapidly while walking up the deserted road soaked in his warm blood.

Like a raging maniac, Terrance unleashes a blood-curdling scream, **"Aaahhh! Tic Tok, Tic Tok,** give me back my fucking rock! CRYSTAL! I can smell you, Bitch! Watch when I get my claws around your itty bitty neck, I will tear it right off your head, you stupid **WHORE!"**

Trailing red liquid down the road, Terrance suddenly hears a loud horn honking in the atmosphere. As the sound echoes louder and louder in his direction, an exploding atomic bomb unleashes from the bottom of the hill where he had left his demolished vehicle. Noticing a black jeep driving straight at him, Terrance sees a cloud of smoke exiting the exhaust pipe, causing the car to blow a fuse, skidding in a full circle before coming to a complete stop in the middle of the road.

Hearing the screech of tires, Terrance stood in a slant, grimacing at the driver. Enveloped in a cloud of smoke, John quickly makes his way out of his jeep to find Terrance submerged with fresh blood, snarling at him as yellow ooze seeps from his exposed socket.

Feeling as though something walked right through him, John's heart begins to hammer against his chest, leaving him frightened, disturbed, and distressed all at the same time. Time stood still while induced anxiety corrupts his inner thoughts. John's terrified mind could only conjure up the worst possible scenario to where his girlfriend might be just by staring into Terrance's cold-blooded demonic orbs.

"What the hell happened to you, Terrance?" John asks, sternly walking towards him with caution. "What did you do? Where is Crystal?"

"She's gone! The bitch escaped!" he half shrugs with a sadistic simper. "You should have had her on a tighter leash, but don't you worry, Mr. Latin lover, when I find your precious whore, she is dead!"

"Whore? Whore?" John hears the unsanitary word whisper repeatedly with a taunting monotone in his ears. His face twist in anger and rage by the vile, indecent, and distasteful name Terrance calls the woman he loves.

"What did you call her? WHAT DID YOU CALL HER?" John groans, reaching out and grasping Terrance by the neck tightly. "Tell me where Crystal is, you asshole!"

Watching Terrance's diamond-shaped eyes dilate, blood begins to flow from his nostrils, trickling onto his lips. Letting loose his slippery tongue, Terrance licks the sweet, silky fluid before transitioning into his demon form, causing painful blisters to protrude from John's hand.

Aroused by the bone-chilling scream that escapes John's lips, Terrance smashes an elbow into the side of his skull, the soft spot high on the temple. Obtaining a handful of John's hair, Terrance suspends his body in the air then slams him violently onto the concrete floor, cracking his spine.

"Snap crackle pop!" Terrance sneers, grimacing at John's paralyzed body lying pathetically on the road. Hooking his claws in the back of John's collar, Terrance drags him down the road, heading towards the Wicker Cove Church.

❊ ❊ ❊

The swirling vapor of fog creates a thick veil as Justin and Sheriff Mills continue driving through Hangman Road. Neglecting to turn on his siren, Sheriff Mills is startled by a bright light coming towards him at high speed. Unable to shift gears on time, the unknown vehicle crashes into them on impact, causing their patrol car to flip over the guard rail.

In an instant, both Justin and Sheriff Mills' body lunges forward in a ferocious blur as the vehicle tumbles down the forest hill, plowing into a river. As the water rises, the car begins to sink slowly.

CHAPTER THIRTY-THREE

SHE WHO HOLDS THE STONE

WICKER COVE CHURCH

Midnight's awakening scowl of revenge cast an unnerving aura above the Wicker Cove Church. An unending circulation of fog hangs like a heavy, suffocating sheath as Terrance drags John down the road by his wavy brown locks. As he scrapes his bloody fingernails across the concrete ground, John's head bobbles back from the injury he sustained at the hands of his arch-nemesis. Gushes of blood fall from his head as he begs Terrance to released him from his grip.

Upon entering the cryptic sanctuary, Terrance hears dripping sounds coming from above the cracked ceiling. Drip, Drip, Drip, like a heartbeat; thick air fills with unwholesome odors while tiny droplets descend onto the soiled red carpet that stretches from the entrance to the altar.

With each step, Terrance admires each black candle he lights throughout the church, symbolizing the demons of the dark and the resurrection of his father, and the first coming shifters. Spotting two shadows that looked somewhat like figures, Crystal hears heavy footsteps lurking inside. Hidden behind the rustic pine wood wing-style podium, tears of pain run down her blood-stained cheeks as she silently shields her mouth with both hands.

Tormenting John, Terrance mimics his cries for help as he slowly drags him down the aisle on the soaked carpet. Like a suction cup to wet mud, John's feet retract grime and swamp worms cohabitating within the floor covering. Twitching his nose in disgust, Terrance glares at the scathe lectern. He catches a whiff of sweet nectar mix with a repugnant metallic smell.

An egregious titter escapes Terrance's blood filled gaping mouth. "You can't hide from me, bitch! Not while I have your precious Johnny boy!" he says, walking past pew after pew, twiddling John's hair between his talon fingers.

Hitting her head against the altar, a surge of pain creeps along her body as if it was on fire. "Shit," she groans under her breath.

It was brilliant, Crystal thought. Terrance vindictively planned to lure her to the church, knowing that John would feel her absence and come looking for her. "Now what?" she asks herself as she slowly rises from behind the podium. As Crystal frighteningly watches Terrance transform back into his human form. She realizes that John should not be the sacrificial lamb for a fate only promised to her.

Gripped by the back of his neck, John lets out a whimper as Terrance presses his talon nails into his skin. An arrogant smirk horrifyingly crosses Terrance's face.

"Hide and seek is over now, CJ!" he says, observing the claw marks on the left side of her cheeks. "Aww, look what I did to your face; I guess beauty isn't forever, huh?"

"Let him go, Terrance! John has nothing to do with this!" Crystal cries out, walking around the altar.

Backing away quickly, Terrance roughly handles John's limp body. His throat in agony, blood drains from John's mouth as he gasps for air, whispering Crystal's name in intervals.

"John has nothing to do with this, Terrance! It is me that you want, so please let him go!"

"Sure! I'll let him go, CJ, but first, you have to give me the necklace," Terrance demands with a sadistic tone to his voice while propping John up to his feet.

"FINE! I'll give you my necklace! HERE!" Crystal belts out in anger, unclasping the amethyst stone from her neck.

"Crystal, no!" John says breathlessly, gazing at Crystal with a lifeless look in his amber, green eyes. "Please don't take it off!"

Tears flowing from her eyes, Crystal pleads with him. "John! If I don't— if I don't surrender the necklace, he will kill you!"

A gurgling sound escapes John's lip as he struggles to stay conscious. "Baby, if I have to die to save you, then that's what I have to do."

Crystal's eyes held John's in a way she never knew possible. He loved her; she always knew that; she knew John would do anything to keep her safe. The love of a man willing to sacrifice himself to make sure she survived was more than she could bear. A life without John is a life she no longer wanted.

Digging his right claws into the flesh of John's back, Terrance uses his left hand and grapples him firmly by the top of his head. "Aww, you want to die for your bitch? Well,—wish granted!" he says, snapping John's neck with a single

"NOOOOOO!" The caterwauling of Crystal's gut-wrenching sobs echoes throughout the church.

"CRACK"

The sound of the snap sends Crystal to her knees while watching John slowly fall to the ground. Letting out a heart-wrenching scream, Crystal weeps, feeling her heart rip out of her chest.

Running over to John's lifeless body, Crystal takes hold of him and cradles him in her arms. A sharp pain fills her body and radiates through her foot. As her vision fades, she catches a glimpse of her boyfriend's broken neck before everything around her goes dark.

Giving a round of applause, Terrance walks past Crystal. "Gosh, I am a sucker for happy endings! Aren't you?"

"You KILLED John! You evil son of a—"

"Shut up, BITCH!" Terrance shouts, hitting Crystal with a bold fist to the head. The spiral blow sends her tumbling back, knocking her head against the rustic marble floor.

THE BROTHER'S CURSE

Yanking Crystal by her left foot, Terrance proceeds to drag her towards the aisle. She yells in excruciating pain. Her nose leaks blood onto the floor as her back feels pins and needles from the hard-hit she endured.

Positioning her body in front of the podium for the ritual **"Le sang du grand père né de la bête statuée."** Translation: The beast of the great father birthed of the statute beast.

Terrance gets on top of Crystal, leaning his knees against her chest.

Loud sounds rush into Crystal ears as her body cuts wind; her stomach feels like it has fallen out of her body as she approaches the end. With equal measures of fury and terror, Crystal sees her chance to rebel. Bringing her knee up, she knocks it hard into Terrance's groin. Grabbing her wrist, Terrance slaps Crystal across the face.

As warm streams of tears run down Crystal cheeks in blankets, Terrance fiery eyes ignite into a flaming glow. He moans at her, "Any last words, CJ?"

Sensing an overwhelming desire to give up, Crystal visions the last scene of her life imprinted upon her mind without the oxygen to sustain it. *There has to be a way to stop this, a way to destroy the stone without dying,* she thought to herself. Then she remembered the passage in the shapeshifter book that read, **"The chosen girl cannot wear the amethyst stone necklace during the ritual while the brothers dip the stone in her blood."**

Without warning, her body jolts as Terrance clasps his hand over her pendant. Before he snatches it off Crystal's neck, he groans with intense pain as she penetrates her teeth into his right hand, forcing him to withdraw his left that grips the stone. With one last shot to free herself from permanent demise, Crystal takes hold of the amethyst stone and stabs herself in the chest.

A sudden beam of radiation circles Crystal as the stone drenches in her blood. The lavender glow releases a burst of cosmic energy, forming dying embers of fire that causes Terrence to combust.

The celestial luminosity causes the amethyst stone to shatter, leaving shiny particles floating in the air. In disbelief, Crystal touches her chest, realizing the stone disappeared. Covered in human organs, Crystal turns onto her stomach, gasping for air. Slowly rising from the floor, she sees John's lifeless body lying in the middle of the aisle in a punitive stance.

Glancing at him, Crystal is startled by the sounds of footsteps entering the sanctuary. She swiftly shifts her body around and sees Alexandria and Derrick running towards her.

"Crystal!" Alex cries out, "oh my God, we found you—we found you. Thank God we found you," she weeps while embracing her.

Suddenly losing her balance, Crystal's legs give out, and she stumbles to the floor. Badly bruised, Crystal's weak state can no longer keep her on her feet. Grasping hold of her, Alexandria wraps her white wool coat over Crystal and steadily brings her back to her feet.

In dismay, Derrick unleashes a terrifying screech when he sees his best friend, John, lying in a pool of blood with his eyes open. Disconnecting his eyes, Derrick chokes up with grief while walking towards Alex and Crystal.

"Crystal, what happened? Where is Terrance? Did he do this to you?" Alex asks, staring at the deep claw wound on her sister's face.

Unable to reply to her sister, Crystal nods her head and mumbles incoherently, "Take me to the hospital, please," she utters as her eyes begin to close.

COBBLETON MAIN ROAD

Silence prevails as Simone and Tilly drive further away from Lakeview Falls. Staring at her grandmother focused on the road, Simone groans inwardly. "Where are we going, Grandma Tilly! You haven't said anything since we left the university."

"You want to talk? Fine, it's time that we discuss our fate, Simone."

Changing lanes, Tilly passes the forest pathway, "there's more to that shifter story than you could ever imagine, Simone. Everything you read in that book was only part of something far more sinister." she says, winking at her.

"How did you—?" Simone gasps shell shocked.

"Oh, I knew you had it, but that's not the entire prophecy."

"What do you mean, Grandma?"

"Simone, there's more to what you read. The book does not foretell Crystal's demise. Only the chosen will figure it out. These events that are occurring are dark, painful, and there are no happy endings, my precious granddaughter."

"How do you know what's happening to Crystal, Grandma Tilly? What are you not telling me?"

"My sister had possession of that extraordinary amethyst chariot stone."

Simone begins to feel an ache in the pit of her stomach. "What does that mean, Grandma?"

"Crystal's grandmother, is my older sister, which means—"

"Crystal is my cousin?" Simone exclaims, shaking her head in disbelief. "No, no, that can't be true. Tell me it's not true, Grandma Tilly! Tell me that you would never keep a secret like that from me!"

"I'm sorry, Simone, but it's true, and that's why I have to protect you!"

"Protect me? What about protecting Crystal, Grandma? We have to go back and find her! She needs us!" Simone says, scowling at Tilly.

"It's too late to save Crystal, Simone! We can't saved her!"

"That's bullshit, and you know it! Grandma Tilly, Crystal, is our family. We can't leave her like this! We have to go to that church!"

Having no other choice, Grandma Tilly reveals the truth about the origin of the amethyst stone necklace and what it does to the last Wiccan girl if she successfully destroys the stone.

Refusal of acceptance in her eyes, Simone places her hand over her heart. Feeling a tightening to her chest, she begins to sob at the mortifying consequences of Crystal's fate.

❊ ❊ ❊

LAKEVIEW MEMORIAL HOSPITAL

Admitted to Lakeview Falls Memorial hospital, Crystal's primary doctor advises her to stay overnight for extensive observations. While she lies asleep in her hospital bed, Alexandria and Derrick take turns napping in the main lobby's waiting area. The silence was eerily unnatural, like a gaping void filled with no words nor sounds. Then suddenly, one female nurse approaches the kiosk check-in touch screen computer and clocks out. She leaves her station unattended to grab a sandwich and a beverage from the lower level cafeteria.

As the red exit light flickers down the somber dim-lit hallway, the sound of sensible shoes squeaks on the pristine white linoleum floor. Strolling towards Crystal's hospital room, Jason slowly props the door open.

Disobeying Tilly's warning about leaving Lakeview Falls, Jason decided to search for Crystal. He desperately wanted to know if she was out of harm's way. If Crystal had miraculously destroyed the purple amethyst stone, then he needed proof. Proof that his life would be free from the constant fear that his brother would hunt him down to kill him for not completing their father's mission.

Entering the room with a silent step, Jason observes a white curtain hanging from a track on the ceiling. Smelling the strong scent of rubbing alcohol, he advances closer, drawing the curtain to the side. He smiles at the sight of Crystal sleeping peacefully. Noticing transparent cords hanging down for the nurse's call button and the IV solutions attached to a silver pole beside her bed, Jason reads the time on her heart monitor, **1:43 A.M, date: NOVEMBER 1, 2025.**

A deep sigh of relief escapes Jason's mouth while a massive wave of emotions engulfs him all at once. "Crystal's birthday is over, and she is alive, and that is all that matters," he tells his inner self as he took a seat beside her on the pale turquoise bed sheets. Frowning at the square-shaped bandage on the left side of her face, Jason smells the metallic odor of blood that secretes from it. Realizing the stone is missing from her neck, he is ecstatic that Crystal found a way to destroy the diabolical pendant.

"You did it, Crystal. You did it," Jason whispers in her ears.

Kissing her softly on the forehead, Jason is startled by Crystal clasping him by the throat with her clawed like hands puncturing each side of his neck.

Staring at her while blood trickles down his neck, Jason is horrified to see Crystal's eyes turn into a bright fiery red glow. Using his hands to fight her off, Jason desperately cries out for help as he struggles to pry her claws out of his neck.

Evil gnawed at Crystal's insides like venom. She sneers at Jason. "Hello, son! Daddy's back!" she says, releasing diabolical laughter so sinister, it echoes throughout the hospital room.

❋ ❋ ❋

EPIPLOGUE

She found herself paralyzed and unable to move in her hospital bed. I felt her eyes scurry back and forth behind her eyelids as her fragile heart races, like a runaway train going faster and faster. Each muscle of her body tightens with incredible force, awakening my demonic soldiers and me, allowing us to explore the inner being of this extraordinary vessel.

Her pure essence is unbothered by our diabolical presence, which makes us gain a hold of every limb she possesses. How will my soldiers and I create havoc if we are now locked in a human? Can it be that the ritual to release us failed at the hands of my offsprings?

As we absorb her consciousness, the metallic aroma enters the room, alerting us that we were no longer alone. Who dares to interrupt my final stage of consumption?

A sudden warmth encircles us as I hear footsteps inch closer. It was my son who defied my rules and neglected the duties set forth to resurrect me. He disobeyed my commands and

allowed love to taint his immortality. And now I shall cause him pain and heartache as punishment for disrespecting his Father.

I hear him softly whisper to her before connecting his lip against her forehead. At that moment, I opened my eyes and felt a surge of power and total dominance. Two hundred years have passed, and I am finally free. Free to reign terror and inflict pain to my mortal enemies.

Awaken by the chosen blood that touched the place, I was imprisoned and damned for eternity. The chosen girl is now my temporary vessel to do as I please.

A nefarious expression pinned upon my face as I firmly grab my son by his throat. His heart, once quickly beating, is now slowing in tempo. He claws his fingers at my hands uselessly and uses his last breath to scream for help. I hear the ragged gasps escape his throat while he slowly slips away. I've waited for this moment to reunite with my precious boy and show him how much daddy misses him. The day has come for you to pay for what you've done; you and those two witches. Once I've conquered my quest to devour everyone. I and only I will be the master and ruler of Lakeview Falls.

It is I who seeks vengeance and drain the souls of the weak to possess the town that so rightfully belongs to me. He who wishes to destroy me shall meet the hands of hell.
For I am Crystal, and she is me, and we are

MASTEMA

ABOUT AUTHOR

Christine M. Germain is a Haitian American author of young adult horror fiction. Born March 8, 1981, in Brooklyn, New York, she found her passion for writing in 1993 and wrote her first horror story at twelve. Watching horror movies and reading young adult horror fiction novels influenced her passion for writing a story with a protagonist that looked like her. In the movie world, African American women were never portrayed as a strong lead in horror films or books. Instead of waiting to see if that would happen, she decided to create a story that she would love to read and watch on the big screen that catered to more diverse characters.

Admiring authors such as Stephen King and R.L. Stein, Christine pursued her writing journey majoring in literature and graduated with a performing arts degree. Known for an imagination unlike any other, Christine is ready to take you to a thrilling shapeshifter world with the first novel of her Saga, "The Brother's Curse."

QUOTE

Storytelling is imagining yourself in character and embarking on a world you never knew existed. When you set your mind free, you open yourself up to the unknown.

Christine M. Germain

Made in the USA
Las Vegas, NV
08 February 2021